LIFELESS

Also by this author

SLEEPYHEAD
SCAREDY CAT
LAZYBONES
THE BURNING GIRL

You can visit the author's website at:
www.markbillingham.com

LIFELESS

Mark Billingham

LITTLE, BROWN

A *Little, Brown* Book

First published in Great Britain in June 2005
by Little, Brown

A CIP catalogue record for this book is available
from the British Library.

HARDBACK ISBN 0 316 72752 0
C FORMAT ISBN 0 316 72753 9

Typeset in Plantin by M Rules
Printed and bound in Great Britain by
Clays Ltd, St Ives plc

Little, Brown
An imprint of
Time Warner Book Group UK
Brettenham House
Lancaster Place
London WC2E 7EN

www.twbg.co.uk

For Mike Gunn.

And for his son, William Roan Gunn.

'Hell is a city much like London.'
Percy Bysshe Shelley

'No one told me grief felt so much like fear.'
C. S. Lewis

PROLOGUE

12 January

I won't waste any time asking how you've been, because I know, and I don't much care. I'm sure you care even less about me, plus you'd have to be stupid not to figure out that things have been less than rosy for some of us. You'd have to be stupid (which I know you're not) not to work out what I want.

I don't think I'm better than you. How could I? But I'm guessing you're a bit better off. So that's basically why I'm asking. I just need a bit of help. I don't have a lot left aside from unpleasant memories. Oh, and the one, more concrete reminder, of course. The 'evidence', which I'm sure each of us still has.

I can't afford to care how despicable it makes me sound, having to come to you like this. Desperation drives a steamroller across self-respect. Besides, you could never hate me more than I hate myself for what happened back there. For dredging it all up again now in search of a few hundred quid.

That's all I need . . .

You'll notice a lack of address. I'm not being mysterious; I just don't really have one at the moment. I'm busy wearing out the welcomes of what few friends and family I've got left.

I'll write again to fix up the where and when. We can arrange a time and place to meet then, OK?

Anonymity is all very well of course, all very James Bond, but unless you've been keeping tabs on each of us, I can't see why you should have a bloody clue who I am. Which one, I mean. You'll find out soon enough, obviously, but it can't hurt to keep the suspense going for a bit, can it?

Could be any one of four, right? Any member of the crew. I'd be amazed if a single one of us is particularly well off.

So . . . for now,

Happy New Year

PART ONE

BREAKFAST AND BEFORE

The first kick wakes him and shatters his skull at the same time.

He begins to drift back towards unconsciousness almost immediately, but is aware of the intervals between each subsequent kick – though actually no more than a second or two – warping and stretching. It gives his brain, which is itself already beginning to swell, the time for one final, random series of thoughts and instructions.

Counting the kicks. Counting each smash of boot into flesh and bone. Counting the strange and, oh God, the glorious spaces in between.

Two . . .

Cold, in the early hours of the morning and damp. And the attempt to cry out is agonising as the message from the brain dances between the fragments of bone in what had once been his jaw.

Three . . .

Warm, the face of the baby in his hands. His *baby. The face of the child before it grew and learned to despise him. Reaching in vain for the letter, dog-eared and greasy, in the inside pocket of his coat. The last link to the life he had before. Groping for it, his flappy fingers useless at the end of a broken arm.*

Four . . .

Turning his head, trying to turn it away from the pain towards the wall. His face moving against the floor, the stubble-rasp like the breaking of faraway waves. Feeling the blood, warm and sticky between his cheek and the cold cardboard beneath. Thinking that the shadow he'd glimpsed, where the face of his attacker should have been, looked blacker than black. Slick, like tarmac after a shower. Thinking that it was probably a trick of the light.

Five . . .

Seeming to feel the tip of the boot as it breaks through the delicate network of ribs. Aware of it in there, stamping around, distorting his organs. Kidneys – are they his kidneys? – squeezed out of shape like water-filled balloons.

Sinking fast through six, seven and eight, their impact like crashes at a distant front door, vibrating through his shoulder and his back and the tops of his legs. The grunts and growls of the man standing above him, of the man who is kicking him to death, growing quieter and further away.

And, Christ, what a jumble, such a scramble of words. Riot of colours and sounds. All slipping away from him now. Fuzzing and darkening . . .

Thinking. Thinking that this was a terrible and desperate kind of thinking, if it could still be called such a thing. Sensing that the shadow had finally turned away from him. Luxuriating then, in the bliss as the space grew, as the knowing grew that, sweet Jesus, the kicking had finally stopped.

Everything so strange now, and shapeless and bleeding away into the gutter.

He lies quite still. He knows there's little point in trying to move. He holds on tight to his name and to the name of his only child. Wraps what's left of his mind around these two names, and around the name of the Lord.

Prays that he might cling on to the shape of these few, precious words until death comes.

ONE

He woke up in a doorway opposite Planet Hollywood, with a puddle of piss at his feet that was not his own and the sickening realisation that this was real, that there was no soft mattress beneath him. He exchanged a few words with the police officer whose heavy hand had shaken him roughly awake. Began to gather up his things.

He raised his face slowly skywards as he started to walk, hoped that the weather would stay fine. He decided that the emptiness at the centre of him, which might have been simple fear, was probably even simpler hunger.

He wondered whether Paddy Hayes was dead yet. Had the young man charged with making the decision pulled the plug?

Moving through the West End as it shook away the sleep and slowly came to life was always a revelation. Each day he saw something he had never seen before.

Piccadilly Circus was glorious. Leicester Square was better than it looked. Oxford Street was even shittier than he'd thought it was.

There were still plenty of people about, of course. Plenty of traffic. Even at this time the streets were busier than most others in the country would be during the rush hour. He remembered a film he'd seen on

DVD, set in London after most of the population had been turned into crazed zombies by some plague. There were bizarre scenes where the whole city appeared to be utterly deserted, and to this day he didn't really know how they'd managed to do it. Computer tricks, like as not. This – the hour or so when the capital showered, shaved and shat – was about as close as it ever came. Far from deserted, but quite a few zombies shuffling about.

Most of the shops would be shut for another hour or two yet. Very few opened their doors before ten these days. The caffs and sandwich bars were already up and running, though. Hoping to pull in passing trade for tea and a bacon sandwich, for coffee and croissants, in much the same way that the burger vans and kebab shops had tempted those weaving their way home only a few hours earlier.

Tea and a sandwich. Normally he'd have spent the previous night gathering enough together to get himself something to eat, but today someone would be buying him breakfast.

Halfway along Glasshouse Street, a man in a dark green suit stepped out of a doorway in front of him and tried to pass. They moved the same way across the pavement, and back again. Smiled at each other, embarrassed.

'Nice morning for a dance . . .'

The sudden knowledge that he'd clearly encountered a nutcase caused the smile to slide off the man's face. He turned sideways and dropped his head. Shuffled quickly past muttering, 'Sorry' and, 'I can't . . .'

He hoisted his backpack higher on to his shoulder and carried on walking, wondering just what it was that the man in the suit couldn't do.

Return a simple greeting? Spare any change? Give a toss?

He walked up Regent Street, then took a right, cutting through the side streets of Soho towards Tottenham Court Road. A strange yet familiar figure, stepping in unison alongside him, caught his eye. He slowed then stopped, watching the stranger do the same thing.

He took a step forward and stared into the plate glass at the reflection of the man he'd become in such a short time. His hair seemed to be growing faster than usual, the grey more pronounced against the black. The neat-ish goatee he'd been cultivating had been subsumed under the scrubby growth that sprouted from his cheeks and spilled down his throat. His red nylon backpack, though already stained and grubby, was the only flash of real colour to be seen in the picture staring back at him from the shop window. The grease-grey coat and dark jeans were as blank, as *anonymous*, as the face that floated above them. He leaned towards the glass and contorted his features; pulling back his lips, raising his eyebrows, puffing out his cheeks. The eyes, though – and it was the man's eyes that told you *everything* – stayed flat and uninvolved.

A vagrant. With the emphasis on vague . . .

He turned from the window to see someone he recognised on the other side of the road. A young man – a boy – arms around his knees, back pressed against a dirty white wall, sleeping bag wrapped around his shoulders. He'd spoken to the boy a couple of nights before. Somewhere near the Hippodrome, he thought. Maybe outside one of the big cinemas in Leicester Square. He couldn't be certain. He did remember that the boy had spoken with a thick, north-east accent: Newcastle or Sunderland. Most of what the boy had said was indecipherable, rattled through chattering teeth at machine-gun speed. Head turning this way and that. Fingers grasping at his collar as he gabbled. So completely ripped on Ecstasy that it looked as though he was trying to bite off his own face.

He waited for a taxi to pass, then stepped into the road. The boy looked up as he approached and drew his knees just a little closer to his chest.

'All right?'

The boy turned his head to the side and gathered the sleeping bag tighter around his shoulders. The moisture along one side of the bag caught the light, and grey filling spilled from a ragged tear near the zip.

'Don't think there's any rain about . . .'

'Good,' the boy said. It was as much a grunt as anything.

'Staying dry, I reckon.'

'What are you, a fucking weatherman?'

He shrugged. 'Just saying . . .'

'I've seen you, haven't I?' the boy asked.

'The other night.'

'Was you with Spike? Spike and One-Day Caroline, maybe?'

'Yeah, they were around, I think . . .'

'You're new.' The boy nodded to himself. He seemed pleased that it was coming back to him. 'I remember you were asking some fucking stupid questions . . .'

'Been knocking about a couple of weeks. Picked a fucking stupid time, didn't I? You know, with everything that's going on?'

The boy stared at him for a while. He narrowed his eyes, then let his head drop.

He stood where he was, kicking the toe of one shoe against the heel of the other until he was certain that the boy had nothing further to say. He thought about chucking in another crack about the weather, making a joke of it. Instead, he turned back towards the road. 'Be lucky,' he said. He moved away, his parting words getting nothing in return.

As he walked north, it struck him that the encounter with the boy had not been a whole lot friendlier than the one earlier with the man in the green suit who'd been so keen to avoid him. The boy's reaction had been no more than he'd come to expect in the short time he'd spent living as he was now. Why should it have been? A wariness – a suspicion, even – was the natural reaction of *most* Londoners, whatever their circumstances. Those who lived and slept on the city's streets were naturally that bit more cautious when it came to strangers. It went without saying that anyone who wasn't abusing or avoiding them was to be viewed with a healthy degree of mistrust until they'd proved themselves. One way or another . . .

It was a lot like prison. Like the way a life was defined behind bars. And he knew a fair bit about how *that* worked.

Those who slept rough in the centre of London had a lot in common, he decided, with those sleeping in whitewashed cells at Her

Majesty's pleasure. Both were communities with their own rules, their own hierarchies and an understandable suspicion of outsiders. If you were going to survive in prison, you had to fit in; do what was necessary. You'd try not to eat shit, of course you would, but if that's what it took to get by, you'd tuck right in. What he'd seen of life since he began sleeping rough told him that things were pretty much the same on the streets.

The café was a greasy spoon with ideas above its station. The sort of place that thought a few cheap sandwich fillings in Tupperware containers made it a delicatessen. The reaction, within a minute or two of him shambling in, sitting down and showing no obvious intention of buying anything, was predictable.

'Hey!'

He said nothing.

'You going to order something?'

He reached across for a magazine that had been left on an adjacent table and began to read.

'This is not a dosshouse, you know.'

He smiled.

'You think I'm joking . . .?'

He nodded towards a familiar figure outside the window as the fat, red-faced proprietor came around the counter towards him. With impeccable timing, the man he'd been smiling at pushed through the door, just as the café owner was leaning in menacingly.

'It's OK, he's with me . . .'

The threatening expression on the proprietor's face softened, but only marginally, when he turned from the tramp's table and looked at the Metropolitan Police warrant card that was being thrust at him.

Detective Sergeant Dave Holland pocketed his ID, reached across and dragged back a chair. 'We'll have two teas,' he said.

The man sitting at the table spoke in earnest. '*Mugs* of tea.'

The owner shuffled back towards the counter, somehow managing to sigh and clear his throat at the same time.

'My hero,' the tramp said.

Holland put his briefcase on the floor and sat down. He glanced round at the two other customers: a smartly dressed woman and a middle-aged man in a postal uniform. Back behind his counter, the owner of the place glared at him as he took a pair of white mugs from a shelf.

'He looked like he was ready to chuck you out if I hadn't come in just then. I was tempted to stand there and watch. See what happened.'

'You'd have seen me deck the fat fucker.'

'Right. Then I'd've had to arrest you.'

'That would have been interesting . . .'

Holland shrugged and pushed dirty blond hair back from his forehead. 'Paddy Hayes died just after eleven-thirty last night,' he said.

'How's the son doing?'

'He was pretty upset beforehand. Wrestling with it, you know? Once he'd decided, once they turned off the machines, he seemed a lot calmer.'

'Probably only *seemed*.'

'Probably . . .'

'When's he going home?'

'He's getting a train back up north this morning,' Holland said. 'He'll be getting home around the time they start the PM on his old man.'

'Won't be too many surprises there.'

They both leaned back in their chairs as the tea arrived with very little ceremony. The fat man plonked down two sets of cutlery, wrapped in paper serviettes. He pointedly nudged a laminated menu towards each of them before turning to empty the ashtray on the adjoining table.

'You hungry?' Holland asked.

The man opposite glanced up from the menu he was already studying. 'Not really. I had a huge plate of smoked salmon and scrambled eggs first thing.' His eyes went back to the menu. 'Of *course* I'm fucking hungry.'

'All right . . .'

'I hope you've brought your chequebook. This could get expensive.'

Holland picked up his tea. He cradled the mug against his chin and let the heat drift up to his face. He stared through the narrow curtain of steam at the dishevelled figure sitting across from him. 'I still can't get used to this,' he said.

'What?'

'This. You.'

'*You* can't get used to it? Jesus!'

'You know what I mean. I just never imagined you anything like this. You were the last person . . . You *are* the last person . . .'

Tom Thorne dropped his menu and crossed stained fingers above it. The decision made. He stared hard across the table.

'Things change,' he said.

TWO

Lots of things had changed . . .

What everything was bloody-well called for a start. When he'd returned to work, it had seemed to Thorne that in the short time he'd been away they'd decided to change the name of just about everything. The Serious Crime Group, in which Thorne had been a detective inspector on one of the nine Major Investigation Teams in Murder Command (West), was now part of what had laughably been christened the Specialist Crime Directorate. *Directorate*, for crying out loud. Did the people who pushed pens around and decided these things really think that changing something's name made a scrap of difference to what it actually *did*?

Directorate, group, pool, squad, team, unit . . . posse, gang, shower, whatever.

Just a bunch of people, of mixed ability, scrabbling around in various degrees of desperation, trying to catch those that had killed. That were still killing.

Or, if they were really lucky, those that were planning to kill.

The Specialist Crime Directorate. Thorne remembered a vacancy advertised by a well-known supermarket in something called 'ambient replenishment'. The job had turned out to be stacking shelves.

Naturally, the structure Thorne came back to had changed as well. Each MIT on the Murder Squad was now composed of three detective inspectors, each at the head of a smaller, core team and each with that much more paperwork, that much more administrative responsibility and that much more time spent behind a desk. Each with another few hours of their working life spent ensuring that staff morale was high while levels of sick leave stayed low, and that actions were carried out within those very necessary constraints of bloody time and sodding budget, and so fucking on and so fucking forth . . .

'I know this stuff has all got to be done, and I know it's got to be done properly, but there have to be priorities. Don't there? For Christ's sake, I've got two Asian kids with bullets in their heads and some nutcase who seems to take great delight in sticking a sharpened bicycle spoke into people's spines, but I'm being prevented from getting out and doing anything about it.'

'Listen . . .'

'Every time I so much as set foot outside the office, one or other of my so-called colleagues starts bitching about having to do my share of the fucking paperwork and it's getting stupid. I just want to do the job, you know? Especially now. You can understand that, can't you? I'm just a copper, that's all. It's not complicated. I'm not a resource, or a facilitator, or a fucking homicidal-perpetration-prevention operative . . .'

'Tom . . .'

'Do you think whoever shot those two kids is sitting at home doing his paperwork? Is this lunatic I'm trying to catch filling in forms? Making a careful note, no, making *several copies* of a careful note about how many different bicycle spokes he's used, and how much they cost him and exactly how long it took him to get them just sharp enough to paralyse somebody? I don't think so. I don't fucking think so . . .'

The man sitting in the armchair wore his usual black hooded top and combats. There was a selection of rings and studs in both ears, and the spike below his bottom lip shifted as he moved his tongue around in his mouth. Dr Phil Hendricks was a pathologist who worked closely with Thorne's team. He was also the nearest thing Tom Thorne had to a best friend. Violent death and its charged aftermath had forged a strong bond between them. He'd caught a taxi to the flat in Kentish Town as soon as Thorne had called.

Hendricks waited just long enough to be sure that Thorne had run out of steam, without giving him the time to get up another head. 'How are you sleeping?' he asked.

Thorne had stopped pacing, had sat down heavily on the arm of the sofa. 'Do I sound tired to you?'

'You sound . . . hyper. It's understandable.'

Thorne jumped up again, marched across to the fireplace. 'Don't start that lowering-your-voice shit, Phil. Like I'm not well. I'm right about this.'

'Look, I'm sure you're right. I'm not there enough to see it.'

'*Everything's* different.'

'Maybe it's you that's different . . .'

'Trust me, mate, this job's going tits up. It's like working in a bank in there sometimes. Like working in the fucking City!'

'What happened when you saw Jesmond?'

Thorne took a deep breath, placed the flat of his hand against his chest, watched it jump. Once, twice, three times . . .

'I got a lecture,' he said. 'Apparently, these days, there's a lot less tolerance for dead wood.'

Lots of things had changed . . .

Hendricks shifted in the armchair, opened his mouth to speak . . .

'Dead wood,' Thorne said, repeating the words as if they were from a foreign language. 'How fucked is that from *him*? Pointless, tight-arsed tosser!'

'OK, look, he's all those things, we know that, but . . . maybe the caseload *is* getting on top of you a bit. Don't you think? Come on, you're not really dealing with the work properly, with *any* of it.'

'Right, and why's that, d'you reckon? What have I just been telling you?'

'You haven't been telling me anything; you've been shouting at me. And what you've *actually* been doing is making excuses. I'm on your side, Tom, but you need to face a few facts. You're either completely out of it or you're ranting like an idiot, and either way people are getting pissed off with you. Getting *more* pissed off with you . . .'

'Which people?'

Then, despite what Thorne had said a few moments earlier, Hendricks lowered his voice: 'You weren't ready to start work again.'

'That's bollocks.'

'You came back too soon . . .'

It was not much more than eight weeks since Thorne's father had died in a house fire. Jim Thorne had been suffering from advanced Alzheimer's at the time of his death, and the blaze had almost certainly been no more than an accident. A misfired synapse. A piece of tragic forgetfulness.

There were other possibilities, though. Thorne had been working on a case involving a number of powerful organised-crime figures. It was possible that one of them – that one man in particular – had decided to strike at Thorne via those closest to him. To inflict pain that would stay with him far longer than anything of which a simple blade or bullet was capable.

Other possibilities . . .

Thorne was still coming to terms with a lot of things. Among them, the fact that he might never know for sure whether his father had been murdered. Either way, Thorne knew he was to blame.

'I would have come back earlier if I could,' Thorne said. 'I'd've come back the day I buried him. What else am I going to do?'

Hendricks pushed himself out of the chair. 'Do you want some tea?'

Thorne nodded and turned towards the fireplace. He leaned against the stripped-pine mantelpiece, staring at himself in the mirror above as he spat out the words. 'Detective Chief Superintendent Jesmond is thinking about a few weeks' "gardening leave".'

Standing in front of Trevor Jesmond's desk that afternoon, Thorne had felt like he'd been punched in the stomach. He'd dug down deep for something like a smile. Deeper still for the flippant comeback. '*I've only got a window-box . . .*'

Now the anger rose up again, but quickly gave way to a perverse amusement at yet another ridiculous euphemism. '"Gardening leave",' he said. 'How nice. How fucking cosy.'

It made sense, he supposed. You could hardly call it what it was: some pointless, hastily invented desk job designed to get shot of anyone who was causing a problem. Anyone embarrassing, but not quite sackable. *Gardening* sounded so much better than *burned out* or *fucked up*. So much more pleasant than *drunk*, *traumatised* or *mental*.

Hendricks walked slowly towards the kitchen. 'I think you should take it,' he said.

The next day, Thorne had discovered how the odds against him were stacking up.

'I'm in a corner here, aren't I?'

Russell Brigstocke had looked down at his desktop. Straightened his blotter. 'We'll find you something that won't drive you too barmy,' he said.

Thorne pointed across the desk at his DCI. A jokey threat. 'You'd better.'

It was a close call as to which of them had been more embarrassed when the tears had suddenly appeared. Had sprung up in corners. Thorne had pressed the heel of his hand quickly against each eye, and wiped, and kicked the metal wastepaper basket halfway across Russell Brigstocke's office.

'Fuck . . .'

Scotland Yard.

Perhaps the single most famous location in the history of detection. A place synonymous with the finest brains and with cutting-edge, crime-fighting technology. Where mysteries were solved and the complexities of the world's most twisted criminal minds were examined.

Where for three weeks, Thorne had been forced to sit in a room no bigger than an airing cupboard, going quietly insane, and trying to work out how many ways a man could kill himself using only standard office equipment.

He had thought, understandably, that the *Demographics of Recruitment* could not possibly be as boring as it sounded. He had been wrong. Although, the first few days hadn't been so bad. He'd been taught how the software program – with which he was supposed to turn hundreds of pages of research into a presentation document, complete with block graphs and pie-charts – worked. His computer instructor was about as interesting as Thorne had expected him to be. But he was, at least, someone to talk to.

Then, left to his own devices, Thorne had quickly discovered the most enjoyable way to pass the time. He was just as quickly rumbled. It didn't take someone long to work out that most of those websites being visited via one particular terminal had very little to do with the recruitment of ethnic minorities, or why more dog-handlers seemed to come from the south-west. Overnight, and without warning, Internet access was denied and, from then on, outside the job itself, there was little for Thorne to do but eke out the daily paper and think about methods of topping himself.

He was considering death from a thousand papercuts when a face appeared around the door. It looked a little thinner than usual, and the smile was nervous. It had been four weeks since Thorne had seen the man who was at least partly responsible for putting him where he was, and Russell Brigstocke had every right to be apprehensive.

He held up a hand, and spoke before Thorne had a chance to say anything. 'I'm sorry. I'll buy you lunch.'

Thorne pretended to consider it. 'Does it include beer?'

Brigstocke winced. 'I'm on a bloody diet, but for you, yes.'

'Why are we still here?'

Thorne hadn't even clocked the name of the place as they'd gone in. They'd come out of the Yard, turned up towards Parliament Square and walked into the first pub they'd come to. The food was bog-standard – chilli con carne that was welded to the dish in places and tepid in others – but they had decent crisps and Stella on draught.

A waitress was clearing away the crockery as Brigstocke came back from the bar with more drinks.

'What's all this in aid of, anyway?' Thorne asked.

Brigstocke sat and leaned towards his glass. Took a sip of mineral water. 'Why's it have to be in aid of anything? Just friends having a drink.'

'You weren't much of a friend a few weeks ago, in your office.'

Brigstocke made eye contact, held it for as long as was comfortable. 'I *was*, Tom.'

The slightly awkward silence that followed was broken by murmured 'sorry's and 'excuse me's as a big man who'd been wedged into the corner next to Thorne stood and squeezed out. Thorne pulled his battered, brown leather jacket from the back of a chair and folded it on to the bench next to him. Relaxed into the space. The pub was busy, but now they had something approaching a bit of privacy.

'Either you want to have a good moan about something,' Thorne said, 'or you want to talk about a case that's pissing you off.'

Brigstocke swallowed, nudged at his glasses with a knuckle. 'Bit of both.'

'Mid-life crisis?' Thorne asked.

'Come again?'

Thorne gestured with his glass. 'Trendy new specs. Diet. You got a bit on the side, Russell?'

Brigstocke reddened slightly, pushed fingers through his thick, black hair. 'Might just as well have, the amount of time I'm spending at home.'

'The rough-sleeper killings, right?' Thorne grinned, enjoying the look of surprise on Brigstocke's face. 'It's not like I've been in Timbuktu, Russ. I spoke to Dave Holland on the phone a few nights ago. Saw a bit in the paper before that. A couple of bodies, isn't it?'

'It *was* a couple . . .'

'Shit . . .'

'"Shit" is bang on. Deep shit is what we're in.'

'There's been a lid on this, right? It literally was a "bit" I saw in the paper.'

'That was the way it was being played until last night. There's going to be a press conference tomorrow afternoon.'

'Tell me . . .'

Brigstocke leaned across the table and spoke, his voice just loud enough for Thorne to hear above Dido, who was whining from the speakers above the bar.

Three victims so far.

The first body had been found almost exactly a month earlier. A homeless man somewhere in his forties, murdered in an alleyway off Golden Square. Four weeks on, and his identity remained unknown.

'We've spoken to other rough sleepers in the area and can't get so much as a nickname. They reckon he was new and he certainly hadn't made any contact with local care services. Some of these people like to matey up and some just want to be left alone. Same as anybody else, I suppose.'

'DSS?'

'We're still checking missed appointments, but I'm not holding my breath. They don't all sign on anyway. Some of them are on the street because they don't want to be found.'

'Everyone's got some official stuff *somewhere*, though. Haven't they? A birth certificate. Something.'

'Maybe he had,' Brigstocke said. 'He might have left it somewhere for safe keeping, in which case that's where it's going to stay. We also have to consider the possibility that he kept it on him, and whoever killed him took it.'

'Either way, you've got sod all.'

'There's a tattoo, that's about it. It's pretty distinctive. It's the only thing we've got to work on at the moment . . .'

There was less of a problem putting a name to the second rough sleeper, killed a couple of streets away a fortnight later. Raymond

Mannion was a known drug abuser with a criminal record. He had been convicted a few years earlier of violent assault and, though there was no ID found on the body, his DNA was on record.

Both men had been kicked to death. They were of similar ages and had been killed in the early hours of the morning. Both Mannion's body and that of the anonymous first victim had been found with twenty-pound notes pinned to their chests.

Thorne took a mouthful of beer and swallowed. 'A series?'

'Looks likely.'

'And now there's been another one?'

'Night before last. Same area, same sort of age, but there are differences. There was no money left on the body.'

'Unless it was taken.'

'That's possible, obviously. No money was *found* on the body.'

'You said differences. What else?'

'He's still breathing,' Brigstocke said. Thorne raised his eyebrows. 'Not that the poor bugger knows a great deal about it. Name's Paddy Hayes. He's on life support at the Middlesex . . .'

Thorne felt a shudder, like cold fingers brushing against the soft hairs at the nape of his neck. He remembered a girl he'd known a few years earlier: attacked and left a fraction from death by a man who'd murdered three before her. Helpless, kept alive by machines. When they'd found her, the police thought that the man they were after had made his first mistake. It was Thorne who had worked out that this killer wasn't actually *trying* to kill anyone. That what he'd done to this girl was what he'd been attempting with the rest of his victims. It was one of those ice-cold/white-hot moments when Thorne had realised the truly monstrous nature of what he was up against.

There'd been far too many since.

'So you think Hayes is part of the pattern or not?'

'It's a bloody coincidence if he isn't.'

'How did you get his ID?'

'Again, nothing official on him, but we found a letter jammed down inside a pocket. Someone from the day centre where he hung out took a look at him and confirmed the name. They had to take a damn good look, though. His head looked like a sack of rotten fruit.'

'What sort of letter?'

'From his son. Telling his father just how much of a useless, drunken bastard he was. How he couldn't give a toss if he never set eyes on him again.' With a finger, Brigstocke pushed what was left of an ice cube around his glass. 'Now the son's the one who's got to decide whether or not to pull the plug . . .'

Thorne grimaced. 'So I take it you're not exactly on the verge of making an arrest?'

'It was always going to be a pig,' Brigstocke said. 'When the first one wasn't sorted within a week it started to look very dodgy, and as soon as the second body turned up they were passing the case around like a turd. That's when *we* ran out of luck and picked the bloody thing up. Just after you went gardening, as it happens.'

'Maybe God was punishing you.'

'Somebody's fucking punishing me. I've had officers on fourteen-hour tours for three weeks and we're precisely nowhere.'

'Grief from above?'

'Grief from *everywhere*. The Commissioner's on our backs because he's getting it in the neck from every homeless charity and pressure group out there. They seem to think because we aren't making any obvious progress that we must be dragging our feet. That, basically, we don't care.'

'Do we?'

Brigstocke ignored him. 'So now it's a *political* issue, and we're fucked because the homeless community itself has bought into this idea that we're not trying very hard. So they've more or less stopped talking to us.'

'You can hardly blame them, though.'

'I'm not *blaming* them. They've got every right to be suspicious.'

'They've got every right to be *scared*, if there's a killer out there. These are people who can't lock the door, remember.'

They said nothing for a few moments. Dido had given way to

Norah Jones. Thorne wondered if there was an album titled *Now That's What I Call Scampi in a Basket.*

'There's another reason they're not talking to us,' Brigstocke said. Thorne looked up from the beer mat. 'There was a statement taken early on from a kid sleeping rough. He reckoned that a police officer had been asking questions.'

Thorne jammed a fist under his chin. 'Sorry, I'm probably being a bit bloody thick, but . . .'

'It was *before* the first murder. He claimed that a police officer had been asking questions the day before the first body was found. Showing a picture. Like he was looking for someone.'

'Looking for who, exactly? I mean, this is the victim you still haven't identified, right?' Brigstocke nodded. 'So didn't this person who was supposedly looking for him mention his name?'

'We could check if we had such a thing as a name and address for the kid who gave the statement. Honestly, nothing about this is simple, Tom.'

Thorne watched Brigstocke take a drink. Took one himself. 'A copper?'

'We've had to tread a bit bloody carefully.'

'Keep it out of the press, you mean?'

Brigstocke raised his voice, irritated. 'Come on, you know damn well that's not the only reason we don't want it plastered all over the papers . . .'

'"It is considered good practice to deliberately withhold details of the MO used by the offender."' Thorne yawned theatrically as he quoted from the most recent edition of the *Murder Investigation Manual*, the detective's bible.

'Right, like the money left on the bodies. So we know the other killings weren't copycats.'

'You can't be sure about Paddy Hayes,' Thorne said.

'No . . .'

Thorne knew that there were certainly sound procedural grounds for keeping things quiet. But he also knew that even the *possible* involvement of a police officer in a case such as this would make the Job's top brass extremely jumpy.

Thorne could see that the next day's press conference made sense. The third body had undoubtedly forced a swift and radical change in media strategy. Now, the public had to be told – but only up to a point – what was going on. It was all spelled out in the *Murder Investigation Manual*: the public had to be reassured, advised, appealed to.

The Met, of course, was also doing the smart thing by covering its arse. God forbid any more bodies should turn up and they had forgotten that the public also needed to be *warned*.

'So, what do you think?' Brigstocke asked. 'Any bright ideas?'

'I think you need to forget about mineral water and go and get yourself a proper drink. A beer gut's the least of your worries.'

'Seriously . . .'

'*Seriously*?' Thorne swilled what little beer there was left around the bottom of his glass. 'You should have tried picking my brains before you bought me three pints of Stella, mate.' He puffed out his cheeks, let the air out slowly. 'My afternoon of recruitment demographics is shot to shit as it is.'

THREE

It was a forty-minute tube ride home from St James's Park. As soon as he walked through his front door that evening he took the CD from his Walkman and transferred it into his main deck. It was part of a boxed set of out-takes and demos from the *American Recordings* sessions, released a few months after Johnny Cash had died in 2003. Thorne cued up 'Redemption Song' – a cover of the Bob Marley classic that Cash had recorded with Joe Strummer. Neither of them had lived to see its release.

Thorne moved around the kitchen, making tea, wondering at how Marley and Strummer could both have gone so young, while Mick Hucknall and Phil Collins were still walking around.

Though he'd been joking with Brigstocke, Thorne hadn't actually got a whole lot done that afternoon. He'd stared at columns of figures, had stabbed perfunctorily at his keyboard, but all the time he'd been thinking about Paddy Hayes and the machines that were keeping him alive. Thinking about the letter the man had carried in his pocket. About the *damn good look* those who knew him had needed before they were able to confirm his identity.

Thorne carried his tea through to the sitting room. He sat and considered everything that Brigstocke had told him, and why. Now that those who were seemingly being targeted had stopped talking to the police, the investigation would stutter and stall very bloody quickly. In all probability, it would grind spectacularly to a halt.

Russell Brigstocke had to have been pretty desperate to come to him for advice in the first place. From what Thorne had heard about the case, that desperation was well founded.

So, what do you think?

In the silence between the tracks, Thorne could hear the distant hum of traffic from the Kentish Town Road, the rumble of a train on the overground line that ran to Camden Town or Gospel Oak. He felt suddenly nostalgic for those few months earlier in the year when he'd shared the flat with Phil Hendricks, whose own place was being treated for damp. It had been cramped and chaotic, with Hendricks dossing down on the sofa bed, and there'd been a good deal of arguing. He remembered the two of them drunkenly rowing about football the day before Hendricks had moved out. That would have been a couple of weeks before the fire . . .

Before the fire. Not 'before my father died'.

That was the way his mind tended to go: the comforting way, towards the absolute. There *was* a fire. The fire was a fact. So was his father's death, of course, but even to form the phrase in his head was to invite in the doubt and the torment to fuck with him for a time. To crack open the carapace of everyday nonsense and force that fissure wider, until it gaped. Until Thorne could do nothing but shut himself down and wait for the churning in his guts and the pounding in his head to stop.

He guessed that Hendricks had done the post-mortems on Mannion and the first victim. That he'd also do the PM on Paddy Hayes when the time came. Hendricks hadn't mentioned the case when they'd spoken, but then Holland had been a bit cagey about it, too. Thorne knew that they were trying to protect him. They believed he was better off where he was. Uninvolved.

Grief and work, so everybody seemed to think, were mutually exclusive. Each got in the way of the other.

Any bright ideas?

Perhaps, though he wasn't sure how bright it was.

Moving to the window, Thorne could feel the draught creeping beneath the sash. Not so long ago the country had been at a standstill for a week as temperatures climbed towards three figures. Now, three weeks into August, and the summer was on its last legs. He thought about how those that lived on the streets were at the mercy of the seasons. How that first hint of autumn would change everything. For those that slept outdoors, that had no other options, a harsh winter could be far more serious than any amount of burst pipes or shunts on black ice.

Not so long ago . . .

Thorne blinked and remembered the feel of the pew beneath him. The smell of himself, sweating in a black suit. No more than three rows filled and most of them there to support him. Feeling a bead of perspiration roll behind his ear and creep down inside the tight, white collar. Knowing he would soon have to stand up and say something . . .

He couldn't carry on with what he was doing now. He wasn't ready to go back to what he'd done before. He could work through grief, or he could grieve at work, but guilt choked the life out of everything.

He moved quickly to the phone and dialled.

'You should think about sending an officer in undercover. Among the rough sleepers.' Thorne wasn't sure if Brigstocke was thinking about his suggestion or had just been stunned into silence. 'It makes sense,' he continued. 'Nobody's talking to you. I can't see there are many other options.'

'It'll take too long to set up.'

'I don't see why; it isn't complicated. You're sending one officer on to the streets, into that community. All we need to set up is a simple line of communication with him.'

'I'll talk to Jesmond, see what he thinks. See if he can *find* anybody. Thanks for the call, Tom . . .'

'Give it some thought.'

A shorter silence this time and then a snort. 'How much more have you had to drink since lunchtime?'

'I can do this, Russell. I did the course . . .'

'Don't be so bloody stupid. An Undercover Two course?'

'Right . . .'

'And how many years ago was that?'

Thorne tuned Brigstocke out momentarily. Elvis was rubbing herself against his shins. He wondered who would feed her if he was away for a while. The woman upstairs would do it if he asked her nicely. She had a couple of her own cats . . .

'I'm hardly going deep inside an organised-crime firm, am I?' Thorne said. 'I can't see how this can be high risk. We're talking about gathering information, that's all.'

'*That's all?*'

'Yes.'

'So you haven't really thought about this bloke who's going round kicking people to death?'

'I want to help catch the fucker, yes.'

'What, you think you can . . . draw him out or something?'

'I don't see how I could . . .'

'Some crap like that?'

'No . . .'

'How does putting yourself in danger help anyone, Tom? How does it help *you*?'

'I'm just going to sleep rough, for Christ's sake,' Thorne said. 'Presuming for a second that this killer *is* still around, how can it be dangerous if he doesn't know I'm there?'

He heard the click of a lighter on the other end of the phone. There was a pause and then the noisy exhalation of smoke.

'The mouse doesn't know there's cheese on the trap,' Brigstocke said. 'But we still call it bait . . .'

FOUR

If a man jumped out in front of him with a severed head in one hand and a blood-spattered axe in the other, gibbering about how the voices in his head had made him do it, Detective Superintendent Trevor Jesmond would be a little out of his depth. He was not, however, a man who thought the *Murder Investigation Manual* was boring, and when it came to 'Communications Strategy' – Chapter Seven, Section Seven, Sub-section Two (Managing the Media) – there was nobody to touch him.

'Let me stress again that the victim of this despicable crime is among the most vulnerable members of our society. His attacker is someone whom we believe has killed twice already. Make no mistake, we will do whatever it takes to apprehend this man before he has a chance to kill again.'

They were gathered in the Press Room at Colindale Police Station; five minutes away from the Peel Centre, where the Murder Squad was based in Becke House. Thorne watched from the back. Staring across the heads of several dozen assembled hacks. Leaning one way and then another to get a clear view of the stage between an assortment of camera tripods.

‘Is this latest victim expected to live?’

‘Mr Hayes is in a critical condition. He is presently on life support at Middlesex Hospital. Without talking further to those doctors caring for him, I’m not in a position to give any more information than that.’

There can’t have been too many people in the room who couldn’t work out that Paddy Hayes was fucked.

‘You’ve suggested that the attempted murder of Mr Hayes is connected to the two other murders of rough sleepers. That this latest attack is part of a series . . .’

Jesmond held up a hand, nodded. He was acknowledging that the journalist was right, but only up to a point. He was also stopping him before he ventured too far down that avenue of questioning. Of course, they’d had to come out and admit that the murders were connected. When the tabloids were putting two and two together, the Met could not afford to appear dim by looking as if they hadn’t.

‘We must assume there’s a connection, yes,’ Jesmond said.

‘So we’re talking about motiveless killings, then? Random attacks?’

A grim half smile. ‘DCI Brigstocke and his team believe that they are hunting a killer who has struck before. The investigation is proceeding, vigorously, along those lines.’

He was playing it very nicely. Striking that essential balance between reassurance and warning. It was, of course, crucial not to alarm the public.

Thorne knew, as Jesmond must have known, that, irrespective of what was said, the papers would print stories about a serial killer. It would shift copies quicker than Posh and Becks, and Fleet Street editors didn’t have any qualms about alarming anybody.

It was a phrase Thorne hated. He had caught, and *not caught*, a number of those who had murdered strangers, and none had borne the slightest resemblance to the creature conjured up by the words ‘serial killer’. All the men and women he’d known who had taken more than one life had done so with what they believed to be good reason. None had thought themselves superhuman, or hunted their victims when the moon was full. They had motives for what they did that had nothing to do with being locked in a cellar when they were children, or made to dress up in their mother's clothes . . .

'As always, we are seeking the co-operation of the public in helping to put an end to these appalling attacks.'

The appeal was textbook stuff. Jesmond gave out the salient facts, insisted that anyone with information, anyone who was in the vicinity, had a duty to come forward. It would, more than likely, prove useless. There can't have been many people hanging around in dark alleyways in the dead of night, and if there had been, it was unlikely, for one reason or another, that any of them would want to come forward. Still, it had to be done, and it had to be specific: dates and times and localities. The last thing they needed was a bland, generalised plea that gave out the wrong message.

We haven't got the first idea who's doing this, but somebody out there must know something. Please help us . . .

'We *will* catch this man,' Jesmond said, winding up. Public confidence was important but so was his own, and he made a point of showing it. Hearts and minds were not won by being mealy-mouthed. His body language and the expression on his face were determined and dynamic. Thorne could easily picture him learning how to project the image, on a weekend course at a country-house hotel. It was as though he were inviting those present to take a bloody careful note of the message, written in foot-high letters across the smart, blue Metropolitan Police backdrop: '*WORKING FOR A SAFER LONDON*'.

Thorne knew that it was smoke and mirrors.

The press conference was there as much as anything to project an image of confidence and efficiency, but Thorne knew that the investigation was in trouble. He knew it was easy enough to marshal resources, to gather significant numbers of officers and be gung-ho about catching a killer when it was only for forty-five minutes in front of the media.

Thorne wondered how anybody was ever fooled.

He hung around in the car park, waiting for Jesmond. Trying to work out the best way of making the approach.

At the sound of the door, Thorne looked up to see two men coming out of the station. Recognising one of them, he tried immediately to turn away without being seen, but he was a fraction too late. He had little choice but to smile and give a small nod. The man he'd been trying to avoid nodded back and Thorne was horrified to see him start to walk over, bringing with him the other man, whose face was vaguely familiar.

Steve Norman was a Senior Force Press Officer, a civilian. He was small and wiry, with a helmet of dark hair and an overinflated sense of his own importance. He and Thorne had crossed swords on a case a couple of years earlier.

'Tom . . .' Still six feet away from him, Norman extended a hand.

Thorne took it, remembering an ill-tempered meeting when Norman had jabbed a finger into his chest. Remembering that he'd threatened to break it . . .

'I hadn't expected to see you,' Norman continued.

So, the gardening leave had become common knowledge. Thorne nodded back towards the main building. 'Conference went well, I thought.' Norman had been heavily involved, of course. Thorne had seen him, lurking at the side of the stage looking pleased with himself. He'd stepped up at one point and whispered something to Russell Brigstocke.

Norman put a hand on his friend's arm and looked towards Thorne. 'Do you two . . .?'

Thorne leaned across. 'Sorry, Tom Thorne . . .'

The man stepped smartly forward and they shook hands. He was mid-fortyish, taller than Thorne and Norman by six inches or more, and thickset.

'This is Alan Ward, from Sky,' Norman said. Thorne could see how much he relished making the introduction.

'Good to meet you,' Ward said. He had large, wire-framed glasses beneath a tangle of dark, curly hair that was three-quarters grey. He put his hand back into the pocket of what Thorne would have described as a denim blazer.

'You too . . .'

Several typically English moments of social awkwardness followed. Thorne would have left, but for the fact that he didn't want to seem rude and had nowhere to go. Norman and Ward, who had clearly been in mid-conversation, were also too polite to excuse themselves immediately. They stood and carried on talking, while Thorne hovered and listened, as though the three of them were old friends.

'I can't remember you at one of these before, Alan,' Norman said.

'It's news, so we're covering it.'

'Bit below your weight though, isn't it?'

Ward stared over Norman's head as he spoke, looking around as if he were taking in a breathtaking view. 'We aren't bombing the shit out of anybody at the moment, thank God, so I'm just here giving the lads on the crew a bit of moral support. Keeping an eye on one or two of the newer guys.'

There was a bit of chuckling, then a pause. Thorne felt like he should say something to justify his presence. 'What is it you do then, Alan?'

Norman took great pride in answering for Ward. 'Alan's a TV reporter. He's normally working in places a little more dangerous than Colindale.'

'Tottenham?' Thorne asked.

Ward laughed and started to speak, but again Norman was in there first. 'Bosnia, Afghanistan, Northern Ireland.' Norman listed the names with great pride, and Thorne realised that he was showing off, like a kid with a new bike. That, however close a friend Ward actually was, Norman got off on knowing him.

Thorne looked at Ward and could see that he was embarrassed, that he and Norman were not really close friends at all. The glance Thorne got back, the momentary discreet roll of the eyes, told him Ward thought Norman was every bit as much of a tit as he did. Thorne took an enormous liking to Alan Ward immediately.

Suddenly it was Thorne's turn to feel embarrassed. 'I thought you looked familiar,' he said. 'I've just realised. I've seen you on the box, haven't I?'

Norman looked like he would wet himself with excitement.

'Have you got Sky, then?' Ward asked.

'I tend to use it for the football mostly I'm ashamed to say.'

'Who are you, Arsenal?'

'God, no!'

At that moment, over Norman's shoulder, Thorne saw Trevor Jesmond emerge. Jesmond looked across, froze, then quickly tried – as Thorne himself had done a few minutes earlier – to spin away without being spotted. Thorne raised a hand, horrified that he and Jesmond shared anything at all in common.

'Well then . . .' Norman said.

To the press officer's obvious delight, Thorne said hasty goodbyes. Ward shook his hand again, and gave him a business card. As Thorne walked away, the reporter said something he didn't altogether catch about getting free tickets for matches.

He caught up with Jesmond just as the Detective Superintendent reached his car.

'Shouldn't you be at Scotland Yard?'

'I was wondering if DCI Brigstocke had said anything to you, sir.'

Jesmond pressed a button on his key to unlock the car. He opened the Rover's door and tossed his cap and briefcase on to the passenger seat.

'My sympathies for recent events are a matter of record . . .'

'Sir . . .'

'But if they have left you in an emotionally charged state, where you are not presently fit to work as a member of my team, what on earth makes you think you'd be able to function efficiently as an undercover officer?'

'I don't think what I'm suggesting is . . . complicated,' Thorne said. 'I think I'm perfectly able—'

Jesmond cut him off. 'Or perhaps that's it.' He blinked slowly. His lashes were sandy, all but lost against his dry skin. He might have been trying to appear knowing and thoughtful, but Thorne watched the thin lips set themselves into what looked to him like a smirk.

'Perhaps your emotional state is precisely *why* you think you should be doing this. Perhaps it's why you consider yourself suitable; why you consider this job suitable for *you*. Have I hit it on the head, Tom? Are you going to be dossing down in a hair shirt?'

Thorne could say nothing. He flicked his eyes away and watched the light slide off the chromed edge of the car's indicators, catching the buttons of Jesmond's immaculate uniform.

'Look, I'm not saying it's a *completely* stupid idea,' Jesmond said. 'You've certainly had stupider.'

Thorne smiled at the line, seeing the glimmer of possibility. 'This one's not even in the top ten,' he said.

'On the plus side, even if you screw it up, I can't see that we have a great deal to lose.'

'I can't see there's *anything* to lose.'

'Give me a day or two, yes?' Jesmond stepped between Thorne and the car door. 'It won't be solely my decision anyway. I'll have to talk to SO10.'

'I really think we can get something out of this,' Thorne said.

'Like I said, a day or two.'

'We can get it quickly as well. There's no need for a long lead-up time. We just do it.' He stared at Jesmond, trying hard to look relaxed even as his stomach jumped and knotted. 'Come on, you've seen some of these down and outs. Staggering around, ranting at the world with a can of cheap lager in their hand. You know me well enough. How hard can that possibly be?'

FIVE

The mood of the café owner had obviously not improved as he cleared away the plates. Holland had eaten toast before he'd left home, but had done his best with a bacon sandwich. Thorne had made short work of the fullest of full English breakfasts.

'The eggs were hard,' Thorne said.

'So? You ate them, didn't you? If you don't like the place, you can fuck off.'

'We'll have two more mugs of tea.'

The owner trudged back behind his counter. The place was a lot busier now, and he had more to do, so it was difficult to tell whether he had any intention of ever bringing the tea as requested.

'Can you find something to arrest him for?' Thorne said. 'Being fat and miserable in a built-up area, maybe?'

'I'm not sure who he hates more, coppers or tramps. We're obviously not doing much for his ambience.'

Thorne stared hard across the room. 'Fuck him. It's hardly the Ritz, is it?'

'I picked up a couple of papers on my way here,' Holland said. He reached down for his bag, dug out a stack of newspapers and dropped them on the table. 'Our picture of Victim One's on virtually every front page today.'

Thorne pulled a couple of the papers towards him. 'TV?'

Holland nodded. 'All the national TV news broadcasts as well. Both ends of *London Tonight*. It's pretty comprehensive . . .'

Thorne stared down at the *Mirror*, at the *Independent*, into a pair of eyes that had been generated by a software program, but nonetheless had the power to find his own, and hold them. Victim One was long-haired and bearded. His flat, black-and-white features were fine, the line of jaw and cheekbones perhaps a little extreme to be lifelike. But the eyes, like the heavy bags beneath them, looked real enough. Dark, narrow, and demanding to be recognised. It was a face that said, *Know me*.

'What do you think?' Holland asked.

Thorne looked at the text that accompanied the pictures. The crucial facts rehashed: a brutal reminder of just how much was known about this man's death when nothing at all was known about the life that had been stolen from him.

Then, the reproduction of the tattoo. The vital collection of letters found on the victim's shoulder. It had been hoped early on – as Brigstocke had told Thorne in the pub – that this might help identify the body, but that hope had proved as temporary as the tattoo itself was permanent.

AB-
S.O.F.A.

The decision not to print a photograph of the tattoo had been taken on grounds of taste. A similar decision with regard to the victim's face had not been necessary: they'd had no choice but to computer-generate, and not just because the face itself was unrecognisable. It was unrecognisable *as a face*: every feature had been all but kicked or stamped clean off the victim's head. The unmarked face that was confronting thousands of people, that very minute over their cornflakes, had been fashioned by a microchip from little more than bone and bruise.

'It's like King's Cross,' Thorne said. 'It's what they did with the victim they couldn't put a name to.'

The fire at King's Cross Underground station in November 1987 had killed thirty-one people, but only thirty bodies were ever claimed. One victim had remained anonymous – in spite of numerous appeals to those who might have known who he was. Thorne remembered that face, too: the sketch on the poster in a hundred tube stations; the clay reconstruction of the head that was lovingly fashioned and paraded in front of the television cameras. Ironically, the dead man, known for years only as Victim 115, had finally been identified just the year before, nearly twenty years after his death, and had turned out to have been a rough sleeper. Many commentators in the press claimed to have been unsurprised. It was obvious he was homeless, or else someone would surely have come forward much earlier, wouldn't they? Thorne wasn't so sure. He doubted that material belongings had a great deal to do with being missed. He thought it was perfectly possible to have a roof over your head, a decent car and two nice holidays a year, yet still go unacknowledged and unclaimed if you had the misfortune to find yourself trapped on a burning escalator.

Thorne reckoned it was less to do with being unknown than with being un*loved*.

'I think we're in with more of a chance though,' Holland said, looking at the picture. 'The quality of this is far higher. It's got to ring a bell with somebody.'

'Let's hope somebody loved him enough.'

Thorne handed the *Independent* back across the table and turned the *Mirror* over to the sports page. He wondered how many footballers had been accused of rape since the last time he'd read a newspaper.

SIX

Thorne leaned in close and stared at himself in the small, square mirror. A week without razor, soap or shampoo didn't seem to have made a great deal of difference. Seven days during which he'd tried to start looking the part, while a pair of stroppy sorts from SO10 – the unit that ran undercover operations – had done their best to put him through a refresher course.

It had all been fairly straightforward. As Thorne had been keen to stress to Brigstocke, the job would be purely about intelligence gathering. There would be no real need to fabricate a detailed back-story – to create what those who worked in this area called a 'deep legend'. When necessary, tax details, Land Registry records and electoral rolls would be doctored, but there would be no need for any such elaborate preparations in this case. Whatever the reason for them being there, those who ended up on the street tended to re-invent themselves anyway; to keep their pasts to themselves. They were starting again.

Thorne took one last look, slammed the locker-door shut and hoisted the rucksack on to his shoulder.

'Once you've been out there a couple of weeks you'll see the difference. Black snot and a proper layer of London grime that won't wash off easily . . .'

Thorne turned to look across at the man standing by the door. 'Who am I fucking kidding, Bren?'

Brendan Maxwell was to be the only person connected with the homeless community who would know what Thorne was doing. What he really was. Maxwell worked as a Senior Outreach Officer for London Lift, an organisation providing counselling and practical help for the city's homeless, in particular those more entrenched rough sleepers who were over twenty-five.

He was also Phil Hendricks' boyfriend. Thorne had been privy to the ups and downs of their often stormy relationship for the last few years and had come to know the tall, skinny Irishman pretty well. Aside from Hendricks himself, and those few officers on the investigation who had been briefed, Maxwell would be – for however long the operation lasted – the only real connection Thorne had between his two lives.

'Don't lose the key,' Maxwell said. 'There aren't any spares.'

Thorne put the key into the front pocket of his rucksack. The locker, where he would leave spare clothes, was one of fifty or so provided for the use of clients at the Lift's mixed-age day centre off St Martin's Lane. The organisation's offices were on the top floor, with the lockers in the basement, along with washing and laundry facilities. On the ground floor were the advice counter, a seating area and a no-frills café serving hot drinks and heavily subsidised meals.

Maxwell walked over. He had short blond hair and wore a brown corduroy shirt tucked into jeans. He cast an amused eye over Thorne's outfit, which he'd already referred to sarcastically as his 'dosser costume'. The sweater and shoes had come from Oxfam and the black jeans were an old pair of Thorne's own.

The grey coat had belonged to his father.

'There's all sorts out there,' Maxwell said. His accent was heavy and the disgust was audible beneath the arch, jokey tone. 'There isn't really a *look*, you know? You could be wearing a three-piece suit and spats, but if you've got a can of Tennent's Extra or a needle in your arm, you'll fit right in.'

'I'll bear that in mind.'

There was a scarred, metal rubbish bin mounted to the wall. Maxwell moved across and took out the stuffed, white bin-liner. Began tying a knot in the top of it. 'This is very bizarre . . .'

'What?'

'First thing I do, with a lot of the younger ones anyway, is give them a reality check. You know? They're straight off the coach or they've hitched here from wherever and some of these kids really do think the place is paved with gold. I swear to God. It's my job, very gently you understand, to point out to them how very wrong, how completely fucking stupid they are. It's usually a waste of time, but even if they tell me to piss off, they find out themselves quickly enough.' He pointed towards a high, dirty window behind a mesh of black metal. 'It's dogshit and fucking despair holding the pavements together out there. A reality check?' He looked across at Thorne. 'Not much point with *you*, is there?'

'Not really.'

Maxwell dropped the bin-bag on to the floor. He reached into his back pocket for a new roll, tore one off. 'Phil thinks you're mental, by the way.'

'I know.'

'I can't say I disagree with him. Why all this De Niro shite?'

'All this what?'

'You know what I mean . . .'

'What are you on about?' Thorne said. 'I've got a mobile phone in my pocket and I'm wearing thermal underwear.'

Maxwell smiled. 'Fair play. You could still go a bit easier though, spend the first couple of nights in a hostel.'

'The men who were killed were all sleeping rough. They died outdoors.' Thorne caught the smell of hot food drifting down from the café. 'Besides, if I'm going to do this, I might as well bloody *do* it.'

Maxwell picked up the full bin-bag and walked to the door. 'Listen,

I'm not having a go, Tom, and I'll be around if you need any help, but don't make any mistake about it. However much you *think* you're doing this, you can always walk away.' He opened the door, then turned back into the room. 'You can dirty yourself up and spend a bit of time kipping on cardboard, but you've got the option to cut and run any bloody time you feel like it. Any time you like. Jump in a taxi back to your flat and your cowboy music.'

Thorne was getting irritated, but had to smile. *Cowboy music.* That was one of Hendricks'. 'I'll see you upstairs,' he said. 'I'd better grab some food before I make a move.'

Maxwell nodded and stepped out into the corridor. 'Stew's good . . .'

It had seemed like as good a spot as any.

Three steps up from pavement level and fairly sheltered. Odd as it was to sleep surrounded by giant black-and-white photographs of actors and extravagant quotes testifying to their skill and comic timing, Thorne figured that a theatre doorway was a safe bet. As long as he waited until the show had finished and the place had shut its doors for the night, he probably wouldn't be bothered. Plus, of course, theatres – unlike shops – tended not to open first thing in the morning.

Two days shy of September, it was a relatively mild night, but within half an hour of lying down, his arse was dead and it felt as though a corpse's feet had been pressed against his neck.

Thorne hitched up the sleeping bag and leaned back against the doors. He'd felt ready to drop only an hour before. Having walked around since the day centre had closed its doors at four o'clock, he'd been stone-cold dead on his feet by the time he'd staked his claim to the theatre doorway. Now, suddenly, he was horribly awake. He thought about getting his gear together again and walking some more, but he didn't want to run the risk of losing his pitch. He'd seen one or two characters earlier in the surrounding streets, mooching around, looking like they were searching for a good spot to spend the night. For a second he decided that reading a book might help him sleep, and then he remembered where he was and what he was doing. It struck him that the first few days would be about similar moments of desire and realisation. About feeling spoiled and stupid every few minutes.

Remembering, and perhaps forgetting, the thousand everyday things that he would be going without.

Music, TV, decent food. But it wasn't even so much about these obvious things themselves. He would eat. There was a television in the day centre if he had a desperate desire to watch *Richard and Judy*. It was getting used to such things not being available whenever he felt like them. It was a question of choice, and space. Somewhere to lie down, to feel comfortable, to have a piss . . .

He started to make a list in his head of all these things and it didn't take him long to work out exactly what it was that he needed. He couldn't believe that he'd been so stupid as not to get it organised. Christ, he'd have had a beer at home, wouldn't he? He decided that tomorrow night he'd make sure he stashed a couple of cans in his rucksack. Maybe something even stronger.

He sat, bored and scared, letting his head drop back against the polished wooden doors and staring at the photographs all around him. Listening to people shouting and to cars accelerating away. Smelling the aftershave on his father's coat.

It was, he guessed, not even one o'clock yet. People still walked past his doorway every few minutes or so. Thorne wondered how long it would be before he no longer bothered looking up at them.

★ ★ ★

In retrospect, his one regret about killing the Driver was that he hadn't given the pathetic twat time to get a proper look at him. He'd have liked to have seen the shock register, just for a second, before the first kick had . . .

Mind you, there was no point dwelling on it. Most of them had been so out of it, so away with the fairies, that they hadn't registered much of *anything*. The Driver was in such a state, he wouldn't have recognised him anyway, likely as not. He could smell the beer on the poor sod, alongside that stink they all had. That tangy, tramp stink. Sharp and musty at the same time, like cats had been pissing in a charity shop.

He turned off the bathroom light and moved into the darkness of the bedroom. He thought about checking to see if there was any metal on MTV, maybe working out for twenty minutes. He decided against it and began to undress; it was easy enough to do a bit more in the morning. He'd eaten late and the food hadn't had a chance to go down.

Things in London had been fairly straightforward up to now, so it annoyed him that this last one, Hayes, had survived. It sounded, from what they'd said on the news and in the paper, that he wouldn't survive for very long, but still, it rankled with him. It made him swear at the mirror and kick out at stuff. You did a good job and you took a pride in it. That mattered. It was important that you did what was required.

He flicked on the TV. The light from the small screen danced across his clothes as he folded them carefully on to the chair at the foot of his bed.

He'd already made up his mind to do another one. This one would be just for him, would go some way towards making up for botching the last one. It wasn't strictly necessary, but it couldn't do much harm. It would cost him another note, of course, but twenty quid a pop wasn't a lot for reinforcement *that* bloody good.

He climbed beneath the blanket in his vest and pants and began jabbing at the remote. Having looked at what was showing on all the stations a few times, it was obvious that there was nothing he fancied, but he carried on regardless. Moving methodically through the channels with the sound down.

★ ★ ★

When he'd finished, Thorne tucked himself in and turned from the wall to find himself being studied.

'You want to be careful, mate. There's one or two coppers round here'll do you for that. Take great delight in doing it, an' all . . .'

He stood directly opposite Thorne on the other side of the road, with a grey blanket wrapped around his shoulders. Early twenties was Thorne's best estimate. He had delicate features set below spikes of blond hair and his cheeks hollowed dramatically as he dragged hard on a cigarette.

'I can show you a place thirty seconds from here which is a bit more private, like, and a lot bloody safer. Of course, there's always McDonald's if you want to go before midnight, though there *is* one down towards Trafalgar Square that sometimes stays open a bit longer. With a piss, like, there's always *somewhere*, but there's nothing quite like seeing them golden arches when you're bursting for a shit.' He reached up a hand from beneath the blanket to take the cigarette from his mouth.

Thorne said nothing for a few seconds. The boy seemed friendly enough, but still, Thorne sensed that caution would be best. It would certainly *look* best. 'Right,' he said. His voice was flat, with just a hint of aggression in the delivery.

The boy looked to his right. 'You're in the theatre doorway, yeah? Just round the corner there?'

Thorne nodded, began to walk slowly towards it.

'Just so as you know, that's Terry T's spot.' He began to move in the same direction as Thorne, walking parallel to him on the other side of the narrow street.

'So, where is he?'

'He's gone visiting, so you'll be all right for the time being. He'll be back at some point, though, so just as long as you know, yeah? As long as you know that's Terry T's spot.'

'Well, I know now. Thanks.'

The boy crossed the road, moving over to Thorne in a couple of strides and walking alongside him. 'It's a good spot, like. Sheltered . . .'

'That's why I took it,' Thorne said. 'I think I'll move around a bit anyway, see how it pans out.'

'Only Terry can be a right psycho, like. Goes a bit mental sometimes and, you know, with him being so enormous and that . . .'

'Mental *how* exactly?'

The boy chucked his cigarette into the road and hissed out a laugh. 'I'm winding you up. I'm kidding, like. Terry's all right, plus he's my mate, so I'll square things if he does get a bit funny with you.'

Thorne had seen the joke coming, but had let the boy have his moment. 'Thanks,' he said.

They rounded the corner and Thorne was relieved to see that his sleeping bag and rucksack were still there. He'd decided to risk leaving them for a minute or two while he'd gone to answer the call of nature. The relief must have been clear to see on his face.

'Don't worry, mate, people only tend to nick what they can sell. Nothing valuable in your bag, is there?' Thorne shook his head. 'Don't worry about your sleeping bag though, you can pick one of them up anywhere. Salvation Army's got thousands of the bloody things, or you'll just see 'em lying around, so you can help yourself. You want to watch out for scabies, though, that is *not* fucking pleasant.'

'Cheers . . .'

'Best not to cart that much around at all if you can help it. Leave your stuff somewhere else, you know, one of the day centres or whatever. Trust me, even a plastic bag with some old papers and a pair of socks in it gets dead heavy if you're carrying it around all the time, like.'

Thorne climbed the marble steps and sat down in the doorway. 'How come you're such a font of all fucking knowledge? You're only twelve.'

The boy laughed again, nodding his head and spitting out the laugh between his teeth. 'Right, mate, you're right, but it's like dog years on the streets, so I'm a lot older than you where it counts, you know?'

'If you say so.'

'How long you been around, then? I've not seen you . . .'

'First night,' Thorne said.

'Fuck.' The boy pulled the blanket tighter around his shoulders. He repeated himself, drawing out the word, respectfully.

'So, what? You're the welcoming committee, are you?'

'Nearest thing to it, yeah, if you like.'

Thorne watched the boy rummage beneath the blanket and emerge with another cigarette. He could see that the boy was much taller than he'd first appeared.

He'd walked with hunched shoulders, eyes down, as though he could tell exactly which way he were going by looking at the cracks in the stone slabs, by studying the pattern of discarded chewing gum on the pavement.

'You look like the Man With No Name,' Thorne said.

The boy finished lighting up, blew out a thin stream of smoke. 'You what?'

Thorne pointed towards the blanket around the boy's shoulders. 'With that. Like Clint Eastwood in the movie, you know? *The Good, The Bad and The Ugly*.'

The boy shrugged and thought for a minute. He shifted his weight from foot to foot, rocking from side to side. 'He the one did those films with the monkey?'

'Doesn't matter.' Thorne shoved his feet down inside the sleeping bag. 'Good time for your mate Terry to go visiting.'

'Why's that, then?'

'One less for this nutter to go after. This loony that's killing rough sleepers.'

The boy's cheeks sank into shadow again as he took a deep drag. He held in the smoke until he needed to take a breath. 'I suppose. He's still got plenty to choose from.' His mood had changed suddenly: fear, suspicion or perhaps a bit of both. It was hard for Thorne to work out which.

'Did you know any of them?' Thorne asked the question casually, through a yawn. 'Any of the blokes who were . . .?'

'I knew Paddy a bit, yeah. Mad as a snake, like, but totally harmless. Paddy was happy with God and a bottle.'

'So you don't reckon he could have fallen out with somebody? Nobody had a reason to give him a kicking?'

The boy looked straight at Thorne but it was as though he'd heard a totally different question. He nodded once, twice, quickly. Repeated what he'd just said: 'God and a bottle . . .'

'Right.'

'What's your name?' Another, equally sudden, change of mood and tone.

'Tom.'

'I'll see you around, Tom . . .'

'What about you? You might look like the Man With No Name, but you must have one.'

'Spike. Because of the hair, you know? Like the vampire in *Buffy*.'

Now it was Thorne's turn to be the one on whom a reference was lost. 'OK, but what's your real name?'

The boy cocked his head, looked at Thorne as though he too were a harmless old nutcase. 'Just Spike.'

Then he turned, hoiked up his blanket and began walking north towards Soho.

SEVEN

The mobile phone Thorne had been issued with was permanently set to vibrate, and had been shoved deep inside the pocket of his overcoat. It had been agreed that Thorne and Holland would talk twice every day, morning and evening. Contact either way could, of course, be made at other times if necessary, and a face-to-face meeting, with either Holland or Brigstocke, would take place, all being well, once a week.

Thorne had already spoken to Holland by the time he walked into the London Lift day centre, just after the place opened at nine o'clock. He found himself in a small holding area between the front entrance and a larger glass door. The young Asian man on duty at the reception desk eyed him through the glass for ten, maybe fifteen seconds, before pressing the button that allowed him through the second set of doors.

'All right?' Thorne stepped up and leaned against the counter.

'I'm good, mate. You?'

Thorne shrugged and scribbled his name in the register that had been passed across to him. The receptionist, who wore an ID badge that said *RAJ*, tapped a couple of keys on his computer and Thorne was buzzed through the steel door into the café area.

A fair number of the grey or orange plastic chairs – scattered around tables or lined against the walls – were already taken. Most people sat alone, nursing hot drinks and rolls, and though a few had gathered in groups, the sound of a knife scraping across a plate rose easily above the muted level of conversation. Considering how busy it was, the place was oddly still and quiet. Thorne knew that half as many people would be making twice as much noise in the Starbucks across the road.

He moved to the end of a short queue, studied the price list on the blackboard behind the counter. He saw a familiar figure rise from a table across the room and nod. Spike walked across, moving a little slower than he had done the night before.

'Found this place quick enough, then?'

'I saw an outreach worker,' Thorne said. 'Came along last night after you left, told me if I got down here first thing, I could get a decent breakfast.' The second lie of the day came easily. He'd told the first on the phone half an hour earlier, when Dave Holland had asked him how his night had been.

Thorne looked around. It was a big room, and bright. One wall was dominated by a vast, glossy mural; notice-boards ran the length of another.

'You signing on?' Spike asked.

Thorne nodded. He wouldn't be going to the dole office, but he'd taken the decision early to live on the equivalent of state benefit. He would exist on the princely sum of forty-six pounds a week, and if he wanted any more he was going to have to find his own way to come up with it, same as anybody else sleeping on the street.

He took a step closer to the counter, remembering what Brendan had said about *De Niro shite*.

'The rolls aren't bad,' Spike said. 'Bacon could be crispier.'

'I just want tea.'

Thorne's instinct at that moment was to put his hand a little deeper into his pocket and offer to buy tea for Spike, too, but he stamped on the natural impulse to be generous. The idea was to fit in, and he knew damn well that, where he was, nobody would make that kind of gesture.

They reached the front of the queue and Spike stepped in front of him. 'I'll get the teas in.'

Thorne watched Spike hand over forty pence for two cups of tea and realised that there was precious little he could take for granted.

They walked over to a table, Thorne a step or two behind Spike, thinking, *He must want something*. Then, *Fuck, I'm doing it again.*

'You get much sleep?' Thorne asked.

Spike grinned. 'Haven't been to bed yet, like. Busy night. I'll crash for a couple of hours later on.'

'Where d'you bed down?'

Spike seemed distracted, nodding to himself. Thorne repeated the question.

'The subway under Marble Arch. I only come into the West End during the day, like, to make some money.' The grin again, spreading slowly. 'I commute.'

Thorne laughed, slurped at his tea.

'It's not bad this place,' Spike said. He leaned down low across the table and dropped his voice. Thorne could just make out the last gasp of an accent. Somewhere in the south-west he reckoned. 'There's not many centres around like this, where under twenty-fives and over twenty-fives can hang around together. Most of 'em are one or the other. They prefer it if we don't mix.'

Thorne shook his head. 'Why?'

'Stands to reason, when you think about it. The older ones've picked up every bad habit going, haven't they? You take somebody fresh on the streets. After a couple of weeks knocking about with someone who's been around a while, he'll be a pisshead or he'll be selling his arse or whatever.'

It made sense, Thorne thought, but only up to a point. 'Yeah, but look at us two. I've got twenty-odd years on you and you're the one that's been around.'

Spike laughed. Thorne listened to the breath rattling out of him and looked into the pinprick of light at the centre of his shrunken pupils, and thought:

You're the one that's picked up the bad habit . . .

Thorne had seen it the previous night: the glow from a streetlamp catching a sheen of sweat across Spike's forehead, heightening the waxy pallor of his skin. This morning, it was obvious that he'd not long got his fix. Thorne knew that without it he'd have no chance of getting any sleep.

'Can you not get a hostel place?'

'Not really bothered at the moment. When I wake up covered in frost, like, I'll be well up for it, no question, but I'm all right where I am just now. Been in plenty of hostels, but I'm not really cut out for 'em. I'm too . . . chaotic, and that's a technical term. "Chaotic". I'm fine for a few days or a week, and then I fuck up, and end up back on the street, so . . .'

Spike's speech had slowed dramatically, and his gaze had become fixed on a spot above Thorne and to the right of him. Slowly, he lowered his head and turned, and it was as though the eyes followed reluctantly, a second later. 'I think . . . it's bedtime,' he said.

Thorne shrugged. A junkie's hours.

Spike slid his chair slowly away from the table, though he showed no sign of getting up from it. On the other side of the room voices were raised briefly, but by the time Thorne looked across, whatever had kicked off seemed to have died down again.

'Maybe see you back here lunchtime.'

'Maybe,' Thorne said.

'Had enough yet?' Brendan Maxwell asked.

Thorne ignored the sarcasm. 'Tell me about Spike,' he said.

As soon as the breakfast rush had started to die down, Thorne had wandered out. Holland had told him earlier that Phil Hendricks would be coming in, and Thorne was keen to see him. He'd headed surreptitiously towards the offices. The admin area was on the far side of the top floor, and Maxwell had given him the four-digit staff code to get through each of the doors. There were coded locks on every door in the place.

With the open-plan arrangement of offices offering little privacy, Thorne, Maxwell and Hendricks had gathered in a small meeting room at the back of the building. If anyone wandered in, it would look like a case-worker–client conference of some sort, but Thorne wasn't planning to hang around very long, anyway. It was just a quick catch-up.

Maxwell was perched on the edge of a table next to Hendricks. 'He's not quite twenty-five, so Spike's not one of mine yet, but I couldn't tell you anything even if he was.'

Hendricks looked sideways at his boyfriend. To Thorne, it seemed like a look that was asking Maxwell to lighten up a little. To bend the rules.

'Come on, Phil,' Maxwell said. 'You know how it works.' He turned back to Thorne. 'Look, I had a long chat with your boss about this. There are major confidentiality issues that have to be considered.'

'Fair enough,' Thorne said. Brigstocke had made the position very clear to him. Unless he had good reason to think it would directly aid the investigation, Thorne would be given no personal information about other rough sleepers.

'It's just the way we do things. I've had Samaritans on the phone trying to trace someone on behalf of parents. People who just want to know if their kid's alive or dead. The person they're looking for might be downstairs drinking tea, but I can't say anything. I can't tell them because maybe they're the reason why the kid's on the street in the first place, you know?'

'Just talk to this kid if you're interested,' Hendricks said.

Maxwell nodded his agreement, leaned gently against his partner. 'Spike's not shy, I can tell you that much. You'll get his life story if he's in the mood to tell you.'

For a few moments nobody said anything. Hendricks and Maxwell were usually a demonstrative couple physically, but Thorne sensed that, at that moment, Hendricks was a little uncomfortable with Maxwell's arm resting on his shoulder.

There had been periods in the past when the relationship between the three of them had become somewhat complex. Thorne thought that Maxwell could, on occasion, be jealous of the platonic relationship he shared with Hendricks. At other times, after a beer or three, Thorne was not beyond wondering if it were he himself who was the jealous one. Right that minute, he was too tired to think much about anything at all. He took a moment. He knew that if he was going to last the course, this was a level of tiredness he was going to have to get used to pretty bloody quickly.

'So, what's happening?' he asked Hendricks. Having spoken to Holland, he was practically up to speed, but Hendricks' take on things, as the civilian member of the team, was always worth getting. 'Anything I should know?'

Hendricks looked thoughtful, then began listing the headlines. 'Brigstocke's talking to a profiler. They're re-canvassing the area where Paddy Hayes was attacked. Everyone's waiting around for the next body to show up, to be honest. Oh, and Spurs lost three–one at Aston Villa last night.'

'Cheers . . .'

There was a knock and a man stepped smartly into the room. He was somewhere in his late forties with neatly combed brown hair and glasses. He wore jeans that were a fraction too tight and a blue blazer over a checked shirt.

The man took in the scene quickly, then addressed himself to Maxwell. 'Sorry, Brendan. Can I have a word when you've got a minute?'

Maxwell pushed himself away from the table, but before he could say anything the man was already on his way out.

'Bollocks,' Maxwell muttered.

Hendricks leaned towards Thorne, spoke in a theatrical whisper. 'Brendan's new boss.'

Maxwell looked none too pleased. 'He's not my boss. He's just the arsehole who controls our budget.' He walked to the door, stopped and turned back to Thorne. 'I was wrong about it taking a couple of weeks, by the way. You look pretty rough already.'

Thorne watched him leave. There'd been a smile on Maxwell's face, but it hadn't taken all the edge off the comment.

'Don't worry about it.' Hendricks rubbed his palm rapidly back and forth across his shaved head. 'He's just in a shitty mood because he isn't getting on with . . .' He pointed at the door.

Thorne nodded. 'The arsehole. He sounded pretty posh.'

'Horribly posh. There's a big consortium running all the outreach stuff now, and they want people with more of a business background. Brendan and a few of the others can't even fill in a claim form for their expenses, so this bloke's been shaking things up. There's a bit of tension.' Hendricks was clearly struck by something hugely funny. 'It's like Brendan's you, and this new bloke's Trevor Jesmond.'

Thorne scowled. 'Then Brendan has my deepest sympathy.'

'Actually, this new bloke's not *quite* as bad as Jesmond.'

'That would be going some . . .'

'Stupid bugger had some high-powered banking job before this. Jetting all round the world for multinationals, oil companies, whatever, and he chucks it all in. Takes a massive pay cut to come and work for the care services.'

'Bloody do-gooder.'

'Mind you, you could be a *paperboy* and you'd still be taking a pay-cut . . .'

Thorne stretched, yawned noisily. 'I'd better get back out there. I'm sure you must have things that need cutting up.'

'I'll find something.'

'Brendan told me you think I'm mad,' Thorne said.

'Only moderately.'

'I didn't see what else we could do. Still don't.'

Hendricks opened the door. 'I'm not worried about the *investigation* . . .'

They both turned at the sound of rain blowing against the window, exchanged the comically world-weary look of a practised double act.

'Brendan really doesn't approve of this,' Thorne said. The silence told him that this was something Hendricks didn't need to be told; that this was an issue he and Brendan had probably argued about. 'Listen, I know how seriously Brendan takes his job, and I know that all he cares about is getting his clients off the streets. So tell him this when you two kiss and make up later on . . .'

'Before or after?'

'I'm serious, Phil. Remind him why we're doing this again, will you? Tell him that there's someone else out there who wants to get rough sleepers off the street, and this fucker's got his own way of doing it . . .'

By lunchtime, the London Lift's café area was busy again. The tables had been pushed closer together and somewhere between thirty and forty people sat eating, or queuing for food at the counter.

Thorne carried a plate of stew across to a table and got stuck in.

Around him were a few faces he recognised. He exchanged nods with one or two people he'd run into during the course of the day so far: an old man he'd walked the length of the Strand with; a Glaswegian with a woolly Chelsea hat and no teeth; a scowling, stick-thin Welshman who'd become aggressive when he'd thought Thorne was stealing his begging pitch, and had then turned scarily affectionate once Thorne had explained that he was doing no such thing. On the opposite side of the room, Thorne saw Spike, sitting with his back to him with his arm around the shoulders of an equally skinny girl.

Again, it was quieter than it might have been. By far the loudest noise came from a big, white-haired man at the other end of the table from Thorne. The man beamed and frowned – pushing a spoon distractedly through his food – far more intent on the two-way conversation he was having with himself on an invisible radio. Every half a minute or so he would hiss, imitating the sound of static, before delivering his message. Then, a few seconds later, he would move his hand, switch the 'radio' to the other ear, and give himself an answer.

'This is London calling the President,' he said.

Spike went to the counter to collect his pudding. On the way back to his table he saw Thorne and shouted a hello. Thorne briefly waved a spoon, then carried on eating. The stew was thick with pearl barley and the gravy was tasteless, but at £1.25 for two courses, he had little cause for complaint.

Once he'd finished eating, Spike walked over, hand in hand with the girl, to where Thorne was sitting.

'This is Caroline,' he said. 'Caz.'

'Nice to meet you. I'm Tom . . .'

The girl had red-rimmed eyes and hair like sticky strands of dark toffee. She wore a faded rugby shirt under a zip-up top, and nervously spun multi-coloured beads and thin leather bracelets around her wrists.

'Spike and me are engaged,' she said.

Spike and his girlfriend sat and talked to Thorne while he finished his lunch. They told him about the time when they were asleep and they'd been sprayed with graffiti, and how another time they'd been pissed on by a gang of teenage boys. About how Caroline had once been propositioned by a woman off the telly and told her to go and fuck herself. About the flat they were planning to move into together once they had a bit of luck.

'It's well fucking overdue, you know?'

'I do know,' Thorne said.

Spike did most of the talking. Thorne figured that this was about as close to normal as the boy ever got: a few hours of balance, of *numbness* between being wasted and needy. It was a window of opportunity that Thorne knew would get smaller and smaller as time went on.

'Everyone deserves a bit of luck, don't they?'

When Caroline did speak, it was in a low mumble. Her voice had the flat vowels and slightly nasal tone of the West Midlands, but Thorne could hear a stronger influence.

Smack had an accent of its own.

There was a sudden, loud hiss from the other end of the table. The big man was receiving another message. Thorne stared at his red face and fat, flapping hands.

'That's Radio Bob,' Spike said. He leaned in and shouted, 'Oi, Bob. Say hello, you cunt . . .'

A pair of small dark eyes blinked and swivelled and settled on Thorne. 'Houston, we have a problem,' Radio Bob said.

Spike sniffed and pointed to a man sitting on an adjacent table. 'And that's Moony,' he said. 'He knew Paddy as well.'

'Did he?'

Spike shouted, beckoned over a skinny character with a sparse, gingery beard. His straw-coloured thatch hid the clumps of dandruff far better than the vast lapels of his dirty brown sports jacket.

'This is Tom,' Spike said.

Moony fiddled with the top of what looked like the plastic Coke bottle he had jammed into his pocket. Cooking-sherry was Thorne's best guess. It was certainly a long time since the bottle had seen anything as benign as Coca-Cola.

'Give me a minute or two,' Moony said, sitting. The voice was high and light; effete, even. 'Just one minute, and I'll tell you what you do. I'll tell you what you *did*, I should really say. In your previous life. I'm never wrong, never. I've got a knack for it . . .'

Thorne spooned stew into his mouth, grunted a marginal interest.

Spike hauled Caroline to her feet and moved towards the counter. 'I'm going to get some tea.' He screwed up his face, put on a posh voice and brayed. 'Perhaps a crumpet, if they have such a thing.'

Moony watched them go, expressionless, stroking the neck of his bottle.

Thorne wondered if Moony was a surname or a nickname, but knew better than to ask. If the latter, then its origin was not obvious. Haggard and pockmarked, he certainly didn't have a moonface. Maybe he was partial to showing people his arse when he'd had a few too many. If so, a sighting might well be on the cards, judging by the state of him. By the stink of him.

'You knew this poor bastard that was half kicked to death, then?' Thorne spoke without looking up from his dish. 'Haynes, was it?'

'Hayes, right. Paddy Hayes. I knew Paddy well enough, certainly. On a life-support machine, according to the television, but we all know that means "vegetable", don't we?'

'Right.' Thorne had spoken to Holland about Paddy Hayes first thing that morning. There was no change. None was expected.

'Not that he can think anything now, of course, but if he could, I wonder if he'd still think that everything happened for a reason. I wonder if he'd still be on good terms with Him upstairs. I wonder if he'd be all *forgiving.*' He scoffed, pointed a finger heavenwards. 'Mysterious ways, my arse.'

Thorne folded a slice of tacky white bread in half and began to mop up the last of his stew.

'I knew the second victim too, you know.'

Raymond Mannion. Found fourteen days after the first victim. Killed three streets away. Thorne looked up, but just for a second, doing his best not to appear overly interested.

'Ray and I talked a great deal,' Moony said. 'A great deal.'

Thorne pushed a dollop of soggy bread into his mouth and wondered who it was that Moony reminded him of. He realised that it was Steve Norman, the press officer: Moony had that same self-importance that Norman had been full of when he'd introduced Thorne to his friend from Sky. He was enjoying himself.

'What did you talk about?' Thorne asked.

'When you've got as much time to talk as *we* had, you tend to cover the entire spectrum. He was drug-fucked, so there were occasions when he couldn't string a sentence together, but we discussed most things at one time or another.'

'Did you talk to him on the night he was killed?'

'*Hours* before he was killed, mate. Just hours before.'

'Christ.'

Moony lowered his voice. 'Which is how I know he was scared.'

'Scared of what?'

'Like I said, he was a junkie, so I thought it was just that at first, you know? Then I could see that something had really put the wind up him. Or some*one* had . . .'

There was certainly an element of grandstanding to the way Moony was telling it, but Thorne thought he could smell truth as well as bullshit.

'He'd said something before about someone asking him questions. It was just after that first bloke was killed he told me this, the one they can't identify.'

'Did you know *him*?'

Moony shook his head.

'So who was asking your friend these questions, then?'

A flash of gold in his mouth, and a snigger that carried the smell of booze right across the table. 'Well, this is the thing, isn't it? Ray reckoned it was a copper, reckoned that he was looking for the bloke that turned up stiff a couple of days later.'

Thorne let a look that said *I'm impressed* pass slowly across his face, while his mind raced. Mannion was a druggie. What he told Moony, if he told him anything at all, could easily have been down to a dose of everyday delusional paranoia. But what if this wasn't a story cooked up in a dirty spoon? Was it at least possible that Raymond Mannion was terrified because he knew something, because he'd seen something? Did he think that someone he'd spoken to had kicked one rough sleeper to death and might fancy coming back for him?

'So this is what he tells me,' Moony said. 'And every time I run into him after that, he looks like he can't decide whether to leg it or shit himself and, lo and behold, suddenly it's Ray who's the one with his brains kicked all over the shop and a twenty-quid note pinned to his fucking chest.' He leaned back, pleased with himself. 'You've got to admit, it's bloody strange.'

Thorne grunted. He did think it was strange, but he was already thinking about something else, something Moony had just said. There was only one thing it could possibly mean . . .

He became aware of Moony talking again and looked up. 'What?'

'She's pretty fit,' Moony said. He nodded across to where Spike and his girlfriend were talking to one of the care-workers. The three of them were laughing, drinking tea. '*Her*. One-Day Caroline.'

Thorne's mind was still in several places at once, but one part of it was curious enough. 'Why d'you call her that?'

Moony looked pleased with himself again, like this was something else he was going to relish passing on. 'Because she's always bleating on about how she's going to get herself clean "*one day*". Then, when she tries to give up, *one day* is usually as long as she lasts . . .'

Thorne looked over, watched Caroline absently trailing her fingers down Spike's arm as she listened to the care-worker, nodding intently.

He pushed his chair away from the table. 'So, come on then,' he said. 'You've had more than a couple of minutes. What did I do before this?'

Moony looked suddenly serious, as if he were getting in touch with something significant, something profound, deep down in his pickled innards. 'It's business, definitely business,' he said. 'Some sort of financial thing. Accountancy or stocks and shares. I reckon you were loaded and then you lost the fucking lot. I'm right, aren't I? I'm never fucking wrong.'

'Bang on, mate.' Thorne raised his hands. 'You are absolutely bang on. That's seriously spooky.' He stood and walked away, leaving Moony nodding slowly, gently patting the bottle in his pocket as though it were his pet. Or his muse.

Out near the reception desk, Thorne all but bumped straight into the man who'd walked in when he'd been talking to Maxwell and Hendricks that morning. Maxwell's new boss . . .

'Oh, hi, I'm Lawrence Healey.'

The tone was not one Thorne had been on the receiving end of for a few days. It was brisk but friendly; respectful, even. Healey proffered a hand and Thorne shook it, wondering for just a second or two if the man knew he was really a police officer.

'Brendan tells me you're new.'

'New-ish,' Thorne said.

'Well, I know how you feel. I'm a new boy myself. If there's anything you need, anything you want to talk about, you mustn't be shy about it. Yes? You know where we are . . .'

Thorne said that he did, and that he certainly wouldn't be.

As he moved towards the exit he could still make out the hiss and blather of Radio Bob's broadcasts, coming from the café, on the other side of the door behind him.

'*Are you receiving me? Are you receiving me . . .?*'

EIGHT

London stank of desperation.

This time of night, of course, it smelled of all sorts of things: fags and fast food; piss and petrol. Still, in spite of all the money that was clearly being spent – the wealth on display in the rows of Mercs, Jags and Beamers, and in the ranks of overpriced restaurants – you could catch the whiff of desperation almost everywhere. Pungent and unmistakable. Classless and clinging, and far stronger than anything being rubbed on to wrists, or rolled across armpits, or sprayed over shoppers by those grotesquely made-up hags in Harrods and Selfridges.

Where he was walking, the desperation was of the common or garden variety. A need for warmth, food or a fix. A need for comfort. But some of the rarer blends of that distinctive scent were around as well, drifting through the West End, there if you could nose them out beneath the everyday stink of chicken and vomit and beer.

From Oxford Street and Tottenham Court Road, it floated south – the stale desperation for a smarter phone and a younger partner mingling with those more basic, bodily needs, reeking in Soho and the Circus – before moving along Piccadilly, where the drive to be better dressed, better off and better *than* gave off the sharpest stench of all. It was a world away from the gutters and the shitty cut-throughs, of course – from the alleyways that were presently his own area of operation – but he knew that the desperation was of an even headier kind in Old Bond Street and the Burlington Arcade . . .

It was already clear to him that things had changed since he'd killed the Driver. Walking around within that rough square bordered by Oxford Street, Regent Street, Shaftesbury Avenue and Charing Cross Road, he'd noticed that more of them were settling down in pairs. Looking out for each other: one asleep and the other keeping at least one eye open.

It was understandable. More than that, it was commendable.

Word would probably have spread faster than head lice anyway after the Driver had been killed. After the second one, for certain. But now the television and the newspapers were all banging on about the danger to what they'd all taken to calling the city's 'most vulnerable citizens'. It was tricky to see it clearly in a community as shifting – as *tidal*, they said – as this one was, but panic was starting to set in.

Now, *that* was another smell he knew far better than most people.

He also knew very well that panic wouldn't save anyone. Panic was what you saw in the eyes of dead men and what stained the floor beneath them.

Moving past Charing Cross Station for the second time that evening and on towards Waterloo Bridge, he peered up every likely-looking side street and into every pool of shadow, humming a song from the mid-eighties. Something about panic on the streets of London. He couldn't remember who the song was by.

It wasn't as if he was going to have any problem finding someone alone and fucked-up and begging for a good kicking. The very nature of these people would work against them in the end. If they were cut out to stick together, to bond with others, you'd hardly see them curling up in puddles and sleeping in their own shit, would you?

Singling one of them out would be easy enough.

They were the leavings; the ones who had failed at everything and would ultimately fuck up at the most basic task of staying alive. Failure was their strong suit, and, at the end of the day, helping one more of them do what they were obviously good at wasn't going to cost him a great deal of sleep.

How could you take someone's life when they didn't really have one in the first place?

⋆ ⋆ ⋆

Moony was two bottles dead to the world, but he still woke up the second the boot was placed across his neck.

'Jesus!'

The sole was wiped slowly across a cheek, then lifted. 'I thought it was your mate Paddy who was the religious one.'

As Moony turned to look up, Thorne bent and grabbed hold of the conveniently wide lapels. He dragged him fast across the narrow street, leaving sheets of cardboard and blankets trailing in his wake. Moony yelped like a throttled dog.

'Hey!' A figure took two tentative steps towards them from the end of the street.

'Fuck off,' Thorne said, and the figure did as he'd been told.

Thorne slammed Moony into a wall plastered with posters for boy bands and nightclubs, pushed him hard on to his arse and squatted down close to him.

'Oh my Christ,' Moony said, breathless.

'There you go again,' Thorne said. 'Strange how people turn to Him when they think their number's up.' He pressed a palm against Moony's heart. 'That's going ten to the dozen, that is.'

'What do you . . .' – three gulps of air – '. . . fucking expect?'

'You thought I was the man who killed Ray, didn't you? The man who kicked Paddy's brains into the middle of next week.' Thorne took a handful of the loose flesh around Moony's chest and dug in his fingers. 'You thought you were about to get some dosh pinned on to you, right?'

Moony squealed and grabbed at Thorne's fist but Thorne calmly raised his other hand and slapped him twice, a little harder than he might have slapped someone who was unconscious. Moony's hands flew to his face and he stopped struggling.

'Only it's the money that's bothering me,' Thorne said. 'Well, not the money itself so much as the fact that you knew about it. Do you see what I'm saying?'

Moony shook his head.

'There's been nothing on the news about any money being pinned to the victims' chests. Nothing in the papers either, as far as I can remember.'

'I don't understand . . .'

'My guess is it's one of those things they're keeping back, you know? They do that sometimes, the police. They keep certain facts out of the press so they can weed out the cranks and the copycats.'

'I must have read about it somewhere.'

'No. You didn't. Not unless it was written on the side of a beer can. There are only two reasons why you'd know about money being pinned to the chests of the victims, and as I don't think you're the murderer . . . You're *not*, are you?'

Moony was starting to snivel.

'I thought not. Which means that you must be the kind of snot-gobbling tosspot that steals money from the body of a dying man.'

'No . . .'

Thorne grabbed an ear, and twisted. 'Tell me.'

'I thought Paddy was just pissed, that's all.' Moony spluttered out his confession between sniffs and yelps. 'I didn't know he was hurt.'

'You lying little turd. There was blood everywhere.' Thorne knew that now he was revealing a knowledge of the facts few would be privy to, but he also knew that Moony was too far gone, and too terrified, to take it in or realise its significance.

'I didn't know he was that bad . . .'

'You didn't *care* how bad he was. You just wanted the money.'

'I needed it . . .'

'Did you take anything else?'

Moony tried to turn away but Thorne yanked on his ear again, turned his face back around. 'There was a watch.'

Long since sold, Thorne knew, and the money – a fraction of whatever the watch might have been worth – spent on cider or sweet sherry.

'Taking the money and the watch is bad enough,' Thorne said. 'The fact that you robbed a man who was supposed to be your friend, whose life was bleeding away into the gutter, makes me sick, but it doesn't surprise me. What I *really* can't understand is why you didn't call the police. Why you didn't tell anybody . . .'

'I told you, I didn't think he was—'

Thorne could feel the cartilage buckle beneath his fingers as he closed his fist hard around Moony's ear. 'If you tell me that again, I'll rip this off.'

Moony gurgled his understanding.

'See, I'm guessing that if you'd called an ambulance, if they could have got to Paddy a little earlier than they did, he might not be hooked up to a machine right now. I'm not a doctor or anything, but there's got to be a chance.'

'No . . .'

'No, you're probably right. Chances are he was already brain dead by the time you started going through his pockets. But you couldn't possibly have known that, could you? You just thought he was . . . what, exactly? Moderately badly injured? Serious but hopefully not critical? So you took what you wanted and left him there to die because, basically, at the end of the day, you didn't give a fuck. Simple as that.'

The recognisable rumble of a diesel engine grew louder as a black cab drove slowly past the end of the street and stopped. Thorne heard a door slam, the exchange of voices before the cab moved off again.

'Leave me alone,' Moony said.

'I will, but what if I was to hurt you first?'

'Please . . .'

'What if I was to injure you in some way? I don't know what exactly, something serious but hopefully not critical.' Thorne watched Moony's eyelids flutter and close. He caught the sudden, sharp smell of urine that drifted up from his crotch. 'If I was to do that and then leave you alone, do you think anyone would help *you*? What d'you reckon?' Thorne leaned in close to Moony's face. 'Would anyone give a fuck?'

Because the average rough sleeper wasn't usually to be seen blathering into a state-of-the-art mobile phone, Thorne had been finding discreet locations from which to check in with Holland. Tonight, he couldn't be bothered, and besides, the phone was small enough to fit easily into his palm. So, sitting in his theatre doorway with it pressed close to his ear, he figured he looked no stranger than Radio Bob, muttering happily into an invisible handset . . .

'So Hayes was definitely a victim of the same killer,' Holland said. 'If he had the money on him.'

Thorne swallowed a mouthful of lager. 'Looks that way,' he said.

'More than "looks", I would have thought.'

'Whatever . . .'

'We've got two murders, *three*, if you count Paddy Hayes, and I think we can—'

'I'm not arguing.'

'You've still got a problem with the whole serial-killer angle, though?'

'Look, Raymond Mannion was terrified. I've got a witness.'

'Of course he was scared—'

'Not in the general way you mean, because there was a killer around. He was scared of *someone*. I think he was killed because of what he knew or what he'd seen.'

'It's a leap.'

'Which means that the killing of the first victim takes on a greater significance. Don't you think?'

'Maybe . . .'

'Come on, Dave. While everyone's looking for all the usual perverse, serial-killer motives, it's worth considering that there might just be something a bit more basic going on here.'

'That's just it, though. Everyone here *is* looking for the perverse serial-killer motives. That's our major line of inquiry at the moment.'

'Right.'

'Well, it has to be until we've got something better to go on, doesn't it?'

'So what's Brigstocke's profiler come up with?'

'Not a lot at the moment.'

'What? Not even the "white, male, started fires as a child and tortured small furry animals" cobblers?'

'What do you want us to do about Moony?'

'Nick him.'

'For what?'

'I don't care. Being a reprehensible shitbag. Think of something . . .'

'It'll be hard to make a theft charge stick when all we've got is what he told you. There's no material evidence. How *did* you get him to tell you, by the way, or don't I want to know that?'

'Look, there's always a chance Moony might sober up and start asking awkward questions, so let's just get him off the street. Give him a nice, warm cell and a bottle of Strongbow and he won't complain.'

'Fair enough . . .'

They chatted for another few minutes, but Thorne spent most of the conversation thinking about what Holland had just said. About the question he'd asked, only half-jokingly.

Don't I want to know that . . .?

As the last major case Thorne had been working on before his leave had moved towards its resolution, he'd been involved in things, he'd *done* things, far worse than slapping a few answers out of someone.

Holland talked and Thorne talked back, but he was thinking about the smell of flesh beneath the weight of a hot steam-iron. Thinking about what Jesmond had said about wearing a hair shirt. Thinking about how good the beer tasted . . .

He woke violently, knowing for certain that he was being watched.

The room he'd been standing in began to go fuzzy around the edges and then to disappear. Of the men in there, one had been his father;

near enough, but not quite as he'd been before the Alzheimer's. There'd been no violent mood swings, no inappropriate language. Instead, there'd been only a priceless look on his old man's face: a bemused half smile at knowing that he'd said something funny without having the first idea why. So the three of them – his father, his father's friend Victor and Thorne himself – had begun to laugh, until the laughter had become all that mattered. So that even the first, delicate wisps of smoke creeping underneath the door had seemed completely hysterical.

Thorne sat bolt upright, breathing heavily.

His tongue was thick and vile against the roof of his mouth. He couldn't tell New York from New Year, let alone the difference between concern and contempt on the faces of the young couple staring at him. So he shouted at them, calling them cunts and telling them to fuck off, before dropping back hard against the door behind him and then down.

For a while, he stared out at the street through a curtain of drizzle. Then, he closed his eyes. Hoping there might be some way back into that room filled with laughter and smoke.

NINE

For Robert Asker, it had begun with the simple, overpowering conviction that there were people living beneath the shower tray . . .

He'd heard them, their voices muffled at first by the rush of the water and then a little clearer, but still indistinct, once he'd turned off the shower. He'd stood stock-still and dripping wet above the plughole and stared down. He'd seen the faintest orange glow, a light of some sort, way down in the pipes. He knew what it meant: they had to be living in the pipework, which meant that they could travel quickly and talk to him from almost anywhere in the house.

It wasn't long before they were using the network of major drains and sewer pipes to follow him when he was outside, when he was away from home. Then he began to hear the voices at work and in his car. It was like several voices at once, each cancelling out the others so that he could only make out one word in ten and could never really get the gist of what they were saying. What they were trying to tell him.

Of course, it *really* began when he told his wife about the voices. That's when he lost control of everything. It all began to fall apart from that moment onwards . . .

It wasn't long after he told her, that he got laid off. From then on it was hard to know whether her attitude stemmed from anger at his getting himself sacked or frustration at his ramblings, at his insistence on what he was hearing. Either way, he was damn sure that she was withdrawing from him and that she was taking his daughter with her. He noticed that she was keeping the girl with her more and more, that she would always take her along, even if she was popping out for just a few minutes.

She was afraid for their daughter to be left alone in the house with a madman.

He wasn't sleeping. They spoke loudest of all at night, and he paced the house with his hands over his ears and with the music turned up so loud that people several houses away would phone the police at regular intervals.

She made him talk to people, to half a dozen different doctors, but nothing they gave him made any difference, except for making him moody, which meant that he started to shout. He shouted because he was sick of not being listened to and he shouted to make himself heard above the constant chatter of the voices. Once he'd started shouting, it was only a matter of time before she left.

It all happened quickly enough. Job, wife, child, house . . .

There was hospital for a while after that, several of them, but the drugs only made him unresponsive, almost catatonic, and the voices were still there, growing in number and urgency. Barracking as he plummeted towards the tender mercies of the community. Towards the net he was destined to slip through.

It wasn't until he was on the street that he discovered the radio. Left to himself he found out how to tune in the voices to make their messages clearer. He also learned how to turn down the volume of the voices when he needed a break, and most importantly of all, he found out how *he* could talk to *them*. He never actually turned the radio off; he couldn't do it, even if he'd wanted to. The best he could manage was to tune it out for a few minutes at a time, but he was loath to do that in case he missed those transmissions he was always hoping to hear: the message offering him his job back; the message from his wife saying that she understood now, and that she was coming back; a message from his daughter . . .

Robert moved slowly past the design stores and clothes shops on Long Acre. Listening, then talking. Laughing every now and then.

He felt all right now, despite everything. It was shitty and he got ill with his guts, and with leg ulcers sometimes, but he was on the air. Radio Bob was as happy as he'd been at any time since he'd first seen that small circle of light, liquid and winking in the belly of a waste pipe.

'There are three basic types of begging,' Spike said. 'There's a couple of other odd ones, there's the specialised varieties, like, but at the end of the day you've got your three main types. I'm not talking about getting cash – there's loads of ways to do that. I'm talking about just *asking* people for it, right?

'There's your simple hungry-and-homeless style, which is what I do most often, which is what we're doing now. It's the best if you're a bit out of it 'cause you can just nod off sat there, and people will still chuck a few coins down if you look pathetic enough. That's the pity approach, like.

'Then there's the hassle approach, which involves a bit more spiel. You can chase after people on the street, which they're trying to clamp down on 'cause it's antisocial or what have you. Or you can do what Caroline does sometimes, which is to blag a tube ticket and wander through the carriages making a bit of a speech and holding a cup out. You're appealing to the punter's better nature with that one, or else they might just give you the cash to make you fuck off, but either way that can be a good earner.

'Or you can just go for the straight-up, in-your-face way of doing things. None of this "I need some money to get into a shelter" or "Please help me get a hot meal" or shit like that. You just look someone in the eye and ask them for a bit of change because the truth is that you're fucking gagging for a can of Special Brew. Some people prefer that . . .'

Thorne thought about it and decided that, as the person being asked to hand over the cash, it was definitely *his* favourite approach. Like most people, though, his normal reaction, however he was being asked for money, was to look away and mutter nonsense, or pretend that he hadn't heard. He'd certainly ignored his fair share of beggars on the tube.

'Right, thanks,' Thorne said. 'I'll bear all that in mind.'

They were sitting against the wall just inside the entrance to Tottenham Court Road tube station. The sign scrawled on a strip of cardboard in front of them said, 'PLEASE HELP' and the small plastic bowl in front of that contained a handful of coins. One-, two- and five-pence pieces.

'Tell me about some of these other ways,' Thorne said. 'Loads of ways to get cash, you said . . .'

Spike leaned his head back. A poster for a new Brad Pitt movie was backlit behind him. 'Yeah, well, there's a few. Busking, *Big Issue*, whatever . . .'

Busking was out of the question, but Thorne had wondered about selling the *Big Issue*. He wasn't sure how many of those who made money selling the magazine slept rough.

'Don't you have to register or something to do that? Get a badge?'

Spike shook his head and leaned forward. He straightened the cardboard sign that was already sodden around the edges. It was chucking it down outside and the floor around them was becoming increasingly wet as rush-hour travellers brought the rain in on their way down from the street to the ticket hall.

'Look, there's selling the *Big Issue* and selling the *Big Issue*, like. Some people just get hold of one copy and sell it over and over again. You tell people it's your last one and most punters won't have the heart to take it. It's a good scam.'

'I might give that a go.' Thorne looked up at a young, black woman coming down the steps towards them. She looked quickly away and stayed close to the far wall as she moved past them and on down the next set of stairs.

'Or there's poncing used travelcards and selling them on. I used to do a fair bit of that. That's a good one an' all, but they're starting to clamp down a bit.'

'Right . . .'

'Oh, shit.'

Thorne followed Spike's gaze and watched a dumpy, dark-haired man walking down the steps in their direction. He was dressed in a grey hooded top and black combats, but it was the way he *wore* the clothes more than anything that identified him as a copper quicker than any warrant card could have done.

'All right, Spike?' the man asked.

'I *was*.'

'Be fair.' The police officer held out his hands. 'There's two of you, so you're actually causing an obstruction. Someone could get hurt.'

'Whatever,' Spike said.

'Where's your girlfriend today?'

Spike ignored the question. He pointed down the corridor towards the platforms, from where the less-than-melodic sound of voice and guitar had been echoing for the previous hour or more. 'Why don't you do something useful and go and hassle the arsehole who's murdering "Wonderwall" at the bottom of the escalators?'

'I'll see what I can do.' He turned, looked down, squatted on his haunches next to Thorne. 'I'm Sergeant Dan Britton from the Homeless Unit at Charing Cross. You're new, yeah?'

There was no sign of any ID being produced. Maybe this was one of those coppers who didn't think that everyone merited an official introduction. This and the counsellor-meets-children's-TV-presenter voice were not facets of a winning personality, but it didn't really matter. In that utterly irrational yet completely straightforward way that Thorne had – that he was convinced most people had if they were honest – he'd marked Britton down as a tosser before he'd so much as opened his mouth.

'New-ish,' Thorne said.

'Well, if you have any problems, just come down to the station and ask for someone from the Homeless Unit.'

Thorne remembered what Lawrence Healey had said to him. There seemed to be no shortage of people offering their help.

'Can you do anything about the price of heroin?' Spike said. 'It's fucking extortionate . . .'

Britton ignored him, carried on talking to Thorne. 'Any problems, yeah?'

'Right,' Thorne said.

Staring at the floor in front of him, Spike raised a hand, slowly, like a sullen schoolboy with a question. 'Actually, there *is* something that's a bit of a bloody nuisance . . .'

Thorne could hear the mischief in Spike's drawl, but Britton took the bait.

'What?'

'It's this bloke. He appears to be going round killing people like me and I was wondering, you know, if you might be able to help with that. Sorry to be a bother, like . . .'

Britton made a poor job of hiding what, to Thorne, looked a lot like embarrassment. He stood up and gave Spike's outstretched leg a nudge with his scuffed training shoe. 'Come on then, off you go. It's getting busy down here and people'll be tripping over you.'

Spike climbed slowly to his feet and Thorne did the same.

'Don't worry,' Thorne said. 'For some reason, people are careful to keep as far away from us as they can.'

They'd taken half an hour or so, wandering slowly along a darkening Oxford Street, saying very little. They'd seen a couple of familiar faces, waved at Radio Bob talking animatedly to himself outside a sandwich bar. They were loitering just inside the entrance to Borders when Spike suddenly began talking as if the earlier conversation had never ended. As if no time had passed at all.

'Begging's getting bloody tricky now . . .'

Thorne had seen the same thing with his father when the Alzheimer's had begun to take hold. He knew that naturally occurring chemicals could be every bit as potent as the ones that people stole, and killed, and sold themselves for.

'Is it?'

'If you just sit there with your hand out, you get moved on, and if you're too pushy, you run the risk of getting an ASBO, like.'

Thorne knew what Spike was talking about. The Anti-Social Behaviour Act, launched in a blaze of Blairite glory, was supposed to curb the activities of nuisance neighbours, of tearaway teenagers and of others who blighted the lives of the majority living in the inner cities. Overly aggressive begging certainly came within the remit of the legislation, but it had become clear pretty quickly that certain councils were using their own interpretation of 'aggressive' in an effort to eradicate beggars of any description. Westminster Council, in particular, was chucking Anti-Social Behaviour Orders around like they were parking tickets – making a sustained effort to criminalise begging, the consumption of alcohol on the street, and any other activity liable to offend. God forbid they should upset those honest, upright citizens who might be confronted by such indecent behaviour on their way home to beat their children and drink themselves into a stupor indoors . . .

'Plus, there's the asylum seekers,' Spike said. 'A lot of them use their kids, or borrow other people's, and if punters are going to give their change to beggars, like as not they'll give it to them. So, you know, you need a bit of extra dosh, you have to be clever. You have to get a bit naughty now and again.'

'*Naughty?*'

'Yeah, naughty. Now, I mean, there's degrees of naughtiness, like . . .'

Thorne nodded. He'd seen just about every sort.

'Some of the ones with a real bad habit can get a bit desperate, you know? There was this one bloke used to put on a crash helmet and run into the chemist's with a claw hammer. I seen him one time running out carrying the dangerous-drugs cabinet on his back. Lugging this dirty great metal box up the fucking street. Another mate of mine used to go into shops just before they closed and hide, like. Then, after they shut up he'd rob the place, then break *out*.'

'Breaking and exiting . . .'

Spike cackled, enjoying Thorne's joke, repeating it a couple of times. 'I'm just talking about a bit of nicking, yeah? A spot of light shoplifting. Marks & Spencer is the best. You used to be able to nick stuff, take it back and they'd give you the money for it. These days they just give you vouchers, but you can sell them easily enough. Say you sell twenty quid's worth of vouchers to some punter for fifteen? You're sorted, and they get an extra fiver's worth of pants and socks, right? Caz is ace at all that stuff . . .'

Thorne was fairly sure he'd need to supplement his forty-six pounds a week somehow, but wasn't convinced that shoplifting was the best way to do it. It wasn't any sort of ethical problem: minor offences would be countenanced as part of his undercover role. It was more about avoiding the hassle of getting caught. He hadn't nicked anything since he was thirteen or fourteen, and that had been a short-lived shoplifting career. He could still remember the look on his old man's face after he'd been marched back from the local branch of WH Smith by a beat bobby.

'You all right?' Spike asked.

'I'm fine.'

He could still remember the look . . .

'I got done for nicking an Elton John album from Smith's when I was a kid.' Thorne hadn't intended to say anything at all, but once it had started coming out of his mouth he felt good sharing the memory. 'They didn't actually prosecute me in the end, but it put the shits up me, I can tell you. My dad went fucking mental.'

'Did he belt you?'

'No, my mum did.' Thorne remembered his mum's largely unsuccessful efforts to instil a bit of discipline. She'd used her hand on the back of his leg, or sometimes a spiky blue hairbrush, but her heart had never really been in it. 'The look on my dad's face was far worse, though.'

'Were you scared of him?'

Thorne was about to make some crack about his father being afraid of *him*, but stopped himself. He thought about how, towards the end, his father had spent most of his time afraid. Thorne hated the idea that this might be the way he remembered him.

'Fucking hell,' Spike said. '*Elton John?*'

Thorne stared blankly back at the security guard who was eyeing them from a corner. 'He was better then . . .'

They stepped back out on to the street and stood for a minute, unsure exactly what to do next. Suddenly Spike raised his arm and pointed back in the direction they'd come. 'My sister works there.' He flapped his hand towards Tottenham Court Road and beyond. 'In the City. Working with stocks and bonds or something. She's got a posh flat in Docklands.'

Thorne was surprised, more at what Spike had said than the fact that he was following Thorne's lead, and talking about his family. Thorne had clearly been wrong in assuming that people who lived like Spike couldn't possibly have any close relatives near by.

'Do you see her?'

'I've seen her a couple of times since I started living on the street. Both times she got a bit upset.' He began to step from foot to foot, rocking, as Thorne had seen him do on the night he'd first met him. 'I've not seen her for a while, like.'

Thorne wanted to know more, but before he could say anything Spike began moving away quickly.

'Let's have something to eat . . .'

Thorne hadn't eaten for eight hours. He hurried to catch up.

Spike pointed ahead again. 'There's a McDonald's back up here on the right. Shall we go mad?'

'I knew there was more to this place than just somewhere to have a shit.' Thorne shoved the last of the cheeseburger into his mouth and chewed enthusiastically. The food tasted fantastic.

Spike was on his third Crunchie Macflurry. Chocolate and ice-cream. Standard smackhead fare.

'The H-Plan diet,' Spike said, grinning. The ice-cream coated his teeth, making them far whiter than they were normally.

'What about that copper Britton, then?' Thorne asked. 'What's he like?'

'He's all right.'

'*All right?*'

'Yeah, well, he's about the same as the rest of 'em, isn't he? None of that lot down Charing Cross can make their minds up what bloody side they're on, like.' Spike was talking faster, running one word into the next. His face was suddenly grey and Thorne could see the goose pimples standing out across the backs of his hands. 'Can't decide if they're there to help us or sweep us off the street.'

'Where is Caroline, anyway?' Thorne asked.

Spike grunted. '*What?*'

'That copper was asking, wasn't he? I haven't seen her all day. You two fallen out?'

'She had to go and meet her case-worker. He keeps trying to encourage her to get a hostel place, but she's even less keen on 'em than I am.'

'She's "chaotic" too, right?'

'Not really. She's just got a problem with institutions. Spent a lot of time in care when she was a kid and stuff. In homes. It was things that happened to her in institutions that put her on the street in the first place, d'you know what I mean?'

Thorne thought that he probably did.

There were few women visible among the community of rough sleepers. So far, Thorne had seen no more than a handful. He'd asked Brendan Maxwell about it, who had explained how a great number of women ended up among the vast population of the city's 'hidden' homeless.

Spike used language that was a little more basic.

'See, a lot of girls *can* get a bed for the night, but they have to share it with some fat, sweaty cunt whose wife doesn't understand him. Selling their arses, them and a few young boys, right? That's what these case-workers are worried about. Don't have to worry about Caroline, though. She'd rather starve.'

'It's not food that's the problem though, is it?' Thorne said.

Spike took another mouthful of ice-cream, and was off on another tangent. He and Thorne began to speculate on just how shitty you'd have to look to be refused entry to various London restaurants. Dressed as they were now, Spike decided that there'd be little or no problem in any KFC or Pizza Hut. Thorne thought they'd have no chance whatsoever of making it past the doormen at The Ivy or Quaglino's, but still had a fair way to go yet before they were considered too shitty to be allowed into a Garfunkel's.

'McDonald's is a one-off, though,' Spike said. 'I reckon you could order a burger in here stark bollock naked with your underpants on your head and a turd in each hand and they'd still ask you if you wanted fries with it.'

It was genuinely funny, but even as Thorne laughed he was watching Spike press his hands hard into the sides of his face. The boy pushed the skin back towards his ears. He pinched up pieces of sweaty skin and tugged at them, as if the flesh on his face no longer fitted.

Bob knew the image of himself that came across.

He was well aware what others thought, but it didn't really bother him. In fact, he played up to it, muttering a bit more than he otherwise would, putting on a bit of a show by giving them all that 'Come in, come in, this is Radio Bob calling the mother ship' rubbish. He'd seen a film set in a prison once, and while everyone else was getting brutalised, they tended to leave the loonies alone. Most people were a little bit scared of them. So he let them all think it was harmless and that he was communicating with aliens, or receiving transmissions from God, or whatever.

Nobody could even begin to guess at what he actually heard. They couldn't possibly know that the voices rising above the constant hiss in his head had real things to say: news and rumours and secret theories; politics, history and religion spoken of in strong accents and strange languages. Profound, frightening things that would cause him to giggle or weep, or fill his pants where he stood.

He never passed on any of this information, of course. If he did, everyone would *know* he was a nutcase.

He was just drifting off when the man appeared above him. Losing himself in the soporific hiss, with only the faintest of voices breaking in occasionally from far away, the words no more than a distant rhythm.

If the man spoke to him before he struck, Bob didn't hear anything.

When it began, the shadow like a bludgeon, it was as if he could feel each part of it in isolation: the laces and the metal eyelets tearing the skin around his mouth and nose; the flesh of lips and nose flattening; the force that drove his head back against the wall shattering bones on both sides of his skull.

Then, finally, those messages he had waited so long to hear began to come through.

Something had been booted loose or realigned and suddenly the wave of pain became a frequency he had never received before. He couldn't make out all of his wife's words, but the tone of her voice told him everything he needed to know. The lilt of sorrow was unmistakable.

He tried to shut out everything else – *every other sound* – and listen harder. The voices were still so familiar. There was something wet in his ear, something warm and sticky on his handset. His daughter's voice was deeper than he remembered, and that made sense because she would be older now. As it began to break up, only one word in three, and then in five, was clear, but it was more than enough. It had faded away, though, before he could try to answer. Before he could send out any message of his own.

Then, it was only the swing of his attacker's leg. Imagined, as he'd already ceased being able to see anything at all. The swing and the stamp and the desperate breath kicked out of him.

Aware, in those final few seconds before everything went dark. Aware, for the first time in as long as he could remember, that no one was talking to him.

TEN

The fat café owner had managed an even more miserable expression when he'd sloped across to deliver Holland's change.

Holland watched him walk back and begin stabbing at the buttons on his till. 'What are your plans for today?'

'No plans,' Thorne said. 'I'll just carry on drifting around, see who I run into.'

'So, much like you'd be doing if you were in the office, then?'

'The lack of any formal structure to the day is quite appealing, as a matter of fact. If it wasn't for the cold, and the hunger, and the fact that you haven't actually got anywhere to sleep, this homeless lark wouldn't be too bad.'

'Some people'll do anything to avoid paperwork.'

'That's definitely a bonus.'

'When this is all over, you *will* have to write up a report,' Holland said. 'You do know that, don't you?'

Thorne's arm snaked across the plastic tablecloth and he tipped the change from the plate into his hand.

Holland watched him pocket the cash. 'That's cheating. It'd take you a couple of hours' begging to make that.'

'I'm only doing it to piss him off.' Thorne nodded towards the proprietor. 'You think that's bad?' he said. 'He'll have a face like a smacked arse when he doesn't get a fucking tip . . .'

Outside, they stood on the pavement and stared across at a newsagent's on the other side of the road. A blown-up front page from *The Sun* was stuck in the front window: '*HOMELESS MURDERS: THE FACE OF THE FIRST VICTIM*'.

'He's the key to this, you know?' Thorne said.

'Let's hope there *is* a key.'

'Well, it won't be found by any profiler. I'm telling you, it's all about the first victim. The killer was looking for him.'

'Speculation, based on highly unreliable hearsay.'

'Unreliable or not, it also suggests that the second victim wasn't selected randomly, either. Mannion was killed because he'd seen something, because he knew something.'

They moved a couple of steps apart to let a woman in a smart business suit through and into the café behind them.

'Look, it's understandable,' Holland said. 'I see why you're fixing on the unidentified victim—'

'I'm not *fixing*—'

'But three more people have been killed since then. Raymond Mannion, Paddy Hayes, Robert Asker. I know you don't want to hear this, but whoever's responsible *is* a serial killer, whether you like it or not. By definition, if nothing else.'

'There *is* nothing else,' Thorne said.

'There's the money he leaves on the bodies. Like it's all he thinks the victims are worth. It's a signature.'

'If I was Ross Kemp and this was a two-part thriller on ITV, then maybe I'd agree with you. Come on, Dave, we've both been after people like this before and you know bloody well that the only signature most of them ever leave is a body. This is somebody saying, "Look at me! I'm a serial killer."' Holland went to say something himself, but Thorne cut across him. 'Yes, I know, he *is*.'

'Even if you're right and the first victim *was* killed for a specific reason, that's not what it's about now, is it?' Holland got no response, pressed on. 'Say he killed Mannion to cover up, and Hayes to make it look like something random. What about Asker, and whoever's next? He's obviously started to enjoy himself now, hasn't he?'

'Maybe . . .'

They looked over at the picture in the newsagent's window; at the face staring back at them from across the road. This was a face that had been generated by a computer, and yet it had something of the same expression Thorne had seen many times already in the previous couple of weeks. The post-mortem had confirmed that this man was not a drug addict, and yet there was the same look Thorne had seen on Spike's face, and on Caroline's, and on a handful of others. It was a look that was difficult to describe. That he could best place at a tipping point, somewhere directly between terrified and dangerous. Thorne knew he was projecting, yet he was sure he saw something around the mouth, and in the eyes, of course, that demanded a reckoning. Or perhaps it was a plea to be reckoned *with* . . .

'Where are you sleeping tonight?' Holland asked.

'Don't know yet.' Thorne had spent the last week moving around, bedding down in a series of different locations, but in terms of shelter and security, his original choice had certainly been the best. 'I might go back to the doorway at the theatre.'

'That's the closest you've been to culture for a while.'

'There's an Andrew Lloyd-Webber musical on. It's as close as I ever want to get . . .'

As he watched Thorne go, Holland had to remind himself that the scruffy figure walking slowly back towards the West End was, theoretically at any rate, still his boss. There'd never been a great deal of 'yes sir, no sir' flying about between them, except when Thorne was in a really bad mood. He was not normally the type to demand, or to dish out that type of deference. Even so, Holland was aware that over the last couple of weeks he'd begun speaking to Thorne differently and that it had nothing to do with his own recent promotion to sergeant.

It shamed him, but if Holland was being honest, his attitude had far more to do with what Thorne had become, with the part he was playing, than with anything that might have happened to *him*.

He watched Thorne pull the dirty red rucksack up on to his shoulder before turning the corner. It had never been easy to read the man, but physically at least he was pretty bloody close to being unrecognisable. Holland knew that it had only been a fortnight, and that it was probably his imagination, but had he seen a stoop there, and something genuinely shambling in the gait?

It worried him more than a little, because Tom Thorne might well be sleeping in a theatre doorway, but he was no actor.

Peter Hayes sat on the train back to Carlisle, thinking of little but how desperate he was to get home and to kiss his son. He decided that this was because he'd watched his father die a few hours earlier, having just turned off the machine that had been keeping him alive.

For the umpteenth time since he'd been given it, he smoothed down the pages of the handwritten letter and read. The words he'd scrawled in such an adolescent fury a dozen years before seemed rather clumsy now, their intention no more or less than to wound.

He looked up from the page and out of the window.

To wound. It was hard to imagine that they had done otherwise. So why the hell had the stupid, drunken fucker held on to the bloody thing?

You left us like a snake, like we were shit, so you could crawl into a bottle and forget we were there at all. You fucking coward. Crawling, beery snake . . .

He read the passage over again, each faded loop and slash of his handwriting like a decaying tooth to probe. Like a mouth-ulcer to gnaw at.

The buffet trolley was coming down the aisle towards him and he decided that he'd have tea, and perhaps a sandwich. He'd wait and see what they had.

He'd wait and see just how hard the questions would be to answer, and how many times he'd ask them of himself. Questions about his judgement back then. About whether he'd pushed his father away until there'd been nobody for the poor old bugger to turn to except God.

He put the letter away.

He ordered tea and a chicken sandwich. He watched the scenery change as the train carried him further north, and counted the minutes until he could hold his son again.

PART TWO

BLOOD AND PETROL

1991

There are two groups of men, four in each group.

The differences between the two groups are striking, though the greatest differences are not the most immediate.

Four men are sitting and four standing. The men on the floor are spaced out on the ground, each several feet from the next. Not within touching distance. They are all wearing drab, olive-coloured clothing, though they're not dressed identically: two have boots on their feet and two are wearing sandals; one has a hat but the other three are bare-headed. The black hair plastered to their skulls is all that can be seen of the men for the most part, until one of them raises his head and takes a bite from what looks like a chocolate bar. He chews mechanically.

The rain and the darkness make everything appear slightly blurred and hard to make out clearly.

In contrast to the first group, the men who are standing are dressed identically. Nothing of these men's faces can be seen beneath the goggles and the multi-coloured kerchiefs or *shamags* that cover their mouths. Two are standing together, one of them flicking through a sheaf of papers which flaps noisily in the wind. The other pair are placed like bookends: one at either end of the row of men on the floor.

Each is pointing a pistol.

The man who is holding the papers waves them in the air, and shouts something across to the men on the floor. It is hard to make out all the words above the noise of the rain: '. . . are keeping . . . Do you understand?'

The man on the floor who is chewing looks up at him, then back to the men who are sitting next to him. They all look up, their faces wet. Two of the others are also eating, but none of them says anything.

The rain is fat, and black. Sputtering and hissing as it drops on to heads and hands and bodies. The man with the papers shouts louder: 'We are keeping these. Do you understand?' And the man who is chewing nods quickly, twice.

Nothing else is said for a while, and some time passes, though it is impossible to say how much. It is suddenly raining more heavily, and the dark hair and the olive clothes of the men on the ground are slick with it.

The men who are standing use their sleeves to wipe the water from their guns.

The light is even poorer than before, but the dull circle in the sky is most certainly the sun rather than the moon. It is dimmest, shittiest daytime, and now all the men with goggles are carrying pistols and pointing them.

It's virtually impossible to tell the four men who are standing apart from one another. Their faces are hidden, but even if they weren't, the light would make it hard to read their expressions clearly. Yet, despite all this, the difference between them and the group of men on the floor is suddenly blindingly obvious.

The men with guns are much more afraid.

ELEVEN

'That isn't Christopher.'

'Are you sure? It's understandable if you're not, what with the face being so—'

'No, I'm sorry. I'm sorry that I can't help you, I mean . . . But that's not him. That's not my brother's body . . .'

Susan Jago turned away as the sheet was lifted and placed back across the dead man's face. Even though Phil Hendricks tried to be as gentle as he could, the noise of the drawer clanging shut seemed to hang in the air, as awkward as the pause that followed it.

DI Yvonne Kitson put a hand on the woman's arm. 'Dr Hendricks will show you out,' she said. 'Phil . . .?'

Hendricks led Jago to the door and through it. Unlike the heavy steel drawer that had been built to take the weight of the dead, the door closed behind them with a soft snick.

'Fuck,' Kitson said.

Holland groaned. 'She sounded so positive on the phone. And I thought we were in, you know, when she first saw his face.'

Jago's hand had flown to her mouth a second after the breath she'd sucked into it. She'd shaken her head and gasped, 'Oh, Christ.'

'That could just have been shock at seeing the body,' said Kitson. 'Or most likely relief.'

'I suppose.'

'It's a natural reaction.'

'It feels terrible, though, doesn't it?' Holland walked slowly over to the wall of steel drawers. 'Wanting it to be him so much. Is *that* a natural reaction?'

There had certainly been a mood of celebration when Jago had called two days before. She'd seen the picture in the papers and on the TV and was fairly positive that she could identify the man who'd been murdered two months earlier. She was confident that the first victim of the rough-sleeper killings was her missing elder brother. Brigstocke had said it sounded as much like a decent break as any he'd ever heard, and the case certainly needed it. The powers that be were thrilled. More than a pint or two had been downed in the Royal Oak that evening.

Holland stuck a thumb inside his sleeve, rubbed at a smear on the metal. 'Wanting the body to be her brother's. It feels selfish . . .'

Kitson shrugged and walked across to where her coat and handbag were hung in the corner of the mortuary suite. There was a small red sofa and a low table, a box of tissues on a pine shelf. 'It's going to feel a damn sight worse telling Russell Brigstocke that we didn't get a result. I'd as good as promised him a name.'

Having made pretty much the same promise, Holland would be the one to break the bad news to Tom Thorne. Kitson didn't know about Thorne working undercover. As far as Holland was aware, below the level of the DCI, he was the only person who *did* know.

He wondered why that was.

Maybe he'd been included because of what was perceived as some kind of special relationship between himself and Thorne. Maybe they just thought that dogsbody and go-between were his special areas of expertise . . .

'I'm sure the DCI will take it in his stride. He must be getting used to disappointment by now.'

Kitson turned sharply. 'Sorry?'

'On this case, I mean.' Holland could see that Kitson was annoyed, that she'd misunderstood him somehow. He tried to back-pedal: 'It's been a bastard from the off, hasn't it?'

'I don't care what it *has* been. Christ, what sort of attitude is that?'

'I wasn't implying anything, Guv . . .'

Kitson shoved her arm through the straps of her bag, lifted it up on to her shoulder. 'Sorry, Dave. I'm just cheesed off and a bit snappy.'

She walked towards the door and Holland followed.

'Is everything all right?' Even as he asked, he guessed it was a pointless question. Kitson rarely revealed anything of her private life any more.

'My eldest got sent home from school yesterday for punching another kid. Some little toe-rag who was picking on his younger brother.' She looked at Holland, unable to keep the grin at bay. 'Of course, secretly I'm *hugely* proud of him . . .'

Holland smiled and opened the door for her.

Kitson had really got herself back together of late. A couple of years earlier she'd been seen as very much the role model for high-achieving female officers: on the fastest of fast-tracks with job and family seemingly balanced perfectly. Then the news got out that her old man had caught her screwing a senior officer and had walked out, taking their three children with him. Though she'd got her kids back soon enough, everything else had unravelled very bloody quickly. It wasn't the affair itself as much as the fact that it had become common knowledge that made things so tough, but she'd eventually come through it.

She'd proved how bloody-minded she was, if nothing else.

In the last few months she'd started to return to her old self. Progress through the ranks would not be quite as mercurial from now on, but she didn't seem overly concerned. She'd even begun seeing someone new; someone who most certainly was not a copper. 'He wouldn't know the Criminal Justice Act from the hole in his arse,' she'd announced gleefully.

Thorne had raised his head wearily from a copy of *Police*. 'Neither would a lot of coppers . . .'

It was odd, but Kitson's life had taken a turn for the better at around the same time that Thorne's had begun its free fall. Now, with Thorne not around, Kitson was more or less running the show day to day; reporting to Brigstocke, who, as nominal Senior Investigating Officer, was kept busy enough dealing with the press and the pressure from above.

Stepping out of the mortuary suite, Holland could see Hendricks and Jago on a bench at the other end of the narrow corridor. Jago was sobbing and shaking her head. Hendricks had his arm around her shoulder.

Holland and Kitson walked towards them, talking quietly to each other as they went.

'Like I said, relief.'

'If she's crying like that *now* . . .'

Kitson looked sideways at him. 'She won't have any tears left if her brother ever *does* turn up dead.'

'I got the impression she's expecting him to.'

They arrived in front of the green plastic bench. Jago looked up at them. Managed to blurt out a broken 'sorry' between sobs.

'Don't be silly, Susan,' said Holland.

'I know you're desperate to get out of here,' Kitson said. 'I just wanted to be certain about a few things.' She gave Hendricks a look. He moved to the end of the bench and Kitson slid in next to Jago. 'The thing is, I don't quite understand why you thought the picture was your brother in the first place. I know it's not a real photo, but you sounded so certain when you called us.'

Jago took a few seconds, brought the crying under control. 'It does look like Chris . . .' The accent was marked. 'Look' rhyming with 'spook'. She'd come down on the train that morning from Stoke-on-Trent.

She nodded back towards the mortuary suite. 'That poor sod probably *did* look a lot like Chris. It's hard to tell, you know? I haven't seen him in so long now that I've no idea what he might look like any more, if he's lost weight or grown a beard or whatever . . .'

'I can see that, but even so . . .'

'It's definitely not him, 'cause there's no scar.' She rubbed her right arm, just above the elbow. 'Chris caught his arm on some barbed wire, there, when he was a kid. Trying to get a ball back.'

'Right . . .'

'And the tattoo was wrong. I was so sure it was the same, you know? Then, when I saw it, I could tell it was different. Maybe it was the position of it. It might have been a bit lower down Chris's arm than it was on . . . that bloke.'

'How exactly was it different?'

Jago started crying again, snatching breaths between the sobs. She raised her eyes to the ceiling and chewed her bottom lip.

Holland looked down at her. He'd thought she was somewhere in her early thirties, but seeing her now he wondered if she might be younger. The mascara that was smeared all over her face made it difficult to tell one way or the other. She had very dark hair and extremely pale skin. Similar colouring to the dead man lying in a drawer along the corridor.

'How was the tattoo different?' Kitson asked again. 'Different letters? Colour? Was it laid out differently?'

Hendricks drew Jago a little closer, nodded his encouragement.

Between sobs: 'I don't . . . know.'

'You're certain it *is* different, though?'

'Yes . . . I think so.'

Kitson glanced up at Holland, raised an eyebrow. When she spoke again, her voice was still low and soothing, but Holland could hear the determination.

'Look, we know the man in the mortuary isn't Chris, which is great.' Holland caught Hendricks' eye and had to look away for a second, embarrassed by the lie. 'But I have to ask you if you recognised him at all. Had you ever seen him before?'

The shake of the head was as definite as it could be.

'I'm only asking you because of the tattoo. It's such a unique design. Do you understand, Susan? Why would someone have a tattoo so similar?'

Again she brought the crying under control, pressing a sodden tissue hard into both eyes.

'There was a time, years ago, when Chris and his mates all went out one night and got one. They got pissed up and got their tattoos at the same time. They got the same sort of thing done. I don't know why. I don't know what it means.'

Excitement flashed across Kitson's face. 'Chris and his mates? Is the man in the mortuary one of your brother's mates, do you think? Is that possible?'

Jago shook her head. 'I told you, no. I've never seen him before . . .'

The excitement had gone by the time Kitson had stood up. She nodded to Holland. 'We'd better be getting back.' To Jago: 'Do you want us to arrange a cab for you?'

Hendricks moved his arm from her shoulder and took hold of her hand. 'Why don't I give you a lift?'

'Could you?'

'Yeah, no problem. I'll run you to Euston . . .'

She looked up at Holland and Kitson. 'I'll have to sort out my ticket when I get there. I'm not sure what train I'm allowed to get, because I got an open return.' Her eyes were red beneath a film of tears, but Holland thought he could see real happiness in them for the first time. 'I thought it was Christopher, you see? I didn't think I'd be going straight back.'

Thorne raised his hands, backing away. Though he could make out precious little of what the man was saying, the words 'fuck', 'off' and 'bastard' were clear enough, so he picked up the gist of it.

'Calm down, pal,' Spike said.

The man hurled another torrent of incoherent abuse at them and wheeled away, just managing to avoid walking straight into the wall behind him.

Spike hawked into the gutter and picked up his pace. 'Fucking old tosser has a right go at me every time I walk past.'

Thorne caught him up. They were walking north up Greek Street, towards Soho Square. The two of them had hooked up in a greasy spoon for breakfast and been mooching around fairly aimlessly ever since. Now, it was raining and they were keen to get indoors; Spike had said he knew somewhere warm where they could get a cup of tea.

'Why?' Thorne said. 'What's he got against you, then?'

'He's a boozer, so he doesn't want anything to do with the likes of me, does he? With a junkie.'

It was a word Thorne was used to hearing spoken with distaste. Spike said it casually, as if it were just another word to describe himself, like 'blond'.

In a little under three weeks, Thorne had seen enough to know exactly what Spike was talking about. The homeless community had its divisions like any other; its imagined hierarchies. There were, by and large, three main groups: drug addicts, drinkers and those with mental-health problems. As might be expected, there were one or two who could claim membership of all three groups, but on the whole they stayed separate. And those with mental-health problems tended to keep themselves to themselves, so any antagonism festered mainly between the drinkers and the addicts.

'It's mad,' Thorne said. 'The boozers can't stand the junkies; the junkies hate the boozers; nobody much likes the nutters . . .'

'And we all hate the asylum seekers!' Spike cackled, loving his own joke, flicking his fingers together like a young black man. 'It's a right old mix, though. I fucking love it, like. You've got your immigrants, you've got blokes who used to be in the army, you've got blokes who've been inside. There's all sorts on the street, mate. All sorts.'

Thorne wasn't going to argue.

They'd reached Oxford Street, where they waited for a gap in the traffic and started to cross. 'You're right, though, it *is* a bit mental that we don't all get on.' Spike spun round, pointed back towards where they'd had their altercation. 'Mind you, you saw what that boozer was like. They're a mad, smelly bunch of fuckers. No offence, like . . .'

'Eh?'

'See, that's another reason why the two of us wouldn't normally get on, apart from the age difference thing. A junkie and a boozer. You *are* a boozer, right?'

For as long as he could remember, people had liked to imagine that Thorne drank a lot more than was actually the case. It was something expected of people who did what he did, saw the things he'd seen. The truth was that he liked expensive wine and cheap beer, and though he and Phil Hendricks could put a few away in front of the football, he didn't have anything like a drink problem . . . not really.

Yes, he'd drunk a little more than normal of late for obvious reasons, and he *was* drinking on the street, but only because the undercover role demanded it. As it was, he'd taken to buying piss-weak lager and pouring it into empty cans of Tennent's Extra and Special Brew. No self-respecting alcoholic would be seen dead with a can of Carling or Sainsbury's own-brand first thing in the morning.

'I mean, it's not like you're *always* drinking,' Spike said. 'But I've smelled it on you.'

Thorne ran a hand through his hair and shook away the water. He winked at Spike. 'I like a drink . . .'

They walked on past the Wheatsheaf and the Black Horse. Past the Marquess of Granby on Rathbone Street. This pub was a favourite of Thorne's, as it had once been of Dylan Thomas. The Welsh poet had been a regular visitor and enjoyed trying to provoke guardsmen, who had popped in to pick on, or pick up, homosexuals.

Spike suddenly cut left, and within a minute or two they were in one of the quiet side streets behind the Middlesex Hospital, where Paddy Hayes had finally died almost a week earlier.

'It's like it is in prison,' Thorne said. 'The way the groups don't get on. Everyone thinking they're better than everyone else. The white-collar brigade, the dodgy businessmen and the conmen think they should be kept separate from the "real" criminals. The honest-to-goodness armed robbers think they're better than the murderers. *Everyone* hates the sex-offenders . . .'

Spike stepped ahead and turned round, talked to Thorne as he was half skipping backwards, away from him. He looked like an excited, adolescent boy. 'So, were you inside, then?'

In retrospect, it hadn't been the cleverest thing in the world he could have said, but Spike's presumption wouldn't do him any harm. He decided to just say nothing.

'Listen, I'm sorry,' Spike said. 'I didn't mean to pry, like, and you don't have to say nothing if you don't want to.'

He stopped suddenly, stood still for a second or two before heading up a narrow alleyway. Thorne followed.

It was the sort of crooked cut-through that London was riddled with; that hadn't changed in hundreds of years. The windowless buildings seemed to press in on either side, closer to each other at the top than they were at street level. The black bricks were greasy, and the floor was rutted and puddled.

A figure stepped into view at the other end of the alleyway and Thorne froze.

'S'all right,' Spike said. He walked towards the man who had clearly been waiting for him, while Thorne stayed where he was, and watched.

It happened quickly enough: hands emerging from pockets, taking, handing over and put swiftly back again.

While Thorne waited for Spike to finish his shopping, he thought about those different groups within the community of rough sleepers. The junkies, the drinkers, the nutcases. He realised that as far as the dead men who had been identified went, there was one from each group: Mannion was a drug user, Hayes was never seen without a bottle and Radio Bob had certainly had mental problems. Was this a coincidence? Or could it be part of the way the killer selected his victims?

Thanks to that woman who'd called to say the dead man might be her brother, they could well have a name for the first victim by now. Did he fit into this pattern at all? The post-mortem had not told them much. There'd certainly been no evidence of drug use or excessive drinking . . .

Thorne turned and walked slowly back towards the street. He wondered what *his* own internal organs, furred and fucked up as they probably were, might one day tell an eager pathologist. What they might have to say for themselves.

He remembered a slight judder; the squeak of the belt as his father's coffin had slid forward, a second before the organist had picked up her cue.

Stopping and leaning against a wall, he hoped that when the time came, his innards would be there undisturbed and intact. Melting nicely. Burning along with the rest of him, having said fuck-all of any consequence to anyone.

'Why did you never report your brother missing?' Hendricks asked.

'I just kept expecting him to pop up again. He always has done before.' Susan Jago had a red vinyl overnight bag on her knees. She twisted the handles around each other as she spoke. 'Chris has been doing this on and off for years. He'll go a bit funny and vanish off the face of the earth for a while, then come waltzing back like there's no problem.'

There were a variety of routes from Westminster Hospital to Euston Station, and Hendricks had mentally tossed a coin. He was driving along Victoria Street towards Parliament Square and from there he'd head north up Whitehall and keep going.

'Was he on any medication?'

'Blimey, he's been on everything at one time or another. You name it . . .'

'Got a loyalty card at the chemist's, has he?'

She laughed and let her head drop back. 'He's a complete mess, Christopher is. Has been for ages.'

Hendricks steered the Ford Focus skilfully through the traffic, though the wet streets weren't making him slow down overmuch. He'd already apologised once when he'd jumped a light and the woman in the passenger seat had sucked in a noisy, nervous breath. Now, he raced to overtake a bus that was pulling out, and she did it again.

'Sorry . . .'

'It's OK.'

'Just trying to get you there a bit quicker. If you miss the next one, you'll have a bit of a wait.'

'Like I said, no one's expecting me back. The kids are at a friend's.'

Despite the weather, Parliament Square was thick with people, and cars were taking an age to get around it. Hendricks had definitely chosen the tourist route.

'Did he never have a job?'

'He had all sorts of jobs, but they were all shit. Couldn't even hold on to *them*. He'd get into a fight at work or just stop turning up. Then he'd be off on one of his walkabouts.' She shrugged, stared out of the window at the crowds under umbrellas outside Westminster Abbey.

'Was there any kind of trigger for Chris's illness? You said he'd been like it for ages . . .'

'I wouldn't call it an illness, exactly. He just gets depressed, you know?'

'It's an illness.'

'OK,' she said.

'I just wondered if there'd been a single event that might have sparked him off? A break-up with someone. A death in the family . . .'

'I don't think so.'

'Nothing you can think of?'

'All of them things happen to everybody, don't they?'

'Yes, but we all have a different brain chemistry.'

'He's always had mates and girlfriends and all that, and a lot of the time he's as happy as anyone is, but for ages now he's just been liable to go off on one. I don't know why. I don't know what causes it. I just want to find him and keep a better eye on him this time. I want to get him some help.'

She was starting to get worked up again, and Hendricks could hear in her voice that tears weren't far away. He thought it was odd, considering how much she clearly cared for her brother, that she seemed to know so little about what was wrong with him. She was vague about the whats and the whens, but then denial tended to do that. He sensed that she blamed herself, that she somehow felt guilty for what had happened, for what *might* have happened, to her brother. He wished that there was something he could do to help her. He thought about the tattoo, about what Kitson had said back at the hospital. If Chris Jago *was* dead – and his sister had obviously thought that was possible – Hendricks thought there might be something he could do to help find him. But first he needed to go home, or back to his office at the hospital . . .

She was staring at him. 'Can I ask you, are you gay?' she said.

Hendricks was stunned at her directness. He took a second, then barked out a laugh. 'Yes, I am.' He was struck by a possibility. 'Was Chris?'

'God, no,' she said. 'I've got a mate at work who is, and you're a lot like him. It doesn't bother me, though.'

They drove on, making small talk until the traffic began to thin out at the top end of the Tottenham Court Road. Hendricks checked the clock on the dash. 'It'll be close, but I think we'll make it,' he said.

Next to him, Susan Jago clutched the handles of her bag a little bit tighter.

Chloe Holland took half a dozen unsteady steps towards her father, and banged her head against the top of his leg. 'Dada . . .'

Holland picked up his daughter and carried her over to the sofa in the corner of the living room.

'Come on then, chicken. A quick cuddle before bed . . .'

His girlfriend, Sophie Wagstaffe, stood in the doorway. 'Don't get her too excited, Dave.'

He thought about saying something about how *any* excitement round the place would be welcome, but he bit his tongue. Its absence was almost certainly down to him. Yes, they were both tired at the end of the day, and fractious, but he was also bringing the frustration of the case home with him. His mood flung a coarse, heavy blanket across everything. He couldn't blame Sophie for being thoroughly fed up.

The little girl pointed to her favourite video, lying on the carpet in front of the VCR. 'Arnee,' she said.

'Barney, yes. Good girl . . .'

His daughter would be a year old in a couple of days.

Chloe had been conceived just in time to stop his relationship with Sophie from falling apart completely. Pregnancy changed the emphasis of everything. The stupid affair he'd had became a weapon that was wielded only rarely, and most of the conversations that took place in raised voices became about the Job. Did he not think that perhaps now he should find something a bit safer? Something that paid a bit more, maybe, before he became completely institutionalised?

Once Chloe had been around for a while, once they'd got over the heart-stopping, joyous shellshock of it, they discussed their future again, though now nobody had the energy to do a lot of shouting. Or to do a lot of anything else. The flat they'd shared for years in Elephant and Castle was far too small, no question, so they talked about moving; about getting out of London altogether. They'd decided that Holland should sit the sergeant's exam, but the increase in pay had been more than cancelled out by a greater caseload. With Sophie back teaching again, and childcare to be paid for, they were no better off. Any move in the short term was out of the question.

'Come on, Dave.'

'All right . . .'

'I need to change her and get her down.'

'Just give me a minute . . .'

The tiredness never seemed to ease up. Just as Chloe had started to sleep that bit longer, he'd been required to do longer tours of duty. His new seniority, together with the seriousness of this particular case, meant that sixteen- and eighteen-hour shifts were becoming increasingly common. He wanted nothing more at that moment than to hug his baby girl tight to his chest, close his eyes and stay where he was until the morning.

'Dave, please.'

That was what was really going on, he thought, when couples stayed together because of the children. The truth was that they were just too exhausted to leave.

It wasn't that bad, of course. He knew that actually he could count himself lucky that Sophie hadn't walked out on *him*. It was amazing that she hadn't packed a bag and done a bunk with someone. Some teacher maybe, same as Tom Thorne's missus. Creative-writing lecturer that had been, years back. Jesus . . .

Holland opened his eyes as he felt Chloe being lifted from him.

'Right, OK then. I need to make a call anyway.'

He watched as Sophie gathered stuff up: the necessary books and an armful of soft toys. He waved his daughter goodnight as Sophie carried her through into the bedroom. If only they could get away, he thought. Just the two of them. Leave the baby with grandparents, then head off somewhere to laze around and fuck each other's brains out in the sunshine. He'd see what he could manage when the case had cooled down a little.

Holland crossed to the door and pushed it shut. He took out his mobile, scrolled through for the number and dialled. He needed peace and quiet to make this call, but he also needed the privacy. He couldn't tell Sophie anything about Thorne working undercover.

Though she'd only met him a couple of times, Sophie had never been a fan of Tom Thorne. She'd decided early on that his would be a bad influence on Holland and had tried, without much success, to make as much obvious to Holland himself. She was not, though, the type to kick anyone too hard when they were down, and had hardly mentioned Thorne's name since she'd heard about the death of his father, and the problems he'd had since. As far as she knew, Thorne had been taken off the squad and given something a little less taxing to do.

Holland waited for an answer, smiling at a memory of Sophie badgering him one night when he'd been cooking dinner. It had been just before the second part of his sergeant's exam, when candidates were faced with hypothetical problems to solve. 'Let the bugger *really* help you for a change,' she'd said. 'If you get stuck, just think about what Tom Thorne would do, then make sure you do the exact opposite . . .'

'Sir?'

There was a grunt at the other end of the line.

'Can you talk?'

Another grunt, but definitely in the affirmative.

Holland told Thorne about Susan Jago having failed to identify the body of the first victim. The reaction had been predictably blunt and blasphemous. Holland guessed that if Thorne, wherever he was, was being watched at that moment by passers-by, his pissed-up dosser act would be highly convincing.

Thorne began to sound a little more upbeat as he spoke about a possible pattern to the killings. He was talking about the different groups of rough sleepers, and a possibility that the killer was carefully selecting victims from among each one.

Holland reached for a pen and a scrap of paper. He began to scribble it down.

'Are you getting this down?' Thorne said.

He'd write it out properly later, pass as full a version as possible on to Brigstocke in the morning. For now he jotted down the bare essentials: 'Killer's basis for choosing. Junkie/Alcoholic/Mental Case . . .'

From next door he could hear Sophie softly singing the 'I Love You' song from *Barney*.

TWELVE

Thorne remembered what Brendan had said about real London grime as he watched it darkening the water. Running to his shins in inky trails and spinning away down the waste in a grey-black gurgle. A knock on the door told him that somebody else was waiting, so he tried to get a move on. It wasn't easy. The flow from the shower head was little more than a trickle, and he had to slam his palm repeatedly into a steel button on the tiled wall to keep the water coming.

As he scrubbed himself, he sang an old Patsy Cline song, quietly enough to go unheard by whoever was outside the door. He didn't know what had put the tune into his head, but it was appropriate enough; he'd certainly been doing a fair amount of walking after midnight. Sometimes he thought that sitting and walking were virtually all that any rough sleeper did when they weren't actually sleeping. Come to think of it, weren't they all that anybody did? Sitting behind a desk or at a till or in a doorway. Walking to work or to the pub or to wherever you could get what you needed to help you through the next few hours. Everyone was sitting and walking and scoring something . . .

There was another knock, louder this time. Something was shouted through the door.

For a final few seconds he stood letting the warm water run across his face and thought about what he'd said to Holland the previous night. Maybe what looked like a pattern was in reality no more than simple chance. Was it likely that the killer would be selecting his victims so carefully when, as Thorne still believed, they were only there to cover up something rather more down to earth? It was perfectly possible, of course, that both theories were true. Even if the later victims *were* there purely as dressing, selecting them in this way would hardly take a great deal of time and effort. The junkies and the drinkers were easy enough to spot as they tended to hang out in their own groups, and you could hardly miss the likes of Radio Bob.

Things had been made nice and easy for him. All the killer had to do was wait, and watch for the people that the rest of the world avoided.

Brendan Maxwell came into the locker room as Thorne was changing back into his dirty clothes.

'Why don't you put clean ones on?' he said.

Thorne shoved a plastic bag containing soap and shampoo into the top of his locker. He turned to a mirror on the wall and stared at himself. 'I'm OK with these.'

'Everyone else uses the washing machines . . .'

'These are fine.'

Maxwell moved so that Thorne could see him in the mirror. He stuck out his bottom lip, shrugged his shoulders and struck a pose. 'You talking to me? You talking to *me*?'

Thorne laughed, stepped right to obscure the Irishman's reflection. 'Fuck off.'

Though he'd been into the café at the London Lift a couple of times, this was the first time Thorne had seen Brendan Maxwell in over a week. The first time since Radio Bob Asker's funeral.

'How was it?' Thorne asked.

'Even grimmer than you'd expect. We took a few of Bob's mates up in a minibus, you know? A couple of the older guys he used to knock around with.' He began to gesture with his hands. 'So, it's us and all of them on the right and his ex-wife and kid plus a couple of cousins or whatever on the left.'

Thorne was thinking there were probably more people there than at the last funeral he'd attended . . .

'It was fucking weird,' Maxwell said. 'Like you've got this poor old fella's two lives right there, one on either side of the church. No prizes for guessing which side was having the most fun, either. There was a bottle of something in a pocket or two, right, and all his mates were going on about what a laugh Bob had been, you know? How they should have been playing appropriate songs in the church like 'Radio Ga-Ga', and how bloody funny Bob would have thought that was.'

He smiled wryly and Thorne reciprocated.

Maxwell's smile became a snort. 'That *would* have been funny, right?'

Thorne had wanted to have something meaningful played at his dad's funeral, but he hadn't been able to think of a particular song or piece of music. He'd never had a chance to ask. They'd settled for some dirge of a hymn that his father would have hated.

Maxwell leaned back against a locker. 'No chance of any laughter, though. No fucking way. No chance of any *joy*. Bob's ex-wife sat there like the whole thing was keeping her from something important like a manicure, and the daughter just cried and cried. All the way through.' He kicked his heel against the metal door behind him. 'They're burying Paddy Hayes day after tomorrow. I'm getting plenty of wear out of the black suit.'

'We're doing our best, Bren.'

Maxwell raised his eyebrows as if to ask exactly what constituted Thorne's or anybody else's best? Thorne was well aware that, although Maxwell was privy to his role within the investigation, he couldn't say too much about how it was progressing.

'We need to find out who the first bloke was,' he said. 'The first victim.'

Maxwell said nothing for ten, maybe fifteen, seconds, then pushed himself away from the locker. 'Good luck with that. Because I want to put the fucking suit away for a while.' He put on the De Niro voice to lighten the mood a little: 'Do you know what I'm saying here?' He stopped at the door. 'Phil's coming in later, by the way, for the fortnightly surgery. I think he wants a word.'

'Fair enough.' Hendricks had been providing an ad hoc medical service to some of the Lift's clients for the last couple of years. Doling out bandages, plasters and, best of all, the odd prescription. He had some cracking stories about the absurd lengths people had gone to to get him to prescribe something. To get him to prescribe *anything* . . .

'He's got a bee in his bonnet about something or other,' Maxwell said.

'About the case?'

'God knows. He wouldn't tell me if it was.'

'Right.'

Thorne looked at him and wondered if that were true. He knew very well that where partners were concerned, the rules about not discussing certain aspects of a case *could* become distinctly bendable. When it came down to it, Thorne really didn't give a monkey's, but he reckoned he knew his friend pretty well: Phil Hendricks would sell state secrets for a blow job or a Thierry Henry hat-trick.

The morning briefing was becoming more like morning assembly all the time.

Brigstocke stopped in mid-sentence, waited for the murmuring at the back of the room to die down. 'What's so fucking important?' he said.

'Sorry, sir. We were just talking about the horse.' The last word was more spluttered than spoken, and the rest of the room immediately broke up.

'Right.' Brigstocke sighed. 'Anyone *not* heard the horse story?'

A few hands were raised among the forty or so in the room. One or two blank faces.

The area car had, by all accounts, been called out in the early hours after reports of a horse running along the A1. Having caught the animal, the two officers were then faced with the problem of getting it anywhere, and hit on the bright idea of *towing* the horse. They wrapped a length of *POLICE – DO NOT CROSS* tape around the animal's neck and while one officer drove, his mate crouched in the open boot of the car and pulled the horse along. This worked fine for a while, with the car gradually speeding up and the horse cantering along quite nicely. *Unfortunately,* what they had fashioned was less of a tow-rope and more of a noose, so that without warning the horse had suddenly collapsed in a heap on the road and begun to shake dramatically. Certain that he'd killed it, the officer climbed out of the boot and walked over to the stricken beast, just in time for the horse to leap to its feet and charge through the nearest hedge, dragging the stunned copper behind him.

Brigstocke wound up by explaining that the officer concerned was recovering in Chase Farm Hospital, while the horse, who was still at large, had last been sighted galloping gaily along a B-road near the gloriously named Trotter's Bottom.

Then he finished his briefing.

'That sort of thing's good for morale,' Brigstocke said. 'Pretty welcome round here at the moment.'

Holland piped up. 'It can't hurt to remind ourselves every so often that it isn't all murder and mayhem.'

'Right, and you told it very well,' Kitson said.

Russell Brigstocke seemed pleased with the compliment as he walked around his desk and sat down in the chair behind. His office was one of three on a corridor that snaked alongside the large, open-plan Incident Room. Holland and DC Andy Stone were based in one of the other two; and, while the man she usually shared it with was on gardening leave, Yvonne Kitson was the sole occupant of the third. These officers – together with office manager DS Samir Karim – had followed Brigstocke into his office. As the everyday core of Team 3, it was their practice to gather here after the formalities of the morning and catch up. To brainstorm and to bitch a little. It was off the record, and what was said was usually nearer the mark than much of the official briefing that preceded it.

'It's not . . . hugely exciting, is it?' Brigstocke said.

Holland and Stone were leaning against the wall near the door. Kitson and Karim had commandeered the available chairs.

Holland replied for all of them: 'We nearly got lucky with Susan Jago. We'll get lucky next time.'

'Right,' Kitson said. 'There's still plenty of calls coming in.'

'Plenty of 'em from fruitcakes.' Brigstocke straightened the picture of his wife and kids that sat on his desk in a scarred, metal frame. This sole attempt at personalising his office had made it far more attractive than most of the other airless, magnolia boxes that honeycombed Becke House. 'Why *do* these morons ring up?'

'I've got three officers on the phones full time,' Karim said.

Stone shrugged. 'It's got to be our best bet, though.'

Brigstocke was not one of them, but there were plenty of senior officers who spoke, who *thought*, only in clichés. As the case stood, they'd have been spoiled for choice. Every available drawing board had been located and gone back to. The book by which things were done was being pawed until its spine cracked. 'Our *only* bet,' Brigstocke said.

There'd been a flurry of activity in the days following Robert Asker's murder, but now, in reality, there was little to be done but donkey-work. The response to appeal posters, press updates and the continuing profile being appended to the picture of the first victim meant dozens of calls to be chased up daily. There were the obvious cranks to be eliminated; those who turned out to be cranks and were then eliminated; and those, like Susan Jago, who were genuine, but proved to be ultimately worthless. The team's dedicated Intelligence Unit, meanwhile, was sifting through endless hours of CCTV footage taken in and around the relevant area. Aside from the predictable brawls and drug deals, and the occasional bout of drunken coupling in a doorway, there was nothing much to merit pressing freeze-frame. It was hard when nobody really knew what they were looking for.

Suspicious behaviour in London's glittering West End? There was plenty of that. Dodgy-looking characters? More than you could shake a shitty stick at . . .

What few officers were left had gone back out on to the streets, but with even less luck than before. If there was any information out there to be gathered, people were keeping it to themselves. The latest death had only led those who might still be at risk to close ranks even further.

There were tighter lips and still greater suspicion.

'Trevor Jesmond was less than thrilled with last night's *Standard*,' Brigstocke said.

Kitson groaned. 'It was silliness, Guv, that's all . . .'

'It just got blown up,' Karim said.

Close enough to the same responses Brigstocke had heard when he'd raised the subject at the main briefing. But it was still embarrassing . . .

The day before, an officer had been trying to question a group of older rough sleepers by the Embankment. When they'd become what he deemed to be over-aggressive, he'd panicked and handcuffed one of them to some railings. The old man's case-worker had contacted the team at Charing Cross, and although the mess had eventually been sorted out, some bright spark had called the *Evening Standard* and the old man had cheerfully recreated the incident for a photographer.

Russell Brigstocke had spent an hour on the phone the night before, having his ear chewed. He looked up at the four in front of him. 'This is not how we deal with this community. Especially not now.'

'It was a one-off,' Holland said. 'I know it looked bad . . .'

Brigstocke shook his head, unimpressed, and looked over at Kitson. 'Spread the word, will you, Yvonne? These people were vulnerable enough before some nutter started killing them. We're starting to look like fucking idiots.'

He leaned back in his chair, exhausted at a little after ten in the morning. Hendon and beyond were the colour of oatmeal outside his window.

Thorne had spent most of the morning begging. Sitting against a wall at the top end of Regent Street, with a blanket across his legs and his rucksack laid out in front to catch the coins. He'd picked a spot nice and close to a cashpoint, and while he wasn't expecting too many banknotes to come his way, people *did* already have their wallets out, so he'd done fairly well.

He had also turned down a fairly lucrative offer of work . . .

A man in Timberland boots and designer casuals had squatted down and asked if Thorne would be interested in making some real money. It was messy work, as it turned out, but certainly paid better than begging. All Thorne had to do was catch a tube up to Camden or Hampstead – a travelcard would be supplied – and spend a few hours going through the bins at the back of one or two big houses. Thorne could guess how it worked. He'd be paid a few quid an hour and then anything useful he dug up and handed over – credit-card slips, bank statements, whatever – would be sold on for a very healthy profit. You could get fifty notes for someone's credit-card details; passport documents and the like were worth even more. The homeless were perfect for the job, of course. They were smelly and shitty already, so why would they object to rooting through someone's garbage?

Thorne had told the man that he'd think about it and the man had given him the name of a pub where he could be contacted. Someone would certainly be making contact with him once Thorne had passed the details on . . .

When a five-pound note fluttered down on to his rucksack, Thorne looked up and saw Hendricks looming above him.

'A cup of tea's bloody extortionate these days,' Hendricks said. 'And coffee's just ridiculous. You won't see a lot of change out of that if you go to Starbucks . . .'

'I'll try not to.'

'So, how's it going?'

Hendricks squatted down next to him, much as the bin-man had done earlier. They spoke in low voices, but Thorne was relaxed enough. If any rough sleeper were to see them talking, it would not look out of the ordinary. Most of them knew Hendricks from the surgery work he did at the Lift.

'If anyone comes by, I'll have to start examining you,' Hendricks said.

'Did you actually *want* something?'

'I just wanted to run this idea by you . . . Well, I've done it anyway, but I wanted to let you know.'

'Is this the bee in your bonnet that Brendan was on about?'

Hendricks rolled his eyes. 'He's a wanker sometimes . . .'

'Are you two not getting on?'

Hendricks was about to say something, but stopped himself. He took a moment and the irritation seemed to disappear. 'He's very down about what's happening, which is understandable. A lot of his clients are obviously upset, so things are tense all round.'

Thorne knew that Maxwell was right to be worried. For anyone left behind after a murder, life was changed, was blighted for ever. The others sleeping rough on the streets were the closest thing these murder victims had to friends and family. Even if the man responsible was caught, readjustment would not be easy. Maxwell and others like him would be the ones who had to deal with the fallout . . .

'So, run it by me,' Thorne said.

'It's this tattoo thing. We know that the tattoo on the first victim isn't unique any more, right? Susan Jago thinks the one her brother's got is a *bit* different, but it's got to be fairly close to identical or she wouldn't have thought it was him. So we can look for it. We can try and find another one. I mean, all this is dependent on her brother being dead, so it might be a waste of time, but . . .'

'Have you talked to Brigstocke about this?'

'It's probably a stupid idea. I was just thinking about how I could do something to help Susan Jago.'

Thorne pulled up his knees, hugged them to his chest. 'Let's hear it, then.'

'It's not complicated. I just went to a few websites. The Pathological Society of Great Britain, the Association of Clinical Pathologists, the Royal College of Pathologists . . .'

'How many bloody pathologists *are* there?'

'I went on to the message boards and described the tattoo. Asked anyone who'd come across anything similar to get in touch. The RCP's got an online database which I can access because I'm a member, so I basically sent out a mass e-mail to pretty much every pathologist in the country. If Chris Jago *is* dead, this might be a way to trace him. Like I said, probably a waste of time . . .'

'Worth a try, though,' Thorne said.

'Actually, it wasn't a *complete* waste of time. I managed to sign up for a course on stem-cell differentiation and I applied for a credit card.'

'There you go, then.'

They looked up and watched as a gaggle of jabbering American teenagers hurried past in a frenzy of clean hair and perfect teeth. When the group had cleared, Thorne found himself staring across the pavement, exchanging blank looks with a man wearing a sandwich board. Thorne had earned enough in the morning to treat himself to the £4.95 all-you-can-eat Chinese buffet being advertised . . .

'Why didn't you go home to have a shower?' Hendricks said.

'You and Brendan really *do* tell each other everything.'

'Seriously, though . . .'

Thorne looked at him as if he were losing his mind. 'I'm supposed to be working undercover, Phil. I can hardly just pop home when I'm feeling a bit grubby.'

'That's crap. This is a transient community, you know it is. People come and go all the time. No one's keeping tabs on you, are they? Nobody's going to bat an eyelid if you disappear for an afternoon. You could jump on a tube and go home for a few hours. Recharge your batteries. You could watch a game and get a decent bloody *curry* if you felt like it.'

'I've got a job to do.'

'It's mental . . .'

'Have you finished?' Thorne leaned forward, began to scoop up the coins from his flattened rucksack. A ten-pence piece fell to the pavement and rolled towards the man with the sandwich board. 'Haven't you got any bodies waiting for you?'

*

The young Trainee Detective Constable would have found conversation on just about *any* topic more interesting than the work he was supposed to be doing, but the salacious detail *was* coming thick and fast.

'I swear, I'm knackered, mate,' Stone said. 'She wants a good seeing to every lunchtime. I've hardly got time to squeeze in a sandwich.'

Karim leered. 'What? She's kinky about *food* as well?'

Stone, Karim and Holland were gathered around an L-shaped arrangement of desks in the Incident Room. The TDC, whose name was Mackillop, sat at a computer, his mouth hanging slightly open.

'You can keep your eighteen-year-olds,' Stone said. 'This woman's divorced, in her forties . . .'

Karim lifted his backside on to the desk, slapped out a complex rhythm on his thighs. 'Single and up for it.'

'She's fit, she knows what she's doing . . .'

'She's *obviously* desperate,' Holland said.

Stone nodded, laughing. 'She's fucking *grateful*, is what she is. And she goes like a bat in a biscuit tin.'

The reaction from the other three was predictably noisy. The laughter began to die down quickly when Kitson was spotted coming across. Mackillop was tapping at his keyboard again by the time she arrived at the desk.

'What am I missing?' she said.

Stone didn't miss a beat. 'Not a lot, Guv. Just talking about that pair of plonkers with the horse . . .'

'Right.' She didn't buy it for a minute.

Holland saw her flush slightly as she picked up a piece of paper from the desk and pretended to read it. He knew very well that Kitson had once been used to this. That the sudden descent of awkward silences on to groups of her colleagues had been an everyday occurrence for her. He felt bad, but there was little he could do. She was one of the boys only up to a point, and even if they *were* happy to tell her what they'd been talking about, the lie had already made it impossible.

What could he possibly say, anyway: 'It's OK, Guv, we were talking about Stoney's sex life, not yours?'

After a minute or two of stilted shop-talk, Kitson drifted away. Soon afterwards, Holland did the same.

The coffee machine had been on the blink for months now, and had been replaced by a cheap kettle, mugs from home and catering-sized packs of tea and coffee from the cash and carry. With Sam Karim in the office, only the foolish or the desperate brought in biscuits.

While Holland waited for the kettle to boil, he considered the way he reacted these days to the racy tales of Stone's love-life. He was generally hugely disapproving or insanely jealous; either way, his reaction was more extreme than it would have been before the baby. He'd decided that, although Andy Stone liked himself a little too much, he was basically all right. He could be flash and lazy and prone to getting only half the job done, but he was a lot better than some.

It was hard to work with someone for a while and then watch them promoted above you, but Holland had been impressed by the generosity of Stone's reaction when he'd made sergeant. Much to his own surprise, Holland had been hungry – at first, anyway – for the 'sirs' and the 'Guvs'. For the deference to rank. Though it didn't kick in properly until you made inspector, Holland made sure he got it where he could. But with Stone he was never really bothered one way or another. Perhaps it was similar to the working relationship he normally had with Tom Thorne: the lack of emphasis placed on seniority, which Holland hoped said something pretty decent about both of them . . .

'Make one for me, would you, Dave?'

He turned to see Brigstocke beside him. Everyone pulled rank when they wanted a cup of tea made.

Holland tossed a tea-bag into his own mug and another into one with 'World's Greatest Dad' emblazoned on the side.

'How was DI Thorne when you spoke to him last night?' Brigstocke asked. 'I know he must have been pissed off when you told him about Susan Jago.'

'*Very* pissed off.'

'Apart from that, though?'

'OK, I suppose . . .'

'I passed that stuff about the different groups on to Paul Cochrane, by the way.'

Holland nodded. Cochrane was the profiler Brigstocke had brought in via the National Crime Faculty. 'Good.'

'He was already taking it into account, in fact.'

'Right . . .' Holland unscrewed the top off the milk. He raised the plastic bottle to his nose and took a sniff.

'I should have had a coffee,' Brigstocke said. 'I'm half asleep.'

Holland poured hot water into the mugs, then the two of them stood for a minute, prodding at their tea-bags with stained teaspoons.

'So, how d'you *really* think Thorne's getting on?'

Holland thought about it, but not for long. 'Not brilliantly,' he said.

They might have been talking about the case, about Thorne's undercover role. But neither of them was.

The lights from the South Bank lay as ragged blades of colour on the water, while the river breathed, black beneath them. Thorne stared out across the Thames from the wide, concrete platform above Temple Gardens. The place had once been popular with prostitutes, but was frequented these days by those with nothing worth selling. At the other end of the bench, Spike and Caroline sat cuddled up.

It was somewhere near midnight, and chilly.

Thorne cradled a beer: the 2 per cent stuff in a Special Brew can. Spike and Caroline were swigging from cans of Fanta. They were both in their early twenties, but when he glanced at them, Thorne thought they looked like they had barely made their teens. They hadn't spoken for a few minutes and suddenly Thorne became aware that

Caroline was crying softly. Spike had put his head against hers, begun to murmur and shush.

When Thorne asked what was wrong, Caroline turned and demanded to know why anyone could be sick and cruel enough to hurt the likes of them. People who wouldn't, who *couldn't,* hurt anyone themselves. She spat, and wiped snot from her nose with her palm, and Spike explained to Thorne – as he'd done the day after they'd found the body – that she had been fond of Radio Bob. That he'd made her laugh and stuck up for her sometimes. Caroline kept asking why, and shouted for a time, while for Thorne, there was little to do but wait for it to stop.

Then, all he could tell her was that the man who was doing these things would be caught. That he would be stopped and punished. He said it slowly, then repeated it until he almost believed it himself.

Later, after Spike and Caroline had left, Thorne sat and finished his beer, and thought about what Phil Hendricks had said.

He knew bloody well that Hendricks had been as unconvinced by that 'work to do' crap as he had been himself. To the right and left of him, cars carried people out of the city centre across Waterloo and Blackfriars bridges. Thorne watched them go, wondering how long it would be before he could consider going home himself. Wondering how long before he no longer felt the dread, squatting in his belly.

Since the loss of his father, he'd increasingly begun to think of *home* as the house where he'd grown up: the big old place in Holloway where his parents had lived until his mum had died six years earlier. Suddenly, his own flat felt like no more than a space in which to store things. A furnished turning-circle he could change in before heading out of the door as someone else. A locker room with Ikea furniture.

Maybe, when this was all over, he should move.

Now there was some money . . .

Down below him a large pleasure boat yawed and creaked against

Temple Pier. Thorne watched a group of people in suits and evening gowns leave, stepping off the boat and moving carefully along the walkway. A necklace of bulbs had been strung between the grey funnels of the boat. When Thorne closed his eyes it swung and shifted; bright for a moment behind his lids, as the beads of light had been against the darkness of the river, before starting to fade.

1991

It's dark still, like the smoke from burning rubber, and now there are only three men sitting on the floor.

The fourth is standing between two of the men with guns and goggles. While one points a pistol, the other drags back the dark-haired man's arms and walks around behind him. He takes out a length of clear, thin plastic and ties the man at the wrists. While this is going on the three men on the floor, whose wrists are already bound, look up and watch. One of them spits and shouts something, and the two other men with guns appear on either side of him. A pistol is jammed, hard, against the man's head, and one of the men wearing goggles and kerchiefs leans down to say something. Then he steps back, raises a boot to the seated man's chest and pushes. The man topples backwards on to the sand, which is saturated now, and solid.

All the men, sitting and standing, are soaked through. The men with goggles raise gloved hands to clear their lenses, while those who are tied can do little but shake their heads like wet dogs.

The dark-haired man, who was last to be tied, is pushed down on to his knees by the two men. A gun is put to the back of his head and he closes his eyes. Nobody moves for a long time until the men who have the guns start to laugh and the barrel of the pistol is raised. The man on his knees slumps towards the floor, moaning, but is hauled back up again. He is kicked between the legs, then allowed to fall.

Some time passes before one of the men with guns begins to wave a plastic bag around. He starts to take things out of it. Dark strips . . .

The man on his knees sees what is happening and his eyes widen. His friends on the floor start to protest, try to move, but guns are smartly raised and levelled. The kneeling man is jerked hard backwards by an arm around his neck.

Then voices are raised to be heard above the noise of the rain. Words are nevertheless lost.

'. . . d'you get it?'

'Say again?'

'Where d'you get it?'

'Brought it with me.'

'. . . reminds me . . . could *kill* a fry-up . . .'

'That stuff fucking stinks, Ian . . .'

Then a few muffled words. Something muttered from close by, the voice somehow far louder than the others but deep and distorted; impossible to make out clearly.

The one holding the plastic bag stretches out an arm. There is something flopping at the end of it. He pushes it towards the man on his knees, who tries to turn his head, but his hair is seized and tightened until he cannot look away.

Then they are placed on his face; laid across his mouth, nose and forehead as he screams.

Rashers of bacon.

THIRTEEN

A few years before, a major inquiry had been launched as to why the murderer of two young girls had been allowed to work as a school caretaker, having been investigated for serious sexual offences on a number of previous occasions. This inquiry revealed a nationwide system that was both unwieldy and seriously flawed. The country's police forces were supposed to be able to cross-reference, check and liaise with one another and with external bodies, yet the inquiry found that effective communication was thwarted at nearly every turn.

This was hard to believe, three decades on from the hunt for the Yorkshire Ripper – a man who had been questioned several times, eliminated on each occasion, and then caught by accident. Mistakes of this nature were understandable, back in those dark days of card indexes and case-notes exploding from mountains of overstuffed files, but *now*?

However many officers were sent on IT courses, and despite the many millions that were spent on tailor-made software and state-of-the-art networking, people still fucked up. Sometimes it wasn't ineptitude so much as incompatibility. Not only were some police computing systems not able to communicate with those of associated services, but often they could not even talk to each other. There were firewalls and brick walls; there were untraceable programs and intractable machines. While a perfectly diligent and proficient detective could store the complete works of Shakespeare on a keyring and send naked pictures of his girlfriend round the world with the click of a mouse, he might easily find himself unable to access intelligence on another floor of the same building.

Computers had become smaller of course, and lighter, but there were still plenty of police officers who didn't trust them as far as they could throw them. In this brave new world, the Met got through as much paper as ever . . .

Hendricks didn't know if there was a name for the electronic equivalent of red tape. He did know it was a reality of British policing, and that it was easy to get caught up in. To get *lost* in. This had been at the back of his mind when he'd decided to do some detection on his own: to switch on a single, steam-powered PC and go looking for tattoos. Much to his own amazement, less than twenty-four hours after his testy conversation with Tom Thorne, he'd got lucky. He'd accessed the site postings and e-mail from his office at Westminster Hospital. There were several dozen new responses. A couple looked like they might be worth following up, most were at least trying to be helpful and a couple were downright weird.

And Graham Hipkiss, FRCP, had left a phone number.

Hendricks reached across his desk for the phone. 'This is Phil Hendricks. I saw your note on the RCP message board . . .'

'Right. I think I've a tattoo that might interest you.'

Dr Hipkiss was a consultant pathologist at a hospital in Nottingham. He described the tattoo, one of several he'd seen on a hit-and-run victim found on the outskirts of the city six months earlier. Though the man – who appeared to have been sleeping rough – had been found alive, he'd died from multiple injuries on the way to hospital. Neither the driver nor the car had been traced, and the police had fared little better in putting a name to the victim. Appeals had been made on *Midlands Today* and in the Nottingham *Evening Post*, but no one had come forward to claim the body. Six weeks after he'd been found in the road, the John Doe was given a simple, Social Services funeral.

Hendricks was certainly interested. He pushed aside a sheaf of student papers and began scribbling down the letters in his notebook, arranging them as Hipkiss read from his original post-mortem notes. They chatted for a few minutes more before Hendricks requested a copy of the post-mortem and thanked Hipkiss for his time.

Then he looked down at the tattoo:

B+
S.O.F.A.

The top row was different from that found on the body of the unknown man in the mortuary downstairs. Hendricks laid out the original tattoo underneath:

AB-
S.O.F.A.

Seeing them together, it became obvious. He flicked quickly through the Rolodex, furious with himself, until he found Russell Brigstocke's direct line.

Thorne pressed his mouth close to the handset, spoke quietly. 'Don't let Hendricks get big-headed about this,' he said. 'It's good news, but it only leaves us with another question. And we still don't know what the rest of it means.'

'Maybe the bottom bit's a club of some sort,' Holland said. 'Maybe the A is for Association. Something Something Football Association?'

'We'll figure it out.'

'We need someone who does crosswords, like Inspector Morse.'

'Inspector Morse never slept in a doorway or got thrashed at table-tennis by a heroin addict.'

'Sorry?'

'I've got to go,' Thorne said. 'Listen, I wanted to wish Chloe a happy birthday. I couldn't get her anything, obviously.'

'How the hell did you remember *that*?'

It was a very good question. Thorne pushed open the cubicle door and stepped out. 'I've absolutely no idea . . .'

When Thorne returned from the toilet, Spike was sitting on the edge of the pool table, his legs dangling.

'I've not moved any of the balls, honest,' he said.

Thorne didn't think for a minute that he had. There was no more need for Spike to cheat at pool than there had been on the table-tennis table half an hour earlier: he'd already been four balls ahead when Thorne had felt the phone vibrate in his pocket and excused himself.

'My shot, right?' Thorne lined up a yellow ball. Missed it by six inches.

There were several people watching. Each duff shot was greeted with a certain amount of half-hearted jeering and a less than flattering commentary.

'No mercy,' Spike said. He put away the remaining red balls, then slammed in the black, acknowledging the apathy of the onlookers by raising the cue above his head and cheering himself.

'Jammy fucker,' Thorne said.

'You need to take me on later in the day, mate. When I'm a bit shakier . . .'

Two men who might have been anywhere between twenty and forty stepped forward to play. Spike asked if they fancied a game of doubles and was impolitely refused.

'The facilities are pretty good in here,' Thorne said.

They walked away up a short flight of whitewashed steps, heading back towards the cafeteria.

'Yeah, not bad.'

'Not bad?' They walked past the TV room, then another that had been converted into a chiropodist's surgery. A woman stepped out, asked if either of them needed anything doing. They kept going up towards the ground floor, the walls of the winding staircase covered with Aids-awareness and drug-counselling posters.

'Junkies don't want a fucking chiropodist,' Spike said. 'There's nothing worth nicking in there, for a start. How much gear d'you think you can get for a box of corn plasters and some verruca ointment?'

'It doesn't mean no one wants to use it, though, does it?'

Spike shrugged. 'Nah, I suppose not. Maybe some of the old boys, like . . .'

The centre would soon be closing for the afternoon and there were only a handful of people left in the cafeteria. Thorne and Spike stopped at a large noticeboard, stared at the jumble of printouts, leaflets and handwritten messages.

'You ever hear of rough sleepers tattooing their blood groups on themselves?' Thorne asked.

'Eh?'

'Their blood groups. You know, AB negative, O positive, whatever. As a tattoo.'

Spike stuck out his bottom lip, thought for a few seconds, then shook his head. 'I've seen most things, like, but . . .'

'It doesn't matter . . .'

Spike pointed at the noticeboard. 'You're right about this place, though, about the facilities. Look at all this stuff.'

There were notices about computer-training sessions, film showings and book groups. There were adverts for the latest performances by an opera company called Streetvoice, a homeless theatre group and a free course of DJ workshops.

'Pretty impressive,' Thorne said.

Spike pulled out a small bottle of water from his pocket, unscrewed it and took a swig. 'There's a place in Marylebone that's even better, but it's a bit further out, isn't it? They do some strange shit there, like. They were giving people free acupuncture last week, which is a bit over the top, if you ask me. I mean, I like needles, don't get me wrong . . .' He cackled, offered Thorne the water.

Thorne took a drink then handed it back. 'Don't some people get a bit pissed off though? Like it's all *too* good.'

'Oh yeah.' Spike spread his arms. 'They reckon laying all this on is encouraging the likes of me to stay on the street. Like there's no incentive for us to get off our arses . . .'

These were the same people, Thorne guessed, who thought life was too cushy in prison. That it was a soft option for many of those inside. He knew that when it had come to *certain* prisoners, he'd been one of those people himself.

'Most places are fuck all like this, though,' Spike said. 'You wait 'til you've been inside a few of the other centres. Some of them are well rough. You been in any of the wet places yet?'

'I don't think so . . .'

'*Wet*. Means you can take booze in with you. Good from that point of view, like, but they're shit-holes, most of them.'

Spike crushed the empty water bottle in his hand. They moved away from the noticeboard and walked slowly towards the exit.

'They can get a bit naughty as well, so you need to be careful. You look like you can take care of yourself, though . . .'

A few months ago, Thorne might have agreed with him. Right now he felt weak and incapable. Then he remembered the anger that had boiled up as he'd dragged Moony from one side of the street to the other . . .

Near the door that led from the café into the reception area, a trophy cabinet was mounted on the wall. There were a number of highly polished cups and shields, and a note taped to the glass showing the position of the centre's five-a-side team in the Street League.

Spike turned to Thorne as though divine inspiration had struck. 'I knew some football fans who had 'em. What you were asking about before. A couple of Chelsea boys who had tattoos with their blood group or what have you. They had blue dotted lines an' all, tattooed around their wrists and necks, saying "cut here" . . .'

Thorne thought about what Holland had been saying on the phone: *Something Something Football Association*. He found it hard to believe that either of the men with the mysterious tattoos was a football hooligan, but it might still be worth considering.

It wasn't as if she hadn't *thought* her brother might be dead . . .

While he was talking to Susan Jago, Stone told himself that it could have been an awful lot worse. It wasn't a bolt from the blue. They were the ones nobody wanted.

I'm sorry to have to tell you that your son/daughter/husband/wife . . . I'm afraid there's been an accident . . . I think perhaps you might want to sit down.

Every copper he knew had their own way of handling those awkward moments, his or her own style. The death message was usually delivered in person, of course, but as this was more of a confirmation than anything, it was decided that a phone call would not be improper. Even so, he'd been annoyed when Holland had palmed the job off on him, but, all in all, it hadn't gone too badly. He'd told Susan Jago about the hit-and-run; about the scar on the dead man's arm that had been detailed in the post-mortem report, and led them to believe that the victim had been her brother . . .

'I don't understand why they couldn't get hold of any of us when they found him.'

'Your brother had no identification, Miss Jago. There was no way to—'

'How bloody hard did they try?'

'I couldn't possibly say, I'm afraid.'

Sam Karim walked past Stone's desk and raised his eyebrows. Stone shook his head, puffed out his cheeks.

'It's just the thought that nobody was with him,' she said. 'You know?'

'Of course. We understand, and we're all very sorry for your loss.' It was a phrase he'd picked up from American cop shows.

'Couldn't they have put something in the press and on TV? Like they did with the man I *thought* was Chris?'

'They did. Locally . . .'

Susan Jago repeated the word on an exasperated breath. There was a pause and Stone waited, expecting there to be tears. They didn't come.

'Right, well, I'm sorry to be . . . you know, the bearer—'

'It's all right. It's a relief in a funny sort of way.'

'I forgot to say, about the tattoos. We know now that some of the letters are a blood group. Your brother had his blood group tattooed on his arm. We wondered if you had any idea why.'

'I'm afraid I don't.'

Stone began to doodle in the corner of his notebook. 'So you don't know what it means?'

'I have to go now. I've got to try and find out where they've buried my brother.'

'Right. I'm sorry . . .'

There was another pause. Then: 'Will you remember to thank Dr Hendricks for me?'

Brigstocke was clearly still on his diet.

'You need to get a few pork pies down you, Russell. You're starting to look gaunt.'

'I can't say that you're looking too good yourself.'

Thorne and Brigstocke had arranged to meet up in Chelsea, a good distance south of the West End. They stood together outside the Royal Hospital, lingering awkwardly for a few minutes like spies who've forgotten their code words, before they started to walk.

'I was going to ask,' Thorne said. 'That fascinating report I did so much work on at Scotland Yard. I do hope someone's polishing it up.'

'I think they binned it,' Brigstocke said.

'Excellent . . .'

They walked through the grounds of the hospital – still an almshouse for more than four hundred red-coated Chelsea Pensioners – past the National Army Museum and down towards Albert Bridge.

'I bet Phil Hendricks is pleased with himself,' Thorne said.

'Actually, he's pissed off because he didn't see it before. AB negative is the rarest blood group of the lot, and even though he typed those letters out himself several times on the post-mortem report, he never made the connection with the tattoo.'

'Tell him well done from me, but that he shouldn't make a habit of it. If he carries on playing detective, I might have to start slicing up corpses.'

Brigstocke laughed. 'Quite right too. God forbid he should make us look like we don't know what we're doing . . .'

'Did you see the PM report on Jago?'

'It was faxed over this morning, and I managed to get hold of the original SIO in Nottingham.'

'And?'

'It was a hit and run. As to whether it was a *deliberate* hit and run . . .'

'We've got two rough sleepers,' Thorne said. 'Both with practically identical tattoos, and both dying violent deaths. What are the odds of there *not* being a connection?'

'I think we're working on the presumption that they're connected.'

'It's just a question of finding the link between Christopher Jago and our friend in Westminster Morgue . . .'

It was a few minutes before seven o'clock and the bridge was already illuminated; the lamps swooping and arcing above the dusty-pink metalwork.

'It blows this serial-killer shit out of the water, anyway,' Thorne said.

Brigstocke looked genuinely curious. 'I really don't see why.'

'The MO, for a kick-off. He runs one over in Nottingham, then six months later he comes down to London and kicks another one to death.'

'More than another *one*.'

'It's the first victim that counts. It's about him and Jago. The others are nothing to do with it.'

'I'm not sure their nearest and dearest would agree, Tom . . .'

Thorne hadn't meant it to come out that way. All the same, he knew he was in danger of focusing too hard on the first victim, and of forgetting those still mourning the other men who had died. He thought about Paddy Hayes' son pulling the plug; about Caroline and the others trying to smile through Radio Bob's funeral.

'So what about this blood-group business?' Brigstocke asked.

On the left of them, Battersea Park lay spread out to the east. Thorne could make out a few joggers and cyclists moving along the avenues. There was some sort of event taking place by the Peace Pagoda.

'I can't see that it's medical,' Thorne said. 'The first victim didn't have any condition that would make it necessary. What about Jago?'

'No, nothing.'

'Right . . .'

'A bracelet's a damn sight easier anyway.'

'What about the football angle?'

Brigstocke had already heard Holland's thoughts on what the initials might stand for, and Thorne had told him what Spike had said about hooligans. 'It's possible, I suppose. We certainly can't discount it.'

'What's your profiler make of all this?'

'Well, it's a bit early. Cochrane's feeding the new information into his report and we should get something in the next day or two. He's been considering the idea that the killer might be someone who used to be homeless himself.'

'And he's basing that on what?' Thorne asked.

'The killer obviously has a knowledge of that community.'

'Because he found a few rough sleepers? They're hardly invisible, Russell.'

'If he *had* lived in that world himself, feeling powerless and marginalised, and escaped it somehow, it's possible that he's trying to wipe out that part of his life. He's showing that *he*'s got the power now. The money's a symbol of that. How he's worth so much more than they are.'

Thorne looked sideways at him, held the look until eventually Brigstocke gave in and smiled; like he wasn't exactly convinced by any of it himself.

'And they binned *my* report?' Thorne said.

They turned into the park and walked down towards the all-weather football pitches. There was a game being played under floodlights and they stopped to watch.

'I'm not a hundred per cent sure the undercover thing's working out,' Brigstocke said.

Thorne, who had arbitrarily picked the team playing in red and begun rooting for them, winced at a particularly high tackle. 'That must have hurt . . .'

'Tom?'

Thorne had heard him well enough. 'I don't know what you mean by "working out".'

'Are you really getting any more out of people than we were before?'

'What about the information I got out of that fucker Moony?'

'It's not hard to threaten somebody, is it?'

As if on cue, words were exchanged and a couple of players squared up in the centre circle, every breath visible in the air as they spat curses at each another. Thorne and Brigstocke watched until they were sure no punches would be thrown.

'All I'm saying is that we should maybe take a view on it,' Brigstocke said. 'It's been three weeks . . .'

'Give me a bloody chance.'

'I'm getting pushed on this . . .'

Thorne turned from the game to look at Brigstocke. 'I don't know if anybody knows anything,' he said. 'And I'm not expecting them to just spill the beans over a can of strong lager if they do. I still believe we need a presence, though, and by being part of that community I'm learning stuff that I think's going to help. I mean, Christ, if you're willing to put faith in your *profiler* . . .'

'A limited amount.'

'You never know, if he's right, by living as a rough sleeper I might be able to get some idea of how the killer thinks. Ask him. I bet he'll tell you it's a good idea.'

Brigstocke couldn't help but look impressed by the cheek of it. 'You've always got an answer, haven't you? Always got some angle.'

'Whatever it takes.'

Thorne turned around and they watched for another few minutes, during which the team in red conceded two soft goals.

'I need to get back,' Brigstocke said. 'I'm in the shit for missing a parent–teacher conference.'

Thorne stayed on, the solitary spectator for a while.

At half-time, the red team's dumpy left-back trotted slowly across to the touchline. His face was scarlet, running with sweat, and the fat on his chest and belly strained against the nylon of his shirt. Thorne watched through the chain-link fence as he wheezed and hawked, bent to take hold of his knees, then threw up on to the AstroTurf.

It seemed as good a time as any to head back to the West End. Thorne turned and walked away, thinking, I know how you feel, mate.

FOURTEEN

There were a surprising number of places that gave out free food if you knew where to go and when.

Spike had given him the low-down early on, and Thorne had thought that it was quite an achievement to keep all those different names, places and times in your head. On any one day in the very centre of London alone, you could get a free breakfast, lunch or dinner in one of a dozen different churches, hostels and ad hoc street cafés. Some operated a ticketing system and with others it was first-come, first-served; some provided full meals while others offered tea, coffee and biscuits, or maybe sandwiches on certain days. With all these possibilities open to those in the know, and with a three-course meal available for little more than a pound at the London Lift, Thorne could not understand why so many were still willing to hang about in all weathers for a bowl of free soup on the street.

Caroline had spoken like someone who knew what she was talking about. 'Some people just don't like going *into* places. You know? They're not happy in buildings, for whatever reason. Centres like the Lift aren't for everyone . . .'

'And cheap's not the same as free, is it?' Spike had added. 'When you've got fuck all and there's free stuff on offer, you take everything that's going.'

The three of them were walking quickly, from the Trafalgar Square end of the Strand, heading for the nine o'clock soup run behind Temple underground station. The street was gaudy with lights: the multicoloured neon from the Vaudeville and Adelphi theatres; the huge yellow lamps across the front of the Strand Palace Hotel; the pulsing red or bright white of the cars, crawling in both directions.

The night was cold again, but as yet mercifully dry.

'You get whatever you can, whenever you can, 'cause there's not a lot to go round,' Spike said. 'Yeah?'

Caroline had slowed to light a cigarette, and was just catching up with Spike and Thorne again. 'Except at fucking Christmas,' she said.

Thorne told them about something he'd read once: a quote from one of those pointless 'It' girls with too many names and too little to do. She'd said something about how dreadful it was to be without shelter at Christmas, and suggested that all homeless people should move to the Caribbean during the winter, and live on fresh fish.

Caroline's laughter quickly turned into a coughing fit.

'Dozy posh cunt,' Spike said.

December was still a few months away, but plenty of shops had already put out the decorations. Thorne had no idea where he'd be when it came. His father's sister Eileen had offered, as had Hendricks. Everyone said that the first one was the most difficult . . .

'It's supposed to be the worst time to be on the street, right?' he said. 'There's always documentaries on the telly. Women in green wellies taking a tramp home for Christmas.'

Spike shrugged. 'It's the same as the rest of the year, just a bit colder. It's every *other* punter that changes.' He put on his best Islington trendy accent: 'It's when people really start to *care* . . .'

They told Thorne about the cold-weather shelters that Crisis and other organisations would open. About the donations that poured in from members of the public, and from some of the more forward-thinking companies. Big-name stores playing Santa and clearing out old stock.

'You can pop along Christmas Day, get yourself turkey and all the trimmings, and as many Gap sweatshirts as you can carry.'

'It's hysterical,' Caroline said. 'You get these poor bastards walking into day centres and hostels all through January with nothing except major drug habits and enormous bags of brand-new toiletries.'

Spike took Caroline's cigarette from her mouth, used it to light one of his own. 'The new clothes thing is ace, though. People who give stuff to Oxfam or whatever seem to think we're all desperate to dress like some old grandad. Fucking cardigans and pyjamas that somebody died in.'

'Nothing wrong with a decent cardy,' Thorne said.

Caroline took hold of his arm. 'Yeah, but you *are* an old grandad, aren't you?'

They drifted across the pavement towards a gift shop and stationer's, whose window was already well stocked with tinsel and tat. They stared for a few seconds.

'Too bloody soon,' Thorne said. There was a Dixon's next door and he turned his attention to the television screens still flickering in the window. A soap-opera, *The Bill*, Sky News. He watched a journalist talking to camera and tried, without the benefit of sound, to work out what he might be talking about. He remembered Alan Ward, the reporter he'd met outside Colindale Station when he'd run into Steve Norman. Thorne decided that if Spurs were at home over the Christmas period – if *he* were at home – he'd take the man up on his offer of football tickets. He thought about the pies and the hot-dogs and the scalding tea at half-time; more attractive, at that moment, than the prospect of watching the game itself . . .

Spike leaned his face against the glass, steaming it up as he spoke. 'I think I might go to my sister's this year. She's got a fantastic flat in Docklands . . .'

Thorne nodded. Spike was constantly telling him things that he'd told him once or twice already.

'I don't care, as long as I'm indoors,' Caroline said. 'This year more than any.'

Thorne knew that she was talking about the murders. For the families, wherever they were, and for those still sleeping on the same streets as their dead friends, this would be that first, difficult Christmas.

'Killing people, or scaring them into leaving,' Caroline said. 'One way and another, he's clearing a lot of us off the street.'

Spike leaned back, drew a face on the window with his finger. 'Maybe he's working for the council.'

As with those places that dispensed more substantial meals, there were soup runs happening across the West End at different times during the evening. There was one at ten o'clock, just around the corner on the Strand, where, with irony far thicker than the soup itself, the homeless were fed within spitting distance – within *sniffing* distance – of the Savoy. Again, it was all about knowing when and where. There were some, with appetites all but destroyed by drugs, who would go all day without eating and get by on two or three bowls of soup; trudging between the various locations with the weary resignation of those for whom eating has long ceased being a pleasure.

There were a dozen or more people already waiting by the time they arrived, including a good few that Thorne had come across before. He recognised faces he'd seen at the Lift, from the streets around the theatre where he bedded down for the night. He met – but only briefly – the disturbing gaze of the man who'd come close to attacking him and Spike a couple of days earlier.

Thorne, Spike and Caroline joined those who were milling around outside a building which was – according to a discreet but highly polished nameplate – the headquarters of British and American Tobacco. Some lurked as close as possible to where they were expecting the van to stop, while others hung back, preferring to wait across the road. They gathered in small groups, talking or staring into space: the pale-faced kids in dirty anoraks, and the entrenched, long-haired and bearded, in dark clothes that seemed smeared across their bulky frames in grease. One group looked like backpackers who'd run out of money. Thorne caught a word or two in an Australian accent and decided that's exactly what they were.

Standing alone on the other side of the road near the tube station was one of the few black men Thorne had seen in his time on the streets. Maxwell had told him early on that there were so few black and Asian rough sleepers because those communities were closer-knit; that they believed in the extended family. Basically, he'd said, it came down to how much people gave a shit. It made sense to Thorne, who knew that were he even able to *find* any of his cousins – first, second or whatever – none of them would be inclined to take him in if he found himself in real trouble. He also knew, of course, that he'd be equally reluctant were he the one being asked to help. He'd seen enough blood to know that it was certainly thicker than water. But he'd also seen enough of it spilled within families to know that the phrase meant less than bugger all.

Spike saw Thorne looking around. 'Told you. There's all sorts . . .'

'Must be great soup,' Thorne said.

It arrived, and it wasn't. Ladled into styrofoam bowls from a huge metal saucepan in the back of a Volvo estate. But it was hot, dished out with a smile and, crucially, with no questions asked. This was another reason why the soup run remained popular, and why teenage backpackers could stand in line with those who'd been sleeping rough for decades.

Caroline crossed the road to a bench and lit up, as a very tall man, six feet five or more and cradling his bowl of soup, sauntered up to where Spike and Thorne were finishing theirs. Thorne put his empty bowl on to the window sill behind him, watched as Spike tossed his into the gutter. Thorne had to fight the urge to march over and pick it up.

The tall man and Spike greeted each other warmly and Spike made the introductions.

'This is Holy Joe.'

The man looked down at Thorne and gave a small nod. He was wearing a Queen's Park Rangers bobble hat and trainers, and what looked like a long brown robe beneath a tightly buttoned donkey-jacket.

'Who was it this time?' Spike asked.

'Nuns,' the man said. 'They're the fucking worst.'

Spike explained that Joe spent most of his time falling upon the tender mercies of a variety of different church organisations: the Jesus Army; the Salvation Army; the Quakers; the Young Jewish Volunteer Corps; the Sisters and Brothers of Just About Anybody. A few weeks at a time of free food and accommodation for the price of a daily Bible class or prayer meeting.

'I've got a hundred and seven crosses in a plastic bag,' Joe said. He took a slurp of soup. 'Wooden ones, plastic ones. There's dozens of Bibles . . .'

'I bet you knew Paddy Hayes,' Thorne said. 'Spike's mate. The one who was killed. He was a God-botherer, wasn't he?'

Joe took a step back into the road, scraped the sole of his training shoe against the kerb as though he were trying to remove dog-shit. 'Yeah, but Paddy was a bit of a lightweight.'

Thorne was still convinced that Jago and the first victim would provide the answer as to why these murders had happened. Why they were *still* happening. But how the killer selected the subsequent victims, if it was anything other than random, might give the police their best chance of catching him quickly. The idea that he was choosing victims from among distinct groups was definitely a strong possibility, but Thorne suddenly wondered if there might be a church connection.

'You can ask this man anything,' Spike said. 'He could do religion and all that shit on *Mastermind*. Your specialist subject, innit, Joe?'

Hadn't Robert Asker thought that he could talk to God on his radio? Maybe he'd been to a meeting or two. Thorne made a mental note to ask Caroline when he got the chance.

Spike was getting excited, shifting from foot to foot. 'Go on, ask him something. He knows the Bible fucking backwards.'

Joe nodded solemnly. 'And the Talmud. And the Koran. I'm not fussy.'

'I can't think of anything,' Thorne said.

'Ask him all the books in the Bible. Ask him to do them in order . . .'

'Too easy,' Joe said.

Thorne thought about his father, who would have loved a game like this. The old man wouldn't have slept until he'd found out the right answer and written it down somewhere. In his last few years he'd taken to ringing Thorne up in the early hours of the morning, demanding lists of answers to all manner of bizarre trivia questions.

'Ask him,' Spike said.

Give me a dozen big cats . . . The three fastest ball-games in the world . . . All the kings and queens of England. Go on, I'll give you the first couple to start . . .

'Go on, anything you like.'

'OK,' Thorne said. He pointed to the bowl in Joe's hands. 'Could Jesus have turned that into soup?'

There was the swish of a revolving door behind them and a man walked quickly from the B & A Tobacco building and hurried across the road. He wore a tailored overcoat and carried a metal briefcase, and his free hand struggled to tuck in one end of a bright red scarf that had caught in the wind.

Holy Joe turned and shouted cheerily after him. 'Oi, mate, got any ciggies for me?'

The man didn't even bother to look up. 'Piss off,' he said.

Back on the Strand, they walked east towards Fleet Street. They passed the 'ghost' Aldwych underground station, half of its boarded-up entrance now home to a Photo-Me booth, and Thorne gave Spike and Caroline a potted history. He told them how the station, originally called Strand, had fallen into disuse a number of times in the century since it had been opened; how a man had been eaten on one of the escalators in *An American Werewolf in London*; and how, during the Second World War, it had been home to the British Museum's collection of mummies.

As they crossed towards St Clement Danes, serene on its traffic island, Thorne pointed towards the spikes and spires of the Royal Courts of Justice, brutal against the night sky beyond the church. As a civil court, it was not a place Thorne knew well, but he *did* know that the man who built its clock was strangled to death when his tie got caught in the mechanism.

'Bloody hell,' Spike said. 'You know some seriously weird shit.'

Thorne thought about everything he'd learned, from Spike more than anyone, in the past few weeks. He thought about the things he'd been shown and the people he'd met. He thought about the knowledge that had been passed on to him.

'*I* know some weird shit . . .?'

Around the back of the church, a number of those who had been at the soup run had gathered to stand around and drink. To kill time until the next one. Caroline and Spike drifted away to talk to a couple of junkies whose conversation, by the look of them, would not be sparkling.

'Gotabeer?'

Thorne turned to see an older man with a shock of white hair and a nose like an overripe strawberry standing far too close to him.

'Gotabeer, mate?'

The words weren't slurred exactly, but ran easily into one as though they belonged together. It sounded both casual and aggressive, the last word fading into a breath like hot fat spitting. Thorne wasn't sure if the man had simply not got him down as a fellow rough sleeper, or was just so far gone that he didn't care who he asked. Either way, the answer was going to be the same.

'Sorry.' Thorne patted the can in his pocket. 'Just got the one and that's mine.'

'You're not drinking it.'

Thorne took the can of Special Brew from his pocket. He was going to fill it with weak stuff later, but what the hell. He yanked back the ring pull. 'Yes I am.'

As Thorne brought the can to his mouth, the man stepped even closer. 'Give us a fucking swig then.'

The man was leaning into him from the side. Thorne could feel the material of the man's filthy bodywarmer against his father's coat.

'Just the one swig . . .'

'Fuck off,' Thorne said.

The man moved back sharply as though he'd been pushed. He squinted at Thorne for ten or fifteen seconds, his feet planted firmly enough, but the top half of his body swaying gently. Then he cocked his head. 'You're a copper,' he said.

Thorne grunted and laughed. Took a mouthful of beer. It tasted vile.

'You're Old Bill. Course you are.' He was starting to raise his voice. 'I *know* you are.'

'Listen, mate . . .'

'I know a piggy . . .'

Thorne thrust the can towards him. 'Here, you can take it . . .'

'Oink! Oink!' He smacked a fat hand against the side of his leg over and over as he shouted: 'You're a *copper*, you're a *rozzer*, you're a rotten, filthy *fucker* . . .'

Thorne was on the verge of driving the base of the can against the old man's head when Spike appeared next to him.

'All right?'

As Thorne turned his head, the man reached out and grabbed the beer.

Spike took hold of his arm. 'Give us that back, you twat . . .'

'Let him have it,' said Thorne.

When Spike let go, the man took a couple of steps back, pulling the can of beer close to his chest. 'He's a copper. I swear he's a fucking copper.'

Spike spoke like he was humouring a mental patient. 'Course he is.' He cupped his hands around his mouth, shouted after the old man, although he was no more than a few feet away. 'You don't know how fucking wrong you are, pal.'

They watched as the man walked to the railings at the edge of the kerb and started to drink.

Spike looked at Thorne. 'You didn't *used* to be a copper, did you?'

Thorne turned and walked away, heading around the narrow strip of pavement that circled the church.

The old man was clearly a headcase, yet Thorne was still unnerved by the confrontation. Was there a chance he *had* been recognised? Could the old man have been someone Thorne had put away years before? It didn't really matter; from what Spike had shouted, it was clear that *he* still believed Thorne had spent time in prison.

He thought back to the case he'd been working on just before his father had died. The case that might have been the *reason* his father had died. He thought about a line he'd drawn, and then stepped across as casually as if he were entering another room.

Ex-offender was exactly right.

He stopped at the front of the church, looked up at the blackened statue of Gladstone, at the defiant bronze figure of Bomber Harris . . .

Something began to suggest itself.

There were other statues around the front of the church. He didn't need to know whom they honoured. Even from behind, the bearing of these men told Thorne *what* they were. He turned and walked back towards the entrance of the church, remembering it even as he saw the three letters, spelled out horizontally on a pale blue cross, beneath the figure of a golden eagle. St Clement Danes was the RAF church . . .

Something blurred started to come sharply into focus.

He thought about the museum he'd walked past earlier with Russell Brigstocke. He remembered something Spike had said when he was talking about the differing backgrounds of people who were sleeping rough:

'It's a right old mix, though. I fucking love it, like. You've got your immigrants, you've got . . .'

And then Thorne knew *exactly* who might have their blood group as a tattoo.

* * *

It was funny, he thought, about old friends.

Sitting in the flat, he thought about the strange ways things could pan out if you came across them again. Funny how it happened as well. It might be that you just ran into someone from your past on a street somewhere, or on a train, or found yourself leaning against the same bar one night. It might be a phone call out of the blue.

Or it might all come about same as this had: it might all start with a letter . . .

It was weird, that was the other thing, how some that you'd never really been close to might turn out, a few years down the line, to be all right. To be the ones you got on OK with. While others – the blokes who you thought at the time would be your mates for ever; who you said stupid, soppy shit to after a few beers; who you felt really *connected* to – ended up being the ones who caused all the fucking headaches later on. And, of course, sod's law, you could never tell first time round which were which.

Time could heal some wounds, *course* it could, but others were always going to fester.

He reckoned that basically there was always a good reason why people lost touch with one another. Sometimes it was an effort to keep a friendship going; when geography was against you or whatever. If the friendship was really worth it, though, you made the effort. Simple as that. If not, you let it go, and like as not the other person was thinking the same as you, and letting it go at exactly the same time.

If an effort was made later to get back in touch, there was a good chance that the party making the effort wanted something. It was certainly true in this case. Very bloody true all round, in fact. But, a decade and more down the road, you want different things, don't you? You want a quiet life and you'll do all sorts of things to keep it that way. You're willing – no, you're *happy* – to fight for what you've got; to keep hold of what you've worked so bloody hard to get.

They all needed each other back then. No shame in that. But life goes on, and people learn lessons, and you didn't need to be a rocket scientist, did you? When there isn't a real enemy around any more, you don't need friends quite so much.

1991

There are no longer any weapons trained upon the four men who have been tied up, and though those who have bound their wrists, and now their feet, are no more than fifty feet away, each allows his gaze, for at least some of the time, to drift towards the floor or to the face of the man nearest to him. The eyes of these men are no longer fixed and popping, as they would be faced with the muzzle of a gun or the blade of a knife.

The sand has become the colour of soil, and their olive shirts are black with the rain and pasted to their skins.

The four figures wearing goggles and helmets are also sitting now, or squatting, close together. Each still carries his gun, but it leans against a thigh or hangs loosely from a hand resting across a knee. Though their position might seem relaxed from a distance, they constantly eye the quartet across from them, and shift nervously. Heavily booted feet are flexed, carving out miniature trenches in the sand, and those on their haunches bob and bend, their arms stretched and stiff against the ground to steady themselves.

Suddenly, one man lowers his *shamag* and spits, a thick trail of it which he pulls away from his chin before lifting the kerchief back into place. He shuffles forward and the others do likewise; they lean close together and talk.

They each have something to say, and though the exchange is heated at first, it settles quickly and the voices gradually lower. The words are getting harder to make out, but they are clearly given greater weight and seriousness, and now the men are close enough to touch one another. It starts with a slap that sounds like a bone breaking and a voice that has become little more than a low growl. Pleas give way to threats. Then promises. One man swears, pushes at a second, and finds himself clutched at like a lover. Heads are shaken quickly and nodded slowly until, finally, each man has a handful of another's jacket or an arm wrapped tight around his shoulder, and they bow their heads so that the helmets smack together. They look like football players in a huddle, desperate to pool their terror and their aggression and turn it into something they can use. Firing up for one last, big push.

And this is when it begins to look like a game.

They all rise to their feet, and after another half-minute, one – chosen or volunteered – steps away from the group. He examines his pistol. In the space that opens up between there is a bright smear on the horizon, fainter as it rises, like red ink creeping up a blotter.

The others watch as the man walks quickly towards the four figures on the ground, though two of those watching turn away at the last moment. They look like players gathered in the centre circle. Some unable to handle the tension of the penalty shoot-out; turning their backs, lowering their heads. Afraid to watch.

The men on the ground begin to move, quickly. They attempt to scramble to their feet, but it's hopeless. They fall on to their backs or faces, and struggle to reach one another. Now their eyes are popping again; wide, and shot with shattered vessels.

Time passes, though probably no more than half a minute, and the man who left the group is on his way back to them.

There's no way of knowing of course what any of them are thinking; those that stand waiting their turn, or the man who trudges slowly back.

But though the goggles and *shamag*s give them all the same blank, robotic expression, it's easy to imagine that the faces beneath are equally expressionless.

He rejoins his friends in their centre circle.

Though three men have begun to scream, and weep, and pray, it's impossible to tell if he's scored or not.

FIFTEEN

The Media Operations Office of British Army HQ (London District) was housed in a building backing on to Horse Guards Parade. It had once been the barracks for hundreds of men, but these days the horses it stabled and the troops who paraded across its courtyards were engaged, for the most part, in ceremonial activities.

As Kitson and Holland had walked towards the reception area, they'd had to pass a pair of Household Cavalrymen on guard duty. The soldiers stood, unblinking in their scarlet tunics, with helmets polished to a mirrored finish, and Holland had only just fought off the childish urge to try to distract them, in the same way that giggling tourists and schoolchildren did all day long. Once inside the office, with a china cup of very strong tea, he confessed this to one of the Senior Public Information Officers sitting behind the desk opposite.

'Oh, they love all that carry-on,' the man said.

The second SPIO, seated behind a desk at a right-angle to the first, was eager to agree with his colleague. 'Especially if it's a couple of teenage girls doing the distracting. You'd be amazed how many saucy notes get stuck into those boys' boots.'

The office, which overlooked Whitehall, was large enough to have housed more than just the two SPIOs, but it was also somewhat dilapidated. Paint was peeling from the green door and eau-de-Nil walls, and though the brown colour hid it, the carpet was probably as thick with dust as the strip-lights above. Several large pinboards were covered with curling charts, sun-faded maps, and, on one, a colour photograph of the Queen in one of those oversized prams she was so fond of travelling around in.

Though many who worked in the building were civil servants, the two men who shared this office were actually retired army officers. This had been made clear early on, when each had introduced the other and had prefaced name with former rank. Ex-Lieutenant-Colonel Ken Rutherford was short and stocky, with silver hair that he'd oiled and swept back. Trevor Spiby, a former captain in the Scots Guards, was taller, and balding. A patch of red skin, which might have been a burn or a birthmark, ran from just below his jaw and disappeared under his collar. Each man wore a shirt and tie, but where Spiby had opted for braces, Rutherford sported a multicoloured waistcoat. Their contrasting appearances gave them the look of an upmarket double act, and this image was furthered by the way that they bounced off each other verbally.

'Tea OK?'

'Be better with a biscuit . . .'

'Are you sure we can't rustle you one up?'

Kitson thanked them and passed. Holland did likewise, the cut-glass accents of the ex-officers making him feel as though he belonged in *EastEnders*. He imagined his polite 'Thank you' sounding like he'd said, 'Get your lovely ripe bananas . . . two bunches for a pahnd!'

'I don't quite understand why you've come to Media Ops,' Spiby said.

Rutherford nodded. 'The Met would normally liaise with the RMP.'

Russell Brigstocke had considered talking to the Royal Military Police, but all that was really needed at this stage was information. He was also wary of the 'can of worms' factor that so often came into play when one force of any kind attempted to make use of another. As far as the meeting itself went, it had been his decision to send Yvonne Kitson along. Most interviews were conducted by officers of DS rank and below, but on this occasion Brigstocke had thought it politic for an inspector to be present.

'It's a simple enquiry really,' Kitson said. 'I just need straightforward information and I don't need to waste a lot of anyone's time. To be frank, it was this office's contact details that were first on the website.'

'How can we help you?' Rutherford asked.

Holland gave a brief summary of the case, concentrating on the deaths of the two men with tattoos, whom they now believed to have been ex-army.

'It sounds more than likely,' Spiby said. 'The blood group is often tattooed, along with other things, of course.'

'Though not too much.' Rutherford was peering over his computer. 'Anyone with too many tattoos can be barred from joining the army in the first place.'

'I don't suppose you'd know what the rest of the tattoo might mean?' Holland handed a piece of paper across. Rutherford pulled on the half-moon specs that hung around his neck. He studied the letters for a few moments and passed it to Spiby.

'They're initials, clearly, but certainly nothing military springs to mind.'

'Do you have any records of the particular markings that certain soldiers may have had?' Holland asked. 'Scars, tattoos, what have you?'

'I'm afraid not.' Spiby looked to Rutherford, who shook his head emphatically. 'There are medical records, yes, but nothing that detailed.'

'DNA?'

'Oh, I doubt it.'

'Dental records, perhaps?'

'Yes, I think so. I'd need to check . . .'

Kitson leaned forward to place her empty cup on Spiby's desk. 'As we only have a name for one of these men, we're very much hoping we can use it to identify the other. Save for the different blood groups, these tattoos are identical, so we're assuming they had them done at the same time. That they served together.'

'It sounds a reasonable assumption,' Rutherford said.

'So if we give you this man's name, we thought you could give us a list of the other soldiers he served with.'

'Ah. *Not* such a reasonable assumption, I'm afraid. First, *we* can't give you anything; you'd need to contact the Records Office. Second, the records just don't work like that. They don't group the men together in that fashion. I'd be amazed if the Met's records worked a great deal differently.'

Kitson sat back in her chair.

'These men who were sleeping rough,' Spiby said, 'they had been out of the army for some time, correct?'

There was a pause. The silence was broken only by the sputtering of the ancient gas fire in the corner of the room. Holland cleared his throat. 'We think so, yes.'

'They were definitely not AWOL servicemen?'

'Not as far as we know . . .'

'It *would* explain why they were sleeping rough. When a soldier is AWOL, they will go to extraordinary lengths to avoid being traced through official channels.'

Rutherford chipped in. 'I'm sure that Army Personnel could cross-check your name against a list of absent servicemen.'

'I don't think that's the case . . .'

'So how far back are we talking?' Spiby asked.

Kitson looked across to Holland. He looked back at her, gave a small shake of the head. 'We're not sure at this stage,' Kitson said.

'When a soldier leaves the army, his records are sent to the Manning and Record Office at the Army Personnel Centre in Glasgow. Some time later . . .' Spiby looked to Rutherford. 'Is it ten years, Ken?'

'Something like that.'

'Some time later, the records are moved to the Services Archive at Hayes. Glasgow would need to recall any file from there if you made an enquiry. You could try that to begin with, but in the first instance they tend to give out only name, date of birth and a confirmation of service.'

'There are constraints on the release of any other information,' Rutherford said.

Holland had started to feel very warm. He undid the top button of his shirt. 'This is a murder investigation, sir. I doubt those constraints would apply.'

Rutherford held up his hands in mock surrender. 'I'm sure you're right, Detective Sergeant, but with all the co-operation in the world I still don't think they'll be able to give you the information you're after. As far as the soldier whose name you *do* have goes, you may still need authorisation from his next of kin. You have that, correct?'

Now Holland was feeling hot. Thinking about who that next of kin might be . . .

'Which regiment did our man serve in?' Spiby asked. 'That might give us a start, at least.'

It was another question Holland couldn't answer. Kitson snapped her head round to stare at him. He could see that she was thinking about Susan Jago, too.

Kitson waited until she'd reached the end of the corridor and turned to walk down the stairs before she let rip. 'They looked at us like we were amateurs. Fuck it, we *are* amateurs. What the hell went on in there?'

Holland said nothing. He was still trying to put it together, trying to remember a sequence of events.

'I don't like passing the buck, Dave, but you were given the job of going into CRIS and writing up the notes for this interview.'

'I did, Guv . . .'

Kitson stopped. 'So why did we not know the answers to those questions?'

Holland had accessed the Crime Reporting Intelligence System first thing that morning. CRIS was a complete record of the case to date: every name, date and statement. There had been nothing relating to

Christopher Jago's service in the army – the year of his discharge, the name of his regiment. Holland had presumed that the data had simply not yet been entered, but that Kitson and Brigstocke must already know the relevant facts. He knew now that he'd fucked up; that they'd all fucked up.

'Dave? Where's the information we got from Jago's sister?' The moment Kitson had finished asking the question, she knew the answer. 'Christ. There isn't any, is there?'

'That's the thing, Guv. I don't think Susan Jago has ever told us her brother was a soldier.'

'Hang on, let's think about this. I know she never bothered to tell us when she came down to ID the body. If the silly cow had mentioned it, we'd have put the whole thing together a bit quicker, wouldn't we? But we've spoken to her *since* then.'

'DC Stone called with the death message.' It was this phone call Holland had been trying to place in a pattern of what had been known, and when.

'Right. So, she'd have talked about it then, surely. Why the hell *wouldn't* she?'

Holland had no idea at all.

Yvonne Kitson was trying to stay calm. It was her team and she was ultimately responsible. She should have made sure. She should have *known* about this. Then it occurred to her that perhaps Susan Jago *had* told them about her brother and that they'd simply failed to process the information. 'Is it possible that DC Stone did not update the CRIS after he'd spoken to Susan Jago?'

Holland knew it was more than possible. There was no record of the conversation on the system. Stone might well have decided that as Susan Jago was no longer important to the investigation, he could get away without doing the update. But that still didn't explain it: Stone had spoken to Jago three days earlier, on the Saturday afternoon; that was hours before Thorne had figured out the army connection.

'It doesn't make sense. When DC Stone spoke to her, we still didn't know about the army thing. So if she *had* said anything, he'd have known it was important and would have passed it on verbally.'

They walked the rest of the way down the narrow staircase, both thinking the same thing: *Why the hell wouldn't Susan Jago have told them?*

'Call Stone and double check . . .'

Holland took out his mobile, dialled Stone's number and got a message. He looked at his watch. 'It's lunchtime, Guv. He'll be in a caff somewhere with his phone switched off.' The lie had come easily, despite the anger he felt. Holland knew very well that whatever Andy Stone was eating, it wasn't lunch.

They emerged into a covered courtyard to find themselves part of a small crowd gathered for the daily mounting of the guard. A row of red-coated Life Guards on horseback stood facing their opposite numbers from the Blues and Royals, identical save for the dark coats.

Kitson and Holland stood with the hushed tourists for a few minutes and watched the ceremony. Cameras clicked furiously as the troops who had ridden down from Hyde Park Corner arrived; the huge horses walking two abreast beneath the arch to Horse Guards.

Holland leaned his head close to Kitson's. 'How come *we* never get saucy notes stuck in our boots?'

But Kitson was in no mood to laugh.

The place smelled of piss and hospital food.

As soon as Thorne had walked through the door he'd remembered what Spike had told him when they'd been talking about the facilities at the Lift; how most places were a lot different. He'd been putting it mildly.

The Aquarius day centre in Covent Garden catered purely for those over twenty-five, but they could easily have upped the lower limit by fifteen years. Thorne hadn't seen a single person younger than himself since he'd got there, and, looking around, it was hardly surprising. The few people he had encountered were old – before their time or otherwise – and he couldn't imagine a twenty-five or thirty-year-old feeling anything other than deeply uncomfortable in the poky, dismal rooms and bare-brick corridors. Where the London Lift was light and well cared-for, everything about the Aquarius reeked of neglect, and a lack of the funding necessary to get rid of the stench.

In the closest thing he could find to a lounge, Thorne sat and tried not to breathe too deeply.

It felt like a doctor's waiting room. A windowless box with a dozen chairs pushed back against its flaking walls, and a table in the centre with old magazines and overflowing ashtrays scattered across it like litter.

Ever since he'd worked out how Jago and the other man might have been connected, Thorne had been absorbed in considering why someone who'd served and possibly fought for their country might return to Civvy Street only to wind up sleeping on it. Might end up spending their days in a place like this. The figures were alarming. Some sources claimed that one in every four rough sleepers was ex-armed forces, with the figure even higher for those who had been on the streets long term. Ironically, squaddies were given the skills that might help sustain them outdoors. They were *trained* to sleep rough. But what led so many of them to end up doing just that?

There would be the same risk factors that applied to anyone else, of course; the same triggers. And it wasn't hard to work out that there would be others, too, unique to a history in the armed forces: post-traumatic stress; difficulties with readjustment; drug and alcohol dependency arising from either of those two things. But these were just chapter headings from a case-worker's textbook. Thorne knew that if he wanted to understand, he would have to find some of these people, and talk to them . . .

A man poked his head around the door, stared at Thorne for a few seconds and backed out again. The room's only other occupant had not even looked up. He sat opposite Thorne in a ratty green armchair, the floor around his feet littered with bits of foam stuffing that had leaked from its cushion. He gripped the wooden arms as though they were keeping him from rising up into the air, and stared at the front of a *Daily Star* that had sat unthumbed on his knees for the past fifteen minutes.

Neither Thorne nor anyone else knew whether Jago and the other victim had been killed because of their army background, or because they were homeless, or because of whatever events had led them from one to the other. Brigstocke had contacted the Ex-Service Action Group in hope of guidance. Meanwhile, Thorne knew that his role gave him an opportunity to talk to those who found themselves where Chris Jago and the other victim had once been.

That said, if Thorne had learned anything over the last few weeks, it was that reaching out to someone was never straightforward.

'This place is a shit-hole,' Thorne said. 'Isn't it? They should just lob a fucking grenade in and be done with it . . .'

The man sitting opposite rose from his chair – letting the newspaper slide on to the floor among the foam debris – and walked out of the room.

Thorne got up and retrieved the paper. He turned to the sports pages and saw that, despite the draw they had scraped with Liverpool the previous Saturday, Spurs were still flirting dangerously with the bottom three.

Then he followed the man out.

Walking fast towards the exit, he thought about his father's war stories. Jim Thorne had been no more than nine or ten when the Second World War had broken out, and his army experience had taken him no further than Salisbury Plain. But he'd been happy to pass on the fact that he hadn't seen a pineapple until he was eighteen, and recalled nights spent below ground while the bombs fell on north London with a clarity that remained undimmed even at the end. Thorne knew this sort of thing was not uncommon, but still he marvelled at how his dad could describe every inch of an air-raid shelter, then forget to put on any underwear.

'*For pity's sake, Dad . . .*'

'*I forgot. I fucking forgot the bastard things!*'

Thorne's father had told him, often, that he'd enjoyed his time as a soldier; that he'd needed the discipline and the routine. Thorne wondered if the problems of many of those who left the army each year stemmed from an inability to deal with the chaos, with the lack of any pattern to their lives in the real world. It would certainly explain why so many regained the order they craved in another way, by moving quickly from army to prison.

He wondered if Jago or the other man might ever have done time . . .

Approaching the exit, he saw the man from the lounge, and something in the stance reminded Thorne of his father's friend Victor. He had a few years on Jim Thorne, had seen active service, and Thorne wondered what a soldier of Victor's generation would make of all this. He knew about how men with shellshock had been mistreated after the Great War, but did that compare with the fate that awaited so many who'd returned from Sarajevo, Belfast, Goose Green?

Thorne remembered reading somewhere that more British soldiers had committed suicide since returning from the Falklands than had been killed during the entire conflict.

The man from the lounge was standing at the door, arguing with someone who looked like a case-worker. Thorne hovered, pretending to study the row of tatty paperbacks on a shelf, not wanting to push past the men in the doorway.

'We were supposed to fill those forms in together,' the case-worker said. 'It's important, Gerry. You promised me you'd bring them in today.'

Gerry was clearly agitated. 'I forgot. I fucking forgot the bastard things . . .'

Back at Becke House, Holland made sure he got to Andy Stone first.

'Guess how many ways you're in the shit?'

The smile slid off Stone's face.

'I've tried to call you half a dozen times since midday.'

'The phone was off for an hour at the most, I swear,' Stone said.

'That's only one of the ways. Why didn't you update the CRIS after you spoke to Susan Jago?'

'When?'

'After you rang with the death message. Last Saturday afternoon.'

Stone opened and closed his mouth, looked at the ceiling.

'You're a fucking idiot,' Holland said. And he knew that *he* was too, and that Kitson felt much the same way. She was already in with Russell Brigstocke, and Holland wasn't so sure that the DCI would be quite so ready to blame himself. 'I walked into a meeting this morning, unable to answer the simplest question, because we hadn't got any of the information about Chris Jago that we should have been given by his sister.'

'I'm not with you . . .'

'When you spoke to Susan Jago last Saturday, did she tell you that her brother had been in the army?'

'No.'

Holland toyed with being pissy just for once and demanding a 'sir', but he decided against it. 'She said nothing about his service history at all?'

'Fuck, don't you think I'd have told you if she had?'

'I *thought* you'd have updated the CRIS,' Holland said. 'Looks like I can't take anything for granted.'

The implications of what Holland was telling him were starting to dawn on Stone. 'So she never said anything to *anybody*?'

Holland answered with his eyes. 'I thought Kitson had the information and *she* thought *I'd* got it off the system. It was never on the system in the first place.'

'Bloody hell.' Stone leaned back against a desk, folded his arms. 'After Thorne came up with the idea that the tattoo was an army thing, I did think it was strange that she hadn't mentioned it. I just thought someone would have checked with her. I thought someone would be getting in touch to ask her about it, you know?'

'Well, nobody did.'

'Hang about. Has it not occurred to you that she didn't say anything about him being ex-army because he *wasn't*. It's only a theory, isn't it . . .?'

Holland shook his head, adamant. 'He was ex-army. That's an army tattoo.' Even as he said it, Holland was aware that this was still conjecture, but he knew instinctively that it was true. And, equally, instinct told him that Susan Jago had been deliberately keeping the information back from them. Yes, they *should* have checked, but they'd been so fired up by Thorne's theory that they'd neglected to get the simplest piece of procedure right. But the fact remained that Susan Jago had volunteered nothing. Holland had already called Phil Hendricks, asked about his and Jago's conversation in the car on the way to Euston, and she'd evidently said nothing to him either.

'So, how pissed off is Kitson about this CRIS thing?'

Holland had already taken a step towards Brigstocke's office. He needed to tell them that he'd spoken to Stone and confirmed their suspicions. That they needed to talk to Susan Jago urgently.

Stone shouted after him. 'I just presumed someone had called her . . .'

Thorne had sat through many tedious hours on stakeouts; in strategically chosen attic rooms or in the backs of unmarked vans. He had felt time drag as slowly as he'd ever imagined it could, and that was with the benefit of company, and coffee. With the prospect of a beer and a warm bed when it was all over.

Time spent on the streets passed like something that was spread over you; marked out in footsteps that could only grow heavier. And heavier still. There were moments when it felt like *no* time could have passed; when you found yourself staring into a familiar window or treading the same stretch of pavement yet again. It was only the blisters and the burning through the joints at the end of each day that made you certain it had passed at all.

Thorne settled back against the door of the theatre and thought about a couple of boys he'd seen in a narrow side street when he'd left the day centre: their skinny fingers cradled around the smoking rock; a flattened and gouged-out Coke can used as a crack-pipe.

He had come to understand just why so many of those with drink and drug problems had turned in desperation to such comforts *after* they'd begun sleeping rough. If anything – bottled or burned – could numb the pain of hours that spread like tumours, or speed up the ticking steps, then Thorne saw clearly that it was something to be clutched at and cherished.

He reached behind him, felt for the can in his rucksack. At least he still had the prospect of beer . . .

Deep inside his pocket, the tiny mobile phone was still cradled in his hand. When he'd spoken to Holland earlier, when he'd been told that they would be bringing Susan Jago down from Stoke for an interview, he'd told him to check whether her brother had ever been in prison. It couldn't hurt to ask.

From the sound of it, it wouldn't hurt to ask the woman a great many things. There had to be a very good reason why she was being secretive, and now they had to hope they would find it. Thus far, luck and guesswork had allowed them to take a few, faltering steps – in who knew what direction – but Susan Jago might provide the hand shoved firmly in the back. The push that would give them the impetus to catch up with a killer.

As Thorne took out the phone and dialled, he wondered whether Chris Jago had been a good soldier. He also wondered if he'd known the driver of the car that had killed him.

The man who answered the phone recited his number slowly, then asked who was speaking.

'It's Tom. I'm sorry for calling so late . . .'

'It's not late, son. Don't worry.'

It had gone midnight, but Thorne's apology had been no more than a courtesy. If anyone had spent longer than he had on the phone to his father in the small hours, it had been Victor. Thorne had been fairly certain that he'd be awake.

'So, what's up?' Victor asked.

'Nothing, really. Just calling for a natter . . .'

Even as he spoke, Thorne thought that, in truth, there was nothing very much worth talking about; nothing that would have any bearing on the case at any rate.

'That's fine, son. It's good to talk. Let me just go and turn the radio off . . .'

Thorne watched as a pair of young women on fuck-me heels clattered past on the pavement opposite. It was far too cold for belly-tops and bare midriffs . . .

'That's better.'

If anyone had ever told him where Victor had originally come from, Thorne had forgotten, but he spoke with the faintest of accents. Somewhere Eastern European, by the sound of it. It struck Thorne that he had no idea *which* army Victor had fought for. He realised that actually, there were a great many things he didn't know about his father's best friend. Things that he wanted to know. Like whether Victor had any family. What he had done before he retired. Where he had met his father, and how long they had known each other, and why he was the only one of his dad's mates who hadn't suddenly developed a busy life when the old man started going loopy.

'Tom?'

'What?'

'You're not doing a lot of nattering, son.'

'Sorry. So, how've you been? Keeping yourself busy?'

'Oh, yes, I'm always busy,' Victor said. 'What about yourself? How's the job?'

'You know . . .'

'When the phone went I thought it was him, you know? Just for a few seconds. Calling up with some quiz question, or one of his jokes, or trying to find out the word for something he'd forgotten. Remember how he used to do that?'

Thorne closed his eyes. He'd seen some film or read a book in which memory could be wiped out with a pill. Right now, even though good memories would be erased along with the bad, he'd take it.

'It's OK,' Victor said. 'I miss the silly old bugger as well, you know?'

Thorne felt suddenly as though he were only seconds away from sleep. 'I'm fine, honestly, Victor. I really didn't ring to talk about him.'

Then a low, amused hum. 'Course you didn't . . .'

SIXTEEN

Becke House was not a fully functioning police station. There were no cells – other than those the detectives were required to work in – and no formal interview suite. As with anyone else who had to be questioned, or held, Susan Jago was taken to Colindale. It had the necessary facilities in abundance, and the added advantage of being just five minutes up the road.

'How long d'you think this is going to take?' Jago said.

Holland opened the door and showed her inside. 'I'd say that was very much up to you, Susan . . .'

It was a narrow room and windowless, but cleaner than most. Jago dropped her handbag down by a chair and nudged it under the table. She looked up at the digital clock on the wall. Though she'd caught an early train from Stoke and been collected by uniformed officers from the station, it was already a few minutes after eleven o'clock. 'I was hoping I could get back to pick the kids up from school.'

'I'm not sure that's very likely,' Holland said. He reached across for her jacket and hung it on a coat-rack behind the door.

When Kitson entered the room, Holland took her coat, too. She nodded at Jago. 'Thanks for coming down so quickly.'

Susan Jago looked different from the last time they'd seen her. Her dark hair had been dragged back into a ponytail and there was no make-up to get ruined by tears. She looked more confident, certainly, but also harder. Holland had already gone through the Judges' Rules with her outside. He'd explained that she was not under arrest, that she was free to leave at any time, and that she was entitled to legal representation. She'd laughed at him as if he were being silly. Now, he went over the same ground for the benefit of the tape. The date was stated and the names of those present given for the record.

Jago glanced up at the camera high in the corner. The hardware had been recently upgraded. Now, as well as being recorded on two audio cassettes, the interview was being simultaneously filmed and burned on to a CD ROM. She looked back to the racks of shiny, wall-mounted equipment. 'I bet that lot cost a fair bit,' she said.

Kitson didn't want to hang around any longer than anybody else did. 'Miss Jago, did your brother, Christopher David Jago, ever serve in the British Army?'

If there was hesitation, it was only fractional. She answered slowly and surely and with pride in her voice. 'Yes, Chris was a soldier.'

'So why did you choose not to tell us that?'

'When?'

'Let's start with when you came to London to identify a body that you believed to be that of your brother.'

'This is going to sound stupid, but nobody asked me.'

'You're right,' Kitson said. 'It does sound *very* stupid . . .'

'Well, I can't help that. I didn't think it was relevant.'

Holland spoke up. 'Surely, if you were looking for your brother, any information about him, about his past, would have been relevant, wouldn't it?'

'Look, I just wanted to know if it was him, and when it wasn't, I just wanted to get the hell out of there and go home. Nothing else seemed very important.'

Holland stretched out his legs, then withdrew them quickly when his feet made contact with Jago's. 'You had a long chat with Dr Hendricks on the way to the train station, didn't you? You were perfectly happy at that time to talk about your brother's history with drugs, about his mental problems, but, again, you never saw fit to mention his past in the army.'

She reached towards her handbag. 'Can I smoke in here?'

'I'm afraid not.' Kitson raised a finger casually towards the smoke alarm on the ceiling, neglecting to mention that it never contained any batteries. The no-smoking rule was her own. She hated cigarettes anyway, but also believed that keeping an interviewee on edge would deliver better results more often than not.

Jago smiled weakly. 'What happened to the good cop sliding the fag packet across the table when the bad cop goes out of the room?'

'We're both bad cops,' Kitson said.

'Miss Jago.' Holland tapped a finger on the tabletop. He wanted an answer. 'You never mentioned your brother's army history during the conversation with Dr Hendricks. Is that correct?'

She nodded.

'For the tape, please . . .'

'Yes, correct. I never mentioned it, but I don't see why one's got anything to do with the other.'

'Don't you?' Kitson asked. 'How many ex-soldiers do you suppose end up sleeping on the streets, Susan? As opposed to ex-footballers, say? Or ex-bank managers?'

Jago shrugged.

'Let's move on a bit,' Holland said. 'A couple of days after that first trip to London, you were contacted by Detective Constable Stone, who told you that we had information about your brother's death.'

She shifted suddenly on her chair, as though there were something uncomfortable on the seat beneath her. 'Right, like it was good news. A fucking phone call from some smarmy, low-rank moron who'd obviously drawn the short straw, telling me Chris is dead. And now you're going to sit there and ask me why I didn't say anything about him being in the army again, aren't you? Well, I'm sorry if I had other things to worry about, like what I was going to tell my mother. Like how I was going to find out where the council had buried my brother . . .'

Holland could see by the look on Kitson's face that she was in no mood to be messed around. 'Let's not waste any more time with this, all right? I'm going to stop saying "forgot to mention" and "neglected to inform" and I'm going to call it what it is: lying. You lied to us, and you withheld information that might have been important to a murder investigation.'

Jago slapped her palms against her jeans and raised her voice. 'They're not the same thing. They're fucking not. You tell me when I lied . . .'

'What about the tattoos?'

The skin around her mouth slackened suddenly, as if the ponytail had been keeping it taut and had suddenly been removed.

'I haven't done anything wrong.' She held Kitson's stare, but her voice had lost all of its stridency.

'You were asked on a number of occasions, by myself, by DS Holland, and by DC Stone during your telephone conversation on 17 September, if you knew what the significance of the tattoos was. On each of those occasions you said that you did not.'

'*On each of those occasions* I was hardly thinking straight, was I?'

'You lied.'

'No.'

'You knew very well they were army tattoos.'

'I never lied. I've already explained that the first time I was messed up. I'd just seen a dead body, for crying out loud, I'd been looking at some poor sod with most of his face kicked to shit. Then, later on, when he asked me about the tattoos on the phone, I was in a complete state, wasn't I? Because I'd just found out that Chris had been murdered as well. How was I expected to think straight?' She shook her head, kept shaking it, but both Holland and Kitson could see immediately that she knew what she'd just said.

'That's a strange way of putting it, don't you think, Susan? Your brother was the victim of a hit-and-run driver, wasn't he? You'd been given no other information than that. You were told it was an accident. Yet you just said, "Chris had been murdered as well". Like the first victim had been murdered . . .'

Outside on the street a car was being revved up, and somewhere along the corridor a telephone was going unanswered.

Kitson leaned forward. 'Why did you lie to us?'

It hadn't taken very long. Susan Jago had been prepared, certainly, had been gearing herself up to front it out, but no amount of hard-faced posturing could mask the agony she felt inside. Once she started talking, it came quickly, like poison from a boil that's been lanced.

'I didn't think it mattered, I swear I didn't. It's like I told that pathologist bloke in the car, I just thought Chris had gone walkabout – you know? – and that he'd come waltzing back when he was ready. So why would knowing what he'd done before matter to anyone except me and him? I just wanted to forget all of it. I managed to convince myself that I didn't know much about his past and that it wasn't hurting anybody to leave it like that.' She looked from Holland to Kitson and back again. 'Then I found out he was dead, and I knew there were two of them. When I knew they'd both been murdered, I wanted to come clean about it all. I wanted to tell, honestly I did, but it was like I'd got so caught up in the lie that I couldn't figure out a way to make it right again . . .'

'Did you recognise the man you saw in the mortuary?' Kitson asked.

She raised her eyes, every trace of bravado long gone. 'I could really murder that fag now.'

'Did you recognise him, Susan?'

'Yes. He was in the crew with Chris. But on my children's lives, I never knew his name. I just saw a photo of the four of them together once, that's all.'

'What crew?' Holland said.

'Chris was a Tanky. He was in the 12th King's Hussars. That's a cavalry regiment—'

Kitson raised a hand, needing to slow things down a little. 'Four of them, you said. Why four?'

'There's four in a Challenger crew. That's the tank Chris and his mates were on. It was the four of them that went out and got those tattoos done just before they were flown out. The blood groups and those letters, which is just a piss-take, by the way, because they all hated the Royal Tank Regiment. There was some stupid rivalry, because they thought the Royals were posh, and the Royals' motto is "Fear Nought", right? So Chris and the others got their own mottos done, as a joke: S.O.F.A. – Scared Of Fuck All . . .'

Holland was struggling to take all of it in, but he could sense its importance. The room seemed to constrict suddenly and grow warmer. It felt as though his ears were popping. 'We've got plenty of time to get all this down, Susan. Can you just tell us why you wanted to keep it a secret?'

Jago reached down and lifted her handbag on to her lap.

'You can have that fag in a minute, Susan,' Kitson said.

But it wasn't a cigarette packet Jago took out. It was a videotape. She placed a hand flat on top of it; then, after a few seconds, she pushed it across the table.

'I'll tell you anything you want to know,' she said. 'Anything I can. But I won't watch it . . .'

1991

There are two groups of men, four in each . . .

Now all of them are gathered together. Those who were previously tied up are sitting much closer together, with the others squashed in around them, squatting or stooping. Though only four of these eight men are dead, the entire group is momentarily still.

Posed and posing.

Behind this bizarre tableau, for the first time the hulking figure of the tank is visible. Its side and its muddy track, streaked with petrol-rain, provide the perfect backdrop. It also offers something to lean the dead men back against.

After a few seconds we hear the voice from close by. Shouted this time. The words are just discernible above the relentless pop and spatter of the rain: 'Put your arms around them . . . Give the fuckers a cuddle.'

Two of the soldiers do as they've been told. They lean forward and each throws an arm around the shoulder of a corpse. The other two soldiers remain still, with their heads lowered.

'I can't see faces . . . *Lift their heads up*.'

One of the soldiers is down on his haunches between two bodies, an arm now around each one. He looks across to one of those who has not moved. 'A bit late to pussy out now.'

After a few moments, the soldier who has been challenged stoops to grab the hair of the dead man and pull back his head. Close-up we see that the corpse's eyes are half closed and the jaw is hanging slack. Rain pours into the open mouth, spills from the side.

'Uh-oh . . . losing one . . .'

The body on the far right starts to tip to one side and slowly fall. The soldier behind, who has still not joined in, half reaches out a hand, then pulls it away at the last moment and allows the dead man to drop to the ground.

'For fuck's sake . . .'

It isn't clear at first. The rain and the shadows, the dark sand and hair make it hard to distinguish. Then, on the body of the fallen man we see the patch that is wetter, blacker; high on the side of the head, and just starting to spread an inch or two across the sand.

'Watch . . .'

A soldier has pressed his face against that of a dead man. He raises a hand and wraps it around the neck. He swivels the head around, one way and then another.

'Gottle of geer, gottle . . . geer . . .'

His friend laughs, pulling off a glove. He leans across and presses a finger to the back of the corpse's head. He looks at the stained fingertip, rubs it against his thumb for a second or two, then dabs it against the dead man's forehead.

A small red spot that starts to run.

'That's better. Want to make sure they let him in to Heaven.'

The soldier who'd let the body drop stands suddenly and reaches over. He grabs the soldier who is still putting his glove back on and drags him to his feet. Screams into his face.

'That's Hindus, you ignorant prick. Not Muslims.'

'All right . . .'

'Not fucking Muslims!' He pushes him away and the two soldiers stand and look at each other. The horizon is a glowing strip behind them.

Then, the camera drifts away, and down.

And white noise . . .

SEVENTEEN

Holland jabbed at the remote and stopped the tape.

After something close to half a minute, during which nobody spoke, Holland got up and moved across to the television. He crouched down by the VCR and ejected the cassette.

Brigstocke turned to the man sitting next to him. 'What d'you reckon?'

'I reckon it's something worth killing for,' Thorne said. 'Worth killing to keep hidden.'

'It's fucking horrible.' Holland stuffed the cassette back into a large Jiffy bag and sat down again. 'That's the fourth time I've seen it and I'm still glad I haven't eaten anything today.'

The three of them were sitting in beige armchairs, gathered around a coffee-table in the TV room at the London Lift. Though he'd moaned initially, complaining that he'd be in the shit if Lawrence Healey ever found out, Brendan Maxwell had eventually agreed to open the place up for them out of hours. It was just after seven on a Thursday night. Nearly thirty-six hours since Susan Jago had handed over the videotape.

'What about the sound?' Thorne asked. 'You can't make out a lot of what's being said. One voice is completely distorted early on, when they're doing that shit with the bacon.'

Holland grimaced. 'That's really hideous . . .'

'We're sending it to the lab at Newlands Park,' Brigstocke said. 'Having heard some of the things they've done with 999 recordings, I reckon they can enhance the dialogue for us. We might find out what everyone was saying.'

'So what *do* we know?' Thorne asked.

Holland took out a notebook, though he didn't really need it. 'It's the first Gulf War. Chris Jago was posted there from Bremenhaven in northern Germany in October 1990. The date on the tape tells us that what we saw took place on February 26th, 1991. As to exactly where . . .'

'I'm not sure it really matters,' Brigstocke said.

Thorne scratched at what had become a pretty decent beard. 'What does Susan Jago say?'

'She says her brother didn't want to go along with any of it,' Holland said. 'She says that he was the one at the end doing the shouting.'

'Of course she does.'

'It's impossible to tell who's who, so I doubt we'll ever know.'

'Like I said before, I'm not sure it really matters,' Brigstocke said.

Thorne shook his head, let it drop back against his chair. 'Nobody tried very hard to stop it. They were all involved on some level.'

'We *do* know one of the others is our mystery man in Westminster Morgue.' Holland picked up his briefcase and took out a grainy 10 × 8 photograph: a still from the video showing the four British soldiers; the moment before one of them moved forward from the group and checked his gun; just before the killing began. Holland laid the photo on the table, tapped at it with a fingernail. 'With a bit of luck, we'll have names for all of them by this time tomorrow.'

Brigstocke looked at Thorne. 'Holland and Kitson are going to pay the twelfth King's Hussars a visit tomorrow.'

'You're going to *Germany*?' Thorne asked.

Holland's expression soured. 'Bloody regiment got shifted back here five years ago, didn't it? They're based near Taunton now, so I get to go to Somerset instead. Shame. I could have done with a new overcoat.' Officers were given allowances of a few hundred pounds, usually in Marks & Spencer vouchers, if they were travelling to countries that would be warmer, or in this case cooler than they might be used to . . .

'Nice to see you've still got your priorities sorted, Dave,' Thorne said.

Holland stood and walked towards a varnished-pine bookcase in the corner. He laid a hand on top of the Jiffy bag as he passed the table. 'God knows what they're going to make of *that* mind you.' He sank down to his haunches in front of the bookcase and peered through the locked glass doors at the rows of videotapes and DVDs inside.

'It's going to be interesting, all right,' Thorne said.

'That's one word for it.'

'How are you going to play it?' Thorne looked across at Brigstocke and received a small shake of the head in return.

'You've got some good stuff in here,' Holland said. 'All the *Scream* movies. A lot of Jim Carrey stuff . . .'

Thorne pointed to the Jiffy bag. 'I think I'd rather watch *that* again.'

They all laughed, but nobody's heart was really in it. Least of all Thorne's.

'Why don't you find us a caff, Dave?' Brigstocke said. 'Bring us some teas back.'

Thorne had eaten no more than Holland, but for different reasons. Now he wanted a variety of cakes and sandwiches with his tea, and in the end Holland had to write it all down. When he'd gone, Thorne turned to Brigstocke. 'What was all *that* about?' He mimicked the strange shaking of the head that had gone on just before.

'I need to get this rubber-stamped by Jesmond first thing in the morning,' he said. 'He's gone higher up, but for what it's worth I've told him I don't think we should tell the army about the video just yet.'

Thorne considered this for a moment or two. 'It makes sense.'

Brigstocke looked relieved that Thorne was agreeing with him, but explained himself anyway. 'What's on this tape is a bloody big deal, and once the army gets hold of it they might well think they've got better things to worry about than a few murders.'

'You're worried they'll try and find some way to cover it up?'

Brigstocke looked worried about *something*, certainly. 'I don't know. Look, when our case is put to bed they can do what they want with it and I'll be happy to co-operate in any way I can. Right now, though, that tape's just evidence in my murder investigation, and I need their help.' He looked down at the photograph on the table. 'I need the names of those men, and if the army knows about this tape I'm not sure we'll get given them very quickly. See what I'm saying?'

'Like I said, it makes sense.'

'It does, doesn't it?'

It was obvious that Brigstocke was still nervous about having made such a potentially dangerous decision. He needed reassurance, and Thorne could understand why he'd sent Holland out before he'd gone looking for it. Thorne wanted to tell him that he was handling the situation well, that he was making a good job of a miserable case. He wanted to tell him that he wasn't the only one in the room who needed reassurance. The moment came and went . . .

'Jesmond might well bottle it,' Brigstocke said. 'If he orders us to hand the tape over, we'll hand it over and see what happens. The Met's worked well enough with the RMP when we've had to. It'll probably be fine . . .'

'Or it'll be like we never had the tape in the first place.'

'We'll see . . .'

'What about the sister?' Thorne asked.

'She's back home but we got pretty heavy with her. She thinks there's a charge of conspiracy to pervert hanging over her.'

'Is there?'

'We'll let the CPS decide. It'll be a difficult one to call, because she never actually *did* anything. She was lying to protect a dead man.'

Thorne had never met Susan Jago. He imagined her as hard-faced and cunning. He pictured thin lips and dead eyes; features she'd have shared with one of the men behind goggles and a coloured kerchief. A man who'd tied up prisoners and executed them. 'She didn't know he was dead when she lied, though, did she?'

The two of them sat back in their chairs, waiting for Holland to return with the food and hot drinks.

'It's just such a fucking relief,' Brigstocke said. 'To have a motive. It's got to be blackmail, agreed?'

Thorne nodded. 'It's the only thing that explains why it's happening now.' It was the obvious conclusion. Someone was willing to kill to prevent this tape getting out. A threat had been made to expose what had happened fifteen years before, and whoever had been threatened had reacted violently. Thorne looked at the picture of the four soldiers. Whoever was doing the blackmailing, the killer had decided to take no chances . . .

Brigstocke sat up, leaned down to study the photograph alongside Thorne. The conditions when the picture was taken, alongside that of the broken down image itself, had combined to give it the strange quality of a double exposure. The figures, dark green against grey, seemed incomplete, almost spectral. Brigstocke traced a finger along the row of soldiers. 'We know two of those four are dead, right? If the other two are still alive, we need to find them.'

'Especially if one of them's the killer,' Thorne said.

'I don't think it's very likely.' Brigstocke sat forward. 'A blackmailer's going to target someone with money. Someone who's done pretty well for himself. Right? Based on what we know so far, that doesn't sound like your average ex-squaddie . . .'

Thorne had to agree that it made good sense. He thought about the voice on the tape, distorted on occasion, and too close to the mike. The voice that had seemed to be giving the orders. 'Well that only leaves one option,' he said, nodding towards the blank screen. 'We're looking for whoever was behind the camera.'

By the time they'd finished at the Lift and Thorne had gone on his way, Holland and Brigstocke were off duty for the night. Brigstocke had gone straight home, and Holland knew that he should really do the same. Instead, he'd called the office to see who might still be around, and, finding that Yvonne Kitson had not yet left, had arranged to meet her for a drink. He'd jumped on the tube and headed all the way back north to Colindale, to meet the DI in the Royal Oak.

Inside half an hour they'd put away a couple each and begun to loosen up a little.

'Where are the kids tonight . . .?' As Holland was asking the question he realised he was unsure what he should call Kitson. He couldn't remember having a drink with her on her own before, and something about it – and perhaps about the fact that they were drinking so fast – seemed to alter the dynamic between them.

'Tony's got them. He picks them up from the childminder if I'm on a late one.'

'Right.' Holland hadn't heard Kitson mention her new bloke's name before.

'And "Yvonne"'s fine, by the way,' she said. 'I think we're off the clock in here.'

They took sips of white wine and lager-top and looked around at the pub's brightly lit and unwelcoming interior. The place had no frills, but was still very busy. As it happened, being very much the local for the Peel Centre, there were usually just as many coppers in the place as were to be found up the road in Becke House.

'What about you, Dave? You were somewhere near Leicester Square, weren't you?'

'That's right.' Kitson still had no idea that Thorne had gone undercover, and so obviously had not been informed that Holland and Brigstocke had gone into the West End to meet up with him and show him the tape. 'Some old boy told one of the local lads he'd seen something on the night of the last murder. Waste of bloody time . . .'

'That's only a few stops from Elephant and Castle, isn't it? You could have been home in quarter of an hour.'

A copper, whose face he'd seen before in the pub and at various times around Becke House, came to the table and asked Holland if the empty chair opposite him was taken. Holland shook his head, watched the man take the chair across and join a group who looked like they were settling down to make a night of it. He turned back to Kitson. 'It's not fair on Sophie. I'm bringing such a lot of shit home with me at the moment, you know? Like I'm walking it through the flat and getting it everywhere. Dirtying everything . . .'

'Is this about the tape?'

'It's mad, I know. We see loads of horrible stuff, right? It's just seeing it happen like that. Watching them do it.'

'It's how you're *meant* to feel, Dave. You should be worried if you didn't.'

'This is going to sound stupid, but I don't want to pass any of it on to Chloe. *I* have to deal with it, but there's no reason why she should, is there? It's like passive smoking or something. I don't want her anywhere near anything that might affect her, and right now it's like I'm choking on it. I feel like I'm carrying it around on my clothes and in my hair. Passive evil . . .'

Kitson smiled as she raised her glass to her lips.

'Told you it was stupid,' Holland said.

Kitson shook her head. 'It's not that,' she said. 'I curse my three sometimes, but perhaps I should be grateful I've got so much chasing round to do. I'm too busy sorting out football kit, and nagging them about homework, and running a taxi service, to worry about bringing work home with me.'

'Maybe me and Sophie should have a few more kids,' Holland said.

Kitson drained her wineglass. 'My shout . . .'

While Kitson was at the bar, Holland thought about the way Susan Jago had fought to protect her brother; to defend him, even in the face of the sickening evidence. He wondered what Jago's mother would think about what her son had done. He'd confronted the parents of those who had committed the most shocking acts and knew that in most cases they never stopped loving their children. They couldn't, any more than he could conceive of not feeling as he did now about his daughter, no matter what she did. For the families – especially the parents – of those who killed or abused, faith could be destroyed. But love, he knew now, was unconditional. When your children did such things, you did not stop loving them. You simply began hating yourself.

Kitson was coming back to the table with the drinks and she smiled as he caught her eye. Holland thought suddenly that she looked quite sexy. Asked himself what the hell he was thinking . . .

'What were you doing,' Kitson asked some time later, 'in 1991?'

Holland did the maths. 'I was sixteen, so I suppose I was going out a lot. I can remember coming back late from parties or clubs a couple of times and sitting up watching the bombing on TV. What about you?'

'I was just finishing college,' Kitson said. 'We were all dead against it, obviously. Not as much as with the last one, but there were still plenty of protests. We thought it was all about oil.'

A cheer went up as someone hit the jackpot on the fruit machine in the corner. Holland leaned forward, spoke up to make himself heard above the rhythmic chink and clatter of the payout. 'It doesn't matter whether you're a copper or a killer, does it?' He swallowed a mouthful of beer. 'How well do we really know anybody?'

Kitson raised her eyebrows. 'Bloody hell . . .'

Holland reddened slightly. He hadn't meant it to sound so stupidly portentous. 'I never had you down as a lefty, that's all,' he said.

'Watford Polytechnic was hardly Kent State.'

Holland laughed, though he didn't understand the reference. 'Even so . . .'

'And I never had *you* down as someone who takes such a lot of the job home with him.' She smiled, nodding towards Holland's glass. 'Speaking of which . . .'

'What?'

'If you *do* want to have any more kids, you'd best finish that, go home and get down to it . . .'

'You look wankered, mate,' Spike said.

Thorne grinned and swayed to one side, waving a young woman past as if he were a bullfighter. 'I *feel* wankered,' he said. 'Bladdered, fucked, off my tits . . .'

'How many of those have you had?'

Thorne had just about got used to the taste of Carlsberg Special Brew, but he hadn't been prepared for the kick. It was somewhere past chucking-out time and he'd been drinking steadily since he'd left the London Lift. Since he'd said goodbye to Holland and Brigstocke and begun trying to walk off the memory of what he'd seen on that video-tape.

'Not enough.' Thorne could feel the weight of the cans in his ruck-sack. 'Plenty more, though . . .'

Walking hadn't done the trick, so he'd gone straight into the nearest Tesco Metro and handed over a quarter of his weekly money in exchange for eight cans.

'You should save a couple,' Caroline said.

He'd met up with Spike and Caroline on Bedford Street and they'd walked aimlessly around Covent Garden ever since. Thorne had announced that he wanted to go to sleep an hour before, that he had to get back to his theatre, but somehow he never quite kept going in any one direction and it seemed stupid to doss down anywhere while there was still a can open.

'Have one!' Thorne tried to reach behind into the rucksack, his arm flailing.

'I keep telling you, I don't want one,' Spike said. 'I'll take one off you to sell, mind you . . .'

'You can piss off,' Thorne said.

Caroline pulled a face. 'That stuff tastes fucking horrible . . .'

'I don't understand why you two don't drink.' Thorne held up the gold and red can and read the writing; the *By Royal Appointment*. 'If it's good enough for the Danish court . . .'

'Prefer to save our money, like,' Spike said. 'Spend it on the good stuff.'

Caroline took Thorne's arm and hooked her own around it as they walked. 'I'll have a vodka, mind you, if there's one on offer.'

'I bet fuck all gets done in Denmark,' Thorne said.

Spike cackled.

'Be nice to get dressed up one night, wouldn't it?' Caroline reached out her other arm and drew Spike towards her. 'Go out somewhere and dance, and drink vodka and tonic or a few cocktails . . .'

Spike leaned over to kiss her and Thorne pulled away from them.

He whistled. 'Give her a snog, for Christ's sake, and tell her you love her.' He was aware of how he sounded: the words not slurred exactly, but slow and singsong; emphasised oddly, like he was speaking through a machine. 'Go on, put your arms round her . . .'

'*Put your arms round them . . . Give the fuckers a cuddle.*'

Thorne stopped dead and shut his eyes. The can slipped out of his hand on to the pavement. 'Fuck . . .'

Caroline and Spike walked over.

'We need to get you bedded down,' Caroline said.

Thorne looked down at the thick, golden liquid running away across the kerb. He pushed the toe of his boot into it. His stomach lurched as he watched it spread and darken, leaking from the wound and staining the sand.

'I want to go to sleep,' he said.

Spike pushed him forward. 'I thought you boozers were supposed to have some kind of tolerance . . .'

Sleep hung around, but refused to settle. Instead, thoughts collided inside his thick head like oversized dodgems moving at half speed . . .

Atrocious was a meaningless, fucked-up word. A crappy meal could be atrocious, yes, or a shit football team or a bad movie. *Atrocious* didn't come close to describing the thing itself: the atrocity. That's what they were calling it. Brigstocke and the rest of them. Not murder. An *atrocity*. All about the context, apparently . . .

There were rats in the skip around the corner. He could hear them digging into the bin-bags. Chewing through styrofoam for crusts, and wrappers slick with kebab fat.

He'd probably seen things as bad in Surbiton semis and Hackney tower-blocks, or at least the aftermath of such things. He'd certainly *known* of worse – of acts that had left a greater number dead – happening in that war and in others. He'd watched them on the news. Weren't those things *atrocities*, too?

He belched up Special Brew, tasting it a second time. Moaning. Biting down into each sour–sweet bubble.

Why was what he'd seen on that piece-of-shit tape any worse than when a bomb fell through the red cross daubed on a hospital roof? These were not civilians, were they? This was soldiers killing soldiers. Yet, somehow it *was* worse. You knew perfectly well that things went wrong, that machines went wrong, and that people fucked up. But this wasn't fucking up; this was basic bloody horror. This was inhuman behaviour from those who'd been there – who were *supposed* to have been there – in defence of humanity.

He shifted, driving an elbow into the rucksack behind him and pulling at the frayed edge of the sleeping bag. He could smell himself on the warm air that rose up from inside.

If anything, what he'd seen on that tape, what had happened at the end, was more terrible than the executions themselves. But whoever was behind the camera hadn't filmed the actual shootings. There was no way, from seeing the tape, of knowing if each of the four soldiers had done his bit.

If each one of *ours* had killed one of *theirs* . . .

He hoped it hadn't been the case; hoped that one soldier, or at worst two, had done all the killing. He pictured one of the soldiers lining up the prisoners and trying to kill as many as he could with one shot. If those heavy heads were close enough together, if all those ducks were in a row, would the bullet pass straight through one and into the next? Through two or three maybe . . .?

Now the soldiers themselves were being hunted down and killed. It was hard to feel too sorry for them though, kicked to death or not. They weren't shitting themselves, were they? Sitting there, watching it happen, and waiting their turn.

He lay down flat and turned his head. The stone felt wonderfully cool against his face.

It had to be the man who'd shot the video, didn't it? Surely. That's what he felt in his guts, swilling around with the beer and the tea and the sandwiches. They'd know soon enough; they'd know what was happening when they found the other two soldiers. If they were alive, they could identify whoever had been pointing that camera.

Somebody shot soldiers shooting.

Fucking tongue-twister . . .

Thorne smelled something familiar and opened his eyes.

He had no idea how many hours it had been since Spike and Caroline had dropped him at his doorway and left. He was equally clueless as to how long Spike had been back, sitting there on the steps with a skinny joint in his hand. Without a watch, Thorne relied on his mobile phone to tell him the time. Even if he could have dug it out now in front of Spike, he wouldn't have bothered . . .

'When d'you come back?'

'Just.' Without turning, he offered Thorne the joint. 'Want some?'

Thorne groaned a negative. 'Where's Caroline?'

From the back, Thorne could see the shrug, and shake of the head, but not Spike's expression. 'Busy . . .'

Thorne's eyes had closed for what seemed like no more than a second when he heard something smack against the wall above him and felt something hit his face.

''Fuck's that?'

He sat up, wiping his mouth, and saw the messy remains of a burger scattered on the floor and across his sleeping bag. He saw Spike standing and moving towards two men in the middle of the street.

'What d'you think you're fucking doing?' Spike asked.

The man who answered was wearing a green parka and a blank expression. He slurred, mock-apologetic. 'Sorry, mate, I thought this was a rubbish tip . . .'

The second man was bald and thin-faced. He laughed and casually lobbed something else, whistling as if he'd launched a grenade. Spike stepped aside and watched the cup explode, sending ice cubes and whatever drink was inside spilling across the pavement.

'You arsehole.' Spike came forward, and the first man – taller and heavier than he was – moved to meet him.

Thorne was on his feet now, sobering up very quickly and struggling to free his feet from the sleeping bag. He watched as the man in the parka spread his legs and lowered his face into Spike's.

'You fancy it, you junkie cunt?'

Then things got very out of hand very quickly.

As the pushes are exchanged, and quickly become blows, Thorne begins moving down the steps. At the same time, the bald man charges towards him. Still tangled in his sleeping bag, Thorne all but falls into him, raising his forearms to meet the man's face as they collide.

As they struggle, Thorne is aware of Spike and the other man going at it a few feet away. He hears leather soles scraping against the road to gain purchase, then bodies hitting it as they both go down. Spike's attacker is taunting him as they struggle: calling Spike filthy; a disease; a dirty, AIDS-ridden fucker. Between these words he grunts with the effort of every punch.

Thorne knows that he's being hit and kicked, but he hears rather than feels the impact. The man is lashing out wildly, screaming at Thorne that he's dead as he swings fists and feet. Thorne grabs an arm, fastens one of his own around the man's neck and moves his hands quickly. He can feel the stubble on the man's head as he takes a firm grip of it and brings a knee up hard into his face.

The man slumps . . .

His hands claw at Thorne's coat, pulling off a button as he goes to his knees.

Thorne spins away and in a couple of staggered steps he is on top of the man with the parka. Spike is flat on his back beneath them, his hands raised to protect his head. Thorne tries to grab hold of the arms that are pummelling Spike, to pin them back, but it's hard to get a grip of the shiny material.

A voice shouts something close to him and Thorne feels a hand taking hold of his shoulder. He wheels round fast, pulling back a fist.

'I said that's *enough . . .*'

Thorne paused for half a second, panting and scarlet-faced, the fist still poised to accelerate forward. He was pissed, *very* pissed no question, but still he recognised Sergeant Dan Britton. The officer was wearing the same hooded top and combats he'd been wearing in the tube station. Thorne, fizzing with adrenaline and strong lager, was nevertheless 100 per cent certain that the man who'd taken hold of him was a copper.

He took a breath . . .

Then punched him anyway.

EIGHTEEN

'I was pissed,' Thorne said. 'I didn't know what I was doing.'

'You broke my sergeant's nose is what you did . . .'

The man opposite Thorne wore a blue suit over a white shirt and a tie with golf balls on it. He'd walked into the Interview Room, told Thorne in very blunt language that he was an idiot, and put two coffees down on the table. He'd identified himself as Inspector John McCabe and then sat back, waiting for Thorne to explain himself.

'How's he doing?' Thorne asked.

'Britton? His face is about the same as yours.' McCabe slid the coffee across the table. 'You look like shit warmed up.'

Thorne felt much worse.

He was starting to realise exactly what had happened. The lack of formality, McCabe's attitude, the mugs of coffee. It was becoming obvious what he'd done; and even as McCabe spelled it out, moments from the night before zipped through Thorne's semi-functioning consciousness like a dream sequence in an arty movie. Being pinned against the wall while others scattered; shouting the odds in the van; bleeding on to the smooth counter in the Custody Suite; making it clear that he could find his own way to the cells, thank you very fucking much. Telling anyone who'd listen that they had to ring this phone number . . .

Christ, he really *hadn't* known what he was doing.

'This is the stuff of legend,' McCabe said. He was somewhere in his late forties, but there was very little grey in the helmet of straight black hair. He was clean-shaven and ruddy, with a smile – much in evidence as he spoke – that was slightly lopsided. 'In years to come, the boys at SO10 might well be using this on courses.'

'All right . . .'

'It's the perfect example of how not to do things . . .'

Thorne picked up his coffee and leaned back in his chair. It was probably best to let McCabe get on with it.

'What you do is, you get yourself arrested for something. Something nice and trivial, you know, like *assaulting a police officer*. Then, when things get a bit tasty, because you're a total fuck-up or maybe because you're a bit frightened of spending a night in the cells all on your own, you start announcing that you're actually working undercover and giving out the number of your squad to all and bloody sundry.' A slurp of coffee and the lopsided smile. 'Done *much* undercover work, have you?'

'Are you finished?'

'Only you don't really seem to have grasped the basic concept.'

'I'll take that as a "no" then . . .'

They stared at each other for a few moments.

Thorne was finding it hard to dislike McCabe, much as he thought it would be the appropriate thing to do. Maybe he'd start disliking him later, when the hangover had worn off a little. 'Let me try and guess why you're so tetchy,' he said. 'You clearly *are*, smiling or not . . .'

McCabe said nothing.

'It might be piles, or money worries, or maybe it's because your wife has discovered that you're really a woman trapped in a man's body. If I *had* to choose, though, I'd say it was because you haven't been kept *informed*. Not about the undercover operation, obviously. That's need-to-know . . .'

'Not last night, it wasn't . . .'

Thorne nodded, allowing McCabe the point, then carried on. 'I'm talking about the rough-sleeper murders generally. Maybe as senior officer on a specialist unit that deals with the homeless, you feel that you should have had some involvement. That you should have been consulted more.'

McCabe's smile had disappeared.

'I know fuck all about it,' Thorne said. Decisions about who should be talking to who had been taken before he was ever involved, but he knew how these things worked. It wasn't just computers that had problems talking to each other, and much as Brigstocke had been loath to take this case on, once he *had*, his Major Investigation Team was as territorial as any other. When it came to expertise and information, the idea was to avoid sharing wherever possible. 'You know the game. Everyone takes what they can and tries to give sweet FA in return.'

'Like oral sex,' McCabe said. 'Right?'

'I'm not sure I can remember back that far . . .'

McCabe leaned back, ran a finger and thumb up and down the golf-ball tie. 'I've not been here long, but I've made it my business to get to know this area. To forge some kind of relationship with most of the people who bed down around here every night. Your lot were complaining that no one was telling them anything, that they weren't being trusted, but the dossers *know* the lads on my team. They might have talked to them. *If* we'd been invited to the party.'

'You must have been consulted at some point, though?'

'We were *liaised* with.' He said the word with huge distaste. Like it meant *interfered* . . .

'You're right,' Thorne said. 'It's stupid. Maybe they should have put the two of us together before I went on to the streets.'

McCabe nodded, like he thought that would have been an excellent idea, turning up his palms in weary resignation at other people's idiocy. 'So how's it going, anyway?' he asked. 'It's all gone a bit quiet since Radio Bob was killed.'

Thorne took a mouthful of coffee. Gave himself a few seconds to formulate a response. As far as his own part in things was concerned, the cat was out of the bag and happily spraying piss anywhere it wasn't wanted. Nevertheless, he thought it might be best to keep quiet about other matters. He thought that McCabe had every right to feel aggrieved at being marginalised, and that if he were brought up to speed on the case, he might even prove to be of some use.

Still, something told Thorne to say nothing.

McCabe saw the silence for what it was. 'And it's *staying* quiet, is it?'

'Like I said, you know the game . . .'

The crooked smile appeared again, but Thorne could see that it contained no warmth. 'So you're happy to suck up a bit when it's in your interests. When I'm sitting here deciding whether or not to put the complaints paperwork through on your assault.'

'Listen—'

'But when it comes to talking about your case, you've suddenly got nothing to say. Shame you weren't so fucking tight-lipped last night.'

'Don't I know it.'

McCabe pushed his chair away from the table and stood up. 'Whatever else happens, I hope Dan Britton presses charges. You can take your chances with the DPS . . .'

The Directorate of Professional Standards. The people that investigated corruption, racism, blue-on-blue violence. They'd made headlines a few months earlier after prosecuting a pair of budding entrepreneurs from the Flying Squad who'd been caught trying to sell footage of car and helicopter chases to TV companies. Thorne had been subjected to DPS attention a few times before. He'd made his fair share of work for those who handed out smacked wrists. But the way things stood now, in his career – in his *life* – there were plenty of things he was more afraid of.

'I was in enough shit before I took this job,' Thorne said. 'A bit extra isn't really here or there . . .'

McCabe picked up his mug, and took Thorne's half-drunk cup as well. 'We'll see.'

'Listen, I was taken off the world's most tedious desk job to do this, for fuck's sake, so it's not like I'm committing career suicide, is it?' Thorne turned, spoke at McCabe as the inspector walked across the room. 'You can do what you like, but I've got to tell you, I could have ripped your sergeant's head off and things wouldn't be much worse than they were already . . .'

McCabe paused at the door. 'Things can always get worse, mate.'

'What happens now?' Thorne asked.

'You sit there and wait. Your guvnor's on his way over.'

Thorne turned back to the table as the door slammed shut. He leaned down to the tabletop and lowered his head on to his arms. He felt wiped out by the exchange with McCabe and hoped he might be able to get a bit of sleep before Brigstocke arrived. Even ten minutes would be fucking great . . .

He closed his eyes. He could hazard a pretty good guess at what sort of mood Russell Brigstocke would be in when he arrived. Thorne was fairly certain he wouldn't be bringing coffee.

From what Kitson and Holland had seen on the cab ride from the station, the army had built on, or fenced off, vast tracts of land in and around the lush river valley a few miles from Taunton that was now home to the 12th King's Hussars.

Standing at the main gate, as they'd waited to be escorted to the admin block, they'd been able to hear the boom of guns from ranges a long way distant and see sheep and cows grazing, unconcerned, on the hills that swept away on either side. Such incongruities were everywhere: a fully outfitted soldier in face paint and camouflage coming towards the barrier on a rickety bicycle; a car park full of Lagunas, Volvos and Passats, while fifty yards away, on a rutted patch of tarmac as wide as a football pitch, rows of tanks and other armoured vehicles stood in lines, some grumbling and belching out plumes of black smoke as they were repaired.

Major Stuart Poulter's office was small, but predictably neat and organised: a series of drawings illustrating the development of the modern tank was arranged along one wall; wooden 'in', 'out' and 'pending' trays were lined up along the front of his desk; and kit-bags of various sizes were laid out in one corner, as if he were expecting to be called away at any moment. Poulter was in his early-forties, a little under average height and with a thick head of dark hair worn relatively long. A full mouth and ruddy cheeks gave him an oddly girlish expression, but his body looked hard and compact under his uniform. He was immaculate in gleaming, brown Oxfords, light trousers, and a green sweater with leather epaulettes over regulation shirt, and khaki tie.

As they waited for their tea to be delivered, Holland explained just how confused he'd already become by the terminology; by the unfathomable series of initials and numbers on the signs that hung outside every office on the corridor. He wondered why an RSM was a WO1 while a CSM was a WO2, and even when he'd been told what OC and CO stood for, he wasn't certain what made commanding officer any different from officer commanding. Poulter, who chain-smoked, and smiled rather too much, explained patiently that anyone unfamiliar with the military was bound to find it all terribly bewildering at first.

Then, even though they knew that Poulter had been comprehensively briefed, Holland and Kitson were obliged to spend five minutes or so going over their reasons for being there.

'Just so we're singing from the same hymn sheet,' the major said.

The visit had, of course, been agreed between the army and the Met well in advance; the details hashed out in a series of telephone conversations between officers far senior to both Detective Inspector Yvonne Kitson and Major Stuart Poulter.

Poulter used a brass Zippo to fire up his second cigarette since the interview had begun and leaned back in his chair. 'I still think it would make more sense for the Met to liaise with the RMP on this.' He had a soft, comforting voice, like someone who might read out a weather forecast on the radio. 'But, ours is not to reason why. Correct?'

Once tea had been delivered and they'd got down to business, it became apparent that the system of tracking regimental personnel was every bit as complicated, every bit as arcane, as the command structure itself.

'We only keep any sort of record on soldiers who are still serving,' Poulter said. 'That's the first thing, and it's purely practical. Once they leave here, they're no longer my concern, and I can't really care any more. You should really talk to the AP Centre at Glasgow . . .'

Kitson told him that they knew all about the AP Centre. She explained that they simply needed the *names* of those who had served alongside Christopher Jago. She gave a brief and relatively vague outline of exactly why those names were so important. The existence of the videotape was not so much as hinted at.

'It's basically about tracing the other three on the crew,' Holland said. 'We just need to know how we can get that information.'

'Which crew are we talking about, though?' Poulter asked.

'Like we said, it's the Gulf, 1991 . . .'

'I'm clear about *that*, but this Jago might have been part of any number of crews. Do you understand? Just in that single campaign.'

'Right . . .' Kitson was starting to sense that this wouldn't be straightforward. That even though, this time, they'd come armed with all the relevant information, they were as far out of their depth as they had been when they'd interviewed Rutherford and Spiby at the Media Ops Office.

'I've been all over the UK,' Poulter said, 'and to most parts of Europe, right? I've been to Malaysia and Hong Kong and Belize; to Bosnia, the USA and Australia. And I've been to the Gulf. All in just the last ten years. Do you see what I'm driving at? Soldiers move around, *all the time*. Not only do they change location, but they also get shifted from troop to troop and from squadron to squadron.'

'What gets done with their records if that happens?' Kitson asked.

'It's fairly standard . . . unless, of course, the soldier in question has served at any time with one of the intelligence-based units. The SAS, the Special Boat Service, 14 Int, or what have you . . .'

'What happens then?'

'Well, those records *can* have a habit of disappearing, or at the very least a few chunks go missing. Normally, though, each man has a P-File, which is confidential and contains all the basic info: the courses he's been on, names and dates, his disciplinary record, that kind of thing. That file goes with him if he switches squadrons. There's also his Troop Bible, which gives admin details – passport number and so forth – but, again, that travels with the soldier.'

'So the paperwork is as mobile as they are,' Holland said.

Poulter turned, blew smoke out of the window he'd opened behind him. 'That's about right. And again, it's purely practical. We'd be swamped with the stuff otherwise. I guess you lot have got much the same problem, right? Filling every bloody form in three times.'

Kitson smiled politely, acknowledging the moment of levity. 'Why might a soldier move?'

'Any number of reasons. Troops go where they're *needed*, basically. You might be going to assist another regiment, right? To back-fill wherever it's necessary. On a tank crew, say, you might have trained as a driver, and if a driver on another crew falls ill or whatever, you get shunted across and someone else is moved into your crew and trained up. You work as crew and you also work as engineering support for crew, and if that expertise is required elsewhere, you go to plug that hole. Some commanders like to move their crews around as a matter of course and some don't, but either way it's all change once the ORBAT comes through.' Poulter saw the confusion on Holland's and Kitson's faces and explained: 'Order of Battle. That's any troop movement order, peacetime or wartime, right? Once that comes through, you go. Simple as that.'

Holland had begun by taking notes, but had realised fairly quickly that there was little point. Even so, he drew a line on his notepad, as if underscoring something of great importance. 'I understand all that, but surely when there's a conflict, like there was in the Gulf, it's a good idea to have some . . . continuity.'

'It's certainly a good *idea*,' Poulter said. He looked vaguely pleased, as if Holland had asked the predictably stupid civilian's question. 'When the regiment's deployed, that's when people really start to get switched around. Troops are reorganised all over again in accordance with battle regs.' He stuck the cigarette into his mouth and began to count off these regulations on his fingers: 'You can't go if there are any medical issues, any at all; you'll get left behind if you've got so much as a toothache, right? You can't go if you're underage . . .'

'I'm not with you,' Kitson said. 'How can you be underage?'

'You can join up when you're sixteen and a half, right? After basic training and what have you, we get them at around seventeen, but you cannot be sent to war unless you're eighteen years of age. You're a gunner on a tank crew and the regiment gets deployed to a combat zone, right? If you're a week short of your eighteenth birthday, somebody else is going to get brought in to do your job.'

Kitson nodded. She couldn't help but wonder if the Iraqi Army had been subject to the same regulations . . .

'Then, once you're actually out there, everything can change again. People get injured; that's the most obvious thing. And I don't just mean as a result of enemy action.' He pointed out of the window towards the line of tanks that Kitson and Holland had seen earlier. 'You take a tumble off the back of one of those wagons and you're going to know about it. These things have a knock-on effect as well. One tanky breaks his arm, half a dozen crews can get shifted around.'

In his notebook, Holland circled the full stop beneath a large and elaborately shaded question mark. 'What about soldiers who were in the Gulf and are still with the regiment?' he said. 'Could we perhaps just talk to them? From what you said before, there should be a list of those people somewhere.'

'Yeah, I think that would be very useful,' Kitson added.

Poulter thought for a moment, before rolling his chair back and tossing his cigarette butt out of the open window. 'I'll go and have a quick word with someone about what you're suggesting,' he said. 'If you'd like to wait there, I'm sure I can rustle up some more tea . . .'

Holland closed his notebook before Poulter walked past him on his way to the door.

NINETEEN

Spike had found him within half an hour of Thorne's release from custody.

'Fat Paul, who sells the *Issue* outside Charing Cross, saw you coming out. How was it?'

'Bailed for a fortnight,' Thorne said. 'Gives 'em time to decide if they want to go ahead and charge me.'

Spike looked surprised, as Thorne knew he had every right to be. 'I don't know how you managed to wangle that. Can't see there's much to decide, seeing as how you decked a copper.'

'They're waiting for medical reports or something.'

'Right . . .'

'Plus, if they do me for assault, they know they might have to do one or two of their own.'

Now Spike thought he understood. 'Good thinking, mate. We'll get one of them disposable cameras, make sure we get some photos of your face. It's a right mess, like.'

Thorne had finally got a good look at himself in the Gents' back at the station after Brigstocke had finished with him. He looked every bit as worked over as he felt. One eye was completely filled with blood, while the other was half-closed above a bruise that was plum-coloured and blackening at its edges. There were scratches down one side of his neck, and a graze, livid against his forehead, from where he'd been pressed against the wall.

'Yeah, well.' Thorne could feel the air, cold on his wounds, and the pain that still sang along his shoulder blades where his arms had been driven up hard behind his back. 'There were quite a few of them in the end.'

'What d'you expect? You smack a copper in the face and a lot of his mates want to give you something to remember them by. Sounds like they did you a right favour, though . . .'

Thorne looked at the cut along Spike's cheekbone and the side of his lip that had split and swelled. 'I thought *you*'d be a damn sight worse,' he said.

Spike shook his head, looking smug. 'I kept my head covered most of the time, like. Bastard ribs are black and blue, mind you. Just sorry I never got a chance to stick the fucker.'

'You carry a knife?'

With half his lip as swollen as it was, the smile was as lopsided as McCabe's had been. 'I've always got a weapon,' Spike said.

They were heading north through Soho. The overcast streets were busy with lunchtime shoppers and workers hurrying to grab a bite to eat, or a quick drink to take the edge off the rest of the day. Thorne and Spike walked slowly along in the centre of the pavement. The state of their faces allowed them to cut a swathe through pedestrians a little thicker than might normally have been the case.

'You're lucky they didn't pick you up with it,' Thorne said. He was thinking that, despite what he'd said to McCabe, things *could* have been a lot worse. If he'd been party to an assault with a deadly weapon, there'd have been bugger all Russell Brigstocke could have done about it . . .

'Sorry I scarpered, by the way,' Spike said. 'I had stuff on me. You know how it is, right?'

Thorne knew how it was.

'Otherwise . . . you know?'

'Don't worry about it.'

Spike sniffed and spat. He shoved his hands into the pockets of a scarred vinyl bomber jacket. 'I wanted to say thanks for wading in, you know? For trying to pull the tosser off me. Not that I was in any trouble . . .'

Thorne nodded solemnly, sharing the joke. 'Course not.'

'So,' Spike grinned as a young couple swerved into the street to avoid him, 'as a small token of my appreciation, I've got us both a job . . .'

Half an hour later and Thorne was hard at work. The sign he was holding had a bright yellow arrow drawn on it and bore the legend: 'MR JERK. CHICKEN 'N' RIBS'. The restaurant was situated halfway along Argyll Street, and Thorne and Spike, with their gaudy advertising boards, constituted a cheap and cheerful pincer movement. Spike was at the Oxford Circus end of the street, his sign pointing hungry people one way, with Thorne doing his bit to encourage them in the other direction from a pitch down near Liberty's. Every half an hour or so the two of them would swap positions; pausing for five minutes' chat outside the Palladium.

At a couple of quid an hour, Mr Jerk was happy, and by the end of the day they would have made enough for Thorne to get a decent dinner and for Spike to get himself fixed up.

Thorne stood, propping up his sign; letting it prop *him* up. The features of those who moved past him were anonymous, in sharp contrast to his own, which had been punched into distinction . . .

What he'd told Spike had been at least partly true. Brigstocke had done his bit to placate McCabe and the officer whose face Thorne had rearranged, but nothing had really been decided. There might well be charges to answer, either sooner as a rough sleeper or later, when the operation was all over, as one officer assaulting another. Unlikely as it was that he'd be allowed to walk away from the incident, Thorne was far more concerned with how his stupidity may have compromised the job he was trying to do. McCabe had given assurances that, as far as Thorne's undercover status was concerned, confidentiality would be maintained. But they were worthless: he could not possibly vouch for the discretion of every one of his own officers, never mind those hundreds of others – the beat officers, the Drugs Squad, the Pickpocket Teams, the Clubs and Vice boys – who moved through Charing Cross Station every day. The Met was no different from any other large organisation. There was talk and rumour. There were drunken exchanges and gossipy e-mails. Thorne thought about the man they were trying to catch; the man who might be a police officer. If word *did* get out, would the killer himself be able to hear those jungle drums?

He remembered something Brigstocke had said: '*The mouse doesn't know there's cheese on the trap, but we still call it bait . . .*'

When he'd stormed into the Interview Room at Charing Cross a few hours earlier, Russell Brigstocke was one police officer who certainly *had* looked like he wanted to kill him. The language of each *I told you so* had been predictably industrial, and he hadn't spared himself. He'd also aimed a good deal of invective at his own stupidity for trusting Thorne in the first place . . .

'I must have been fucking mental,' he'd said.

'Maybe it was that diet you were on . . .'

That hadn't helped, and it wasn't until Brigstocke was about to leave that he'd seemed to soften even a little. He'd turned at the doorway, exactly as McCabe had done, and let out a long breath before he spoke. 'At least you look the part now . . .'

Walking up now towards Oxford Street, Thorne could see Spike on his way towards him, spinning the sign in his hand as he bounced along. He looked twitchy, like his blood was jumping. He'd need paying pretty soon.

Thorne remembered the look on Brigstocke's face when he'd spoken; it was somewhere between pity and relief. He'd always been confident that he could look the part. He just hadn't banked on *feeling* it.

*

The soldier standing at the side of Major Poulter's desk wore regulation combats over a green T-shirt, and Holland could not help but be struck by how good the uniform looked on her. As part of the Royal Armoured Corps, the 12th King's Hussars was an all-male regiment. Neither Holland nor Kitson had expected to see any women . . .

'This is Lieutenant Sarah Cheshire, our assistant adjutant,' Poulter said. 'She's the administrative wizard round here, maintains all the databases and so on. If you'd like to tell her exactly what it is you're looking for, I'm sure she'll do her best to sort you out.'

Kitson explained that they needed a list of all those soldiers currently serving in the regiment who'd also fought in the first Gulf War.

'Shouldn't be a problem,' Cheshire said.

Holland's charm was not quite as boyish as it had once been, but he turned it on nevertheless. 'That'd be great, thanks . . .'

Cheshire nodded and turned to Poulter. 'I'll get on it then, sir.' She was no more than twenty-two or three, with ash-blonde hair clipped back above a slender neck, and a Home Counties accent that Holland found a damn sight sexier than the major's.

'That's good of you, Sarah, many thanks. I can't see it taking you too long, to be honest.'

'Sir?'

Poulter looked across his desk at Kitson and Holland. 'Aside from myself, I don't think we're talking about more than, say, half a dozen men left in the regiment.' He smiled at Cheshire; drew deeply on his cigarette as he watched her leave the room.

'Why so few?' Kitson asked.

Holland shook his head. 'I thought there'd be a lot more than half a dozen.'

'Soldiers leave,' Poulter said. 'For many reasons. We lose a lot of men after a major conflict. A lot of them. It's all about pressure, at the end of the day. Pressure from others and pressure inside your own head. If you're lucky enough to have a family, then nine times out of ten they'll want you out. You've been and done your bit, you've been out there and risked your neck, so why the hell go back and do it again? If you were lucky enough to make it back in one piece, the attitude of your nearest and dearest is, "Why push your luck? Get out while the going's good."'

'Understandable,' Kitson said.

'Of course it is, but that's the easy pressure. And having that kind of support system makes it easy to readjust afterwards. For those without that system, and even for many who do have loving families, it's not quite so cut and dried. You come back, your head's still buzzing, you're in constant turmoil, and I'm not necessarily talking about men who've fought hand to hand or anything like that. Any length of time spent in a combat situation, or spent *in constant readiness* for such a situation, is going to leave a good number of men in a fragile mental state.'

'Like post-traumatic stress disorder?'

'In some cases yes, but for many others it takes a different form. Some just crave the adrenaline high they experienced during combat. Back here, they just can't get it, can they? You can see the signs. Silly buggers signing up for parachute jumps and what have you. Anything to get the rush. These guys have got ten, maybe fifteen years of skills and drills, then they come back from combat and they've got sod all to do with them. That's why so many go wild, land themselves in trouble, and end up in prison. It's why they end up on the street, like with this case of yours . . .'

The office door was held open by a tank shell. Kitson watched the smoke from Poulter's cigarette drift upwards, and then out into the corridor. 'You must have to do a lot of recruiting after a war, then,' she said.

Poulter barked out a smoky laugh. 'Quite the opposite. The numbers go through the bloody roof for some reason. Good job as well.'

'Why didn't *you* leave?' Holland asked. 'If you don't mind me asking . . .'

Major Poulter took a moment, then leaned forward to grind out his cigarette into a tarnished metal ashtray. '"Mind" is putting it a tad strongly. But I can't see that it's strictly relevant.' He was trying to smile, but his eyes seemed to have grown smaller suddenly. 'I'm more than happy to answer what I understand to be the important question, which is whether I remember your man Jago, or any of the men in his tank crew. I'm afraid I don't.'

'Fine,' Holland said. 'Thank you.'

'I've already explained how things worked out there.'

'You made it very clear.'

'I may not have come within fifty miles of that crew, and even if I did, it *was* rather a long time ago . . .'

Holland grimaced and saw Kitson do the same as an engine was cranked up to a deafening roar just outside the window. Poulter said something Holland couldn't hear but he nodded anyway. The noise explained why so many of the soldiers he'd seen had been carrying ear protectors, which they kept tucked into the belts of their blue coveralls.

It had become obvious that there was little to do but wait for the list of men who'd been in the Gulf, however small that turned out to be. They weren't likely to get any more useful information out of Poulter, but Holland decided to ask a question or two anyway, just for himself. They had time to kill, after all . . .

'It strikes me that the army does precious little to help these men after they leave.' Holland cleared his throat, spoke up over the noise that was dying as the vehicle moved away. 'It's like they fight for their country, then you wash your hands of them, just when they need the most help.'

'There's a comprehensive army pension system.'

The major had spoken as if it were the end of the conversation, but Holland saw no reason to let it lie. Besides, he'd been doing a little reading up. 'Not if you leave too early, there isn't,' he said. 'Unless you've been wounded, you only get a pension if you do twelve years. That's right, isn't it?'

Poulter reached for another Silk Cut. 'Look, I can't say I completely disagree with you, but I do think the army does its level best in difficult circumstances. No, at the end of the day, pastoral care is probably *not* top priority, but you have to understand that the army has been doing things the same way for an awfully long time.' He summoned up a smile again as he leaned across the desk for something, then waved it around for them to look at. 'I still carry a bloody riding crop around, you see? We wear black ties at dinner and we still get issued with mess kits.' He lit his cigarette. 'Basically, we're still Victorian . . .'

Holland returned the smile. 'Well, the system for keeping records certainly is.'

The lid of the Zippo was snapped shut. 'Some would say that we've got rather more important things to do.'

The slightly awkward pause might well have gone on much longer if Sarah Cheshire had not appeared in the doorway brandishing a piece of paper.

'Come on in, Sarah,' Poulter said.

She walked over to the desk. 'It's not a long list, I'm afraid. There are seven men who served in Gulf War One who are still with the regiment.'

Poulter looked pleased with himself. 'I was more or less spot on, then . . .'

'Three of these are presently away on attachment elsewhere, leaving four, including Major Poulter, on site at this moment.'

Cheshire handed the list to Poulter, who looked at it, then passed it across the desk to Kitson.

'Thanks for that,' Holland said. He was pleased when Lieutenant Cheshire held his gaze a little longer than was necessary; then embarrassed when he felt himself start to redden.

'You already know that *I* can't help you,' Poulter said, 'but you're more than welcome to talk to the others on the list. You might be able to cross-reference any useful memories, but I have to say I think you'll be very lucky . . .'

'We haven't had a lot of luck so far,' Kitson said.

'As I explained earlier, these men might not have served together, and even if they *did*, it was a fair while ago.' He turned to Holland. 'How long have you been with the Met, Detective Sergeant?'

For some reason, Holland felt his blush deepen. 'Just over ten years.'

'Right, ten years. And how many of your fellow cadets can you remember?'

Holland could do little but shrug. Poulter had a very good point.

Cheshire took half a step forward. 'I did have one idea,' she said. She directed her suggestion towards Poulter. 'I was wondering about the war diaries . . .'

'That's good thinking,' the major said. He turned to explain to Holland and Kitson. 'The squadron adjutant would have routinely kept log-sheets, which would then have been collated into a digest of service. They're usually archived somewhere at HQ, aren't they?'

Cheshire nodded.

'They *might* mention Jago and his crew, but only if any of them were commended or listed as casualties.'

'Right, thanks.' Kitson felt fairly sure that neither of those things would apply.

'Thinking about it, old documentation might prove to be your best bet.' Poulter was warming to his theme. 'A lot of soldiers do hang on to stuff. You'd be surprised . . .'

'What about letters home?' Cheshire asked. 'If the men on this list are still with the same wives or girlfriends, they might still have the letters they wrote to them from the Gulf.'

'Right, that's another good thought. Soldiers often talk about their mates, or moan about the ones in the troop they can't stand, or whatever. If it's just the names you're after, that might be worth a try.'

Kitson agreed, of course, that anything was worth a try, but suddenly *everything* was starting to feel like a straw to be clutched at.

Once again, she thanked them for their suggestions. It was polite and it was politic, but with the mood she was in – as dark as the shadow that was moving rapidly across the whole investigation – it was hard to tell if they were genuinely trying to help.

Or simply trying to look as if they were.

They boarded the train back to London early; made sure they got themselves a table. Each of them had bought something to eat and drink on the concourse, and, as they waited to leave, both seemed happy to sit in silence, to concentrate on taking sandwiches from wrappings and stirring sugar into coffee. It wasn't until the train was pulling out of the station that Yvonne Kitson passed what would prove to be the journey's most pertinent reflection on their day.

'Nothing's ever fucking easy,' she said.

While Kitson tried to sleep, Holland leafed through a magazine, but nothing could stop him thinking about Thorne for too long. Late the night before, Holland had taken the call from the custody sergeant at Charing Cross. He'd passed on the news – along with the irritation at being woken up and the alarm at what Thorne had done – to Brigstocke, who had, presumably, passed it on in turn to Trevor Jesmond. It was a chain of conversations into the early hours that might well be used later to string up Tom Thorne . . .

Holland thought back to when he'd last seen him, walking away from the London Lift after they'd sat and watched the Gulf War tape. Thorne had seemed right enough at the time. Then Holland remembered how badly he himself had needed a drink; how much he'd appreciated the chance to sit in the pub with Yvonne Kitson and pour some of it out. He doubted if Thorne had anyone he could have shared a drink with and discussed what he'd seen. Anyone who could have told him that he'd drunk enough.

Against all prevailing wisdom, Thorne had been someone he'd looked up to since he'd first begun working with him, but even Holland had to admit that the DI's future was looking far from rosy. He might well be taken off this case straight away, and even if he was allowed to carry on, what would he come back to when it was all over? He'd been shunted off to the Yard when it became obvious that he hadn't recovered from the death of his father; that he wasn't himself. This latest misadventure wasn't going to help his case for returning to the Murder Squad, which, as anyone with any sense could see, was always going to be an uphill struggle. There were plenty for whom Thorne's presence on the MIT was even more unwelcome when he *was* himself.

Stupid, stupid bastard . . .

Holland stared out of the train window and realised that they'd stopped moving; that the train had been stationary for several minutes. He looked at his watch. He'd rung home to say he would be back late, and now it was getting later all the time. Sophie wouldn't be overly bothered, he knew that. He increasingly felt that she was happier when he wasn't around. But he'd be annoyed if he missed out on seeing Chloe before she went to bed.

The train began moving with a jolt. Kitson opened her eyes for a second, then closed them again. Rain was streaking the window, and some tosser in the seat behind was talking far too loudly on his mobile phone.

Later, Holland would call and tell Thorne how things had gone at the regiment. Find out how things had gone for him, too. How the daft sod was doing . . .

He flicked through the pages of *Loaded*, staring at pictures of scantily clad soap stars until he started to feel something other than irritation. He picked up the magazine, slid out from behind the table and walked towards the toilet.

TWENTY

Over the years, Thorne had felt more than his fair share of rage and regret, of lust and loathing, but he'd never been overburdened with guilt. He guessed it was because he spent his working life trying to catch those who should have been eaten up with enough of it for everyone. Many who had done the very worst things felt nothing, of course, but most people, even those without a shred of religious conviction, at least accepted that they *should*. For Thorne, it used to be that clear cut.

It wasn't that he never felt guilt at all; it was just that it was usually of the vaguely delicious variety that followed over-indulgence of one sort or another. Its more corrosive strain was one that never burned within him for very long. It could be neutralised by making the call he'd forgotten to make; by stepping forward; by having that awkward conversation he'd been putting off. The pain was short-lived and easily dealt with.

These days, though, Thorne could feel little else . . .

He'd spent most of the afternoon mooching around the Strand; begging for a couple of hours, chatting to a pair of old boys who drank near the Adelphi and hanging around at a lunchtime soup run.

Now, as the day turned from grey to charcoal, he moved quietly among the few tourists still left in the courtyard at Somerset House. This eighteenth-century riverside palace had, at one time or another, been home to the Inland Revenue, the Register of Births, Deaths and Marriages, and Oliver Cromwell's New Model Army. Now it was just another of the city's attractions: a place for visitors to take snapshots of history, or for families to gather in winter, when the water fountains were replaced with a skating rink. Thorne remembered that they'd filmed an ice-skating sequence here for that stupid film with Hugh Grant as the Prime Minister. Yeah, right. Another one of those picture-postcard movies where London looked dreamy in beat-bobby blue and Routemaster red. Where the snow never turned to slush, and the ethnic communities were mysteriously absent. Where, if there was no one sleeping rough, it wasn't because they'd been swept off the streets or were being kicked to death.

When Holland had rung the night before, Thorne had put on a good enough display of frustration and annoyance: at the way things had gone down in Somerset; at the polite enquiries about how they'd panned out for him at Charing Cross nick. In reality, he'd been feeling guilty as hell. He was screwing things up, and not just for himself.

He'd heard it in Holland's concern every bit as much as it had been there, loud and clear, in Brigstocke's curses. In that final comment from the doorway of the Interview Room when he'd talked about Thorne looking the part.

Thorne accepted that he wasn't always completely honest with himself. But why had he ever thought that his going undercover would be a good idea? Had he only convinced himself as a reaction to those who made it clear what a *terrible* idea they thought it was? Maybe everything that had happened in the last year – what he'd done and what had been done to him in return – had skewed his judgement permanently; made it no more reliable than if he were the one now suffering from dementia.

When he was eleven or twelve, his father had taken him skating a couple of times. Thorne had hated it. The Silver Blades at Finsbury Park was nobody's idea of a romantic location, with the frequent stabbings as much a feature of the place as the ice itself. Thorne remembered struggling around the outside of the rink, cultivating blisters, and getting knocked on his arse by older boys with earrings and feather cuts. He remembered getting to his knees, pulling in his hands quickly as the blades flashed by, then looking across to see his dad rushing on to the rink. He'd been embarrassed because his father had broken the rules by coming on to the ice in his shoes. He remembered the look on his father's face, the blush that had spread across his own, as Jim Thorne had skidded towards the boy who'd knocked him down and shoulder-charged him into the barrier. He remembered his dad pulling him off his knees, and brushing away the slivers of ice. Taking him over to hand in his skates. Across to where they could buy hot dogs and limeade . . .

Thorne knew very well that guilt caused such memories to bubble up and burst, the air inside permanently fouled. Guilt poisoned a well that should have been sweet to drink from.

'*I'm fine, honestly, Victor. I really didn't ring to talk about him.*'

'*Course you didn't . . .*'

It took Thorne a few seconds to work out that the vibration in his pocket was his phone ringing. He moved to a corner and stole a glance at the handset; saw that the missed call was from Phil Hendricks. More concern from a friend, and more false assurances. Another small measure of poison.

Thorne needed to find somewhere secluded from where he could return the call. He walked back out on to the Strand and turned east towards Fleet Street. The City would be emptying rapidly now, as the rush hour took its grip of the streets. A hundred yards along, he stopped at a stall selling the late edition of the *Standard.* Stunned, he read what was on the hoarding, then stepped closer to look down at a front page.

After no more than a few seconds, the man behind the stack of papers leaned across. 'Buy one or piss off . . .'

Thorne just stared at the headline.

*

He woke up, cold and clammy, and certain that he'd been crying in his sleep.

The copy of the *Standard* that Thorne had shelled out for was flapping, two steps down from his doorway, the headline partially revealed as the page caught the wind: '*ROUGH SLEEPER KILLINGS. MET GOES UNDERCOVER*'.

A few steps further down, Spike was sitting, much as he'd been two nights previously, just before the trouble had started. He looked high and happy, and he stared at Thorne for a full ten seconds before seeming to notice that he was awake. He pointed towards Thorne's sleeping bag. 'New . . .'

'Yeah. Not *new* new, but . . .'

'S'nice, like. Brown . . .'

By the time Thorne had got back to his pitch after being released from Charing Cross, his sleeping bag – which had been left in the street during the mêlée – was nowhere to be found. He'd picked up this newer second-hand one from the Salvation Army centre on Oxford Street.

Spike stretched out an arm for the newspaper and dragged it towards him. Thorne watched, wondering what his response should be if Spike were to say anything about the headline. As it was, he turned straight to the back and began to flick very slowly through the sports pages.

'You follow a team?' Spike said, eventually.

'Spurs, because I'm stupid. What about you?'

'Southampton. Not properly for a few years, like.'

'Is that where you're from?'

Spike lowered the *Standard*, then folded it. 'Not far away. Just some shitty little seaside town.' He ran his hand slowly back and forth along the crease he'd made in the paper. Stared at a spot approximate to where Thorne was sitting. 'Couldn't wait to get the hell out of it, tell you the truth. And they couldn't wait to get rid of me . . .'

It sounded like Spike had got himself into trouble before he'd come to London. It was the same story to one degree or another in most provincial towns. Kids reached a certain age, ran out of things to do and looked around for something to combat the boredom. It was usually drink, drugs, crime or a combination of all three. Some got out and got lucky. Others were drawn to those places where their blighted lives might flourish among like-minded souls. Many were destined to fare no better in London, Manchester and Edinburgh than they had at home, but they would not be short of company; equally doomed perhaps, but not quite as freakish.

'They let you out on police bail, right?' Spike asked.

'Right . . .'

'But what if you *needed* to be bailed out? If you needed someone to come and get you, to pay to get you out? Would you have anybody?'

Thorne said nothing. Thinking it would probably be Hendricks; Holland at a push. But beyond them . . .

'It'd be my sister, I think,' Spike said. 'It'd have to be. She bailed me out a year or so back, when I got caught with my stuff as well as Caroline's and this other bloke's, and they done me for dealing. So my sister stumped up the bail *and* gave me some extra cash on top of that.' His head dropped, and when he raised it again a smile was smeared across his face. His eyeballs were starting to roll upwards, creamy under the streetlight and cracked with red. 'She wanted to set me up for a bit, you know? To tide me over. I told her I was going to try and get myself clean, but I went straight out and used the money she gave me to score. Surprise, surprise, right? I think deep down she knew I would, 'cause she knows well enough what I'm like. She knows me better than anyone.' He stared at Thorne for half a minute, blinking slowly. 'She knows, right?'

Thorne nodded. From a club somewhere near by came the deep thump of a bass line. It was not 2 a.m. yet.

'I'd really have to be in the shit before I'd ask her for help again. Really deep in it. D'you know what I mean? Because I know bloody well I'd only let her down, and life's hard enough without feeling guilty all the time, right? It's not like she can't afford it, mind you. She's done brilliantly. She's got a really posh job, got herself a flash car and a swanky flat in Docklands and all that. It's just like it's become dead important for me *not* to ask my sister for anything. I'm fucked, right? I know I am. We're all completely fucked. But whatever happens, I'm not going to disappoint her again . . .'

Spike unfolded the paper and turned it over. He stared down at the front page, mouthing the first few words of the headline. Thorne was looking down at him from six feet away, but even if he'd been eyeball to eyeball, there would have been no way to tell if Spike was really taking in what was in front of his face.

If he *was*, something in the story made him suddenly laugh out loud. He cackled and hissed, chortled to himself for the next minute or more.

Thorne could only wish he found it that funny.

TWENTY-ONE

'Dan Britton's not here,' McCabe said. 'In case you've come to apologise.'

Nothing could have been further from Tom Thorne's mind. 'Still pissed off, is he? Maybe he decided to get his own back by opening his mouth . . .'

They were standing on the corner of Agar Street, on the north side of the Strand, a hundred yards or so from Charing Cross Station. Thorne had asked the desk sergeant to pass on a message: he needed to meet Inspector McCabe outside, *urgently*.

'I'll tell him,' the desk sergeant had said. 'He's most likely up to his neck.'

Thorne had leaned on to the counter. 'Tell him I've got information that could help prevent a serious assault . . .'

Outside, the wind whipped the litter in front of passing cars. 'I saw the paper.' The lopsided smile appeared. 'It's unfortunate.'

'It'll be a lot more unfortunate when I break his nose all over again.'

'Don't even *think* about accusing anyone on my team.'

'Well, *someone's* got a big mouth.' Thorne realised what he'd said straight away, and the mileage that the man would enjoy getting from it.

'Talk about pots and fucking kettles,' McCabe said. 'I don't know how long you've been mixing with smackheads and winos, mate, but you're starting to make about as much sense . . .'

McCabe began to walk. He turned right along Chandos Place towards Covent Garden. Thorne watched him, then followed, a hundred yards or so behind. At a corner of the piazza McCabe stopped and Thorne caught him up. They stood on the edge of the Saturday morning crowd that had gathered in front of a heavily tattooed juggler.

'This bloke's good,' McCabe said.

Thorne grunted. There were a lot of people watching, and if one in five of them chucked a bit of money his way, the juggler would do all right for himself. Maybe he'd tell Spike to start practising . . .

'Better than those arseholes who paint themselves silver and stand around pretending to be statues. I think I'd rather have junkies and dossers on the streets than out-of-work actors.'

'Shame our killer doesn't agree with you,' Thorne said.

McCabe turned slightly to look at him, as if he wasn't sure whether Thorne was joking. As if he wasn't sure about Thorne, full stop. 'Seriously,' he said, 'I tried to make certain everyone got the message. I did as much as I could to keep the lid on.'

'Fair enough . . .'

Thorne was starting to calm down a little. It didn't matter whether McCabe was telling the truth or not. There was nothing anyone could do about the leak now. But still, Thorne couldn't help but wonder why anyone would bother going to the paper with the story. 'It's not like it's a royal sex scandal, is it?' he said. 'It doesn't make sense.'

'Not giving Princess Anne one, are you?'

'Come on, they don't pay big money for this kind of tip, do they? So what's the bloody point?'

'Not big money, no,' McCabe said. 'But if it was one of your rough-sleeper mates, they'd settle for a few quid, or a bottle of Scotch. They'd take anything they could get.'

'Nobody I've met on the street has a clue . . .' Then Thorne remembered the drunk outside St Clement Danes: the one who'd known he was a copper, who'd shouted about it until Spike had come along and shut him up. Could he have told the *Standard*? Could Moony have said something to somebody? Either was a possibility, of course, but Thorne was far from convinced.

'You wouldn't know if they did,' McCabe said. 'The Drugs Squad sent a UCO in a year or two back; before my time. He was sussed within five minutes. Silly beggar was buying everyone beer and sneaking off to hotels every night.'

'I've not been that stupid,' Thorne said. He continued quickly before McCabe could say anything. 'Not *quite* that stupid.'

McCabe turned back to the show, his interest waning suddenly. 'If it isn't about money, I haven't got a clue.'

'That's why I was only half joking when I suggested Britton. He's got a motive. I could understand him wanting to make me look like a mug.'

'It wasn't Britton.'

The juggler was tossing meat cleavers into the air. He deliberately let one clatter to the cobbles, making the stunt look that bit more dangerous. The crowd didn't seem overly impressed.

'Whoever opened their mouth did so for a reason,' Thorne said. 'They must be getting something out of it.'

There was one major change to the layout on the whiteboard at the far end of the Incident Room: the list of victims had been divided into two. The names of Mannion, Hayes and Asker now constituted a column of their own. Next to it, in black felt tip, was written: 'Unknown Vic 1' and 'Jago', with a line in red leading from those names to '12th King's Hussars' and another to 'Tank Crew'.

Beneath that were two question marks.

Of the large number of calls and e-mails that Brigstocke had fielded so far that day, he'd hoped that one or two might have gone some way towards replacing those question marks. He'd hoped that, despite everything Kitson and Holland had been told in Somerset, the army would have found some way to dig up the names of the other soldiers who had served on the tank crew with Christopher Jago in 1991.

One already dead. Two who might be, or might *soon* be . . .

As it was, far too many of those calls and e-mails had been about Tom Thorne.

'It's a pain in the arse,' Brigstocke said. He and Holland were sitting in his office, having polished off a lunch of ham rolls and cheese-and-onion crisps brought across from the Oak. 'I've had that tosser from the Press Office on half a dozen times at least. Norman? He reckons he's got papers and TV all over him.'

Holland grimaced. He remembered Steve Norman from a case a couple of years before, when the MIT had been forced to work more closely than they'd have liked with the media. 'Slimy sod deserves something a lot worse all over him.'

Brigstocke didn't think it was funny or he wasn't listening. 'I said as little as I could get away with, but I think they're happy enough to let the story run for a while. Nobody seems desperate to squash it, anyway.'

'It's a bit late, I'd've thought . . .'

'Norman's not an easy bloke to read, but he's sharp enough. We were going round the houses a bit, you know, discussing the story, talking about the UCO.' He raised his fingers, used them to put the initials in inverted commas. 'But I got the distinct impression that he knew we were talking about Thorne.'

There was a knock at the door.

Holland lowered his voice. 'Should he know?'

'He *shouldn't*, but if it was a copper who leaked the story, then it's hardly a major surprise.'

Holland remembered a little more about the case during which he'd first come across the senior press officer; about the way Norman had clashed with one officer in particular. 'Him and Thorne have got a bit of history . . .'

Brigstocke barked out a humourless laugh. 'Is there anyone Tom Thorne *hasn't* got history with?'

Another knock, and, on being invited in, Yvonne Kitson put her head round the door. Holland saw something pass across her face on seeing that he and Brigstocke were ensconced, on guessing that they'd just stopped talking. But whatever she was feeling – curiosity, envy, suspicion – its expression was only momentary. He hoped that when the investigation was over, Kitson wouldn't be too pissed off that he'd been privy to the workings of the undercover operation while she had not. Holland thought he knew her well enough. He was pretty confident that she wouldn't feel slighted; that she'd put it down to the close working relationship he had with Tom Thorne.

'Am I interrupting, sir?'

'No, you're fine, Yvonne. Everyone OK after the briefing this morning?'

'I think so . . .'

Once the story had appeared in the previous day's *Standard*, Brigstocke had been forced to say something to his team. He'd been forced to lie, told them that, yes, there was a UCO working as part of the investigation, but that the officer had been recruited, as might have been expected, from SO10. There was nothing else they needed to know.

There was no reason for anyone to doubt that this was the unvarnished truth. Even if they did, they certainly wouldn't have imagined that the officer at the centre of it all was Tom Thorne.

'You OK, Dave?' Kitson asked.

'Yeah, I'm good . . .'

Thinking about it, Holland might have preferred it if Kitson *had* been the one dealing with Thorne. To be honest, he could have done without the stress.

Kitson and Brigstocke spent a few minutes talking about another case. While the rough-sleeper killings was far and away the most high profile and demanding of the team's cases, there were, at least theoretically, another forty-seven unsolved murders on their books: dozens of men and women stabbed, shot and battered. Murders that were horrific and humdrum. Predictable and perverse. Gangland executions, domestic batteries, hate crimes. From sexual predation to pub punch-ups. Killings of every known variety, as well as a few that seemed to have been created just for the occasion. Some had come in since the rough-sleeper murders had started, but some dated back to long before. Thankfully, a healthy number were in the pre-trial stage, but there were still many that showed no sign of progress, and these were the ones that had been shoved on to the backburner. It always struck Holland as a ridiculous mixture of metaphors: some cases had gone so cold that no amount of time on any sort of burner would do them any good. The top brass had their own way of describing such things: they were fond of words like 'de-prioritising'.

He could almost hear Thorne's voice:

'*De-prioritised in terms of fucking manpower, maybe. In terms of money. Try telling the victim's family that they've been de-prioritised . . .*'

Holland knew that catching the man who was killing the ex-servicemen was the only acceptable outcome; that was *their* priority. He understood the decision not to reveal the videotape at this time. Still, he hoped when the time came, though some or all of those responsible would already be dead, that as much effort would go into investigating the murders of four Iraqi soldiers.

Kitson stopped on her way out. 'I'll let you get back to it.'

'Boy's stuff,' Holland said.

Brigstocke pursed his lips and nodded, mock-serious; masking the bullshit with silliness. 'Right. You wouldn't be interested . . .'

As she walked back towards the Incident Room, Yvonne Kitson tried to keep the irritation in check. She'd had enough of this crap the year before. When her private life had become the stuff of pub chat and water-cooler gossip.

She'd been as rattled as anybody else by Brigstocke's briefing that morning. Everyone had been talking since they'd seen it in the paper, of course, but hearing it from the DCI was something else. She knew very well that undercover operations could succeed only through secrecy, but still, she'd felt as a DI that she could have been taken into confidence. Brought within the inner circle.

She hadn't let Brigstocke or anyone else see how she was feeling, though. That was something else she'd learned the previous year. When Brigstocke had asked how everyone had taken it, she'd lied.

But hopefully she'd done so just a little better than he and Holland just had.

She walked back into a crowded and bustling Incident Room, wondering why it was that people whose job it was to find the truth lied like such rank amateurs.

★ ★ ★

He only came into the West End for work. At other times he couldn't see any point in it. In terms of shopping or entertainment, you could get everything you needed locally, and he preferred not to venture too far from where he was staying. It wasn't that he was a long way away; it wasn't too much of a slog to get into town or anything like that. Central London just wore him out. Once he'd returned home, and the buzz of the job he'd been doing had worn off, he was left ragged and wrung out, with a dull ache, as if a muscle he'd been working on was complaining at the effort.

The West End was greedy.

Everywhere your eyes fell, the place had its scabby hand out in one way or another, from sandwich boards to neon signs and a hundred foreign students with a thousand pointless leaflets. Everyone wanted something, and not just those poor, useless buggers with nowhere else to go. All of them: the people working in shops and behind fast-food counters and the ones in cars and those walking fast along the pavement, tutting and growling, looking like they were ready to kill someone if their progress was halted for even one second. They all wanted something – your money, or your time or your fucking attention – and if you wanted to make absolutely sure they got nothing, that no part of you was touched, it was crucial to stay on top of your game.

He wandered through the streets around Soho and Covent Garden, moving quickly between those places he needed to visit. There was a list of them in his pocket, and he'd worked through most of it already. He turned from Dean Street on to Old Compton Street, heading towards Piccadilly. Past the cruisers and the coked-up media wankers. Past a wild-haired wino, breathing heavily and scowling at the world from the doorway of a fetish-wear boutique.

As he walked, he realised where that dull ache came from. It was the effort of staying self-contained that drained you; of keeping yourself impervious to the offers and the pleas; to the promises of pleasure of one sort or another. It was as though he'd been forced to spend the day permanently clenched, and he knew that when he got home he'd need to spend long hours flicking through the channels or working at the controls of the PlayStation. Sleep wouldn't come until the knots had fallen out.

He wasn't complaining. You went where the job demanded, but still, he was pleased that he'd been able to define what it was that was niggling him. He'd write it down somewhere when he got back. All that stuff about greed . . .

At least it was an appropriate place to be, he thought. Considering why he was there in the first place. After all, if one idiot hadn't got greedy, none of it would ever have been necessary. They would all still be alive. The Driver and the Gunner and . . .

He waited until the man who was walking straight towards him had stepped aside before pulling the list from his pocket and checking the next address.

By the time it was dark he'd be well away, and he'd made an early start so as to be sure of it. He'd been around the West End late on a Saturday night before and it wasn't something he was desperate to repeat unless he had to. That was when the fights broke out and the gutter seemed as good a place to lie down as any; when *all* the alleyways ran with piss and every hidey-hole contained some moron throwing up or sleeping off the excesses.

On Saturday night you couldn't tell who was homeless and who wasn't.

★ ★ ★

The young blonde-haired woman was still unhappy with the background. She waved her hand, urging her subject to move just a little further to the right . . .

There was no shortage of photo opportunities in London. The gasometers of King's Cross were perfect for the seriously arty, as were the estates of Tower Hamlets and Tottenham for a certain sort of documentary-maker. Snap-happy tourists, of course, were spoiled for choice. The Americans and the Japanese on their European tours, the Geordies and the Jocks down for the weekend; they could all point their cameras just about anywhere, and few landmarks were more popular than Eros. Visitors to Piccadilly Circus clicked away oblivious, thinking that the figure atop the memorial fountain was the God of Love, and equally misguided about many of those who gathered around the steps of the monument. The statue was actually meant to be the Angel of Christian Charity, and a number of those within range of his bow were among the city's lost: runaways, junkies and rent boys for whom a little Christian charity was long overdue.

'No . . . further . . . keep moving . . .'

The blonde spoke with a thick Scandinavian accent and kept waving from behind the camera, eager to keep the trio of scarred and scruffy-looking wasters out of her shot. Her boyfriend was growing increasingly impatient, unaware of the three figures on the steps directly behind him.

Spike and Caroline were tucking hungrily into greasy pizza slices, while Thorne sat engrossed in what was happening on the far side of the circus. He watched as a big man in an unfamiliar blue uniform leaned down to talk to a beggar outside Burger King. There was some head-shaking before the man on the ground snatched up his blanket and stalked away.

'Who's that?' Thorne nodded towards the man in the uniform.

Spike stood up and peered across the traffic. 'PCP,' he said.

'Piccadilly Circus Partnership.' Caroline shoved the last bit of pizza into her mouth and wiped her fingers on the back of her jeans. 'A bunch of local businesses pay for a few little fucking Hitlers to keep the streets clean. Someone told me they're in radio contact with the police and there's a huge control room full of CCTV screens in the Trocadero.' She pointed towards the huge entertainment complex on

Coventry Street. 'They're *supposed* to be on the lookout for all sorts of stuff. Cracked paving stones, blocked drains or whatever . . .'

'Yeah, right.' Spike was lighting a roll-up. 'These fuckers think some things smell a damn sight worse than that, like.'

Thorne watched the man in the blue uniform walking slowly across the zebra crossing towards Virgin Megastore. There were plenty of these cut-price coppers to be seen around the West End, differentiated – to any but the trained eye – only by the coloured fluorescent strips across their uniforms and peaked caps. Aside from the PCP goons, there were council-appointed city wardens patrolling the streets in pairs. Then there were the Met's own community support officers. The CSOs had the power to detain rather than arrest, and despite the publicity that had surrounded their introduction a few years previously, they were seen – not least by real police officers – as something of a joke.

'Look at that cocky sod,' Caroline said. 'I bet he goes home and gets his wife to piss on him . . .'

In general terms at least, Thorne shared Caroline's suspicions. He thought that those who wanted to be full-time police officers were dodgy enough. Anyone who couldn't manage that, but still had some overwhelming desire to pull on a uniform and strut around trying to keep the streets clean, almost certainly needed watching.

Spike tried to blow smoke rings, but the breeze pulled them apart. 'Or he makes her dress up as a beggar and handcuffs her to the bed.'

Caroline laughed. 'With a sign saying "Homeless and horny" . . .'

'Dirty bastard . . .'

Thorne thought about the 'policeman' that Mannion and others had mentioned. The one who was supposed to have been seen asking questions prior to the first killing. Was it possible that this man had been one of these ancillary officers? With a few drinks inside you, wouldn't one uniform look much the same as another on a dark night? He thought it was unlikely. They didn't know for sure that the officer described had even *been* uniformed, but if he had, Thorne guessed that most of those sleeping rough around the West End, many of them living on the fringes of one law or another, would know a genuine copper when they saw one.

He turned, and watched a real enough police officer marshalling the queue that was moving slowly into a matinee at the Criterion. He decided that thinking out loud could do no harm. 'Do you reckon this killer might be a copper?'

Spike sat down again. The smoke from his cigarette moved quickly across Thorne's face. 'Fuck knows. It's what a lot of people think.' He turned to Caroline. 'Caz thinks he's a copper, don't you?'

'Got every chance,' she said. 'That's why they've sent this undercover copper in to catch him. It's like in films, when they talk to convicted killers to find out what the one they're after is thinking. It takes one to know one kind of thing . . .'

Thorne nodded, thinking that he didn't understand what went on in his own head, let alone anybody else's.

'I wouldn't fancy doing it,' Spike said. 'Sleeping on the street if you didn't have to, with a killer knocking around.'

Caroline leaned across and touched Thorne's face. The graze on his forehead had scabbed over and the bruises were yellowing nicely, their edges indistinct. 'This undercover bloke'll be all right,' she said. 'If he's as handy with his fists as the coppers that did this, I don't think he's got much to worry about.'

TWENTY-TWO

'Where've you been?' Holland asked. He stepped into a shop doorway to escape the noise of the traffic.

'Sorry. I only just got your message. I fancied a lie-in . . .'

'Where are you?'

'Hang on . . . I can't see a street sign. I'm somewhere round the back of the National Gallery.'

'I was looking for you at the theatre.'

'That's where I normally am.'

'I know. I went in to the London Lift when you didn't return the call and that's where Brendan said you'd be.'

'I moved,' Thorne said.

Holland grunted, relieved that Thorne was OK but pissed off that he'd spent all morning running around like a blue-arsed fly, trying to find him. 'We've had a bit of luck,' he said.

'What?'

'Where can we meet?'

The three of them had walked the length of Oxford Street before Spike and Caroline had gone down into the subways beneath Marble

Arch to catch up on some sleep. Thorne had crossed the road into Hyde Park and sat down on a bench near one of the cafés at Speaker's Corner. This triangle at the north-east corner of the park should have been a pleasant enough place to sit at this time of year. Even if the verge adjoining the bridle path had been freshly churned into mud, elsewhere the autumn crocuses were in full bloom, bright and lively. The railed-in lawns were still lush, and, despite the plastic bags that danced from many of the branches, the leaves provided plenty more colour a little higher up – green and bronze and butter yellow on the ash trees.

Thorne knew that twenty-four hours earlier, as on every Sunday morning, the political pundits, the zealots and the nutcases would have been out in force. They'd have been up on their soapboxes, shouting about freedom and enlightenment, and aliens sending messages through their toasters, each one honouring the tradition of free speech which had been guaranteed on this spot by Act of Parliament a hundred and twenty-five years before. Halfway through this bleak Monday, freezing his tits off and with a headache just starting to kick in, Thorne found it far easier to picture the gallows at Tyburn, which had stood on the same spot for centuries before that. It took less effort to imagine the creak of a body swinging – of twenty-four at one time from the Triple Tree – and the bloodthirsty cries of the crowd than to conjure the voices of debate and discussion.

Holland dropped down on to the bench next to him and nodded towards the corner. A semicircle of pin oaks had been planted on its farthest boundary, fiery red against the off-white brickwork on the far side of Park Lane. 'What would you want to get off your chest, then?'

'Eh?'

'If you had a crowd, and you could talk about anything you liked . . .'

It was one of the main reasons why Thorne enjoyed having Holland around; why Thorne had made himself unpopular with anyone who'd stepped, however briefly, into the former DC's shoes. Holland had the pleasing knack of being able to punch through the hard shell of a black mood with one glib comment or seemingly innocent enquiry; with a stupid question in too cheery a voice. There were occasions, if Thorne was feeling particularly arsey, when he put this down to insensitivity on Holland's part, but more frequently he saw it to be the exact opposite.

'God knows,' Thorne said. 'The way things are going, I think I'll end up as one of the toasters-and-aliens brigade.'

'Sorry?'

Thorne shook his head. It didn't matter. 'What about you?'

'Where d'you want to start? I'd try to win the crowd over to the idea that all children should be taken into care between the ages of one and sixteen. I'd ask them to support my campaign for police paternity leave to be extended to, say, five years, and to include free alcohol and Caribbean holidays. I'd ask if any of them wanted to sleep with me . . .'

'Things a bit sticky at home?'

'How much room is there in your doorway?'

Thorne did his best to smile, and leaned back on the bench. He watched a pair of squirrels chase each other around a litter bin; saw a fat magpie hop lazily away as one of them ran at it.

Holland took off his gloves as he reached down to pull something from his briefcase. 'I'm only joking,' he said.

It was a magazine. Glossy, with a picture of a grim-faced soldier on the front: sand all around and sandbags at his feet; sheets of dust rising black behind him. In bold red lettering across the top: 'GLORIOUS'.

'It's the regimental magazine,' Holland said. 'That's their nickname: the "Glory Boys" or the "Glorious Twelfth". A woman from their HQ sent it. She's the assistant adjutant . . .'

'She sent it to you?'

'Just arrived out of the blue. It's the spring 1991 issue.'

Thorne threw him a sideways look as he began to flick through the magazine.

'I'm sure she was genuinely trying to help.' Holland tried to summon a cocky grin, but blushed despite himself. 'But I think she *did* take a shine to me . . .'

'It's bloody typical,' Thorne said. 'The finest detectives on the force applying themselves twenty-four hours a day, and we get a break because some woman, who's clearly mad or desperate, thinks you've got a nice arse.'

The magazine was a mixture of regimental news and notices. There were letters, quizzes and book reviews; advertisements for modelling kits, financial services and shooting weekends. There were obituaries for those who had long since left the regiment and for some who had died more recently, while on active service.

About half the magazine was taken up by articles and photographs. All these were the work of serving soldiers, and the majority of them concerned what had, in spring 1991, been the very recent conflict in the Gulf: '*Christmas in Kuwait*'; '*Desert Shield – A Trooper's Perspective*'; '*Into the Storm*'.

'That's the one,' Holland said. He leaned across and pointed to where a page had been marked by a piece of paper. 'That's the page she wanted us to see.'

Thorne unfolded the bookmark. It was headed with the regimental crest and Latin motto. The message was handwritten in blue ink: '*Thought this would be a shot in the dark, but I think we struck lucky. The photograph is what you'll probably be most interested in. Lt Sarah Cheshire.*'

'No kiss?' Thorne asked.

'I'm not listening,' Holland said. He pointed to a black-and-white photo that took up half a page of the magazine. 'Our four men are somewhere among that lot . . .'

Two dozen or so soldiers had posed for the camera, arranged in front of, around and in many cases on top of three battle tanks. They all wore desert camouflage and berets. Each carried a rifle and no more than a few of them were smiling. There was a caption to the right of the picture: '*D Troop, 2nd Sabre Squadron. Bremenhaven. October 1990*'.

'Just before they were posted to the Gulf,' Holland said. He reached over again and jabbed a finger towards one of the soldiers. The faces were small in shot, the features indistinct. 'That's Jago . . .'

Thorne looked at the list of names beneath the photograph. Jago's was certainly there, but the list was not structured in any way. It was impossible to tell how the names corresponded to the men in the picture, gathered as arbitrarily as they were.

'How do you know?' Thorne asked.

'We scanned the photo and e-mailed it to Susan Jago. She picked her brother out for us.'

'She pick out anybody else?'

'She told us before that she'd only seen one photo of the crew together . . . and that was years ago.'

Thorne studied the photograph. He thought he could read fear – apprehension, at least – on one or two of the faces, but decided in the end that he was simply projecting. He couldn't see what was in the heads and hearts of these soldiers any better than he'd been able to see what was in the eyes of the four he'd watched committing murder on a grainy videotape. Those men were in front of him at that moment; he was looking at their faces. And now, if any were still alive, there was a way to trace them.

'How did they get away with it, Dave? How did no one find out what they'd done?'

'Maybe someone did,' Holland said. 'The army might have known and hushed it up . . .'

Thorne wasn't convinced. 'Or maybe they just buried the bodies.' He ran that through his mind for a moment; thought about holes being dug in wet sand once the camera had been switched off. Thinking about the tape reminded him of something else. 'Any word back from the lab yet? They were going to try and sort out the sound on the video . . .'

Holland rolled his eyes. 'Believe it or not, we've now sent it to a special unit at the University of California . . .'

'What? They can't do it here?'

'Not if you want a result this side of Christmas.'

'Jesus.' Thorne handed the magazine back to Holland. 'I presume we're going back to the army with these names.'

'Yeah, and this *should* make things piss-easy for them. We know none of them are still serving with the 12th King's Hussars, but we should be able to find out if any have moved anywhere else within the service. And now we've got the names, we can finally get on to the Army Personnel Centre.'

'I think we should start trying to locate them ourselves at the same time, though.' Thorne got to his feet. 'We might find them faster than the army can.'

'That's the plan,' Holland said. 'We just need to get hold of someone with a decent memory. Someone who can remember the other three who were in Jago's tank crew.'

'Start with the rarest names, right? Leave the Smiths and Joneses 'til last . . .'

'Really?' Holland looked across at Thorne like he was telling him how to tie his shoelaces.

Thorne returned the look with knobs on. 'OK . . . Sorry, *Sergeant*.'

'We're shit out of luck as far as that goes, anyway.' Holland pulled on his gloves and stood up. 'Nothing too outlandish, I'm afraid. Not a single Private Parts or Corporal Clutterbuck among them . . .'

They walked south towards the Serpentine.

It had started to drizzle, and Holland reached instinctively for the umbrella in his case, then stopped when he saw Thorne moving through the rain as if he were unaware of it.

'So why did you move?' Holland asked. 'Are you trying to lower the tone in as many places as possible?'

'No choice. The bloke whose pitch I took is coming back. Today or maybe tomorrow. These things tend not to be very specific . . .'

When Thorne had seen him the day before, Spike had been insistent that Terry T was on his way back to London. He'd heard a definite rumour, at any rate, and seeing as how Terry would want his pitch back, it was a good idea for Thorne to look around for somewhere else to bed down. Terry T was a big bloke, after all, Spike had said, and with a seriously vicious temper. Thorne had taken the bait, pretending to fall for the same gag he hadn't fallen for on the first night he and Spike had met . . .

'How's the face feel?' Holland asked. This was the first day he'd laid eyes on Thorne since his arrest, and the first time he'd mentioned Thorne's souvenirs of the occasion.

'What, have you only just noticed it?'

'I didn't think you'd want people banging on about it . . .'

'Because I got my face smashed in?' Thorne's tone was suddenly edgy, and snide. 'Or because of *why*?'

They walked on in silence for a few minutes.

'Obviously, it looks pretty bad,' Holland said. 'The face, I mean. I just wondered if it hurt much, that's all. Thought maybe you could get Phil Hendricks to bung you a few painkillers or something.'

Thorne felt bad that he'd been snappy. 'Don't worry about the face, Holland. It looks like shit, but beneath the bruises my looks remain undamaged.'

'That's a shame,' Holland said.

They came out on to Carriage Drive opposite Hyde Park Corner. Thorne had decided to take the long way back and walk into the West End along Piccadilly. Holland was planning to catch the tube back up to Colindale.

'Do you want to know the worst thing about you being promoted?' Thorne asked. 'I can no longer enjoy the simple pleasure of calling you "Constable" as if it's spelled with a "u" and an extra "t" . . .'

★ ★ ★

Saturday had been a bit hectic, but he'd got what he needed, and the rest of the weekend had actually been very pleasant. He'd taken a boat trip down to Greenwich and wandered around the Maritime Museum. Sitting in a nice pub by the river, he'd had a couple of pints and a Sunday lunch with all the trimmings. Later, he'd poked around a few of the little antiquey places and second-hand shops. He'd bought a computer game and a black suede jacket from the market.

If you could be bothered to look, there were *plenty* of places like that in London, north and south of the river; places with some charm and individuality; with a little bit of character. You couldn't help but wonder why those who ended up on the street chose to congregate like rats around the West End. Were they drawn to the bright lights or something? Did they think it was *glamorous*? He didn't understand it. Surely they could have gone wherever they fancied, slept wherever they liked. Wasn't that one of the few *good* things about being homeless?

For all that he'd learned about the lives of these people – and he'd made it his business to learn a great deal – he couldn't help but think that, for some of them, it was a lifestyle choice. There were a few, of course – the ones who were soft in the head or whatever – who would never be able to cope and were always going to end up on the margins of society, but for others it seemed to be about preference. From what he could see, those people didn't want to help themselves and scorned any offer of assistance from others. It was hard to have any real sympathy with that sort . . .

Bearing in mind what he'd been doing, he knew full well that he could hardly have been expected to think any other way, but that was genuinely his opinion on the subject. He firmly believed that he could do what he'd done and still be, you know, *objective* about what went on in the world. The people who had died had done so for no other reason than simple necessity. What had been done – what he'd *had* to do – was about no more than self-preservation. Well, that and the money, of course.

But nothing else.

He could honestly say that he hadn't borne any ill-will towards anyone he'd ever killed.

Today, with more work to do, he wasn't quite as relaxed as he had been when ambling about in Greenwich. It should all have been done and dusted by now, but when it came to protecting yourself, being safe rather than sorry was the only sensible approach.

He was spending a dreary Monday mastering his new computer game; sharpening up his reflexes and concentrating his mind. He'd get back to the matter in hand tomorrow.

TWENTY-THREE

As a trainee detective constable, Jason Mackillop was desperate for any chance to make an impression. It was easy to get lost on a major investigation such as this one. But it was also possible, if you were in the right place at the right time, with the right people at the end of the phone, to go from donkey to hero in a few minutes. They hadn't talked much about luck on the five-week Detective Training Course at Hendon, but all the trainees knew it was every bit as important as the stuff they had been taught: forensics; crime scene management; handling exhibits; disclosure of evidence; performance in the witness box.

At twenty-three, he was relatively young for a TDC. He was perhaps no more than six months away from being assigned as a full DC, but after the probation, the year on relief, and the two more as a dogsbody on the Crime Squad, he was more than ready to step up. He'd already proved he could handle himself in most formal areas of the job, and catching a break like this one certainly couldn't hurt . . .

Mackillop put down the phone, took a deep breath, and snatched up the piece of paper on which he'd been scribbling. He needed to pass on the information quickly, but for a second or two he wasn't completely certain as to whom. Should he observe the chain of command or just go straight to the most senior officer he could find? If he did, would he risk putting noses out of joint? It was fantastic to impress, but it might be a very bad move to alienate those just a step or two further up the ladder than he was.

He glanced around the Incident Room, feeling the paper warm against his sweaty fingers. They were a good bunch, by and large, with no more tossers than you'd expect on any team of this size: Andy Stone was the sort of bloke you'd like as a mate, but Mackillop was unsure how good a copper he was; Kitson seemed well liked, but she sometimes had that look, like you wouldn't want to get on the wrong side of her; Holland could be a bit distant, though he'd only just been promoted, and was bound to have a lot on his plate. Mackillop had never met Tom Thorne, the team's absent DI, but he'd certainly heard enough about him . . .

Looking around, trying to make his mind up, he saw that Kitson was watching him from a spot by the coffee machine. Her eye flicked from his face to the piece of paper he was now wafting nervously from the end of his outstretched arm.

'All right, Jason?'

'Guv . . .'

Mackillop walked across, decision made, and within a minute he knew it had been the right one. Once he'd finished telling her about the phone call and shown her what he'd written down, Kitson had done exactly as he'd hoped she'd do: she'd congratulated him on a job well done, then pointed him straight towards the DCI's office.

He couldn't see Spike or One-Day Caroline, and guessed they'd be in later, but there were plenty of faces Thorne *did* recognise as he looked around. He saw Holy Joe, and the drunk who'd shouted at him outside St Clement Danes, and others he'd exchanged a story or two with at the soup runs around the Strand.

He asked if any of the unfamiliar faces belonged to Terry T.

Brendan Maxwell craned his head, panned quickly around the café, then went back to his breakfast. 'No, I can't see him. Why?'

'That's his spot I've been bedding down in most nights and Spike reckons he's coming back. So I've got to find somewhere else.'

'Doesn't hurt to move around a bit,' Maxwell said.

Thorne rammed the last of an egg and bacon roll into his mouth and answered with his mouth full. 'S'pose not . . .'

'A lot of my clients have been moving around a bit more lately.' They had been talking quietly anyway, but now Maxwell lowered his voice until it was barely above a whisper. 'Some of them have taken to sleeping in a different place every night, or getting themselves indoors. For obvious reasons.'

'I don't want to go into a hostel,' Thorne said.

He had purposely gone into the Lift early. The battery on his mobile was very low and he was borrowing a charger in Maxwell's office. They'd gone down to the café for breakfast while they waited.

Maxwell took a slurp of tea, then grunted and swallowed quickly as he remembered something. 'Did that copper find you, by the way? He was going to look for you at the theatre, I think . . .'

Thorne nodded. 'He tracked me down eventually.' He remembered Holland telling him on the phone that he'd come here; that Maxwell had pointed him towards the theatre doorway.

Since they'd met the day before in the park and Holland had shown him the magazine, Thorne had been anxiously waiting for news. It could only be a matter of time until they had names. It felt like they were turning a corner and picking up speed. Of course, he'd had the same feeling plenty of times before. Often, it just meant that you hit the brick wall that much faster.

'What's Phil up to?' Thorne hadn't seen Hendricks for nearly a fortnight.

The Irishman pointed a fork towards Thorne's face. 'He told me to make sure you took some painkillers if that was hurting . . .'

'They're fucking ganging up on me,' Thorne said.

Maxwell looked confused for a moment, shrugged when Thorne

shook his head. On the far side of the café, a plate crashed to the floor. Maxwell joined in with the cheer as loudly as anyone else. 'You seeing a fair bit of the city, then?' he asked.

'I'm seeing a lot of it, yeah. But I don't know that "fair" is the right word.'

'Not the stuff you see in the guide books, is it?'

'It's like being on *Panorama*,' Thorne said. 'Only with more killing.'

In the queue at the counter behind them, voices were suddenly raised. Maxwell pushed back his chair and stood, ready to step in, but the man doing most of the shouting was already striding towards the door, telling anyone who'd listen that they could go fuck themselves.

Maxwell sat back down. 'You like all that nasty stuff, though, right? Phil was telling me. All that blood and guts and Black Museum shit.'

Thorne felt slightly irritated. He didn't know if Maxwell was being deliberately obtuse or if Hendricks had just put it across to him badly. Knowing how Hendricks had once tried to explain Thorne's love of country music by telling Maxwell that he liked songs about death and lost dogs, this was certainly possible. 'I like history,' he said. 'In London, a lot of it's just . . . dark.'

Maxwell pushed what was left of his breakfast around the plate. 'Getting darker all the time,' he said.

Thorne sensed a figure looming behind him and twisted his neck round to see Lawrence Healey standing there, clutching a tray.

'May I join you?' Healey asked.

Maxwell put his fork down and threw back what was left of his tea. 'I'm just on my way to a meeting. Tom?'

'Free country . . .' Thorne said.

Maxwell looked across the table before he turned to leave, something Thorne couldn't read in his eyes. 'Let me know if there's anything else you need . . .'

Healey tucked into a bowl of what looked suspiciously like bran. There was a carton of yoghurt on his tray and a cup of foul-smelling herbal tea. After a minute or two of silence and an exchange of awkward smiles, Healey cleared his throat. 'I was going to ask how you were getting on, but, looking at you, I'm not sure there's any real need.'

'You should have seen the other bloke,' Thorne said.

'I saw him yesterday, as a matter of fact . . .'

Thorne didn't know what to say.

Healey's voice, even posher than Thorne remembered, suited a tone of wry amusement very well. 'We have a weekly meeting with some of the officers from the Homeless Unit. Just a chat about anything that's come up.' He stared across at Thorne for a few moments, nudged his glasses a little higher, then went back to his cereal.

Thorne watched Healey eat. He looked fit and tanned under a brushed-denim button-down shirt. That said, most people would have looked well compared to Thorne himself. Or to any of the blotchy or the blasted, the washed-out or pasty-faced characters that moved around them. 'Thanks for the concern,' Thorne said. 'But I really wouldn't bother.'

'You might need some legal advice . . .'

'I'll be fine.'

'We can help you with that.'

Thorne said nothing. He turned and looked at the noticeboard for a while, decided he'd probably give the poetry workshop a miss.

'Things going OK, though?' Healey asked. 'Generally, I mean?'

'I've been better . . .'

'I know.'

'Really?'

'I do understand how hard it is.' Healey's voice was lower suddenly. He reminded Thorne of an over-earnest vicar. Or of Tony Blair. 'It's the adjustment that's particularly difficult . . .'

Thorne had actually found adjusting to other people the trickiest thing of all; to the way other people *saw* him. It was usually one of two reactions: he was avoided or ignored. In the first instance, pedestrians would steer clear, the more sensitive doing their best to make that feint to one side as unobtrusive as possible. In the second, he seemed to become completely invisible, as passers-by simply pretended that they hadn't seen him at all. Both reactions were gloriously British in their sly dishonesty, but no more so, Thorne decided, than some people's when confronted by people whom they actually *knew*. When greeting those they perhaps hadn't seen for a while. There was one phrase that Thorne particularly hated; it could cover a multitude of sins and was trotted out no matter how sick or sad the person on the receiving end appeared. No matter how frightful their clothes or hair, or how much weight they'd put on since the last time you'd seen them:

'*You look well . . .*'

Suddenly a hand fell on to Thorne's shoulder and a rheumy-eyed whippet of a man he'd talked to once or twice leaned down close to him. 'Great days, eh?' The man breathed sweet sherry into Thorne's face. 'Great days . . .'

Thorne had no idea what the man was talking about. He watched him walk away and accost someone at the next table, then turned back to Healey. 'I've met some fascinating people, though,' he said.

'What's it been now? A month or so?'

'Something like that. You lose track.' Thorne wasn't sure exactly how many rough sleepers came within the Lift's remit, but he couldn't help wondering if Healey knew as much about all his clients. 'What about you?'

'Sorry?'

Thorne was thinking about what Healey had said when they'd met in the corridor a couple of weeks before. 'We're both "new boys", remember? How are you settling in?'

'Oh . . . settled now, most definitely. Thank you for asking.'

'Just talking,' Thorne said.

'People can be suspicious of a new broom, you know? You just need to get your head down and get on with it, whatever anyone else thinks. A certain amount of tunnel vision definitely helps.'

The concern in Healey's voice had gone and been replaced by something a little more abrasive. Thorne saw that there was a resolve behind the nice-but-dim accent and the do-gooder appearance. He also understood exactly what Healey was saying. Tunnel vision was something he'd been accused of himself, though it was usually described somewhat less politely.

'It could help get you off the street,' Healey said.

'Maybe it's what put me *on* it.'

'You want to talk about that?'

'Not hugely . . .'

When Healey began removing the foil from his yoghurt carton, Thorne stood up and took his coat from the back of the chair.

'I enjoyed the chat,' Healey said.

Thorne bent to pile his empty plate and cup on to the tray. 'You need to get out more,' he said.

He slid his tray on to a trolley near the food counter, then looked back to make sure that Healey hadn't gone anywhere. He wanted to check to see if there'd been any messages, and as long as Healey was still eating, it was the perfect time to nip up to the office and get his phone back.

Looks played a major part in it; that's how Russell Brigstocke felt anyway. It was like being a hard man; like being feared. Yes, it was about what was inside your head, about having the will to dish out pain, and to take it, but once you had it going on up there, then what you looked like was the next most important thing. The set of your mouth, and the way your eyes absorbed the light – the way they sucked it in and smothered it – counted far more than your size, or how much weight your punch packed.

It seemed to Brigstocke that Jason Mackillop *looked* like a copper. He had short hair and skin that was pitted with acne scars. He was heavyset beneath a blue M&S suit, and he stood awkwardly, as though he were designed to be permanently leaning on something: the roof of an unmarked vehicle; the window sill in an airless interview room; a bar. What Mackillop looked like of course was a casting director's *idea* of a copper, but as most of those who did the job for real looked like financial advisers – Brigstocke himself included, if he were being honest – that was probably no bad thing. At that moment, with the

TDC standing in front of his desk and brightening the day *right* up, he decided that Jason Mackillop was the sort of copper he could do with a damn sight more of.

'Right, let's have those names . . .' Brigstocke said.

The list of soldiers in the *Glorious* photograph had been divided up and Mackillop had been the one who had struck lucky. Among those in his allocation had been the writer of the original article, and not only had First Lieutenant Stephen Brereton been fairly easy to trace, but he'd had no great trouble providing the relevant information. Mackillop had already explained to Brigstocke how Brereton – now a major in the Corporate Communications Department of the MOD – had remembered Chris Jago pretty well. He'd talked about their time in Bremenhaven; about Jago's fondness for German beer and German girls. He'd told Mackillop how each crew in the troop had been tight with each other; how a friendly rivalry between the different crews had been actively encouraged. Brereton hadn't seemed to mind too much that he could not be told why the police were so interested, and had said he'd be happy to have a look through some of his old Gulf War journals and diaries. After no more than ten minutes, he'd called back with the names of the other three men who'd manned a Challenger tank alongside Chris Jago in the early part of 1991.

'That major down in Somerset . . . Poulter? He said that these crews got moved about all the time, that they were sometimes shifted around in battle situations. How can Brereton be certain these are the men who were in that tank on February 26th, 1991?'

'He isn't,' Mackillop said. 'Not absolutely, one hundred per cent, I mean. I gave him the exact date and he told me that his memory wasn't *that* good, but that he thought he'd remember if there'd been any injuries or last-minute transfers, you know? He wouldn't stake his life on it, but he couldn't recall any particular reason why that crew should have been split up.'

'Right . . .' Brigstocke was holding out a hand, waiting to take the piece of paper.

Instead, Mackillop looked at his list, read the names to the DCI: 'Trooper Christopher Jago, he was the Gunner; Lance Corporal Ryan Eales, the Loader/Operator; Trooper Alec Bonser was the Driver, and the tank Commander was Corporal Ian Hadingham. I reckon this was our crew, Guv.' Then he stepped forward and passed the paper across the desk.

Jago. Eales. Bonser. Hadingham.

Brigstocke stared down at the names of four men who surely held the key to solving a series of murders. Four men who themselves had committed murder and who now appeared to be paying for it with their own lives.

'Obviously, we're still in the dark about which one of them is our first victim,' Mackillop said. 'It could be Eales, Bonser or Hadingham.'

Brigstocke nodded. 'Now we've ID'd the crew, we can put a bit more pressure on the Army Personnel Centre—'

'I'm already on it, Guv.'

'I can't actually promote you until you've made DC, you know, Jason.'

Mackillop reddened. 'Well, I'm not on it exactly, but Major Brereton said he'd talk to them and try to get at least the basic stuff to us a.s.a.p.'

'*Basic stuff?*'

'Individual pictures of the soldiers, and maybe some of the details that are in their records: height, weight, colour of hair, blood group with a bit of luck. Hopefully, we should be able to figure out which one our mystery corpse is.'

'Hopefully.' Brigstocke was thinking that they'd need more than a photo. The killer hadn't left any of the victims in a state that was particularly recognisable. 'He reckons he can do that, does he, this Major Brereton?'

'He sounded like there was every chance, yeah. I think they respond better when requests for information come from other soldiers.'

Brigstocke picked up the phone. 'Not like the way most people on the Job respond to each other, then?'

'Guv . . .?'

'You'll know what I'm on about soon enough.' Brigstocke dialled a number, pointed towards the piece of paper. 'Well done on this, Jason. Your luck was in, no question . . .'

'Oh, it was pure bloody jam, Guv, I know that.'

'Luck's no use to anybody unless they use it. It sounds like you dealt with this Brereton bloke very well.'

Mackillop handled the praise like someone with far greater experience. Just a small nod. But Brigstocke caught the spasm of delight on his face, like a stifled sneeze, in the second or two before the TDC turned to walk towards the door.

Brigstocke leaned back in his chair and listened to the phone ringing on the other end of the line. He was as absurdly excited as Mackillop had been by the prospect of giving Detective Chief Superintendent Trevor Jesmond the first piece of genuinely good news in a while.

The four of them – Thorne, Spike, Caroline and Terry T – sat around a table in a grotty café behind the Charing Cross Road. Terry had returned from his travels with a few extra quid in his pocket and had insisted on shelling out on tea and doughnuts for everyone. This, and the fact that he was able to make the word 'cunt' sound like a term of endearment, made Thorne take to him straight away.

'You the cunt who's been sleeping in my pitch?' Terry had said on being introduced. The voice was high and hoarse, ripening a thick London accent.

Thorne had thought about it for a few seconds. 'Yeah, I think that'll be me. Just keeping it warm for you, obviously.'

'Fair play, mate . . .'

Terry T was every bit as tall as Spike had described, but he was also spookily thin. He was, Thorne guessed, somewhere in his late thirties, but he looked a damn sight older, with sunken cheeks, very few teeth and what appeared to be no hair at all beneath a floppy green hat. Like a cross between Nosferatu and the King of the Gypsies. A feather dangled from one ear and he'd taken off his scarf to reveal a heavy-looking, tarnished padlock on a chain around his neck, which had turned the skin beneath it distinctly green.

Terry had seen Thorne staring and reached up to finger the chain. 'Lost the fuckin' key, didn't I?'

'So where you been then, Tel? What you been doing . . .?'

Spike was buzzing, and for more than just the usual reason. He was excited to have his friend back. Thorne felt a peculiar twinge of something that might have been jealousy, though it was probably no more than a sugar rush from the doughnuts.

'Been all over,' Terry said. 'Up north to Birmingham and Liverpool, then even further, mate. Up with the chilly Jockos.'

Spike dipped a doughnut into a glass of Coke, let the drips fall off. 'I thought most of them were here in London.'

'Plenty more where they came from,' Terry said.

Spike rolled his eyes, put on a cod-Scottish accent, and mumbled something incomprehensible. 'It's fucking disgusting,' he said. 'They come down here, they beg on our street corners, they drink our Special Brew . . .'

Terry and Caroline laughed.

'How d'you get around?' Thorne asked.

'Hitching, mostly. Got a couple of free trains by keeping an eye out for the ticket collector and spending a lot of time in the bog.'

'I bet it's a bit colder on the streets up there.'

'I was indoors, mate. Sofa-surfing . . .'

Instinctively, Thorne looked to Spike for an explanation.

Spike held out his arms as if riding a surfboard, repeated the phrase in a silly American accent. 'Sofa-surfing. Moving around, like. Dossing down on people's floors, sofas, whatever . . .'

'Loads of people do it,' Caroline said. She'd poured a small mound of sugar on to the tabletop and had been absently toying with it: drawing patterns in the grains with her finger. All at once she chopped the edge of her hand on to the table and swept the sugar on to the floor. 'You think there's a lot of people sleeping on the street and in the hostels, you can multiply that by tens of thousands . . .'

More of those who, conveniently, could never be counted when the official figures were being produced; more of the so-called 'hidden homeless'. Thorne suddenly wondered if Terry T knew what had been going on while he was travelling. What had happened to some of those who had been unable to hide.

'So how long have you been away, Terry?'

Caroline flashed Thorne a look. He could see that she knew what was going through his mind, but he couldn't be sure what she was trying to tell him.

'Christ . . . it was a few days after that poor bastard got his head kicked in round Golden Square. When was that?'

'A couple of months ago,' Spike said.

'Did they ever catch the bloke who did it?'

Terry couldn't remember the last time he'd seen a paper or watched the news; he knew nothing of those who had died after that first victim. Caroline brought him up to date: she told him about the murders of Ray Mannion and Paddy Hayes; she leaned across to grab one of Terry T's long, bony hands and told him what had happened to Radio Bob.

Spike edged towards Thorne. 'Terry and Bob were mates,' he said. Like it wasn't obvious enough . . .

'Do they know why?' Terry asked eventually.

Spike snorted. 'Not got a clue, if you ask me, like.'

'There's supposedly an undercover copper sleeping rough,' Caroline said. 'To try and catch him.'

'They reckon the killer might *be* a copper,' Thorne said.

There was a small bowl on the table filled with sachets and sealed tubes: sugar, vinegar, mustard, mayonnaise. Caroline grabbed a handful and dropped them into her bag. She closed her eyes and leaned her head against Spike. He drummed his fingers on the tabletop, whistling something between his teeth.

Terry took out a plastic wallet and shook some money on to the table to settle the bill. 'He'll be a dead copper if I get hold of him . . .'

*

They walked up to Centre Point, then stopped and stood about for a quarter of an hour. For a few, strange, minutes, Thorne felt like a teenager again; content to hang around with friends, not doing anything in particular. Just talking bollocks and winding each other up. Happy enough to say nothing at all if the mood wasn't right.

The feeling passed quickly enough. This was not about relishing space and free time and the absence of responsibility. It was about being lost.

They moved off again, crossing Oxford Street and heading north. 'I can't fucking believe I wasn't here,' Terry said. 'I can't believe I missed Bob's funeral.'

Caroline caught up with him. 'Listen, I'm sure you and some of the other lads can get together later and have a few drinks for him, eh?'

'More than a few,' Terry said.

Caroline looked at Thorne. 'You up for that?'

'Better watch him though, Tel.' Spike pointed at Thorne and began to shadow-box. 'After a couple of cans he thinks he's Lennox Lewis . . .'

'I don't really know what I'm doing later,' Thorne said. 'I've got to find a decent place to get some kip.'

Terry turned to him. 'I was only joking about my pitch, mate. Plenty of room in there for two, if you want to stick around for a bit.'

Spike whistled. 'You on the turn, Tel?'

'I'll see . . .' Thorne said.

Caroline punched him on the shoulder. 'Tonight's sorted, so don't bother arguing. It's going to piss down later, so you're coming underground with us . . .'

Major Stephen Brereton had been as good as his word. By mid-afternoon, photos and descriptions of the four men in the tank crew were being faxed through to the Incident Room. Holland and Kitson had stood over the machine as the information came through, inch by inch. They cleared a desk, laid it all out and looked for the answer that they hoped would be somewhere in front of them. Brigstocke had been right in guessing that the photos would not do the job on their own. They were simple head-and-shoulder shots of the four men in uniform, taken shortly after each had enlisted, but enough was likely to have happened since then to change the way each of the men looked.

They studied the information sheets on Hadingham, Bonser and Eales: dates of birth and of enlistment; potted service histories; basic physical details.

'Blood group doesn't help us,' Kitson said, reading. 'Eales and Hadingham are both O positive . . .'

Holland was the one who spotted it. 'Found him . . .'

'Show me.'

Kitson looked over Holland's shoulder and Holland pointed to the description of Trooper Alec Bonser. The Driver.

'He was five feet nine look, same as our John Doe. Eales and Hadingham were both six-footers. The body in Westminster Morgue has got to be Alec Bonser.'

Kitson carried on staring at the sheet of paper.

'It's got to be,' Holland said. 'I don't see any other—'

'You're right, I know.' Kitson pointed to another line of type. 'I was looking for something else. This is good news for *us*, maybe . . .'

Holland saw that Kitson was pointing to the entry under *Next of Kin*: *Barbara Bonser (Mother)*.

Holland let out a long, slow breath and looked around. He could see that Andy Stone, Jason Mackillop and others had been earwigging; that they were hanging on every word. 'What about the death message?' Holland asked.

'I'll sort it.' Kitson gathered up the sheets of paper. 'I'll go and fill the DCI in and get the say-so . . .'

'So we should start looking for Eales and Hadingham, then?'

'Looks like it.' She pulled out one of the sheets, glanced at it and thrust it back at Holland. 'You can make a start on our tank commander while I'm gone.'

As he watched Kitson walk towards Brigstocke's office, Holland wondered what *he* would say to Barbara Bonser if he were in the same position. What his own mother would say if it were *his* death message that was being delivered. He started to sweat, and to feel like he needed to sit down, when he began to wonder how he would react – how he would *really* react – were he ever to be told that anything had happened to Chloe . . .

An hour later the whiteboard had been updated. Blown-up pictures of Jago, Hadingham, Bonser and Eales had been added. The question marks had been removed. They had the names of the two soldiers who might still be alive and finally they had the names of *both* of those who were dead. Now, well into the locate/trace on Ian Hadingham, Holland had come up with nothing. The usual calls and searches to DSS and the National Voters' Register had failed to turn his man up, and though he hadn't expected it to be simple, he was wondering where to go next.

'*This is good news for* us, *maybe . . .*'

It suddenly struck him that he hadn't once put Sophie into any of those painful next-of-kin scenarios that had occupied his thoughts earlier. The realisation came like a fist in the gut; it winded him, and he knew he would be feeling its effects for a while. But at the same time it gave him an idea. A change of direction.

He looked again at Ian Hadingham's information sheet and turned back to his computer.

Brigstocke should have known better. All his years of experience should have told him there were only two chances the day would finish up as well as it had started.

Slim and none.

When he answered the phone and the caller introduced himself by stating his rank, Brigstocke presumed it was the Army Personnel Centre, or perhaps someone from the regimental HQ in Somerset. He was about to pass on his gratitude for their sterling work in getting the details sent across so quickly.

But he was not speaking to an ordinary soldier.

The Special Investigations Branch of the Royal Military Police was the army's equivalent of the CID. It was their job to investigate the more serious offences committed against army personnel and their families. An elite force of fewer than two hundred plainclothes detectives selected from RMP ranks, they had teams in constant readiness to be deployed anywhere in the world. But they were also there to investigate serious crimes committed *by* soldiers; policing their own, in much the same way as the bunch who might well be hauling Tom Thorne across the coals when all this was over. In Brigstocke's mind, this made them spooks; 'rubber-heelers', because you could never hear the buggers coming. If the ordinary squaddie felt the same way about them as the ordinary copper felt about the DPS, Brigstocke guessed they were as popular as turds in a sandpit.

Brigstocke was rarely quick to judge – and was certainly not in Tom Thorne's league – but the SIB man got up his nose from the off. He was a major, which, as far as Brigstocke knew, may well have equated in army terms with his own rank, but there was no reference to it. And certainly no bloody *deference*. He spoke to Brigstocke as if they were colleagues, which, considering he'd never so much as heard of the bloke before, was hugely irritating.

As they were talking – or rather as Brigstocke was listening – he kept wondering if he was on the phone to a copper or a soldier; or some bizarre hybrid of the two. The man certainly had twice the arrogance of either.

And to begin with, at least, he insisted on trying to be jokey.

'It's sod all like they make out on *Red Cap*,' he said. 'The women aren't nearly so attractive, for a start . . .'

'I've never watched it,' Brigstocke said.

The major then went round the houses for a while, chatting about this, that and every other thing: asking Brigstocke how busy he was and comparing caseloads; no rest for the wicked, no thanks for a job well done and you didn't have to be mad to work here but . . .

It took maybe ten minutes before he got to the point: 'So, this business with the tank crew . . .'

Brigstocke repeated what Kitson and Holland had said that first time to Rutherford and Spiby at Media Ops; what they'd said a few days after that when they'd been down to the regiment's HQ in Somerset. He talked about a complex and consuming murder case: two vagrants who, it transpired, had been ex-servicemen, and two others whom they'd been trying to trace. They were trying to catch a killer; there was no more to it than that.

'So, how's it going?'

'We're getting there, slowly. You know how it is . . .'

'You've traced the crew, though. You've got all four names now, yes?'

He'd have got that from the AP Centre. Maybe from Stephen Brereton. It didn't much matter.

'Yes, they came through this afternoon.' *Thinking*: *you fuckers don't hang about, do you?* 'The army's been very helpful . . .'

'Well, of course, why wouldn't we be?'

Brigstocke manufactured a laugh. 'No reason,' he said. 'But if it's anything like the Met, sometimes it's got sod all to do with a desire to help and everything to do with red tape, you know . . .?'

There was a pause then. Brigstocke thought he could hear, through the faint hiss on the line, the sound of pages being turned.

'So, nothing you think we should know about?'

If Brigstocke were the paranoid kind, he might have heard that as *nothing you're not telling us?* If he were really going to town, it might even have been *nothing you're not telling us that we might know already?*

'If I think of anything, I'll get back to you . . .'

Of course, Brigstocke had said nothing at all about the video. He'd been delighted, if a little surprised, that Jesmond, who was normally circumspect about such things, had backed his judgement and authorised him to keep quiet about it.

'I'm sure we'll speak again,' the major said, before hanging up.

They *would* be told about the videotape at some point. Once it ceased being active evidence, it would be handed quietly over, and then it would be up to the Redcaps what they did about it. Then, Brigstocke felt sure, the man he'd just spoken to would be back on the phone. Only this time, he wouldn't be quite as matey . . .

He was still thinking about these conversations, past and future, while Holland was speaking. He'd come into Brigstocke's office and begun to talk about the locate/trace he'd set up on Ian Hadingham.

Brigstocke pushed thoughts of the SIB Major to the back of his mind and concentrated on what Dave Holland was telling him.

'. . . so I went after his *wife* instead,' Holland said. 'Shireen Hadingham was listed as his next of kin. Not much more bloody luck with *her* until I started using her maiden name. She's gone back to calling herself "Shireen Collins" . . .'

'Her and Hadingham split up?'

'Not long after he came out of the army.'

'Did you find her?'

'Yeah. Five minutes. I spoke to her.'

'She confirm the tattoo?' Brigstocke asked.

Holland nodded. 'He was very proud of it, by all accounts.'

On the ceiling, a strip-light that was on its way out buzzed and flickered. Brigstocke could feel the day grinding towards its arse-end. He was aching to get out of the building; to get home and collapse on to a sofa. He wanted nothing more than to open a bottle and let a few children clamber over him for a while. 'Does she know where her ex-old man is?' he asked.

'Oh yes, and she's pretty sure he isn't going anywhere.'

'Get on with it, Dave . . .'

'He's in Denstone Cemetery, just outside Salford.'

Brigstocke stared at Holland. He guessed he wouldn't be opening that bottle for a while yet.

'That's the thing,' Holland said. 'Ian Hadingham killed himself just under a year ago.'

TWENTY-FOUR

Thorne had parted company from Spike, Caroline and Terry T a few hours earlier. Caroline had insisted that they'd see him later – 'back at our place' – before she and Spike had disappeared, and Terry had wandered off in search of strong drink. On the pretence of doing the same thing, Thorne had gone his own way, grateful for the chance to spend some time alone; to get on the phone to Dave Holland and catch up with developments.

Things had been moving bloody quickly . . .

He'd never been one to write a lot of stuff down; certainly no more than he'd had to, and that was quite enough. He'd grown accustomed to carrying around a lot of information in his head, both mundane and monstrous, and to the fact that some of the grislier details had a habit of lodging there, unwanted, like the melody to some anodyne pop song. Working as he was, though there were a few bits and pieces scribbled on scraps of paper in his rucksack, he was having to remember much more than he normally would.

Now there were four more names he was not likely to forget in a hurry. Hadingham, Eales, Bonser and Jago. A quartet of soldiers, of killers. Perhaps of dead men . . .

Thorne had been less than gobsmacked to learn that ex-Corporal Ian Hadingham was already dead. There were no details as yet, but he'd have put money on the fact that this 'suicide' was about as kosher as the 'accidental' hit and run that had killed Trooper Chris Jago. And there was no doubt whatsoever as to how Alec Bonser, the driver of the tank, had died.

That was three out of four . . .

It was by no means clear cut, of course, but it certainly added credence to the theory that the crew was being targeted by the man who had shot the video; that whoever had been behind the camera on that ugly day in 1991 was doing the killing.

The warren of pedestrian subways that ran beneath Marble Arch had probably looked like a good idea on paper; in much the same way that sixties tower-blocks had seemed to make perfect sense until those unlucky enough had actually started to live in them. The tunnels honeycombed from Oxford Street to Edgware Road; from the tube station into Hyde Park, in a maze of long, intersecting corridors from which there were no fewer than fourteen different entrances and exits. By day, these subways were eerie enough. Once darkness had fallen, though the subways themselves were well lit for the most part, anyone with any sense would risk sprinting across four lanes of traffic rather than venturing underground.

When Thorne had been here a few days before, the morning he'd met Holland at Speaker's Corner, an old woman had been sitting on a bench outside Exit 6, feeding the pigeons. It had taken Thorne a few moments to notice her, to make her out clearly behind the curtain of wings, the shifting mass of greys and browns and slick-wet blues that surrounded her. The birds had engulfed the tiny figure, walking across her lap and sitting on her head and shoulders. They swarmed in a grubby mass around her feet and perched on every spare inch of the bench and on the handle of the shopping cart by her side. It had been a disturbing image, as though she might be consumed, but as Thorne had walked past he could see that the woman looked perfectly content. She'd sat there smiling, a cigarette dangling from her lips, talking happily to the pigeons as they flocked to devour only the crumbs from her hand. Thorne had slowed to listen, but whatever the old woman had been saying was lost beneath the noise of the feeding-frenzy.

Now, as he walked towards the subway entrance, there was only a mottled carpet of pigeon-shit around the bench as evidence of the woman's presence. If she were ever to disappear, the Council's Cleaning Department would have to be considered prime suspects . . .

Even halfway down the stairs, the sound changed. The noise of the traffic above became a hum; a low drone broken only by the bleat of a car horn or the distorted wail of an emergency siren. By the time Thorne was in the subway itself, though the noises from the street had receded, those from closer around him had become amplified. The ordinary sound of a cough, of an empty can blown or kicked along, of his own footsteps, was suddenly spookier; a full second passing between the sound itself and its echo, carried back on the wind that didn't so much whistle as growl along the concrete corridors.

The tunnels were about eight feet wide and more or less the same high. Once they might have seemed futuristic, these straight tubes with lights mounted every few feet along the walls, but now they were simply unnerving. Stinking of urine and danger and something sickly-sweet that Thorne couldn't quite place.

The tiles that ran along some walls, and the complex mosaics that were crumbling from others, contrasted with the graffiti-covered metal doors. Thorne guessed they concealed pipework. Small metal speakers were mounted along the ceiling. They were presumably there to carry Underground announcements, but something about the place made it easy to imagine a robotic voice conveying information to the survivors of a nuclear blast.

As Thorne walked deeper into the maze of tunnels, one or two people began to move past him. They all wore rucksacks or carried sleeping bags, and some had large sheets of cardboard folded under their arms. In each corridor there were already a number of people sleeping. At least, Thorne presumed there were; it was difficult to tell, as some of the boxes – the cardboard coffins, eight or ten feet long –

could have been empty, but Thorne was fairly sure that most were inhabited. He wondered if the pigeon woman was down here somewhere. He briefly imagined her, boxed up beneath a blanket of dirty feathers, waiting for daylight; for the sound of claw-skitter and wing-beat.

When she might feel what it was to be needed again . . .

Thorne came to a T-junction and looked both ways. At the far end of the right-hand tunnel he saw two figures sitting against a wall. Spike and Caroline. He watched as Spike stood and whistled to him. He waved and began walking towards them.

Halfway along the tunnel, Thorne walked past a complex arrangement of boxes: two fastened together, one on top of the other, with a third coming off them at a right angle. A middle-aged black man sat near by, proprietorial outside his unique sleeping quarters. He wore a baggy grey hat that perfectly matched his beard, and the colour of his skin. He looked up from a paperback as Thorne passed and gave him a hard stare. Thorne held the look just long enough to make it clear he knew what he was doing and kept on going.

When he reached Spike and Caroline, Thorne sat down. He pointed back over his shoulder towards the man who, he guessed, was still staring at him. 'Neighbourhood watch?'

'Ollie's a cool bloke,' Spike said. 'He keeps an eye out, you know?'

Caroline moistened a Rizla and completed a skinny roll-up. 'He's also got the only two-storey bedroom down here. It's like one of those hamster houses.'

Thorne looked at the two huge cardboard boxes end-to-end against the wall next to them. 'Where do you get these things?'

'Round the back of Dixons,' Spike said. 'They're for fridge-freezers, you know? Those big, fuck-off American ones, right, Caz?'

'We fold 'em up, stash 'em during the day and then put 'em back together last thing.'

'It's flat-pack, like.' Spike had taken the tobacco and papers, was busily rolling a fag of his own. 'Same as you get from Ikea, only cheaper . . .'

Caroline lit her cigarette, inhaled deeply, then pointed to the smaller of the two boxes, letting the smoke go as she spoke. 'That one's yours . . .'

Thorne looked, and realised that Spike and Caroline would be sharing the bigger box. That they'd made the other one up for him.

'We got you some scoff an' all,' Spike said. 'We've already had ours . . . sorry.' He produced a brown KFC bag and handed it to Thorne.

Thorne felt oddly touched. As he reached across for the bag, he was thinking that, in relative terms, there weren't many people he could think of who'd have done as much for him. There were plenty, with far more to their names than these two, who'd have baulked at equivalent acts of generosity.

'Be stone cold by now, like,' Spike said.

Thorne opened the beer he'd brought with him. While he tucked hungrily into the food, the three of them talked. And they laughed a lot. Spike was a natural storyteller and Caroline was the perfect foil; she happily fed him cues and helped him recount tales of life on the street, some of them horrific, despite the humour that Spike was able to wring from their telling. It was no different, Thorne thought, to a copper's war stories; to the gags that flew thick and fast across a room where the walls were smeared with blood and in which one occupant would fail to laugh only because they were dead.

There hadn't been a single night since Thorne had come on to the street when he hadn't sat or lain, desperate for sleep to take away the ache of cold or hunger, and thought that he would give nearly anything for the comfort of his own bed. That he'd have plumbed the depths of depravity for a curry from the Bengal Lancer and a Cash album on the stereo. But, sitting in a stinking subway with two junkies, watching water run down the wall behind them, and with cold KFC settling heavy in his gut, Thorne felt as good as he had in a long while.

'I want to get the stuff for our flat from Ikea,' Caroline said, suddenly. 'And I want a big American fridge.'

Such was the nature of their conversation: tangential; fragmented; comments that referred to conversations long since dead-ended . . .

'Got to get the flat first, like,' Spike said. He pushed his legs out straight, then raised his knees, then repeated the action. 'Yeah? See what I'm saying? Got to get the fucking flat.'

'It'll happen,' Thorne said.

Caroline sniffed once, twice and let her head drop back. She banged it against the wall, over and over again, though never quite hard enough to hurt. She spoke like a child, desperate to cling on to a fantasy; to be convinced that it isn't really the lie she knows it to be. 'When . . . when . . . when . . .?'

'I'm not a fortune-teller,' Spike said.

'Tell me.'

'When we get enough money. You'll have to start nicking stuff from a better class of shop . . .'

'I know how to get the money.'

'Fuck *that*!' Spike was clenching and unclenching his fists; quickly, like he was shaking away a cramp; like he was warming up for something. '*Fuck* that!'

Thorne could see that, all in a rush, things were starting to unravel. Their words were not overtly aggressive, but an agitation, an impatience, a *pain*, was colouring everything they said.

'You talked once about just needing a bit of luck,' Thorne said. 'Remember? You never know when that's going to happen.'

'Right, he's right,' Spike said.

Caroline snapped her head up and stared at Thorne. 'I know it's going to happen, because it *always* happens, and it's always *bad*.'

Spike shook his head, kept on shaking it. 'No . . . no way, no way . . .'

'I don't know anyone who has the good sort,' she said. 'We only have the shit kind. We get luck that's fatal . . .'

They were starting to talk over each other. 'When it comes, we'll have enough money to get everything we want. Everything.' Spike was grinning from ear to ear, jabbering, high and fast. 'We'll get a place with room for loads of fucking fridges and the best sound system and all great stuff in the kitchen and whatever . . .'

'You're dreaming . . .'

'We can have massive parties, and when we feel like it we can check in to one of them posh places in the country and get straight, and then when we're well and truly sorted we can get Robbie back . . .'

Caroline flinched and dragged her eyelids down. When she opened them again, though she made no sound, her eyes were wide behind a film of tears. She cast them down to the floor, her fingers spinning the thin leather bracelets around her wrist.

'He's here,' Spike said suddenly.

As fast as Thorne could turn to see the man walking towards them down the tunnel, Caroline was on her feet and on her way to meet him. It didn't take very long. There were not much more than half a dozen grunted words of exchange before the more important commodities were handed over.

Thorne looked back to see Spike unrolling a bar-towel on the floor, revealing three or four thin syringes, a plastic craft knife and a black-bottomed spoon with a bent handle. He then produced a small bottle of Evian from behind one of the boxes, looked across at Caroline, who was on her way back. Thorne could see the goose pimples clearly, the sheen that he'd thought was grease from the fried chicken.

'Get a move on, Caz, I'm sick . . .'

Caroline sat back down and passed over a matchbook-sized wrap of folded white paper.

Spike snatched up the cigarette lighter, talking ten to the dozen as he opened the wrap, smoothed it out on the floor. 'Great to see Terry again, though, yeah? Told you he was a good bloke, like. He'll be fucking bladdered by now, off his fucking head somewhere with a few of Radio Bob's old cronies. Bunch of nutters, most of 'em, but Terry's not proud who he drinks with, like . . .'

Using a supermarket reward card, Spike flattened out the heroin, shaped it carefully until he was satisfied. He thrust the card at Caroline. 'You cut, I'll choose.'

Caroline moved away from the wall, shuffled towards Spike, and towards the heroin. Now Thorne could see that she was every bit as strung-out as Spike was. Her tongue came out to take the sweat from around her lips. The translucent covers on the subway lights cast an odd glow across everything, but it wasn't this which gave her skin the colour of the old newspapers that blew down the tunnels. 'Don't fuck about,' she said. 'Cook it all . . .'

Spike funnelled the wrap and carefully poured every grain of brown powder on to the spoon. 'You do me first, yeah?'

'Piss off. I'll do myself, *then* I'll do you.'

'No way. You won't be in any fit state to do fuck all then.'

'Just get a move on, tosser . . .'

Spike drew water up into the syringe, then let some out until he had just the right amount. He leaned down, concentrating hard as he released the water into the bowl of the spoon, then used the end of the syringe to mix the heroin into it.

And Thorne watched . . .

He wasn't shocked, but he'd never worked on a drugs unit; he'd never been this close to it before. He sat and stared, gripped by the process. Fascinated by the ritual of it all.

'You got vinegar?'

Caroline reached into her pocket, pulled out tissues, a plastic Jif lemon, the pile of sachets she'd grabbed earlier in the café. She handed a sachet to Spike. He bit off the end, squeezed some vinegar into the mixture and continued to stir.

'What's that for?' Thorne asked.

'This lot was only twenty quid,' Caroline said. 'It's not pure, so it don't mix very easy. The vinegar helps it dissolve a bit better . . .'

Thorne reached across for the plastic lemon on the floor. 'Making pancakes later?'

Spike put down the syringe and picked up the lighter. 'Taste well strange if we did, mate.' He held the flame beneath the spoon, nodded towards the lemon in Thorne's hand. 'It's not fucking lemon juice in there.'

'Anyone tries it on, they get a face full,' Caroline said.

Thorne took the cap off, sniffed, then drew his face sharply away from the pungent kick of the ammonia.

Spike laughed. 'I've got my weapon, she's got her's, like . . .'

Then Thorne became aware of another smell: the syrupy kick of the heroin as it began to bubble on the spoon; the vinegar slight, but noticeably sharp, beneath. He realised that this was the smell he'd noticed earlier. He held his breath . . .

Caroline reached over for the needle. She tore it from the plastic sleeve, and, after pulling off the orange cap, she attached it to the syringe.

'Come on, we're there,' Spike said.

There were a number of cigarette butts, of varying sizes, scattered across the bar-towel. Caroline took one from the bobbly, maroon material and used the knife to cut a thin slice from the filter, then dropped it into the liquid. Thorne thought it looked like those inedible slivers of something or other you got in spicy Thai soup . . .

While Spike held the spoon steady, Caroline placed the tip of the needle flat against the section of filter and drew the liquid through it, up into the syringe. Again, she expunged some of it back into the spoon to be sure she had exactly half.

'For fuck's sake, Caz, get a shift on . . .'

'This is for your benefit, mate, to make sure you get your share.' She lifted the spoon and placed it on the floor, out of harm's way. The handle had been bent in such a way that the bowl rested flat on the concrete.

Spike had already rolled up the sleeve of his faded, red hoody. As Caroline put the needle to his skin, he twisted the material that was gathered above his elbow and made a fist.

Caroline grunted as she dug around for a vein . . .

Spike moaned as she found one; as she drew blood back into the syringe; as the red billowed into the brown, like wax in a lava lamp; as she pushed the plunger.

'Flush it . . . flush the fucker . . .'

Twice, three times, she drew the blood back into the syringe and pressed it back into the vein. By the third time, Spike was nodding; each bounce of his head taking it lower. He raised it slowly, one last time to smile at Thorne, to beam like a baby at Caroline. 'Time for bed, said Zebedee . . .'

Caroline had already begun to clean out the syringe, drawing water in from the bottle and squirting it away on to the floor. She leaned across to kiss Spike, then gave him a push. 'Into your box, you silly bastard . . .'

Spike half fell, half crawled into the cardboard box, until all Thorne could see were the soles of his trainers. After only a few seconds, they stopped moving. Then Thorne watched as Caroline flushed the syringe again. She cursed, announced that the thing was 'juddery', and rooted among her collection of sachets for a pat of butter to smear around the plunger. Her movements were practised and precise, and she bit off the ends of her words as she talked, like they were bitter on her lips.

'Aren't you worried about sharing needles?' Thorne asked.

She shrugged. 'It's only him and me . . .'

'But they're easy enough to get.' He pointed at the bar-towel. 'You've got new ones.'

'Everyone thinks we've got AIDS anyway, don't they?'

Thorne stretched out his legs and opened his mouth, but before he could speak she was shouting at him to be careful, and moving quickly to avert any risk of the spoon being knocked over; of losing the precious liquid pooled in its bowl.

'Who's Robbie?' Thorne asked.

She dipped the syringe back into the spoon, put the needle to the filter and drew up the remainder of the heroin. 'My kid. From before I met Spike. He'll be ten now.' She held the syringe up to the light. 'I lost him.'

Thorne watched as she pushed down a sock and flexed her foot. 'I'm sorry . . .'

She looked up briefly from what she was doing. 'See what I mean about luck, though?' A smile that seemed to hurt appeared for just a moment. 'Mind you, my luck might have been shit, but at least Robbie's hasn't been too bad. It was his good luck to get taken away from me, right?'

Thorne couldn't think of anything to say. He could only imagine how badly she needed what the needle she was holding could give her.

For another few seconds she tried to get the needle into the right position, but it was tricky. She was right-handed and the vein she was after was above her left ankle. She looked up at Thorne, sweat falling off her. 'Could you give me a hand with this?'

'I'm a bit shit with needles . . .'

'Please . . .?'

Thorne had known there might be such moments; he hadn't signed on to go undercover thinking it would be easy. That he would never need to make tough choices. It took him only a second or two to realise that, as choices went, this was actually one of the easier ones.

It was the least he could do . . .

He could feel something shift – in himself as well as in Caroline – as he pushed the drug into her. He swung round when it was finished, so that he was sitting next to her against the wall. He let her head fall on to him as she began to nod. 'I was thinking about this money thing,' he said. 'I know Spike doesn't like to ask, but couldn't his sister help? Just to get you two started, maybe?'

'Sister . . .'

'I know he's funny about it, but it sounds like she wants to help him.'

Now the words dribbled from her, falling in thick, sloppy threads without emphasis or cadence. 'His sister's dead; died fucking ages ago. Years. When he was still at home . . .'

'Caroline . . .?'

It was maybe half a minute before she continued. 'When he was still at home, his dad used to mess with 'em, you know? With both of 'em. Used to hurt him and his sister and he couldn't stand it, so he got out.

'Got the fuck out . . .

'He was older than she was, you see? A couple of years. Older. So he left her there, and then a bit later on . . . six months or something, you'd have to ask him, was when she took a load of pills. Chucked 'em down like Smarties . . .

'Spike was . . . you know? He was very fucked up. There was a nasty scene when they buried her . . . That was the last time he saw anyone in the family. That was it for good then.'

'He knows it wasn't his fault, doesn't he?' Thorne asked.

'Like Smarties . . .'

Thorne could hear someone singing in one of the adjoining subways. He was stroking Caroline's hair. 'I don't think it's hurting anyone that Spike pretends . . .'

Caroline groaned.

'Everybody does it to some extent or other,' Thorne said. 'When they lose someone. People bang on and on about *letting go*, like it's the healthy thing to do, like we don't all need a bit of fucking comfort. We all keep our loved ones alive somewhere . . .'

But she couldn't hear him any more.

At some point during the night, Thorne was woken by something. He reached out to touch the cardboard on every side of him. He was hot and stinking inside his sleeping bag.

From a few feet away, he could hear Spike and Caroline making love. The noises they made, their cries and the movement of their bodies inside the box seemed urgent and desperate. His hand moved to his groin, but did not stay there for very long. He was touched rather than excited by what he could hear: there was a reassurance in their passion, in the simple desire of each to please the other.

Thorne eventually drifted back to sleep, soothed by the rhythm of it and comforted by the affirmation of need. By an honest moment of human contact; by an act of love that had more meaning on cardboard than it might have had on silk.

The next time Thorne woke, he knew the cause straightaway; he could feel the mobile phone vibrating in his coat pocket. He groped for it, getting hold of the thing just as the shaking stopped. The glow from the illuminated screen lit up lines of grime on the heel of his hand; it was 6.18 a.m. and it had been Holland calling . . .

It rang again almost immediately.

Thorne pushed his way out of the box and took a few steps away from where Spike and Caroline were still sleeping. He squatted down, answered the phone with a whisper.

'Dave?'

'Thank fuck for that . . .'

During the short pause that followed, Thorne stood and waited for his head to clear a little. A plastic bag flapped along the tunnel and he shuddered as the draught whipped into him; icy against clammy skin.

'I just wanted to make sure you were alive,' Holland said.

'That's thoughtful, but it's a bit bloody early—'

'They've found another body. We haven't got anyone down there as yet.'

Thorne could smell piss and sugar, vinegar and grease. He glanced up and down the corridor, checking that there was no movement from any of the boxes. He wondered if the body might be that of Ryan Eales; if the killer had finally completed the set.

'Sir . . .?'

'I'm listening,' Thorne whispered.

'A rough sleeper, looks like the usual method, in the doorway of a theatre behind Piccadilly Circus. D'you see what I'm getting at?'

Thorne saw exactly.

'*Just keeping it warm for you, obviously.*'

Now his head was clear, but the rest of him was suddenly leaden. He could feel a prickly heat rising . . .

There was a grunted laugh of relief before Holland spoke again. 'I just wanted to be sure,' he said. 'I thought it might be you . . .'

Thorne leaned back against the wall, breathing heavily. He stared down at the discarded chicken bones and scattered flakes of leprous-looking batter.

And was violently sick.

PART THREE

LUCK OF THE DRAW

TWENTY-FIVE

Holland and Stone stood on the platform at Stockport station, waiting for their connection to Salford. Both had hands thrust deep into pockets, and as they gazed along the track in the hope of seeing the train's approach, they could see the rain coming down in skewed, billowing sheets.

'Fucking hell,' Stone said, miserable. 'I'm still wet from the other night . . .'

Holland nodded, remembering the downpour as they'd gathered at the crime scene, waiting for the sun to struggle up. The rain had hissed off the arc lights, and the only dry body there was curled up and stiffening in the theatre doorway. As with the other victims, there hadn't been a great deal that was recognisable about Terence Turner. He'd finally been identified by a friend thanks to the chain and padlock around his neck. Later, this had been removed with a hacksaw by a mortuary assistant, just prior to Phil Hendricks getting to work and doing some cutting of his own . . .

'I'm going to see if I can grab some coffee,' Stone said. 'D'you want some?'

Holland eagerly accepted the offer and Stone walked towards the station concourse in search of what would be their third cup of the day.

It was a little over twenty-four hours since they'd found the body, and Holland had slept for perhaps three of them.

It was accepted that the first twenty-four hours were 'golden'; that this was when they had the best chance of picking up a decent lead. As far as Holland was aware, at that moment they still had nothing, and he'd be surprised if anything changed. It wasn't always just a killer they were up against. Care and caution could get thrown to the wind in the name of urgency, and adrenaline was easily swamped by fatigue and protocol.

After they'd wrapped things up at the murder scene, a DS from the Intelligence Team had conducted the 'hot debrief' at Charing Cross police station. Every officer who'd been present had run through the notes in their incident report book and made a statement. These would need to be collated and added to the duty officer's report and the log that would later be completed by the DCI. This was all part of the procedure instituted in the wake of the Lawrence Report. There were those who thought it would mean fewer mistakes. Others, including Tom Thorne, were more sceptical. They thought that it was less about doing the right thing than being seen to do it.

Thorne . . .

This was what, for some of them at least, had given the latest murder an unsettling significance, had brought it far closer to home. Those on the team who knew of Thorne's role in the investigation had come to an obvious, and disturbing, conclusion. Holland, Brigstocke and Hendricks had stared at the battered body of a man in a doorway; had watched it being bagged up and loaded into a wagon; had seen the progress of the pathologist's blade through its flesh, and known, as they looked on, that it should have been the body of Tom Thorne that was suffering such indignities.

Holland looked up, watched Stone walking back towards him with the drinks and thought about the phone conversation two nights before . . .

'*That's thoughtful, but it's a bit bloody early.*'

He'd rung from home as soon as he'd been contacted about the discovery of the body. Sophie had been woken by the initial call, and he'd gone into the living room so she wouldn't hear him talking to Thorne.

He'd felt a little embarrassed at how relieved he'd been to hear the miserable git's voice.

It was strange: Thorne had taken longer than anyone else to grasp the significance of just where Turner's body had been found. Maybe Holland had caught him at a bad time . . .

'Train's coming in,' Stone said, still a few feet away.

Holland looked back and saw the train rounding a bend, moving towards them through rain that was getting heavier. The huge wipers were moving fast across the locomotive's windscreen.

Stone seemed to have cheered up a little. He put on a coarse, Hovis accent: 'It's grim up north,' he said.

Holland smiled and took his coffee, thinking that it wasn't exactly a bed of roses back where they'd come from.

'Do you want me to tell you how many of those kicks could have killed Terry Turner on their own? How many different bones were broken? How many of his teeth were actually smashed up into his nose?'

'Only if you want to put me off my lunch,' said Thorne.

They were sitting in a dimly lit pub, south of the river near the Oval. A television was mounted high on one wall. *Through the Keyhole* served only to highlight the lack of atmosphere in the place. Aside from a couple in their thirties who scowled at each other across scampi and chips, Brigstocke and Thorne were the only customers.

Brigstocke knew that, with Thorne looking the way he did, they'd have had a fair amount of privacy even if the place had been much busier. Though the bruises had faded to the colour of nicotine stains, Thorne was still far from a pretty sight. That said, though, he had never been a *GQ* kind of man, and many had given him a wide berth even when he *hadn't* looked like a battered sack of shit. Brigstocke had said as much to him as they'd collected drinks and cheese rolls from the bar.

Thorne held up his Guinness and smiled. 'Cheers, mate.'

'Those clothes are actually starting to smell . . .'

'I think *you're* the one they're worried about,' Thorne had said. He'd nodded towards the couple who'd given the two of them a long, blatantly curious look when they'd walked in. 'They think I'm some sort of over-the-hill rent boy and you're a *very* pervy businessman on a limited budget.'

The jokey tone hadn't lasted long . . .

'You said that going undercover would just be about gathering information,' Brigstocke said. 'We've got that information now. We know who the victims are, and we know why it's happening, so give me one good reason for you to carry on.'

'Because the killer hasn't gone anywhere.'

'We talked about this when you came to me with your stupid idea in the first place . . .'

'Things are much different now,' Thorne said.

'Fucking right they're different.' Brigstocke glanced towards the couple, then across at the woman who stood smoking behind the bar. He lowered his voice. 'The night before last it was *you* he tried to kill . . .'

Thorne put the half-eaten cheese roll back on to his plate. He wasn't hugely hungry. He'd gone to the Lift early and put away a full breakfast while he waited in vain for Spike or Caroline to turn up. Thorne hadn't seen either of them since the previous morning. He'd left the subway when Holland had called with news of the murder, then returned a few hours later to wake them; to tell them that he'd been into the West End and seen the police gathered outside the theatre.

To tell them that Terry was dead . . .

'You're not willing to consider the possibility that Terry Turner being kicked to death in that doorway was a bizarre coincidence, are you?' Thorne looked at Brigstocke. 'I thought not . . .'

'The killer knows who you are,' Brigstocke said.

'Thanks to one too many cans of Special Brew, the world and his fucking wife know there's an undercover copper on the streets.'

'Right, but this bloke knows it's *you*.'

'I'm well aware of that . . .'

'Do you think he knows you personally? Is it someone you've met?'

Thorne stared into his beer. 'He mistook Terry Turner for me, so I doubt it.'

'It was dark. It was pissing with rain. Turner might well have been out of it, asleep, with his back to the killer . . .'

'Terry was a foot taller than I am,' Thorne said. 'I can't see it.'

The door opened and a man walked in leading a greyhound. He climbed on to a stool at the bar and the dog dropped flat at his feet. The man exchanged a word or two with the barmaid, ordered a pint and turned to stare at the TV.

'We can skirt around the obvious question all bloody day . . .' Brigstocke said.

Over by the bar, the greyhound raised his head for a moment, yawned and let it drop again. The dog looked like he couldn't give a fuck, and so did his owner. The man seemed far more at ease than Thorne imagined him to be behind his own four walls: he looked at home; he looked like himself.

'Tom?'

'I'm listening . . .'

'Why? That's what we need to address. Why on earth does he come after you?'

Thorne took a second to collect his thoughts. 'OK, this is the best I can come up with, and you're not going to like it. I reckon he's shitting himself.'

'*He's* shitting himself?'

'I think he's panicking. I think he knows we're getting close. Maybe not to him, not as yet, but he doesn't feel safe because he knows we've put the nuts and bolts of it together. Like you said, we've got the names and we've got a motive. If Eales is still alive, and we can find him, the killer knows he can be identified.'

'So why not just kill Eales?'

'Maybe he already has,' Thorne said. 'Look, all I'm really saying is that I don't think this bloke's that bloody clever. He's felt cornered, he's started to panic and he's reacted, and I don't think there's a lot more to it than that. Who knows? Maybe he thinks I'm such a brilliant detective that he needs to get me out of the way.'

'Now it's getting really far fetched.'

'Whichever way you look at it, it wasn't a very clever thing to do, but I think we're talking about someone who works on instinct, you know? If we're right about the blackmail angle, this whole thing is about him feeling threatened and trying to protect himself . . .'

The pub's business rocketed as a pair of lads came through the door. The dog barked half-heartedly and was silenced by a nudge from his master's boot. The barmaid lit another fag from the butt of the last one, and on TV, a blonde with a smile as overcooked as her tan was promising to find an elderly couple their dream home in the sun.

Brigstocke tore open a bag of crisps and leaned across the table. 'All this stuff he knows. How exactly does he know it?'

'That's the bit you're not going to like,' Thorne said.

'We're back to him being on the Job, are we?'

'I'm starting to think it's likely. If I'm right about why I was targeted, I can't see how else he'd know what was going on, unless he was a copper.'

'*If* you're right . . .'

'He knew more than who I was, Russell. He knew where I'd be.' Thorne pictured Terry T, fingering the padlock at his throat, offering to share the doorway that even now they were still trying to scrub the blood out of. 'Where I was *supposed* to be.'

Brigstocke said nothing for several moments. His face, distorted as it was through his glass of water, made it clear he was finding Thorne's point a hard one to argue against. 'So who are we talking about? How many people knew where you were sleeping?'

'You, Holland, Hendricks. Brendan Maxwell at the Lift. McCabe and maybe one or two others at Charing Cross.'

'Was McCabe's name last for any particular reason?'

'I just think he's worth looking at. Him and a few of his team.'

'Looking at?'

'Maybe we could get a couple of Intel lads on it. Keep an eye on him . . .?'

Brigstocke looked drawn suddenly, like another weight had been added to a load that was already unbearable. 'This kind of thing's easy to suggest. It's a piece of piss in a pub, but actually getting it done is a fucking nightmare. You don't really grasp any of that, do you, Tom? Christ, putting a DI under surveillance on the strength of something like this, on the strength of very little, is asking for trouble.'

Thorne remembered something he'd said to McCabe that still held true. 'I can't speak for you,' he said, 'but some of us are in plenty of trouble already. I don't think a bit more's going to make a lot of difference.'

Thorne stared and Brigstocke stared back at him; a grim expression that stayed frozen on the DCI's face for several seconds, until he stuffed a handful of crisps into his mouth.

Shireen Collins – Ian Hadingham's ex-wife – was a petite, attractive black woman who Holland guessed, once he'd seen her up close, to be somewhere just the right side of forty. She presented a fair bit younger – her hair in corn rows and her clothes suitably sporty – though with half a dozen kids under five running about, a tracksuit and trainers were probably the most practical choices.

She worked as a childminder, and Holland and Stone had arrived to find that she was looking after four children that day. 'Plus two of my own,' she told them, pointing out a boy and a girl. 'Those are mine. The really evil ones . . .'

'They're nice-looking kids,' Stone said.

'The older two, *Ian's* two, are both at school.'

The flat, on the southern side of Salford, was on the ground floor; one of three in a Victorian conversion. 'The people upstairs work all day,' Collins said as she showed them in. 'So we can make as much noise as we like, which is great. Four- and five-year-olds make a *lot* of noise.'

From what Holland and Stone could make out, there were a couple of bedrooms and a large living room that ran off a kitchen–diner. They sat at a long kitchen table, from which Collins had been clearing the remains of lunch when they'd arrived. 'There's a bit left if you fancy chicken nuggets and potato faces,' she said. Having missed breakfast, Holland was seriously tempted, but the offer was declined. In the next room, visible through a serving hatch, the kids were gathered in front of a widescreen TV. Collins leaned through the hatch and issued gentle but firm instructions until there was something approaching quiet.

'They get half an hour with a video after lunch,' she said. 'So that's about as long as *we've* got.'

Holland threw his overcoat across a kitchen chair. 'That'll be plenty, Shireen.'

The conversation was not without interruption – punctuated by high-pitched chatter, cartoonish music and the occasional bout of tears from the next room – but Shireen Collins spoke openly enough. It was obvious that at some point she'd felt a great deal for Ian Hadingham. But it was equally clear that she'd moved on. From their marriage, and from his death . . .

'Ian was always a waste of space unless he was in a uniform,' she said. 'When he'd come home on leave or whatever, he'd just sit about feeling sorry for himself. He'd ignore me and he'd ignore the kids most of the time and to be honest, after a couple of weeks, I couldn't wait for him to get back to his bloody regiment. God, that sounds awful, doesn't it?'

'Have you been talking to my girlfriend?' Holland said.

Collins laughed. She tried to explain how it had felt; how she'd once felt jealous of the bond he'd so clearly shared with his pals in the regiment. How she'd resented it, and fought for her husband's attention, and then, in the end, how she'd simply given up competing.

'What happened after Ian came back from the Gulf?' Holland asked.

Collins laughed again, but rather more sadly this time. 'I'm not sure how much of him *did* come back,' she said. 'It was like he was somewhere else in his head and it wasn't a place where I was welcome. Actually, I'm not sure it was a place I'd've liked very much. I know they all went through a lot out there.'

Holland stared straight at Collins. He did not want to catch Stone's eye; he knew Stone would be thinking the same thing he was: *You have no bloody idea . . .*

'He left the army pretty soon after he came home,' Collins said. 'It was all right for a while, for a year or so, and we even talked about having more kids, but something told me not to. That we'd've been doing it for the wrong reasons.'

'What did Ian do,' Holland asked, 'after he left the army?'

'All sorts of things, but none of them for very long, you know? He worked in warehouses, did some security work, tried to retrain as an electrical engineer, but he couldn't hold down a job. Had a bit of a problem with authority. It'd be fine for a few months, then he'd blow it. He was fired more than once for threatening people.' She opened her mouth to say something else, then changed her mind. 'His head was basically messed up afterwards.'

Stone nodded his understanding. 'So he moved out, right?'

'Right. We decided to separate a few years on from that. He moved out and eventually I got this place. He never went far away, like – he wanted to stay close to the kids and that – but he moved around.'

'He got a flat?'

'Lots of different flats. He didn't seem to like staying put too long; plus, he kept falling behind with his rent and getting chucked out of places.'

'How did he react when you met somebody else?' Holland asked. 'It can't have been very easy . . .'

There was a yell from next door. Collins stood to look in on the children, but sat down again quickly enough. 'Ian wasn't exactly thrilled and he had a bit of a problem with Owen.' She pointed towards her young children. 'Owen's their dad. Things got a bit ugly and Ian was a big bloke. He was handy, you know? So we got the police involved and we decided against actually getting married, and it was fine after that. It was fine for me and Owen, I mean, but things went downhill for Ian pretty quickly.'

'Downhill?' Stone said.

'He started dossing down all over the place. Sleeping on people's floors and in shitty bedsits or whatever. Like he'd stopped caring, basically. He was drinking a lot and pissing off all his mates. Not that he had many left by then . . .'

'Did he see any of his old mates from the army?'

'I don't think so.'

'Any of the lads on his tank crew, maybe?'

'He never talked about it,' she said. 'I wouldn't know if he had, but to be honest I'd stopped really listening to him, you know? He went funny the last few years. He talked a lot of rubbish. Before he died he came round to tell me that he was going to turn it all round. Banging on about how he was going to look after me and the kids, how he was going to see us all right. I never told Owen any of that, by the way. He'd've gone mental.'

Holland couldn't resist a glance at Stone this time. 'Did he say how he was going to turn it round? Was he talking about money?'

'Yeah, I think so, but he always had some stupid scheme or other on the go. He was always on about getting himself sorted again. Silly bastard . . .'

'Tell us about when Ian died, Shireen?'

A boy came to the hatch and asked for a drink.

Shireen smiled; told Holland and Stone about her ex-husband's death as she mixed orange squash. 'It was booze and pills,' she said. 'He emptied a couple of bottles of both in some pissy little room just round the corner from here. They didn't find him for a week because the poor sod had nobody to miss him by then.'

'They never found a note, did they?'

'No . . .'

'You never thought it was odd that Ian killed himself?' Stone said. 'Bearing in mind what he'd said about turning his life around and all that.'

She looked at them, unblinking, and Holland thought he could see the unasked question in her confused expression. He thought it said a lot about how Shireen Collins was getting on with her life that she hadn't really asked them why, a year after her ex-husband had died, they wanted to talk to her about him. He also thought that if Hadingham was as big, as *handy*, as she'd said he was, then it couldn't have been easy for whoever had killed him to have forced those tablets down his throat. Mind you, if Hadingham had been pissed before it happened . . .

Suddenly, there were other children demanding drinks and attention and it was clear that half an hour had been a generous estimate.

'I'm sorry,' she said. 'Maybe you could come back . . .'

They'd taken a cab from the station. Stone asked if there was a number they could call or somewhere they could pick up a taxi. She gave them directions to a minicab office five minutes' walk away.

Holland started pulling on his coat. 'Do you mind me asking what you did with all Ian's things?'

'All the stuff he'd left here had gone long before he died,' she said. 'I gave the clothes and a few of his old CDs to a charity shop. A lot of it just went in the rubbish, to be honest.'

'Were there any videotapes?' Stone asked.

She seemed slightly thrown by the question. 'We had . . . blank tapes for recording stuff on. We still use them, I think, for taping the football or *Corrie* or whatever . . .'

'What about the things Ian took with him when he left?'

'No, they gave me everything that was in the room where they found him; all his personal belongings.'

'You don't remember a video tape?'

She suddenly looked embarrassed. She lowered her voice, and tried to look Stone in the eye, but couldn't quite manage it. 'D'you mean like porno?'

Handing Stone his jacket, Holland turned to her. 'It doesn't matter, really. It's nothing . . .'

It was dry outside, but from the look of the sky it was no more than a lull, so they did their best to make the five-minute walk in much faster time.

'She's going to find out what he did eventually,' Stone said.

Holland shook his head. 'It's not up to us.'

'I don't think she'll be that devastated somehow . . .'

'Maybe she will. On her kids' behalf.'

'Right. I suppose it's going to piss on their old man's memory somewhat. Blow the whole war-hero thing.'

'Just a bit . . .'

'We're bang on about the fucking blackmail, though. That's for definite. Hadingham as good as told her he was coming into money.'

'Yeah. I just wish we had something more than what she says he told her.'

'You've become a damn sight harder to please since you became a sergeant, do you know that?'

'You're always hoping there'll be like . . . I don't know, a photocopy of the blackmail demand he made to whoever topped him or something. You know, by some miracle . . .'

'Her testimony's a confirmation though, isn't it?'

'It's just circumstantial, at the end of the day. I mean, it all helps, I'm not saying it doesn't. It's another piece of it. It's a *big* piece. But it's way too late to get any physical evidence, any forensics or whatever, so I can't see us actually pinning it on the bloke when we get him.'

'What about the tape?'

'Maybe he had it with him, which makes sense if he thinks he's going to make some major money out of it, and the killer took it. Or he never had one, which doesn't really pan out if we're sticking with the blackmail idea. Or it's lost . . .'

'Or he left it at home when he moved out and the bloke his wife was shagging taped *Match of the Day* over it.'

'You know, this is one of the many reasons why I'm a sergeant and you're not.'

'Bollocks!'

The rain came then, suddenly, blowing into them from behind and quickly soaking the backs of their legs. Stone carried on swearing, and though they couldn't have been too far from the minicab office, he started to run.

Holland just kept walking and watching Stone disappear into the distance. He couldn't be arsed to try and catch up.

TWENTY-SIX

Thorne tried and failed to make himself comfortable in the doorway of a tatty souvenir shop on Carnaby Street. There were half a dozen of these places knocking out multicoloured Doc Martens and overpriced T-shirts on a street that hadn't been fashionable in donkey's years.

He could remember when London *had* been the centre of everything. When the city could still get away with it, and swing without looking like someone's dad at a school disco. Once or twice around that time, when he'd have been six or seven, his parents had brought him into town to do some shopping, and though they'd tended to avoid the likes of Carnaby Street and had made straight for the department stores, Thorne could still recall seeing young women in floaty dresses and men wearing bright military jackets. Or perhaps he only *thought* he could. He knew that memory tended to work like that. Maybe he was just filling in the gaps with pictures of Terence Stamp and Julie Christie . . .

Either way, because he had at least been there in the sixties, Thorne had viewed the whole 'Cool Britannia' movement of a few years before with a certain degree of cynicism. With Union Jacks on frocks and cars and album covers, what started as a trend had quickly become little more than a marketing bandwagon to be hijacked by everyone from Marks & Spencer to New Labour. Still, Thorne had to admit that bands had at least rediscovered guitars, that tourist numbers had picked up, and that it had given a creative spark to many kids of Spike and Caroline's age.

It remained to be seen if tourists would be flocking to the West End for very much longer. Beneath a headline that read, 'The Latest Victim', a photo of a younger and altogether healthier-looking Terry Turner dominated the front page of the day's *Standard*. The news was well and truly out that Theatreland had become a killing ground.

Thorne wondered if the killer had seen the newspaper. Did he know yet that he'd killed the wrong man?

Before settling down for the night, he'd been along to Marble Arch, had gone down into the subway to see if he could find Spike or Caroline. He'd got little change out of Ollie, who, if anything, had eyed him with even more suspicion and hostility than when they'd first encountered each other.

'I'm looking for my mates,' Thorne had said. He'd pointed along the corridor, to the corner that was now deserted, but where he'd slept alongside Spike and Caroline a couple of nights earlier.

The old man had glanced up from his book. Narrowed his eyes. 'Look somewhere else . . .'

It wasn't as though Thorne had been expecting to find them. He was well aware that Spike and Caroline kept strange hours. He knew what woke them and what put them to sleep.

In his doorway, Thorne pulled himself upright and moved his arms to the outside of his sleeping bag. He stared at the lit window displays across the street and listened to the dance music that was coming from one of the flats above.

He thought again about where the leak might have come from. He *had* to consider McCabe, whatever Brigstocke thought of the idea. Who else knew exactly where he would be sleeping? It was inconceivable that the information could have come from anyone closer to him. What ate away at Thorne was that, somewhere, he knew that he already had the answer. It couldn't be too hard to figure out who had been responsible; it was a basic two-piece jigsaw. Of course, other rough sleepers knew *where* he was, but they didn't have the other piece of it. None of them knew that he was an undercover police officer. At least, he *presumed* none of them knew. Certainty, of any sort, was a luxury he'd given up along with the rest of them, when he'd taken the decision to sleep on the street.

'*Do you want me to tell you how many of those kicks could have killed Terry Turner on their own? How many different bones were broken . . .?*'

Earlier, with Brigstocke, he'd played it down. He'd had to. But now there was no point pretending that what jumped in his guts and sucked away at his breath was anything other than fear. He'd felt it from that first moment underground, when he'd heard about Terry T's death, and it had settled, content inside him. It had quickly made itself at home, coating the walls; clingy and seeping . . .

Thorne had felt afraid a lot more lately. In the recent weeks and months there had been a general apprehension that he could not name, as well as a perplexing, irrational fear of specific things. He'd become jumpy in crowds; he was suddenly scared of escalators and of heights; he'd started feeling increasingly wary in cars. Thorne knew that some people became more nervous about flying the more frequently they walked onboard a plane, and he wondered if he was moving along the same lines.

Or perhaps this susceptibility to fear in all its forms was simply a part of getting older. His father had been afraid of all sorts of bizarre things. Thorne wondered if he was simply turning into his old man. He'd known it would happen eventually, it happened to just about everyone, but the process seemed to have put on a burst of speed with his father's death. It was as though he were part of some twisted, cosmic equation. He felt like he was changing to fill the hole left by his father's passing.

And there was the other thing: the trick that was played on you after the death of a parent. After the death of your last parent, when you became an orphan. The switch that was thrown . . .

For the first time in his life, Thorne was starting to comprehend the pain of being childless; not to *feel* it, not quite yet, but to understand it. He now knew why those desperate for children spoke of it as a hole that needed to be filled. He had started to feel as though that hole might be inside himself somewhere; growing, but still hidden, waiting only for what covered it to drop away. He'd wondered if having children simply to stop the pain of not having them was a good enough reason. Was it the reason why most people became parents? Certainly, he could now begin to guess at the agony that Caroline must feel at being both childless and a mother at the same time.

Losing parents, and losing children . . .

Thorne's mind shifted to the man behind that video camera. The man who had filmed the deaths of four men: four sons; quite possibly four fathers.

How were they ever going to find him if they didn't trace Ryan Eales? The most obvious place to start would have been the army, of course. They might at least have been able to shed some light on what sort of person was out there. What manner of individual might have stood on the black sand, soaked in shadow and petrol rain alongside that tank crew. It would be very difficult to make advances to the army now of course; not after certain . . . important facts material to the case had been withheld. Brigstocke had confessed to Thorne in the pub that keeping the existence of the videotape secret was a decision he was starting to regret.

Thorne had done his best to be sympathetic. 'We're *all* Sherlock Holmes with hindsight, mate. Don't give yourself a hard time about it.'

'If we don't get a result,' Brigstocke had said, 'there'll be plenty ahead of me in the queue . . .'

The music from the flat above the shop opposite had stopped. It was replaced by the tuneless singing of a trio of football fans who came down the street from the side of the Shakespeare's Head and began to move in Thorne's direction. He shrank a little further back into the doorway and watched them pass.

They didn't see him. Or, if they did, they didn't give a toss . . .

In those few, brief moments of clarity that come before sleep, Thorne thought of someone he could perhaps speak to, a person who might at least provide some insight into what had happened on 26 February, nearly fifteen years before. Thorne would have to be careful how he handled it of course, but nobody had come up with anything better.

He drifted off to sleep, deciding that he'd had worse ideas; thinking that he still had the business card stuffed inside his wallet back at the Lift. Hoping that he'd remember all this in the morning.

TWENTY-SEVEN

DS Sam Karim, who took responsibility for such things, had almost finished rejigging the layout of the whiteboard for the umpteenth time.

Still arranged at its centre were the photographs recently provided by the Army Personnel Centre: Chris Jago, Ian Hadingham, Ryan Eales and Alec Bonser. Portraits of four young men, all taken when they'd first been posted to the 12th King's Hussars.

Holland stood and watched while the shape of the case as it stood that day was laid out. It was hard to equate the quartet of fresh faces – scrubbed and set square, a hint of a smile on one or two – with those whom he knew had been hidden behind rain-streaked goggles and muddy kerchiefs; sweating, contorted; the eyes tight shut at the moment when the trigger was pulled.

Elsewhere on the board . . .

The list of those victims who had been murdered simply to disguise the true nature of the crime: Hayes, Mannion, Asker.

Terry Turner, murdered, it would seem, in error; sharing nothing but initials with the man for whom he'd been been mistaken.

The names of those on the fringes of the investigation: Susan Jago, Shireen Collins.

Those who had provided information, statemented or otherwise: Spiby and Rutherford at Media Ops; Brendan Maxwell; Major Stephen Brereton; Poulter and Cheshire at the 12th King's. One name had now been removed from this list, and from the contact sheet circulated to all officers: Paul Cochrane. The services of the National Crime Faculty profiler had been dispensed with, now that the motive for the killings had become apparent even to those without letters after their names.

'Last but not least . . .'

Karim drew a thick, black line down to a crudely drawn square that contained the only remaining question mark on the board. It was largely symbolic: a simple representation of their prime suspect; the man behind the video camera whom they now thought to be the reason why they were all there in the first place.

Karim stepped back and examined his work. It was far from the whole story, of course . . .

There was a side to the investigation that could not be encapsulated in crude capital letters or delineated by magnets and felt-tip pens. Thorne's contribution to the case was missing: information that had originated from him, or from sources close to him, would remain absent. This was also the case with details of the secondary intelligence operation, the small-scale surveillance that had just been mounted on DI John McCabe and several other officers from the Homeless Unit based at Charing Cross. The authorisation for such surveillance was need-to-know information that Brigstocke had passed on to none but his core team. As with any blue-on-blue operation, there was very good reason.

Somebody always knew somebody . . .

Karim walked away, and Holland approached the board. 'You're an artist, Sam.'

Stone was on his way back from the Gents'. '*Piss*-artist,' he said.

Jason Mackillop looked up from his computer and grinned. Stone moved across to join him, laughing at his own joke.

The whiteboard should have been replaced long ago. Countless murders had been mapped out across its surface over many years. As Holland looked, he could see, in what few white spaces were left, the faintest outline of old markings; the swoops and stabs of the pen just visible beneath the scratched and pitted metal. Death, terrible and tawdry; fury, loss, *grief* reduced to scribbled lines and letters; to names and numbers now long since wiped away and replaced. Holland licked the tip of a finger and reached over to rub at one of the ghost names. A name that had refused to fade completely . . .

'Dave?'

Holland started slightly and drew his finger quickly away. He hadn't been aware of Yvonne Kitson moving alongside him. He turned to acknowledge her, then shifted his gaze back to the board.

They both stared at it for a while.

They looked at the sweep of it; the way that so many were ensnared by the tendrils that snaked from its poisonous root. The names of all those it had touched: the innocent and the guilty and the dead. But one name was now prominent.

'How the hell are we going to find Eales?' Kitson asked.

Holland considered the question. 'Do the Home Office have any psychics?'

If they'd been lucky in tracing Ian Hadingham quickly, it had been more than balanced out by the complete lack of anything even resembling progress in the hunt for Ryan Eales.

The team had run 'full research'. Both the CRIS and CRIMINT systems had been scanned a number of times but had yielded nothing. Traces had been run via the National Voters' Register, the DSS, the DVLC and every local housing authority in the country. All major store-card and mobile-phone companies had been contacted, while the Equifax system – a software package giving access to a huge number of financial databases – was being run repeatedly without success. Thus far, save for a driving licence, a National Insurance number and a last known address that were all equally moribund, full research had come up empty.

The first conclusion, based on the fact that the recently deceased are often fairly easy to locate, was that Ryan Eales was probably still alive. The second conclusion was not quite so comforting.

'He doesn't *want* to be found,' Kitson said.

Holland knew she was right. He also knew that if Eales was lying low, he had very good reason for doing so. 'He's hiding from the killer.'

Kitson wasn't arguing. 'There's every chance. If he reads the papers, if he's been in any sort of contact in recent years with the rest of them, or their families, it's odds on he knows at least a couple of the other three are already dead. If so, he'd be justified in thinking he might be next.'

'And he might well have worked out that we know why . . .'

If Eales knew that the police were looking for him, he could guess that they had seen the videotape, so he would not be in any great hurry to step forward; to face the music for what had happened in 1991.

'It's another thing they're going to be good at,' Holland said.

'Who?'

'They're ex-soldiers. The training means that they're better equipped to survive life on the streets, like Bonser and Jago, but it also means they're good at making themselves invisible, if they need to.'

'Like being behind enemy lines,' Kitson said.

Holland thought of something. He walked to the board and pointed to the name '*Poulter*'. 'Remember what he was saying when we went down to Taunton? If Eales ever served with the SAS, or one of those other intelligence units, he'd be even better at all that undercover stuff. And it would explain why we can't find any half-decent records on him . . .'

They looked again at the photograph of Lance Corporal Ryan Eales.

His was one of those faces whose expression had been softened by a smile. He was square-jawed, with wide, blue eyes and a sprinkling of freckles across a flattish nose. Sandy hair dropped into precisely trimmed sideburns; perfect rectangles below the maroon beret.

'He doesn't look all there to me,' Kitson said.

'They *all* look a bit weird,' Holland said. 'But maybe that's because we're looking at it after the fact. Because we know what happened later on.'

'I think you've got to be slightly odd to join up in the first place.'

'Not a lot of choice for some people,' Holland said.

Kitson shrugged, conceding the point. 'No stranger than wanting to become a copper, I suppose.'

'At least they get to travel . . .'

'Why did you join up, Dave?'

Behind them, Stone finished telling Mackillop the same, vaguely offensive joke he'd been telling everyone for days. The TDC laughed on cue.

'The mental stimulation, I think,' Holland said.

'Don't tell me. It's the Spurs–Arsenal game.'

'Well, as you mention it . . .'

'You want tickets for the match next weekend.' Alan Ward sounded amused rather than pissed off at the imagined imposition. 'I seem to remember I told you I could get them.'

'It's not the tickets,' Thorne said. 'Actually, I just wanted to pick your brains about something. Have you got a minute?'

'Glad to get out of this bloody edit, tell you the truth. Hang on . . .'

Thorne could hear Ward's own voice being broadcast in the background. Then he heard the man himself talking to someone: telling them he wouldn't be long, that he'd be outside if there was any problem.

Thorne had walked east to Holborn and then kept going towards the City. Past Smithfield Meat Market and into the ossified heart of the Barbican. This was the only residential estate in the City. Almost as free from pedestrians as it was from traffic, its looming tower-blocks were connected by a series of elevated walkways. Despite the arts centre, the museums and the smattering of trendy shops and restaurants, there was a strangely hostile feel to the place; something humming in the endless walls of concrete that rose up at every turn.

'Right, I'm all yours,' Ward said.

Thorne stepped into shadow, pooled with water beneath an overhang. Pressed the phone to his ear. The small talk was about as small, and over about as quickly, as it could be. Both said they were very busy without going into any detail. Ward said he'd seen Steve Norman quite recently and asked if Thorne had. Thorne told him that he hadn't, and they chatted about football for another minute or two.

'I wanted to ask you about the Gulf,' Thorne said. 'Did you go over? The first time . . .'

'Yeah, I was there. I was a baby reporter back in '91.'

'Right, good.'

'I wasn't a baby by the time I came back, mind you . . .'

'No, I bet.'

'It was fairly heavy,' Ward said. 'You know? I'd not been involved in anything remotely like that until then. Not that I was doing a great deal other than poncing around in front of the camera. But you still *see* stuff . . .'

'That's what I wanted to talk to you about, really. Not about things you might have seen necessarily, but things you might have heard about.'

There was a pause. 'Is this connected to the rough-sleeper murders?'

Thorne had been right when he'd thought this would need careful handling. Ward was sharp; worse, he was a journalist. It hadn't taken much to pique his professional interest. Thorne guessed that Ward had got a sniff of something straight away; the minute he'd answered his phone, and a copper he'd met once, for five minutes, had reintroduced himself.

'What makes you say that?' Thorne asked.

'Nothing particularly. It's the case I'd presumed you were working on, bearing in mind that we met after the press conference.'

It was Thorne's turn to be professional: 'I'm sure you understand that I can't comment on an active investigation.'

'Of course. But I'm *seriously* intrigued . . .'

Ward laughed then, and so did Thorne.

'While you were out in the Gulf, did you ever hear anything about war crimes or atrocities?'

'*Atrocities?*'

'On *our* side . . .'

Another pause.

'There was some stuff that came out a few years ago,' Ward said. 'In an American magazine – the *New Yorker*, I think. There was an incident, an *alleged* incident, on the road from Kuwait to Basra a few days after the ceasefire, when retreating Iraqi columns were attacked by Apaches and tanks. They called it the Battle of Rumailah, but it was just a massacre, by all accounts. A 'turkey shoot' the magazine said. There were civilians in trucks, there was supposedly a bus filled with school kids . . .'

'Jesus . . .'

'There was another one just before the ceasefire, when four hundred Iraqi troops surrendered to a US scout platoon. Some of them were wounded, bandaged up, in clearly marked hospital trucks. They were gathered together, fed and what have you, then, according to reports, another unit turned up in Bradley armoured vehicles and just shot the lot of them. Opened up with machine-guns. This is supposedly based on evidence given by soldiers who were there at the time, but, having said all that, I don't think anybody's ever been prosecuted.'

Thorne moved into sunlight again. He looked up as a jet roared overhead. From where he was standing, the plane appeared and disappeared between the tower-blocks before emerging into a muddy sky and banking towards City Airport.

'What about UK troops?' Thorne asked.

'In terms of war crimes, you mean?'

'Did you ever hear anything?'

'Stuff goes on,' Ward said. 'It always does. Some of the troops were based in Dubai for a lot of the time. I was there myself later on. You could buy sets of photos in corner shops, you know? Soldiers posing with bodies; with arms and legs. Trophies . . .'

'But you were never aware of any specific incidents?'

Ward suddenly sounded a little wary. There was an amused caution in his voice, as if Thorne had changed the steps to the dance that they were performing. 'I think you're going to have to be a *bit* more specific yourself . . .'

Thorne had known he might have to venture into this kind of territory, and he wondered for a second or two if it was worth plunging into the murk. He hardly knew Alan Ward, and couldn't be certain that anything valuable would be gained from talking to him.

But he was equally unsure there was a great deal to lose . . .

'Did you ever hear of anything involving a British tank crew?' Thorne said. While he waited, Thorne watched a couple on a walkway ahead of him. They seemed to be arguing.

When Ward finally answered, his voice was close to a whisper, and Thorne could hear the excitement in it. 'What have you found?'

'Like I said before, I can't—'

'OK, I get it. Look, there were one or two rumours about something. No more than that, as far as I can remember.'

'About a tank crew?'

'Yeah . . . I think so.'

'So, here's the thing,' Thorne said. 'If someone else was involved, someone apart from the four men in a tank crew, who might it be?' He glanced up again. The couple on the walkway were now embracing.

'I'm not with you,' Ward said. 'It could be virtually anybody. You're not really giving me a great deal to go on.'

'Another individual. A fifth man, present when this incident took place.'

'A fifth soldier, you mean?'

'I suppose so . . .'

'Where precisely are we talking about?'

'I don't really know. We have to presume it's somewhere off the beaten track.'

'*Everywhere* was off the beaten track, mate,' Ward said. 'You just mean that geographically, the incident happened in isolation, right?'

That much, Thorne could be fairly certain of. 'Yes.'

'So we're talking about someone with access to a vehicle, then. An officer, perhaps?'

Perhaps, thought Thorne. They were certainly talking about someone who'd had no problem telling the four crewmen what to do. Someone whose orders had been followed.

Perhaps . . .

It was as positive as they were going to get.

'I have to make a small professional plea at this point,' Ward said. 'Can you make sure I'm first in line if this ever comes out?'

Thorne was slightly nonplussed. Ward was clearly every bit as ambitious as he was sharp. Still, bearing in mind that Thorne had called *him*, it was a reasonable enough request. 'I'm not sure I'll have a lot of say in it, to be honest . . .'

'This is what I do, Tom. Seriously, if there does come a time when whatever this is can be made public, I hope to hell you'll come to me. Like I said before, I'm seriously bloody intrigued.'

'Right . . .'

'Whenever you like, Tom. And it goes without saying that my sources always remain confidential. No names, no pack drill.'

'I've got it.'

'And there *are* perks, of course.'

'Are there?'

'Do you want to see the game next week or not?'

Thorne could think of nothing he'd like more. Cursing bad luck and worse timing, he explained to Ward that, much as he'd love the tickets, he'd be far too busy to use them.

Russell Brigstocke viewed the prospect of a conversation with Steve Norman in much the same way as a trip to the dentist: it was something necessary but usually unpleasant. You could put it off and put it off, but you always had to go through with the bloody thing in the end.

And you had to wash your mouth out afterwards . . .

The nature of the investigation meant Brigstocke had been forced to endure a good deal more contact with the Press Office than would normally have been the case. The media had been all over them since Jesmond's first press conference, and Norman – whatever anyone thought of him personally – had proved extremely adept at his job. He'd kept the media's appetite for information sated, and had called in favours from reporters when they were needed. And one was very definitely needed now.

Using the press had brought them, circuitously, to Chris Jago. Now, as the hunt for Ryan Eales ran out of steam, using it again might be the team's last hope of a result. They had already run a fifteen-year-old picture of Eales in the *Standard* – inside the issue with the photo of Terry Turner on the front – describing the soldier as someone whom '*the police would very much like to talk to in connection with . . .*'

The calls were coming in, but they needed more, and they needed them faster.

'I think I can swing *Crimewatch* again,' Norman had said.

'Tonight?'

Over the phone, the senior press officer's voice had sounded even more nasal, more irritating than it did face to face. 'This is still a major inquiry, Russell, so I think it should be doable. They'll bump something else off until next week . . .'

They'd broadcast a reconstruction of Paddy Hayes' killing on the show – which BBC1 put out live on a Friday evening – a month before, and there had been a further appeal for information after Robert Asker's murder. In itself, this had gone down as something of a coup. The programme-makers were notoriously squeamish, with a distaste for anything overtly graphic. The sensitivities of the viewers had to be their primary concern. Murder was acceptable, but only if it was tastefully done, and not too scary.

Taking the case on to such a show was usually a last resort, but most senior officers still considered it worth doing. It was television, so when they were asked for help, people reacted in much the same way as they would to a phone-in question on a quiz show: the answer might not be the right one, but there was always a healthy response.

'So what do we think?'

'That's great, Steve,' Brigstocke had said. 'Thanks.' The platitude had screamed inside his skull like the squeal of a dentist's drill.

'Just a quick update, yes? Something in the "urgently need to trace" round-up towards the end of the show.'

'That's all we need.'

'We'll get Eales' picture in vision for as long as possible. Wait for the phone lines to light up.'

'Let's hope so . . .'

'Well, even if nothing concrete comes of it, it's as much about being *seen* to do something a lot of the time, right?'

Brigstocke had been desperate to hang up by this point. To rinse and spit. 'I'd better go and talk to the chief superintendent,' he'd said. 'We probably need to put our heads together . . .'

'How clean is your suit?' Norman had asked.

Brigstocke had spoken to Trevor Jesmond after that, talked about tone and message and budget. Then he'd phoned home and asked his wife to set the video. Now, he stepped into the Incident Room and called for hush. The TV appeal would generate a lot of calls. A fair few nutters would come crawling out of the woodwork, but they would all have to be listened to, their information transcribed as if it were the Word of God, and every lead, no matter how iffy it sounded, would need chasing up.

'Usual good news–bad news routine,' he said. 'Most of you can forget about your weekend. Fishing, football, feet up, trip to B&Q with the missus. Not going to happen . . .'

A voice from the back of the room: 'Is this the good news or the bad news?'

Brigstocke shouted above the laughter. 'But the overtime's been approved . . .'

Thorne felt happier, more sure of himself and his surroundings, as the noise of traffic began to grow louder; as people moved around him in all directions and he could taste the fumes. Moving away from the

Barbican's eerie sprawl, he walked up what had once been Grub Street, and thought about his conversation with a man whose profession, in its worst excesses, had come to be associated with the name.

There'd been no thunderbolts of insight, of course; nothing to quicken the pulse overmuch. But there was enough to think about. Thorne had already considered the possibility that the man behind the video camera had been an officer. It was a reasonable enough supposition, but it was still interesting to hear it from Ward; to have the notion validated by someone who'd actually been there. There was no room for more than four men in a Challenger tank. The fifth man had to have got there under his own steam. If Brigstocke could eke any more information out of the army, it might be worth asking which ranks would have routinely had access to vehicles back then.

And there was something else to interest the DCI: '*There were one or two rumours about something . . .*'

If rumours of an atrocity had reached the press at the time, then it was safe to assume that the army would have been fully aware of them. Thorne felt pretty sure that they were every bit as aware fifteen years on. If the army knew at least *something* of what might have gone on on 26th February 1991, that would certainly explain the call from the Special Investigation Branch of the Royal Military Police.

He would enjoy telling Russell Brigstocke that he wasn't *completely* paranoid . . .

The light changed on the pavement ahead of him, and Thorne looked up to see the sky darkening rapidly. He watched a ragged finger of cloud point its way behind a glass high-rise on Farringdon Road, and he followed it back towards the West End.

TWENTY-EIGHT

'Good of you to have made an effort,' Thorne said.

'Eh?'

Thorne looked over at Hendricks, straight-faced. 'The dosser's outfit . . .'

'Cheeky fucker.'

'Honestly, it's nice of you to try and blend in. Maybe you should knock all this medical stuff on the head and try working undercover yourself. You've obviously got a gift.'

'I'm glad one of us has,' Hendricks said.

Save for the metallic aftertaste of bargain burgers, they might have been relaxing over a takeaway from the Bengal Lancer. Were it not for the rain, and the view of huddled bin-bags, they might have been watching TV in Thorne's front room; arguing about the football like a grossly unfit Gary Lineker and a shaven-headed, multiply pierced Alan Hansen.

As it was, they were leaning against a wall on Great Queen Street, beneath a covered walkway that ran alongside the Freemasons' Hall. They traded digs and shared silences, and drank the beer Hendricks had brought with him.

Hendricks tapped his beer can against the building, the frontage of which was decorated with Masonic symbols. 'Probably a fair few coppers hang about in there, don't you reckon? Pissing about with goatskin aprons and rolling up their trousers . . .'

'Talking of which, did you see Brigstocke on the box?'

'Is he a Mason?'

Thorne shrugged. 'Wouldn't surprise me. I know Jesmond is.'

'Brigstocke came across very well, I thought,' Hendricks said. 'Relaxed, you know? He's obviously in charge, but he looks friendly. You want to do whatever you can to help him.'

'He's good at all that stuff. He's been on courses.'

'I don't know what the response has been like.'

'Pretty good, I think,' Thorne said.

Holland had called Thorne within an hour of the broadcast. The programme had shown the original photo of Ryan Eales, together with a digitally aged image of the soldier's face, to give *Crimewatch* viewers an idea of what he might look twenty years on. Calls had begun coming in immediately.

'I wonder if the killer was watching,' Hendricks said. 'Maybe by showing that picture of how Eales might look now we're helping him find him.'

'I shouldn't worry. He hasn't needed anybody's help so far.'

Hendricks grunted his agreement and took a drink. 'I was thinking about the tape . . . Do you reckon Hadingham had it with him when he was killed?'

'Definitely,' Thorne said. 'That tape was Hadingham's leverage. He wouldn't have let it out of his sight. The killer took it after he'd forced pills down the poor bastard's throat; and I think he took Bonser's too, after he'd kicked him to death. It certainly never showed up in any of his belongings or with any of his family after we'd identified him.'

'And the only reason he never got Jago's was that he'd left it with his sister.'

'Meaning?'

'Meaning that maybe Chris Jago wanted to leave that part of his life behind, you know?' Hendricks pressed on, though Thorne was already starting to shake his head. 'Perhaps Susan Jago wasn't bullshitting. Perhaps her brother *was* the one who wanted nothing to do with what happened; the one who was arguing with the others.'

It may or may not have been true, but Thorne wasn't sure it made any difference.

'They each took a copy of that tape, Phil, *each of them*, because no matter who did the shooting, they were all part of it. The fact that they all had the tape was the insurance. It's what kept all of them quiet.'

'Until Hadingham broke rank, and it got all of them killed.'

'Right.' Thorne held up his can, swilled the last of the beer around in the bottom as though it were fine brandy in a crystal snifter. 'And we can only presume that Ryan Eales has got the last copy . . .'

Nothing but the occasional car or pedestrian passed them in either direction. Those on foot moved quicker than normal, while the cars drifted, sluggish as hearses, through the rain. The two of them were sitting close enough to hear the rumble and hiss of the traffic on Kingsway, still heavy in the early hours of Saturday morning; vehicles moving south towards Aldwych and the river, or north towards Holborn, Bloomsbury and beyond.

'So, what are you going to do about Spike and his girlfriend?' Hendricks asked.

Thorne had already told Hendricks that he was worried about them; that he still hadn't seen either of them since Terry T had been killed. He'd asked around and had found out nothing that he hadn't known already. Spike and One-Day Caroline had both been very upset by Terry's death. It had hit them hard, Holy Joe had said. A strange and morbid thought had crossed Thorne's mind then. Would it have hit them as hard if it *had* been him that had been killed?

'I'll just have to wait for them to turn up,' Thorne said.

'I'm sure they will.'

Thorne knew that they would, but he also knew just how addicts could react when bad things happened, things that disturbed their routine or threw them off kilter. He could only hope that when Spike and Caroline did show up, it wasn't as two more names on a long list of drug fatalities.

You do me first, yeah? Piss off, I'll do myself, then I'll do you.

Vinegar and plastic lemons and one dose too many, in a box that looked enough like a coffin to begin with . . .

'Tom?'

'I'm listening.'

'I said, "I'm sure they will".'

Thorne looked up and smiled. 'I know.'

'It's . . . impressive that people in their situation can be so affected by losing someone, you know?' The beer was starting to make itself heard in Hendricks' voice. 'That these relationships can run so deep, I mean. Brendan's always on about this, but I could never really see it until these murders started. How the homeless are a community.'

'Brendan's right,' Thorne said. 'A small and very fucking weird one, that's for sure, but a community same as any other.'

'Will it survive this, d'you think? I mean, I know that people are supposed to bond during times of adversity . . .'

'It's the adversity that glues everyone together in the first place.'

'I suppose so.'

'They'll get through this.' As he spoke, Thorne felt a certainty that would not have been there a few weeks before. He pictured the faces of those he'd met since he'd been on the streets. He'd seen shame sometimes, and anger, in those faces. He'd seen disease and despair and a hunger for any number of things that could be dangerous to be around. But he'd also seen resilience, or at least the strength that can come through resignation. 'A lot of these people are being killed every day,' he said. 'Little by little . . .'

Hendricks reached into his plastic bag, rummaged for two more cans.

'Shit like this just makes you stronger,' Thorne said. 'You move a little closer together. We look out for each other.' He looked over at Hendricks. 'What?'

Hendricks held out the beer, unable to keep a slightly nervous smile at bay. 'You said, "we" . . .'

Thorne reached across and took the can. He'd already drunk three but was feeling unusually clear-headed. He wondered if all that Special Brew – a beer he'd sworn by everything he held sacred never to touch again – had somehow increased his tolerance to the weaker stuff. He popped the ring-pull. 'This stuff must be stronger than it tastes,' he said.

★ ★ ★

If you screwed up on a computer game, nobody minded. You could always have another bash. It was easy enough to go back and start that level again.

He wasn't screwing up; he rarely did because he got plenty of practice. But people – real life, flesh and blood, human fuck-ups – weren't quite as predictable as those he was happily blowing away on screen. The real ones moved around; they weren't where they were supposed to be. And they had an irritating habit of looking much the bloody same in a darkened doorway at three in the morning . . .

He'd planned to be long gone by now. Somewhere sunny and expensive, where people smelled good and the only ones dossing down outdoors were sleeping on the beach because they couldn't find their way back to the hotel. That had been the idea, anyway. Taking Thorne out of the picture was meant to be something of a last hurrah, but it hadn't turned out that way.

When he'd completed the level, he turned off the PlayStation and ejected the game. He sauntered through to the tiny kitchen to make himself some tea. It was important to wind down a little; you had to let the adrenaline level drop and level out if you wanted to get any sleep at all. He sat in his underwear, watched the kettle and waited. Trying to picture the sea. To imagine it like glass, lapping gently at the sand; to look down at himself, lying golden and satisfied, like a pig in shit with all his worries far away. This was something he'd become good at over the years: he'd developed the ability to lose himself, and to watch as he reappeared elsewhere; somewhere safe and still. But as the kettle boiled, the salt water began to seethe and the sea quickly grew rough. The waves became larger and crashed on to his beach, forcing him to move. Soaking the sand . . .

It wasn't time to relax quite yet.

He carried his tea back to the bedroom and lay down.

As soon as he'd seen that newspaper – the photo of a young man called Terry Turner below its lurid headline – he'd realised that he'd made a mess of it. He'd known deep down that he wouldn't be going anywhere for a while. It was a pain in the arse, having to rethink, but to have left would have felt wrong. He knew that if he had done so, he could *never* have relaxed.

He didn't set a great deal of store by much any more, but he still believed in the virtue of a job well done.

TWENTY-NINE

There were no more cans in the bag.

Though Thorne – as far as he could work out – had drunk as many as Hendricks, he felt none the worse for it. He was still worn out and frightened; he was still lost. But for that moment at least he wasn't alone, and he welcomed the clear understanding of his place in the world that chance, or cheap lager, had lent him. It wasn't exactly a pleasant place to be; not where he was in the life he was pretending to have, and certainly not in the life that was truly his to live with. The life which sooner or later he would have to go back to. Face up to.

His place in two worlds . . .

'I think I should make a move,' Hendricks said.

Thorne grunted, waited, but it looked as though thinking about it was as far as his friend was going to get for a while. The rain had stopped, but water was running off the roof of the covered walkway, falling on three sides of him as he sat back against the wall.

He saw something else clearly, something which most people – even if they knew the truth of it – were happier to ignore. He saw the dreadful ease with which the line separating two worlds could be breached.

He had chosen to take that step and could retrace it, but he knew that for those with no choice at all, it was usually a one-way crossing.

'We're only two pay cheques from the street,' he said.

Hendricks turned his head. 'Right . . .'

'Two pay cheques. A couple of months. That's all that separates a lot of us from sleeping in a doorway.'

Thorne had heard Brendan talking about this, so he knew it was likely that Hendricks had heard it many times. But he wasn't talking for Hendricks' benefit, and besides, the man who was now lying next to him seemed perfectly content to listen.

'I mean, obviously it depends on circumstances,' Thorne said. 'On having the right sort of family, or more likely the *wrong* sort of family. It comes down to not having the support when you need it most. You see what I'm saying? You're earning enough to pay the rent, or make the mortgage repayments, right? You make enough money to eat and have a social life. But you've got no capital of any sort, you've got decent lumps owing on your Visa, and on a few store cards, and you're paying for a car on tick or whatever. You get two months' notice and you're fucked. Really, it sounds unbelievable, but you could easily be comprehensively fucked. You might not realise that straight away, but your whole life can go down the toilet in those eight weeks.

'And this is not a fantasy, Phil. This is how a lot of people live. And I'm not talking about poor people either, or drug addicts or piss-heads. These are not people on Channel Four documentaries. These are *average* people. These are average *families* a lot of the time, who can find themselves homeless very bloody quickly. Living in hostels and care homes before you can say P45.

'You've got two months. Normal notice period. Now, the council might pay your rent, but by the time those payments come through, your landlord's thrown you out on your ear because he can't be arsed waiting for his money, right? They might pay the interest on your mortgage, but there's a limit on that depending on how generous your local council is, and banks get stroppy pretty bloody quickly when the cheques start bouncing.

'Two months . . .

'You still owe money on your cut-up credit cards, and you lose the car sharpish because you can't make the payments on that, and it's weeks before the DSS gives you anything. So, bit by bit, you lose everything: job, car, house, credit rating. Wife and kids, if it all goes really tits up. It all just slips away; or it's taken away by force. If you've got good friends or close family who are there for you when this happens, then fine. Likely as not, you'll be all right. You might not fall too far or too hard. But if you haven't . . .

'I've met people, Phil . . . Most of them haven't finished falling yet.

'You'd be amazed how quickly good friends can become distant acquaintances. How fast close family just become people with the same surname. If you're unlucky, you find that blood means fuck all when you're in the shit. When you stink of failure.'

Hearing footsteps, Thorne looked up and saw a young man walking past on the far side of the street, swinging an orange-striped traffic cone at his side. He watched as the man leaned against a shopfront, heaved the cone up to his mouth and made his own Friday night entertainment by blowing trumpet noises through it.

Thorne looked to his right and saw that Hendricks' eyes were closed. 'Are you tired or am I boring?' he asked.

A smile spread slowly across Hendricks' face, then, with one of those sudden bursts of energy unique to men under the influence, he climbed rapidly to his feet and slapped his hands together. 'Right. I'm away . . .'

'How you getting back?' Thorne asked.

'I'll pick up a cab.' Hendricks squinted across the street at the cone trumpeter.

'He's great, isn't he?'

Hendricks turned back to Thorne. 'We must do this again. Well, not *this*, but when you're back, you know, let's have a proper night out. The four of us maybe. You, me, Brendan and Dave. Brendan likes Dave. Actually, I think he fancies him a bit, but he always denies it.'

'That would be good,' Thorne said.

Hendricks was ready to go. He looked from one end of the street to the other.

Thorne pointed to the right. 'Kingsway.'

'Kingsway,' Hendricks repeated. He turned and pointed himself towards the main road. Walking quickly, like someone trying too hard to look sober.

Thorne shouted after him. 'Cheers, Phil . . .'

Hendricks raised a thumb, without turning round.

The drunk with the traffic cone was now playing something vaguely recognisable, though Thorne couldn't put a name to it. Wondering if the man did requests, Thorne toyed with shouting across; asking if he knew the horn part to 'Ring of Fire'.

He took out his sleeping bag and tried to get settled for the night. Opposite, the man with the cone grew in confidence and technique. He played 'Mack the Knife' and 'When the Saints Go Marching In'.

After five minutes, Thorne stood up and shouted at him to piss off.

His eyes snapped open and he stared at the figure standing above him: a shape stooping out of shadow. Thorne cried out and kicked his legs forward, pushing himself away from danger, driving himself back against the wall.

'What's the matter with you, you daft fucker?' the man said.

Thorne gulped up his heart. Felt it thump against his teeth.

'For fuck's sake, you silly twat!'

The breath he'd been holding exploded from Thorne's mouth. 'Oh, Christ, it's you.'

Jim Thorne chuckled. 'You thought I was the killer, didn't you?'

'What am I supposed to think?' Thorne gestured angrily at his father. 'Standing there in the dark . . .'

'Standing in the dark and pissing myself laughing, watching you scuttle away like a fucking girl.'

Thorne was still breathing heavily. He shuffled forward and moved to one side. His father stepped forward and sat beside him, groaning with the effort as he lowered himself on to the concrete.

'Anyway, son, I'm the one person you can be pretty sure *isn't* the killer, right? You've not sussed much of anything out so far, but I should hope you've worked that much out at least. Yes?'

Feeling like a kid, answering the question quietly, the sarcasm sounding childish and petulant as he spoke. 'Yes. *I know that much . . .*'

'You know *all* sorts of things. All sorts. You know who the killer really is, for a kick-off.'

Thorne stared. His father's face was expressionless. 'You've got worse since you died.'

'You know his name, son.'

'Tell me . . .'

'Hold your horses. Let's have some fun with it.'

Thorne saw where it was going. 'Oh, please God, no. Not a fucking quiz.'

'Don't be so boring. Right, list all the people who it *might* be.' He leaned over and tapped at the side of his son's head. 'You've got all the names up there.'

'I'm tired,' Thorne said.

'Come on, I'll give you the first couple to start . . .'

Thorne listened as his father gave him the first name, paused and then gave him a second. Thorne was impatient. He couldn't help asking, though he knew his father would say nothing until he was good and ready. 'Is either of those the man behind the camera? Is one of them the killer, Dad?'

The old man smiled, enjoying his secret. He began to list more names, and with each one Thorne felt himself drifting further towards sleep . . .

Then back towards consciousness. And by the time he'd woken up, thick-headed and shivering, Thorne couldn't remember a single name.

THIRTY

There was nothing like a grisly death or two for putting things into perspective.

Holland sat at his computer, logged on and cast an eye across the daily bulletin. Each morning he did the same thing: scanning the reports on serious crimes that had come in overnight. It was useful to see what other teams were doing of course; to get a sneak preview at what might be coming his own team's way. And to get a graphic reminder – good and early in the day – that, all things considered, life could be a hell of a lot worse . . .

Sometimes, if it had been a slow night, there was little to get excited about. But usually there was something: a body, more often than not, or a missing person who would soon become a body. Something to take Dave Holland's mind off the fact that he was putting on a bit of weight, or to push some imagined slight to the back of his mind, or to make him forget about the row he'd had with Sophie the night before.

Saturday morning's bulletin was usually the best, or worst of the week. Depending on whether you wanted to be seriously distracted or were just interested in keeping your breakfast down.

It had been a vintage Friday night . . .

A man, age and ethnicity impossible to determine: hog-tied and barbecued in the back of a burned-out Nissan Micra in Waltham Forest.

Two teenage boys, one white, one Asian: the first killed, the second fighting for his life in hospital after a stabbing outside a club in Wood Green.

A woman, thirty-four: found at home by her boyfriend after gaffer-taping a twelve-inch Sabatier carving-knife to the edge of a table and pushing her neck against it.

Two murders, perhaps three; possibly even four. The Homicide Assessment Team would already have signed the Waltham Forest killing over to an MIT. They would be waiting to see if the boy carved up in Wood Green recovered. They would certainly be taking a good, long look at the man whose girlfriend had supposedly killed herself so inventively . . .

DS Samir Karim walked past Holland's desk and held up a coffee. 'Ready to get going as soon as I've got this down me . . .'

Holland nodded. He went back to the computer, pulled up the list of visits he'd been allocated to make later that morning and printed them out. While he waited for hard copy to appear, he looked at the details. He studied the names, addresses and comments attached; aware all the time of those other details, still there in the bulletin window, inactive and partially hidden on the screen.

While some had spent their Friday night busy with gaffer-tape, washing blood from their hands or disposing of petrol cans, others had been safe at home in front of the television, disgusted and entertained by *Crimewatch*'s crime-lite version of such events, before picking up the phone – four hundred and twelve of them – to do their bit . . .

'How come *we* never get any of the overnighters?' Andy Stone was pulling on his jacket and moving towards him.

Holland thought that Stone had good reason to be pissed off. Obviously, a great many of the calls that had come in after the programme had been made from outside London, so while those in the office liaised with the relevant local forces, members of the team had been dispatched bright and early. Officers were already on their way to Exeter, Aberdeen, Birmingham and half a dozen other cities. Such interviews were coveted, and with good reason. Holland was one of those who would not have said no to a night away from home; getting a little time to himself and giving his expenses a hammering in the restaurant of a decent hotel.

'Luck of the draw, mate,' he said.

'Couldn't you have swung something with the DCI?'

Holland thought that he probably could have. He wondered why, in spite of fancying the time away, he hadn't even bothered to try. Chances are, Sophie would have offered to pack for him . . .

'So who are you heading out with?'

'I've got Mackillop,' Stone said. He brandished a piece of paper with his own list of names and addresses. 'Me and Wonderbollocks are off to waste our time in Hounslow, Lewisham, Finchley. All the glamour locations.'

'We've got to check out every possible sighting, Andy.'

'I know,' Stone said. 'I'm kidding. Yourself?'

Holland pointed across to Karim, who waved back and dropped what was left of his coffee into a wastepaper bin. 'Me and Sam are going slightly more upmarket.'

'Eales hiding out in Mayfair, is he?'

'Well, we've got a woman reckons she's seen him walking a dog on Hampstead High Street.'

'Why are so many of these calls always from women?' Stone asked before wandering away.

Holland thought it was likely to be something to do with women being more observant, and more likely to respond to appeals for help. More inclined, when it came down to it, to get off their arses and make an effort. They wouldn't even have Eales' name if it hadn't been for that female assistant adjutant going the extra yard.

Seeing Karim heading over, looking ready for the off, Holland began gathering his things together. He guessed that he would be spending much of his day thinking about Lieutenant Sarah Cheshire, and nights away in posh hotels.

'I've put him in one of the rooms upstairs,' Maxwell said.

Thorne nodded. 'I'll follow you . . .'

Maxwell had collared Thorne in the café, explained that Lawrence Healey had found Spike passed out on the steps when he'd arrived to open up. 'Not that unusual,' Maxwell said, as he led Thorne towards the offices. 'Their sense of time gets totally screwed. Sometimes they turn up in the middle of the night expecting to get breakfast and just nod off.'

They walked up the winding stone staircase. Thorne stared at the face of the boy on a drug-awareness poster; the blackness of the mouth inside the smile. He could see that the resilience he'd described to Hendricks was only as temporary as the high.

'Healey actually thought Spike had OD'd,' Maxwell continued. 'He spent twenty minutes walking him round, slapping some life into him.' Maxwell grinned. 'Got a decent slap back for his trouble.'

'Sounds like Spike.'

'Looking at the state of him, though, I'm guessing it's only a matter of time . . .'

They arrived at a door marked 'PRIVATE. COUNSELLING IN SESSION'. Maxwell knocked and pushed it open. 'I'll leave you to it. Give me a shout when you're done.'

'Thanks, Bren.'

Maxwell took a step away then turned, smiling. 'Oh, I couldn't get much sense out of Phil this morning. He had a bit of a headache for some strange reason. But he did manage to tell me about the two of us going out on a double date with you and Dave. Sounds like fun . . .'

Spike's head was drooping, and the smoke from a cigarette rose straight up into his face. He was sitting on a dirty cream sofa, similar to the one Thorne remembered from the room where he and the others had watched the videotape. Looking around, Thorne realised that this room was virtually identical to that one, save for the absence of a VCR, and the fact that there were AIDS information leaflets on the coffee-table, rather than the *Radio Times* and *TV Quick*.

'Thought I'd got rid of you,' Thorne said. He flopped into an armchair, leaned forward and began to drum his fingers on the edge of the table.

Spike raised his head, grinned and spread out his arms; croaked a cheer that quickly ran out of steam. He was wearing cammys and his cracked, vinyl bomber jacket. The T-shirt underneath was stained, dark at the neck, and when he let his head fall back, Thorne could see the small, square wad of bandage and the plaster.

Thorne stroked the side of his own neck. 'What happened here?'

'Abscess burst,' Spike said. 'Stunk the fucking place out . . .'

The worst detective in the world could have seen that Spike was a long way gone. Thorne could only presume that he was carrying his works with him; that he'd managed to fix up somewhere since Healey had found him outside the Lift and brought him indoors. Thorne guessed that Spike had spent every waking hour since he'd last seen him as fucked up as he was now.

'Where've you been?' Thorne asked.

Spike raised his hands to the hair which lay, damp-looking, against his head. He gathered it between his fingers and tried in vain to push it up into the trademark spikes. 'Around. Where have *you* been?'

'I knew you were upset about what happened.'

'What happened?'

'What happened to Terry,' Thorne said. 'I knew the pair of you were upset.'

'I went to see my sister.'

'It doesn't matter where you were. I'm happy you're still in one piece.'

'She gave me some cash money . . .'

It was like talking to someone who was underwater, suspended beneath the surface of a liquid that thickened as they tried to speak. That was *setting* above them.

'Actually, in a way, Terry helped out a bit,' Spike said.

'How's that?'

'I needed gear, course I did, *loads* of it. Both of us did. Most of these cocksuckers are hard as nails, like; wouldn't matter what you said to 'em. But there's a couple of dealers who've sussed that it's always going to be good for business in the long run. They do me a favour one time, they know damn well I'll be back tomorrow . . .

'So I lay it on a bit thick, right? I tell 'em that my mate's been killed, for Christ's sake, and I need to get more stuff. I tell 'em I *really* need a bit extra, you know, because of how horribly fucking upset I am. See? Simple . . .'

Thorne just listened, unable to fill the pauses that grew longer between sentences. He watched as Spike raised an arm up and pointed a finger. Span it around, making a small circle in the air.

'So, Terry dies, and I need the stuff . . . and I get the stuff because I tell everyone how upset I am . . . Then I work out what a sick bastard I am for doing that to get the stuff . . . And I hate myself.' He screwed up his face, put inverted commas round 'hate' with his fingers. 'So then I need even more stuff . . . and round and fucking round . . .'

Thorne waited until he was fairly sure there was nothing else. He had no way of knowing if Spike was aware of the tears, any more than he was of the cigarette that was no more than ash and filter between his fingers. 'Where's Caroline?' he asked.

'Will that bloke call the police 'cause I clocked him?'

'Healey, you mean?'

'She's in Camden . . .'

Thorne laughed. 'I feel like the quizmaster on that *Two Ronnies* sketch.'

Spike looked blank. It had been Thorne's father's favourite: Ronnie Barker as the man on a quiz show whose specialist subject was answering the previous question.

'*What is the last letter on the top line of a typewriter keyboard?*'

'*The Battle of Hastings.*'

'*Hosting a dance or enjoying yourself might be described as having a . . .?*'

'*P.*'

'What's in Camden?' Thorne asked.

Spike began pulling at a loose thread on the cushion next to him. 'Dealer's place.'

'How long's she been there?'

'A couple of days.' He pulled the cushion to him, folded his arms tight across it. 'I took her round . . .'

Round and fucking round . . .

Thorne understood that Spike and Caroline had both been desperate. That each had found their own way of getting as much as they needed. 'Let's go and see her,' he said.

Spike moaned and shook his head.

Thorne stood and stepped across to him. He raised Spike's hand, lifted it until it was over the table, and squeezed until the burned-out nub-end dropped into an ashtray.

'Where exactly are you from?' Stone asked.

The barman turned from restocking an optic. 'Wellington.'

'Have you got some identification on you?'

The barman sighed, started rooting around for his wallet. 'I've got credit cards . . .'

Stone took another glance at the photo he was carrying with him, a composite of the original Ryan Eales photo and the digitally aged version. He looked back at the man behind the bar. 'Forget it, mate. It's OK . . .'

He walked back to where Mackillop was sitting. The woman next to him, who'd called to say that the man behind the bar of her local pub might well be the one they were after, looked up eagerly.

'He's fifteen years too young and he's from New Zealand,' Stone said. 'He's got a bloody accent.'

The woman, fifteen years older than she wanted to be, and from Hounslow, was less than delighted. 'I never said I'd spoken to him, did I?' She sat there for a few seconds more, then snatched up her handbag. 'I suppose I'm buying *myself* a drink, then . . .'

Mackillop and Stone watched her at the bar. 'We could get something to eat ourselves while we're in here,' Mackillop said. 'It's near enough lunchtime.'

Stone looked at his watch and stood up. 'Actually, I'm meeting someone for lunch, so I think we're better off splitting up for an hour or so.'

Mackillop looked thrown. 'Right . . .'

'If we do Finchley next, you can drop me off in Willesden on the way and I'll meet you there.'

'Fair enough.' He followed Stone towards the door. Lewisham, the other location on their list, would have been closer, but Mackillop wasn't going to argue. Especially when it dawned on him exactly how Stone was planning to spend his lunch-hour.

They grabbed cold drinks and a paper from a newsagent's, then walked across the road to a small pay-and-display behind a branch of *Budgens*. 'Fucking New Zealand,' Stone said.

He hung up his jacket in the back of the car, then turned on Capital Gold while Mackillop waited for his chance to nose the Volvo into traffic. 'So, you spend an hour or so in a caff or something, right?'

'I might just grab a sandwich,' Mackillop said.

'Whatever. I'll meet you outside the Finchley address, two o'clock-ish. Maybe just after.'

'How are you going to get there from Willesden?'

'I'll call a cab,' Stone said.

'Straight up the North Circular, I would have thought. Piece of piss this time of day.'

They drove along the London road through Brentford and turned north along the edge of Gunnersbury Park.

Stone sang along to an Eric Clapton track, put finger and thumb together as if holding a plectrum during the guitar break. 'If you get there before me, just park up and wait,' Stone said. 'I'll call to find out where you are.'

Mackillop tried his best to keep a straight face. 'Wouldn't it be simpler if I just tagged along to your lunch meeting?'

'You can fuck right off,' Stone said. 'Mind you, she'd probably be up for it.'

THIRTY-ONE

Thorne sprung for a couple of tube tickets and he and Spike travelled the half a dozen stops to Camden Town. Spike was asleep, or as good as, most of the way, while Thorne was stared at by a young mother who hissed at her two kids and made sure they stayed close by her. When they stood to get off, the woman smiled at him, but Thorne saw her arms tighten around her children's waists.

Spike dragged his feet and was easily distracted as they walked along Camden Road towards the overground station. He stopped to peer into the windows of shops or talk to strangers, few of whom seemed fazed at being drawn into conversations with a junkie and a tramp. As places in the capital went, Camden was pretty much a one-off.

Despite Thorne's efforts to urge him forward, Spike sat down next to someone he actually knew, who was begging outside the huge Sainsbury's. Thorne stepped away from them and stared at his reflection in the glass of the automatic doors. His hair and beard were surely growing at a much faster rate than they normally did. He wondered if it was anything to do with exposure to air, fresh or otherwise. Though the bruises had faded, so had the rest of his face. The marks were still visible against the skin, like ancient tea-stains that stubbornly refused to shift from a pale, cotton tablecloth. He inched across until he was right in the middle of the doors; until he could enjoy himself being split down the middle whenever anyone walked in or out.

A security guard was eyeing him with intent, so Thorne decided to save him the trouble. He moved away and yanked Spike up by the collar of his jacket. Spike's friend moved to get to his feet, caught Thorne's eye and lowered himself to the pavement again.

Thorne wrapped an arm around Spike's skinny shoulders. 'Time to go and see Caroline,' he said.

They walked further away from the high street and the market, minutes from Thorne's own flat in Kentish Town. Halfway between the million-pound houses of Camden Square and the more modest accommodation of Holloway Prison, they stopped. Spike shook his head, like he was about to have teeth removed, and pointed towards an ugly, three-storey block set back from the main road.

'Up there,' he said.

They stared across at the green front doors for a minute or two; at the brown balconies and multi-coloured washing strung from their railings. 'Do you want me to wait here?' Thorne asked.

'Wait here for what?'

Thorne was starting to run out of patience with Spike's sulky attitude; with the drug and with the hunger for it. He wanted to grab him and tell him to get up to his dealer's flat and *do* something. To pull Caroline out of there, or smash the place up, or get down on his knees and thank the poxy shitbag who was fucking his girlfriend so they could get a bit higher for that much longer. Anything . . .

'I don't know,' he said.

Spike leaned against a parking meter. His breathing was noisy; cracked and wheezy. 'You could maybe come up, stand at the end of the corridor or something.'

'Come on then . . .'

They moved across the road like old men, with Spike talking to himself, then spitting at an Astra whose driver had leaned on his horn, furious at being forced to brake. At the base of the low-rise, on a small square of dogshit-and-dandelion paving, a kid on a skateboard looked at Spike as if he'd seen him before and Spike looked back.

As they entered the pungent cool of the stairwell, Thorne looked round, watched the boy pull out a mobile phone as he kicked his board away.

'It's always handy to know when someone's coming,' Spike said. 'The little fucker gets enough cash to keep him in football stickers.' He smacked his palms slowly against the blistered handrail as he led Thorne up to the top floor. 'Everyone's got some sort of habit, like . . .'

Climbing, Thorne watched Spike trying, in cack-handed slow-motion, to smarten himself up. He messed with his hair and stopped to tighten the laces in his trainers. He straightened his jacket and tucked in his T-shirt, and as they emerged on to a concrete walkway, Thorne was still wondering who the effort was being made for.

A door opened, two or three from the end of the corridor, sixty feet away. A man stepped out: thirty or so, short, with dark hair and stubble. He was wearing sandals, and creased grey trousers below a polo shirt.

Spike stopped and waved. The man in the doorway raised up his chin.

'That's Mickey,' Spike said. 'He's from Malta, so he's got brown balls . . .'

Thorne watched the man take a step forward so that he could look down over the balcony.

Spike leaned in with a grin, spelled out the joke loud enough for the man by the door to hear. 'He's a Malteser, like, so he's got brown balls.' He looked round, gave the man another wave.

Mickey smiled. 'Fucking *huge* brown balls . . .'

Spike moved away from Thorne suddenly, and began edging slowly backwards towards Mickey. He nodded at Thorne, once, twice. 'It's OK, mate, I'm good from here.'

'Does your friend want something?' Mickey said.

'No, he's cool,' Spike shouted.

Thorne wasn't sure whether the dealer was talking about drugs or trouble. The man certainly seemed happy enough to provide whatever was required.

'Really, it's fine now,' Spike said.

He was spinning around slowly as he went. He walked backwards then forwards between Thorne and the dealer, partially blocking the view as Thorne caught sight of a second figure emerging through the green door. Thorne stepped to one side to get a better look. To catch Caroline's eye.

She looked as pleased to see him as dead eyes would allow. She tugged on Mickey's shirt and pointed. 'He likes to beat up coppers,' she said.

The dealer smiled. Let the backs of his fingers move down the girl's arm. 'I like it. He gets a freebie if he wants one.'

'Honest, you can go now,' Spike said. He was starting to sound desperate, to look embarrassed that Thorne was there at all. 'We're sorted. Both of us. Right, Caz?'

Caroline pulled fingernails through her hair and walked back into the flat as if she'd forgotten something. Thorne watched Spike drift over to Mickey. Watched the dealer press his fist against Spike's and step back through the doorway.

'See you at the Lift later, then?' Thorne said.

Spike picked at the plaster, tore the stained wad of bandage from his neck and lobbed it over the balcony. As he followed Mickey inside, he stuck up a thumb without turning round, just as Hendricks had done the night before.

Thorne waited half a minute after the door had closed before walking up to it. A curtain was drawn across the only window and he could hear no sounds from inside, so he turned and walked back towards the stairs.

On the way down he took out his phone. He'd felt the vibration of a message coming through as he and Spike had walked from the tube station. It was a text from Phil Hendricks, another gag based around the possible 'double date' with Brendan and Dave Holland . . .

Thorne stopped and stared at the screen.

He'd felt it up to now as something annoying yet unimportant; like something caught in your teeth that you couldn't get at. That you pushed at until your tongue got tired and then gave up on. Suddenly, Thorne knew exactly what had been nagging at him. And he knew why.

'*You know all sorts of things . . .*'

He remembered the voice from a dream and he remembered other voices, too. He remembered what Hendricks had said:

'*Brendan likes Dave. Actually, I think he fancies him a bit . . .*'

And what Maxwell had said back at the Lift only an hour before. And, most important of all, what he'd said to Thorne a week or so before that . . .

He dialled Brendan Maxwell's mobile number, the excitement building in him like nausea. 'Bren, listen, it's Tom. Remember you told me that a police officer was looking for me. A week ago?'

'I'm right in the middle of something . . .'

'It wasn't Dave Holland, was it.' It was more statement than question.

There was a pause. Thorne could hear others talking in the background. Maxwell lowered his voice. 'Sorry, Tom, I'm not with you.'

'This was a couple of days before Terry Turner was killed. You said that a police officer was asking where I was, and you'd pointed him towards the theatre, yes?'

'Yes . . .'

'I know that Holland *had* been in, because he couldn't get hold of me, so I presumed . . .'

'Dave came in the day after, I think. If I'd been talking about Dave, I'd've said so, wouldn't I, because I know him. I'd never seen this other bloke before.'

'Right. And because I'm a fucking idiot, I've only just worked that out.'

'Is this important?' Maxwell asked.

Thorne began to move again. 'How did you know he was a copper?'

'Can I call you back?'

'I just need a minute, Bren . . .'

Maxwell sighed. 'He introduced himself, then he showed me ID. I'm not a complete moron.'

'Do you remember the name?'

Another pause. 'No. Far too many names to remember.'

Thorne swung round fast on to another flight of stairs, began to swear with each step he took.

'Sorry,' Maxwell said.

'How did he get in to see you?'

'Same as anybody else, I think. They called me down from reception and buzzed him through.'

'So he would have signed in?'

'He certainly should have done. They're usually pretty hot on health and safety. Do you want me to go and have a look?'

'I'll be with you in about twenty minutes . . .'

Thorne took the remaining stairs two at a time, feeling each step jar and burn in far too many places. He was aware of the skateboarder's eyes on him as he came out of the covered stairwell a whole lot faster than he'd gone in.

Rosedene Way was a quiet road, five minutes from the tube station and no more than a pitching wedge from Finchley golf course. The Volvo was not out of place among the Saabs and Audis; well-tended hanging baskets far outnumbered satellite dishes on the tidy thirties houses.

Mackillop had driven round for twenty minutes looking for somewhere decent to eat, and had eventually given up. He'd grabbed a sandwich from the M&S at Tally Ho corner and eaten it in the car. Now, he was stupidly early for the rendezvous with Andy Stone, but he was as happy where he was – with the car radio and a newspaper – as he would have been anywhere else.

He looked up at the top floor of the house they would be visiting; it looked like an attic conversion. He dropped his eyes down to the ground floor, where their interviewee lived, then left to where a woman was watching him while her dog relieved itself in the gutter. Saturday afternoon and there were plenty of people around. He smiled at the woman, who bent down smartly, plastic bag at the ready to clear up the mess.

Mackillop thought about what Andy Stone was doing. How long it had been since he'd done the same thing. He'd split up with his girlfriend four months before, and one pissed-up fumble with a Colindale WPC after a lock-in at the Oak was the closest to sex he'd managed since. Mind you, he'd probably get fairly close, at least by association, when Stone showed up, gagging as always to go over the highlights of his performance.

The woman with the dog gave him a good look as she walked past the car; her face like she could still smell the turd in her plastic bag.

He realised that he'd forgotten it was Saturday when he'd been talking to Stone about the best route to take. Traffic could very easily be snarled up on the North Circ. There wasn't a lot of choice mind you; it was a pig of a journey by tube, with at least a couple of changes between Willesden Green and West Finchley . . .

He hoped he wouldn't have too much longer to wait.

When they started playing cheesy country rubbish, Mackillop quickly retuned the radio. Then he opened the *Express* to the crossword, folded it across the steering wheel and dug around in his pocket for a pen.

THIRTY-TWO

Maxwell found the page he was looking for and passed the centre's registration book across. He pointed at the date and entry that Thorne would be most interested in.

The name was scribbled rather than printed, but it was legible enough. 'DS Morley,' Thorne said, reading. 'Detective Sergeant T. Morley.'

'Like I said on the phone, he had a warrant card . . .'

They were alone in a small storage room next door to the laundry; the Saturday lunch rush was at its height and there were plenty of people in the building, both clients and staff. Thorne was fired up, but in spite of all that had happened it was still important, especially *here*, to maintain the integrity of the undercover operation.

Or, at least, as much integrity as he had left . . .

'What exactly did he say?' Thorne asked.

Maxwell sat down on a cardboard box marked 'Domestos'. The room smelled of polish and cleaning fluid. 'Fuck . . . I'm not sure I can tell you *exactly* . . .'

'Did he mention me by name?'

'I suppose he must have done. It was definitely you we were talking about.'

'Me specifically?'

'Yeah, as far as I can remember . . .'

'First name? Second name?'

'I think he knew your first name. I think so . . .'

'It's about whether he was looking for me, or just looking for "the undercover copper". D'you see the difference? It's about how much he *knew*.' Thorne stared at the name on the page, reached for his phone and dialled Scotland Yard.

'He knew enough,' Maxwell said.

As soon as he got through to the Information Room, Thorne gave his name and warrant number. He told the WPC that he needed a check run on an officer. 'The name is Morley,' he said, 'first initial "T". A sergeant . . .'

The woman took down details of Thorne's request, said that she'd call him straight back.

'Any idea how long it's going to take?'

'You know how it works,' she said. 'I've got to check *you* out before I can do anything else.'

Andy Stone thought he'd got this one figured out; that they had an understanding, but she'd really surprised him. He'd thought it was all about sex; that she just wanted a quick session of an afternoon, same as usual. So he'd arranged to pop round for 'lunch'. He'd worked out that he'd have enough time to get there, give her what she wanted and get back in good time to meet up with Mackillop for the next interview. That was the theory, but it hadn't quite worked out that way. The woman had only gone and cooked him a meal. She'd actually wanted to have *lunch*. Not that she hadn't wanted to go to bed as well; she'd left him in no doubt that spaghetti Bolognese wasn't the only thing on the menu. But he couldn't just get straight down to it, could he? Not after packing all that pasta away. So, twenty minutes for lunch, fifteen to chat while they let it go down, then a decent half-hour bout between the sheets. Now there was no way he could make it across to Finchley in time.

He sat on the edge of the bed, pulling on his socks as quickly as he could, and making small talk; sneaking glances at his watch so as not to hurt her feelings. He thought she was starting to like him a bit too much. Maybe the whole cooking lunch thing meant that she wanted to move things on a bit between them. He'd have to give that some serious thought.

Shit: he hadn't even ordered a cab yet. He asked her if she had a number she used, and stood as she moved towards him, naked, to fetch the card from her purse. She lowered a hand to cup his balls through his underpants as she passed, and he stepped back, telling her that he really was going to be fucking late and reaching into the corner for his trousers.

She retrieved the card from her handbag and shouted out the number. Stone dropped back on to the bed, dialled as he watched her walk into the en-suite and bend to run the bath . . .

Fifteen, maybe twenty, minutes behind schedule . . . if he was lucky. He ordered the cab and looked around for his shoes, deciding that he'd call Mackillop once he was on his way.

The rhythmic drone became a high-pitched whine as one of the machines moved on to its spin cycle in the laundry-room next door.

'We're talking about the killer here, aren't we?' Maxwell said. 'Tom?'

'There's every chance.'

'So how did he know to come here and start talking to me as if he knew you?'

Thorne could still not be certain that the killer *didn't* know him. He looked up from the phone that was resolutely refusing to ring. 'That's what I'm trying to make sense of,' he said.

Not that any of it made a great deal of sense. The killer may or may not have known the name of the undercover police officer he was looking for; following Thorne's indiscretions in the aftermath of his arrest, that information was certainly out there. But even if the leak had come from McCabe or one of his team – even if DS T. Morley was one of that team – Thorne couldn't see how the killer had connected him to the Lift.

'It's freaky to think that I talked to the fucker,' Maxwell said.

'You get used to it.'

'Will I have to go to court if you find him?'

'Maybe. Phil can give you some tips . . .'

Maxwell smiled, but he looked uncomfortable. 'Thing is, I don't know if the image I've got in my mind is accurate or not? I don't know whether I'm remembering this bloke or if I'm imagining him. Now that I know what he did, you know?'

'We need to get you to a station as soon as we can,' Thorne said. 'Start trying to put an e-fit together.'

'If I hadn't talked to him, Terry Turner would still be alive, wouldn't he?'

Thorne looked away. '*I* should have put all this together a lot quicker, Bren.'

'If I hadn't told him where you were supposed to be sleeping . . .'

The phone buzzed in Thorne's hand.

The Information Room WPC told him that there were two T. Morleys serving in the Met. 'So I got on to both borough personnel offices.'

'Thank you,' Thorne said.

'Standard procedure. One's on a Murder Squad in Wimbledon. The other's a relief sergeant in Barnet. He's the one that's got a crime report attached to his records. Trevor Morley—'

'Crime report?'

'He's not actually been back at work that long. He was mugged in a pub car park three months ago. Nasty attack, fractured his skull . . .'

Thorne didn't need her to tell him that the mugger had never been caught. Or that, among other things, Sergeant Trevor Morley's warrant card had been stolen during the attack. He didn't need to tell her that the warrant card would have been the reason Morley had been attacked in the first place.

He thanked the WPC for her help. She told him she'd pass a report on to the Information Room's chief inspector, who might well need to get in touch with him. Thorne said that would be fine before he hung up.

'Not a real copper,' Thorne said. 'He was using stolen ID.'

The information didn't seem to make Brendan Maxwell feel any better. 'It had his photo in it.'

'Easy enough to paste in. How closely did you look?'

Maxwell shook his head. About as closely as anybody looked at anything.

'Whether you're remembering his face or imagining it, we still need to get you somewhere and get it down. I'll call someone and get it sorted.'

'I don't know how much detail I can give anyone.'

Thorne started pressing buttons on his phone, searching for Brigstocke's number on the memory. 'Just start with the general stuff,' he said. 'Height, build, colouring . . .'

'He was big. Six foot two or three, and well built. He looked pretty fit.'

'Hair?'

'Medium, I suppose, fairly neat. And he had a beard. Not ginger, but sandy-ish. He was that kind of colouring. Light-skinned . . . blue eyes, I think . . . and maybe a bit freckly, you know?'

Thorne knew.

He felt that rare, yet familiar, tickle of excitement. The shuddery spider-crawl of it at the nape of his neck, moving beneath the hair and the collar of his dirty grey coat. 'Do you recycle?' he asked.

Maxwell looked and sounded confused. 'Yes . . .'

'Where?'

'Out by the wheely-bins.'

Maxwell opened his mouth to say something else, but Thorne was already on his feet and moving towards the door.

THIRTY-THREE

Fucked-up weather and busybodies. Jason Mackillop reckoned they were both about as British as you could get.

It was one of those bizarre, early-autumn afternoons that couldn't make up its mind: sunshine, wind and rain in a random sequence every half an hour or so. Now, it was spitting gently, and Mackillop stared through the streaked windscreen at the man with the plastic carrier bags, who was walking towards the car and staring back with undisguised curiosity.

Stone had called a few minutes earlier to say that he was running late. Mackillop had heard the grin in Stone's voice; the implication that it was all due to his phenomenal staying power. Now Mackillop would be sitting there like a lemon for another twenty minutes or more . . .

The man carrying the plastic bags walked a few yards past the target address, then stopped and came back. He stared until he caught Mackillop's eye. He adjusted the grip on each bag and took slow steps towards the car.

Mackillop leaned on the switch. He let the window slide down as far as possible without letting in the drizzle.

'Can I help you?' the man said.

Mackillop had been about to ask much the same question. He reached into his jacket, produced his warrant card. 'No, I'm fine, thank you.'

The man gave a small nod, hummed a reaction, but showed little inclination to move.

'Do you live there?' Mackillop asked.

'Yes, I do.' He turned and stared back at the house, then span back around to Mackillop. 'It's four flats, actually.'

'I know.'

'I think they made a nice job of the conversion.'

'Right . . .'

The man looked round at the house again. 'I've not lived there for very long, mind you.'

Mackillop decided that it couldn't hurt to get a bit of background information while he was waiting for Stone to show up. The man seemed keen enough to help. 'Do you know a Mr Mahmoud?'

'I'm not sure.'

Mackillop fished under the newspaper on the passenger seat, pulled out his page of notes. 'Asif Mahmoud . . .'

'What does he look like?'

'He's the tenant on the ground floor.'

The man leaned down a little closer to Mackillop's window. The spatterings of rain darkened the material of his knee-length raincoat and baseball cap. 'The one with the dope, right? You can smell it when you come in late sometimes.'

'Right, thanks,' Mackillop said. If the man was right, the likelihood of their visit being a complete waste of time had just rocketed. 'Mr Mahmoud's helping us with something, that's all.'

The man smiled to himself, looked both ways along the street.

'Can I ask which flat is yours?' Mackillop asked.

'Flat D. Up with the gods. All those stairs keep you fit, I tell you that . . .'

'Top floor?'

When the man saw Mackillop looking, *really* looking, at him for the first time, he smiled again, and swallowed. Then his expression became suddenly serious, and he asked Mackillop exactly who he was, which branch of the police he was with and where he was based. Mackillop calmly gave him all the information he asked for.

'Trainee?' the man said. 'Like a junior doctor kind of thing?'

'That's right.'

'Sort of like doing your basic training.'

'Listen . . .'

The man took a couple of paces backwards, to allow Mackillop room to open the car door. 'I'm Ryan Eales,' he said. He held up his plastic bags. 'I need to go and put this shopping away . . .'

Thorne and Maxwell pushed through an emergency exit into a covered service yard at the rear of the building. The recycling bins – half a dozen of them, each filled with clear glass, green glass, plastic or newspapers – were lined up next to three huge wheelies. The place smelled of cat-piss and damp wool, and every available inch of brickwork was covered in graffiti, elaborate and largely illegible. Thorne knelt down, threw the lids off the bins until he found the one he was after, and began pulling out piles of old newspapers.

Maxwell walked to the edge of the covered area, put his hand out into the rain. 'I suppose you'll tell me what you're doing when you're good and ready.'

'I'm hoping we won't need to bother with that e-fit.'

'And last week's copies of the *Sun* are going to help, are they?'

'This might be utter bollocks, of course. I could be way off the mark.'

'From what I've heard, that would be my bet,' Maxwell said.

With a wide range of staff and clientele, the Lift catered for a variety of tastes when it came to reading matter. Thorne dug through back-copies of most of the daily tabloids and broadsheets. He picked up and threw away dozens of freebies aimed at Australians and New Zealanders, music papers, TV magazines and issues of *Loot* until he found something he was interested in.

He seized on a crumpled edition of the *Standard*. The headline disturbed him no less than when he'd first seen it: '*ROUGH-SLEEPER KILLINGS. MET GOES UNDERCOVER*'.

Maxwell looked over Thorne's shoulder. 'That's when the cat came out of the bag, right?'

Thorne opened the paper and began to read. 'This is how he knew . . .'

'Knew what?'

'You asked me back in there. How did he know to come here and start asking questions? I don't think he knew to come *here* specifically, but he knew it would be a good idea to visit places like this one, because they fucking told him. Listen . . .'

He read from the newspaper story: '"*It's understood that the Metropolitan Police has liaised closely with an organisation working with rough sleepers, in order that the undercover officer concerned can integrate with the homeless community as smoothly as possible*".'

Maxwell walked back towards the building, taking it in. He turned and leaned back against the door. 'Bloody hell . . .'

Thorne read on, growing angrier by the second. Not only had the story announced his presence, it had also, unwittingly or not, given a killer the means to find him.

'So he reads that and he works out that somebody must know something.'

'It wasn't rocket science, was it?' Thorne said. 'Somebody at one of the hostels, one of the shelters, one of the day centres. At Crisis, or Aquarius, or here. He just made a list. He visited all of them, flashed his nicked card and asked a few vague questions in the hope of getting lucky and coming across someone who'd been "liaised with". You might have been the first person he talked to or the fortieth. Doesn't really matter . . .'

'So, even though he knew your name, chances are he didn't know *you*?'

'God knows . . . probably not. We can be fairly sure he was getting his information from the newspaper, as opposed to anywhere . . . closer to home.'

There were still many things Thorne couldn't be sure about, like how the killer had known his name. But it was starting to look as though a stolen warrant card was as near as it came to police involvement in the killings themselves. It might therefore be safe enough to take surveillance off McCabe and the others at Charing Cross.

Thorne held up the paper. 'I still don't know who leaked *this*, though.' He tossed the *Standard* towards the mass that had already been discarded and went back to searching through the main pile. He still hadn't found the newspaper he was actually looking for.

Eales' flat was small, but smart and extremely tidy. Once inside, a tightly winding flight of stairs covered in coir matting rose straight into a bed-sitting room, with an arch at one end leading through to a tiny kitchen, and a door at the other, which Mackillop presumed opened into the bathroom.

Eales was putting his shopping into cupboards, while Mackillop sat on a stiff-backed chair in the bed-sitting room, still unable to believe how jammy he'd been.

'I know it's not huge,' Eales shouted through from the kitchen. 'But I don't have a lot of stuff . . .'

Mackillop was buzzing. He felt like he'd been in the Job for years. He couldn't wait to clock the look on Stone's face when he finally turned up; when the DC saw which of them had *really* got lucky that lunchtime.

'You still wouldn't believe what the rent is, mind you . . .'

'It's nice,' Mackillop said, meaning it. His own flat in a modern block was bigger, but strictly functional. He liked the polished floor in this place, the stripped beams in the ceiling and the stained-glass panels in the bathroom door.

'It'll do,' Eales said.

'It'd do for me . . .'

'Good job I've just done a shop.' Eales was walking in from the kitchen brandishing an unopened packet of Digestives. 'Coffee won't be a sec.' He handed the biscuits across and turned back towards the kitchen. 'If your partner's going to be a while, you might as well put your feet up . . .'

While he waited for his coffee, Mackillop continued to look around. Eales had said that he didn't have much, but Mackillop thought he could be fairly positive about at least one of the ex-trooper's possessions; the one which, without any doubt, would be the most valuable. There was a VCR beneath the small TV at the end of the bed, and a number of unmarked videotapes piled on top of it. Mackillop couldn't help but wonder . . .

'Why have you not contacted us, Mr Eales?' he asked.

Eales walked back through, handed a mug to Mackillop, and sat down on the edge of his bed. 'I haven't done anything wrong,' he said.

'You did know we were trying to trace you, though? You didn't seem very surprised to find a policeman on your doorstep.'

'A little, maybe.'

'It was obvious you knew who I was looking for.'

'I didn't know *anything* until I saw it on the TV the other night. I've not seen a newspaper in a while. I've barely been out of the house.'

Mackillop took out a biscuit from the packet on the floor, held it up. 'Except to go shopping.'

'Once every couple of days,' Eales said. 'You've got to get supplies in. And when I go, I don't hang about.'

'You've been keeping your head down?'

'Something like that.'

Mackillop knew why, of course. Even with his life under threat, Eales would hardly have been mustard-keen to go to the police; to explain the reason why he was next on a killer's list. Mackillop also knew that, by questioning him, he was almost certainly moving well beyond his remit. So far, he hadn't been short of luck, but the sensible part of him was wondering just how far he could push it. 'I'm guessing it's not your name on the rent book . . .'

'It's a name I use sometimes.' Eales slurped his coffee. 'I pay the rent, and that's all anyone seems bothered about.'

'You've not used your real name for a while, have you?'

Eales walked over, leaned down to grab a few biscuits, then sat again. 'Have I not?'

'I know that because we've looked. *Everywhere* . . .'

'I didn't think you were here to nick me for not filling in forms correctly.'

'I'm not,' Mackillop said. 'But it's natural to wonder why you might be so keen to stay anonymous.' He watched as Eales downed the rest of his coffee in three or four swift gulps; amazed, as his own mug was still hot to the touch.

Eales stood, gestured with his empty mug. 'I'm going to get some more.'

Mackillop followed him towards the kitchen. 'Mr Eales . . .'

'I've moved around a lot in the last few years.' Eales spoke with his back to Mackillop, taking coffee and sugar from the cupboard, moving across to the fridge for milk. 'I've done a few strange jobs, you know? Worked for one or two dodgy characters . . .'

'Dodgy how?'

'Dodgy, as in secret. I do what they pay me for, I fuck off and I keep my mouth shut. This isn't the sort of work you pick up at the Job Centre, you know?'

Mackillop thought about it, guessed that Eales was talking about working as a mercenary. He watched the man's shoulders moving beneath his sweatshirt. Eales certainly looked as though he kept himself useful. 'We're not really interested in what you've been doing,' he said. 'We're actually here for your own good. But I think you know that, don't you?'

Eales turned, looked at him.

Mackillop was starting to grow impatient with the caginess; tired of going round the houses. Here was someone who'd taken part in a brutal war crime; their only hope of catching a man who'd perpetrated an atrocity of his own fifteen years down the line.

'Do you know *why* we've been trying to find you, Mr Eales?'

Eales began to look a little nervous. He reached for his mug and dropped his head to sip from it. Mackillop waited a few seconds, then pulled out his phone, deciding that maybe it was a good time to see how far away Stone was . . .

Eales moved forward, suddenly enough to slop hot coffee across the floor. To make Mackillop step back. 'Show me your warrant card again. Straight away, please.'

Mackillop did as Eales asked. Watched as he took a few moments to regain control and recover his composure.

'I'm sorry for . . . sorry about *that*,' Eales said. 'You know damn well that I've got every right to be a bit jumpy, so let's not kid each other.' He snatched a tea-towel from the worktop, tossed it on to the spill and pushed it around with his foot as he spoke. 'I knew Ian Hadingham had topped himself last year, all right? *Supposedly* topped himself. And I knew Chris Jago was missing because I'd tried to get in touch with him. So that, on top of Hadingham, was enough to make me nervous. Then I open a paper three weeks ago and see a picture of a dead man who looks very much like Alec Bonser. I see his picture, and I see a picture like *this* . . .' He rolled up the sleeve of his sweatshirt. There were several tattoos: a row of Chinese symbols, two Celtic bands, a lion's head – but the important one was high up, just below the shoulder.

Letters faded to the blue of his eyes:

O+
S.O.F.A.

'I've no idea if he killed Chris Jago or not, but I'm the fourth member of that crew, and I want to stay alive as long as possible, thank you very much. I'm not claiming to be Brain of Britain. I was just a pig-thick squaddie, but it seemed like a good idea to keep a fairly low profile. Like you said, I kept my head down, and I've got away with it. Until now, at any rate.' Eales shrugged, blew on his coffee. 'You lot might want to talk to me, but last time I checked, that wasn't fatal.'

Mackillop felt like straps were being fastened tight across his chest. Dry-mouthed in a second, he sucked in the words and tried to arrange them into the question that was begging to be asked: You've no idea if *who* killed Chris Jago?

But he said nothing. The suspicion that he was out of his depth had suddenly become a horrible certainty. He felt like he was back on the course, that this was part of some elaborate training exercise. It was as if Eales were one of his tutors playing a role and this was the crucial point in the assessment process. The part where he could fuck up everything if he wasn't very careful. Mackillop knew that he was being given the chance to put the big question, but he also knew that the moment belonged by right, and by seniority, to others . . .

Eales nodded towards the mug in Mackillop's hand. 'Do you want another one of those?'

The clever thing to do, the *correct* thing, was to back off a little. To sit tight, and wait for Andy Stone to arrive. Mackillop handed the mug across and turned back towards the bed-sitting room.

THIRTY-FOUR

THE LATEST VICTIM. THE FIRST PICTURE . . .

The newspaper felt a little spongy. It was stained in places by whatever liquid had pooled, brown and viscous, in the bottom of the bin. But the headline remained stark enough; the expression on the face of the young Terry Turner still hopeful, and heartbreaking.

'Weird to see him looking so young,' Maxwell said. 'Without the bloody padlock . . .'

Thorne tore through the pages until he found the one he was after: the photo of another young man, this one in uniform, staring into the camera; wide eyed and half smiling, like it didn't much matter what was coming.

Thorne got up off his knees. 'Look at this.' He folded the newspaper over and handed it across.

Maxwell stared at the picture for a few seconds, at the appeal for information beneath it, then turned back to Thorne. The expression on his face made it clear that he wasn't sure what he was supposed to be looking at; what he was meant to be seeing.

'Could that be him?' Thorne asked.

Maxwell went back to the photo. '*This* bloke?'

'Could he be our Detective Sergeant Trevor Morley?'

'How old's this picture?'

'Just look, Bren . . .'

Maxwell did as he was told. Let out a long, slow breath . . .

Thorne moved quickly across to stand alongside him, nodded down at the photograph. 'That was taken when he joined up in the late eighties.' He suddenly remembered the digitally aged version that had been broadcast the night before; that Hendricks had talked about watching. 'Did you not see this on *Crimewatch* last night?'

'I was out,' Maxwell said.

'Shit . . .'

'I was out on the streets, *doing my fucking job*. Fair enough?'

'Just stick twenty years on his face, all right? He'd be late-thirties now, somewhere round there. Hair longer, obviously. A beard. From what you said, the colouring's the same, right?'

'Sandy, but with some grey. And the freckles are darker, but I suppose that would have happened . . .'

'Look at the mouth,' Thorne said. 'The smile would almost certainly be the same.'

'Maybe. Yeah . . . this could be him.'

'*Could be*, or *is*?'

'Jesus. I should have looked at this properly when I saw it the first time. I read about what had happened to Terry; that's all. I never really took this in.'

'Well, now's your chance. Come on, Brendan.'

Maxwell stabbed at the page. 'The face has filled out a bit and it's lined. Not wrinkles exactly; hard lines, like creases, you know? Like it's weathered.'

It was good enough . . .

Thorne knew that they'd made a huge mistake; that they should at least have *considered* the possibility of this for longer and not dismissed it as quickly as they had. Though the evidence had certainly pointed towards the man behind the camera, they'd got it the wrong way round.

'It's me . . .'

'What?' Maxwell turned, thinking that Thorne was talking to him, but he saw that Thorne had his phone pressed hard to his ear.

'We've been idiots, Russell,' Thorne said. 'Ryan Eales isn't the next one on the list. He's the one who's been working his way *through* it . . .'

Ryan Eales turned side on, leaned against the wall in the archway between kitchen and bed-sitting room. 'Bit of luck that I came back when I did. That you were sitting outside in your car like that.'

'We'd have knocked on your door eventually,' Mackillop said.

'I might not have answered it.'

Which would, Mackillop thought, have been understandable. All in all, things had turned out pretty well. It was equally likely that, if there had been no reply, and the man in the ground-floor flat turned out to have been the pothead Eales said he was, that nobody would have bothered coming back. Mackillop laughed. 'I suppose we should be grateful that you'd run out of biscuits,' he said.

'Right . . .'

The weather had changed suddenly yet again. Sunshine was screaming in through the big bay window and a smaller skylight towards the bathroom, flashing where it kissed the white walls and the varnish on the honey-coloured floorboards. From where he was standing, near the top of the stairs, Mackillop saw the gleam from two pairs of boots, highly polished and placed side by side between bed and wardrobe. He saw magazines neatly piled beneath the bedside table and freshly ironed shirts folded symmetrically on a chair next to the bathroom door. 'You can tell the person who lives here's ex-army,' he said.

Eales seemed to find this funny. 'How come?'

'The boots.' Mackillop pointed across to them. 'The way they're arranged; the way everything's laid out. Neat, you know, and well organised.'

'It's just the way we're taught to do things.'

'It must take a lot of effort, though.'

'Not really,' Eales said. 'You do things a particular way because it makes sense. Being organised and tidy makes things simpler.'

Mackillop considered this. 'I thought about the army myself before I joined the Met. For a short while, anyway.'

'You'd've been good.'

'You reckon?'

'Chances are, if you're a good copper.'

'Getting there,' Mackillop said. He felt himself redden slightly. Looked around the room once again. 'Yeah, definitely a soldier's place . . .'

Eales smiled. 'Look underneath the bed.'

Mackillop glanced across, then started to move when Eales nodded his encouragement. As he bent down, he could see that the base of the bed was actually a drawer. He pulled it out and found himself staring at a collection of military memorabilia: a dress uniform, pressed and folded; a gas mask; badges and medals displayed in open cases; bundles of photographs. And weapons: grenades, guns, knives, a highly polished bayonet . . .

'Bloody hell!'

'Don't worry, the guns have been decommissioned,' Eales said. 'Firing pins removed and barrels drilled.'

Mackillop reached towards one of the pistols. 'May I?'

'Help yourself. That smaller one's a Browning nine millimetre. It's Iraqi.'

Mackillop's hand hovered above the gun. He wondered if it had once belonged to one of those soldiers he'd seen kneeling in the desert. Taken from him before another was put to the back of his head. He picked up the bayonet instead.

'That's seriously sharp, by the way.'

'I bet.' Mackillop stood and held the bayonet up in front of himself. In the skinny mirror of its blade he could see the reflection of the bathroom door, the TV and VCR, the black wire that snaked across the floor from the PlayStation to the controller.

'Nice, isn't it?' Eales said.

'This might sound morbid, and a bit . . . geeky or whatever.' Mackillop turned the hilt, throwing a sliver of reflected sunlight across Eales' face. 'Has this thing ever . . . killed anyone?'

Eales walked across and took the bayonet from Mackillop's hand. 'This?' he said. He examined the blade as if he were seeing it for the first time, leaned forward and slid it into Mackillop's belly. 'Not until now . . .'

The policeman's hands flew to the hilt, wrapped themselves tight around the soldier's; hands that were bigger and stronger and drier. He tried to push, and when he opened his mouth he produced only the gentle pop of a bubble bursting.

'You ready?' Eales asked. 'Here we go.' He nodded, counting quietly to three, before twisting the bayonet and dragging it up hard, through muscle, towards the sternum.

Mackillop sighed, then sucked the air quickly back in, as if he'd just dipped a foot into a hot bath or touched a sensitive filling.

There was only the sound of breathing for a while after that, laboured and bubbly, and the low moan of boards beneath shifting feet, as both sets of fingers grew slippery against the hilt.

'Luck always runs out in the end,' Eales said.

And he never broke eye contact, not for a moment. Holding fast to what was bright in Jason Mackillop's eyes, which seemed to blaze, just for that final second or two, before it went out. Like the last dot of life as a TV screen fades to black, shrinking quickly from a world to a pin-prick.

And then nothing.

PART FOUR

FINISHED FALLING

THIRTY-FIVE

At first, he told everyone later, he thought that Mackillop had simply got tired of waiting for him and buggered off . . .

By the time Andy Stone's taxi had finally worked its way through the Saturday afternoon traffic and reached the house where Asif Mahmoud lived, the Volvo was nowhere to be seen and Jason Mackillop wasn't answering his phone. Stone had visited the ground floor flat. He'd been told by Mr Mahmoud that though he hadn't seen any police officers, he had heard comings and goings. Someone had come into the house a short time earlier, then left again fairly soon afterwards. Stone had immediately knocked at the other three flats in the building – including, of course, the one on the top floor – but had received no reply.

Confused and pissed off, he had decided to head back to Becke House, so had made his way to the tube station. It wasn't until thirty minutes later, when he got above ground at Colindale, that the message had come through about Ryan Eales . . .

'How long d'you think Stone missed him by?' Thorne asked.

Holland was pulling sheets of paper from his case. He looked up. 'Impossible to say for sure. It must have been pretty close, though.

Hendricks has the time of death at somewhere between one-thirty and two-thirty . . .'

'I was calling Brigstocke just after two,' Thorne said. 'We should have moved faster. *I* should have moved faster.'

When, after an hour, TDC Mackillop could still not be contacted, a team had been dispatched back to West Finchley. While the car – which was found in a side street behind Finchley Central Station – was being towed away, witnesses described seeing it parked outside the house on Rosedene Way. A woman who'd been walking her dog gave an accurate description of Mackillop, and a man who lived opposite gave a statement saying that he'd seen the driver of the car talking to someone on the street.

More officers had gathered, serious and uneasy, as the Saturday began to dim. An armed unit was called into position. Residents were evacuated and the road was sealed off, before finally – five hours after he'd driven into Rosedene Way – the door to the top flat at number forty-eight was smashed open, and Jason Mackillop was found . . .

Thorne had never met the murdered trainee. He wasn't sure whether that made it easier or not to deal with his death, but it certainly made it easier to idealise him as a victim. Thorne didn't know if Mackillop had bad breath or a foul temper; if he fancied himself or was close to his family. He'd never seen him at work, or fallen out with him, or heard him talk about anything important. Thorne knew only that he was naive, and keen, and almost ridiculously young. This *not knowing* made Jason Mackillop less real than many victims. But it didn't mean that the dirty great slab of guilt that had been laid down on top of the others, had any less weight.

'He shouldn't have gone in there on his own,' Holland said.

Thorne looked wrung out by exhaustion and anger. 'That doesn't help.'

'It's all Andy Stone's got to hold on to . . .'

It was Monday afternoon; two days since Ryan Eales had murdered Jason Mackillop and fled. Police, continuing to investigate the killings of homeless men in and around the West End, had taken a room at the

London Lift to conduct interviews, including one with a rough sleeper known only as Tom.

Thorne and Holland were catching up.

'He must have got out of there in one hell of a hurry,' Holland said. 'No money in the place, but he seems to have left more or less everything else behind.'

They were in a poky, self-contained office in one corner of the bigger, open-plan admin area: a small sofa and a chair; a desk with a grimy computer and several heaps of cardboard files. The day was grey outside the frosted glass of a thin window. Thorne took the sheets as they were handed to him. 'He knew that after what he'd done it wouldn't much matter if we got hold of this stuff. And it's not like any of it gives us a *name*, is it?'

Holland passed yet more paper across: photocopies of documentation found during the search of Eales' flat. All indicated that, although Eales had killed the other three men in his tank crew, as well as Radio Bob and Terry T and the others, he'd actually been working with somebody else. Or rather, *for* somebody else . . .

The man behind the camera.

Thorne had been made aware of all this within hours of the entry into Eales' flat, but this was his first look at the material evidence. He flicked through the bank statements and credit-card slips as Holland talked.

'Half a dozen different accounts, in four different names, and he managed to empty all but one of them before he did his vanishing act. Major payments into one or other of his accounts within a few days of Jago's death, and Hadingham's "suicide". Money paid in after each killing.'

'All in cash?'

'All in cash, and completely untraceable to anybody. He was well paid for what he did.'

'He was very good at it,' Thorne said.

Holland dug out another piece of paper from his case and held it out. 'And very good at not being caught . . .'

Thorne took the sheet and began to read.

'I meant to tell you about this,' Holland said. 'Then, when everything kicked off on Saturday afternoon, you know, I thought it could wait.' He pointed. '*That*'s how they got away with it. Remember, we were talking about what they did with the bodies of the Iraqi soldiers? When we went to Taunton they told us about these war diaries, and at the time I didn't think it was worth chasing up, because our boys would only have been mentioned if they'd been wounded or commended . . .'

Thorne saw where it was going. 'You're shitting me . . .'

'I just double checked.'

Thorne read the words aloud. '"*Callsign 40 from B-Troop, under the command of Corporal Ian Hadingham, engaged with and destroyed an enemy tank, killing all four on board . . .*"'

'The Iraqi tank surrendered,' Holland said, 'or was captured or whatever. Then, after they'd shot them, Eales and the others just put the bodies back in the tank and blew the thing to shit. Whether anybody ever found out or not . . .'

'They got *commended*?' Thorne looked as though he might be close to tears of one sort or another. 'Christ on a bike . . .'

Holland was rummaging in his briefcase again. 'Something else that just came through. We finally got the transcript back from that lab in California: the techies who enhanced the sound on the video.' He passed across the sheaf of papers, and closed his case.

Thorne took what was handed to him without really looking at it and placed it on the desk with the rest of the paperwork. He groped for the swivel chair behind him and slid clumsily on to it. 'Another couple of loose ends tied up. It's all good, I suppose . . .'

'None of it gets us anywhere, though. Right?'

The silence that hung between them for the next few seconds was answer enough.

'So what's happening indoors?'

'Everyone's busy,' Holland said. 'Fired up, like you'd expect, you know, but . . .'

'Aimless,' Thorne said.

'The Intel unit's digging around. Hoping that the paper trail might throw up an address or something. Somewhere Eales might hole up.'

Thorne was dismissive. 'He's long gone.'

And Holland didn't argue. He suspected that the brass had already taken the decision to scale down surveillance at all ports and airports.

The fact was that Mackillop's death and Eales' flight had torn the guts out of the investigation, and everyone knew it. It might, in other circumstances, have been what united the team and drove it on with renewed vigour, but this was more coffin-nail than spur. Though they wanted Eales more badly than ever, they had to accept that, for the time being at least, they weren't likely to find him. And, despite what they now knew, there was little chance, without Eales, of ever catching the man who'd bankrolled at least half a dozen killings over a year or more. Overstretched budgets were always important factors, as were limited resources and time constraints, but once a team lost the *appetite* for it, everything else became secondary.

'What did Brigstocke say?' Holland asked. He had a pretty good idea, of course, and wondered if he was overstepping the mark by asking. But he guessed correctly that Thorne had long since forgotten, or stopped caring, where such marks were.

'He was "officially" telling me that the undercover operation was to be wound down. That I should go home and have a bath . . .'

Thorne was obviously making light of it, but Holland wasn't sure whether to smile or not. 'When?'

'I'll stay out another night, I think.'

'OK . . .'

'There's a few people I need to say goodbye to.'

'Then what?'

'Then a decent curry, a good night's sleep, probably a very pissed-off cat . . .'

'That's not what I meant,' Holland said.

Thorne smiled. 'I know it isn't.'

Brigstocke had called the evening before, when the dust kicked up by Mackillop's murder had begun to settle. He'd made it clear that he was brooking no argument as far as pulling Thorne off the street was concerned, so Thorne didn't waste any time by initiating one. Eales had gone. There would be no more killings. There was no longer any point. When it came to exactly what Thorne would be returning to, Brigstocke was a little less dogmatic. It may just have been that the decision had yet to be taken, but it was equally likely that Brigstocke had simply fought shy of delivering one blow on top of another.

As things stood, if it *was* to be a continuance of his gardening leave, Thorne would give in to it without much of a fuss. The thought of going back to the team, back to how things had been before, unnerved him. He felt as though he'd lost his way during some long-distance endurance event; as if he were staggering, miles off the pace, in the wrong direction. He couldn't do anything else until he'd completed the course, however laughable his finishing time was. He knew he couldn't really compete, but he needed to cross the line . . .

'"I don't know" is the simple answer,' Thorne said. 'I don't know what *they* want. I don't really know what *I* want.'

Holland filled the pause that followed by reaching for his coat. 'Do you think Eales spoke to whoever's paying him before he left? Warned him?'

'Maybe, but I don't think he had a great deal to warn him about.' Thorne gestured towards the papers on the desk. 'There's nothing there that incriminates anybody. I think Eales knows how to keep his mouth shut. How to keep secrets.'

'Probably a good idea. Considering how many people died because one greedy fucker couldn't.'

Thorne eased his chair round slowly, one way and then the other. 'We set so much store in trying to get hold of Eales, thinking that he'd tell us the name of the man behind the camera. I'm not actually sure it would have done us any good.'

'You don't think he'd have given him up?'

'Eales is still a soldier,' Thorne said. 'Name, rank and serial number, right?'

Holland picked up his case and crossed to the door. 'Are you sticking around here for a bit? I need to get back . . .'

Thorne grunted; he didn't look like he was ready to go anywhere.

Holland recalled walking through the café on his way up and seeing the addict Thorne had been spending so much time with. The boy had been sitting with his girlfriend, whose name Holland had never learned. Holland thought about what Thorne had said earlier; wondered how difficult he might find it to say some of those goodbyes. 'Your mate Spike's downstairs . . .'

Thorne nodded, like he already knew. 'We're supposed to be playing pool.'

'We can have a game some time, if you want,' Holland said. He hovered at the doorway. 'Later in the week, maybe. That pub round the corner from your place has got a table, hasn't it?'

'I'll give you a call, Dave,' Thorne said. 'When I've got myself sorted.'

He sat for a few minutes after Holland had left and let his mind drift. Sadly, however hard he tried, it wouldn't drift quite far enough.

For want of anything else to do, he reached for the documents scattered across the desk and began to thumb through them. It always came down to paper in the end. Filed and boxed up in the General Registry. And it felt as though this case was heading that way pretty bloody quickly; not cold exactly, but as good as. The case, such as it was, would be handed over to the Homicide Task Force, or perhaps the brand-new, FBI-style Serious and Organised Crime Association. These were the pro-active units responsible for tracking down and charging prime suspects who had gone missing. Thorne felt fairly sure that Eales was already abroad; that he would not make himself easy to find. The world was becoming smaller all the time, but it was still plenty big enough.

He stared down at the bank statements; at the payments, each one representing a man Ryan Eales had killed. He looked at the amounts and was unable to stop a part of his brain making the perverse calculations: fifteen hundred pounds per kick delivered; something like that . . .

He thought back to the case he'd been working on the previous spring: to the hunt for another man who'd chosen murder as his profession; book-ended by two fires, twenty years apart. A young girl dead, and an old man. Now, here was Thorne, sitting in the old man's coat and gnawing at the decisions he'd taken. At the series of judgements, considered and otherwise; from one burning to another.

He pulled the Gulf War transcript to the front and glanced down at it. The printed dialogue and descriptions were horribly effective prompts. His mind called up the associated images from the videotape in an instant as he read: the groupings of the men, and the rain striking the sand like black candle-wax, and luminous horror like a cat's-eye in the darkness.

A soldier waving papers taken from the Iraqi prisoners. No sign of what was to come. '*We are keeping these.*' (LOUDER) '*Do you understand?*'

While decisions – including that which would determine his own future – were being made, Thorne wondered if the Met had taken one to hand the tape over to the army. He wondered too, in spite of all the bickering between the Met and the RMP that would surely follow, if the army themselves would be very surprised. Had Eales and his fellow-crewmen effectively covered their tracks in 1991?

'*Where d'you get it?*'

'*Say again?*'

(LOUDER) '*Where d'you get it?*'

'*This?*' (SOLDIER HOLDS UP BACON STRIPS). '*I brought it with me.*'

Or was that commendation in the war diary little more than an exercise in sweeping shit under the carpet?

'*That reminds me, I could kill a fry-up . . .*'

'*That stuff fucking stinks, Ian . . .*'

Thorne read the next line . . .

And stared, breathless, at the page. At five words, spoken out of vision. A phrase that told him everything.

He knew who the man behind the camera was.

Thorne shut his eyes and pressed himself back in the chair, thrown by the excitement and the terror of being suddenly and completely without doubt. It was a sensation he'd almost forgotten: the sickness and the surge of *knowing*.

Then, quick and painful as a low punch, Thorne knew something else: that the man who had paid Ryan Eales to commit murder would walk away from it as surely as Eales himself had so far managed to do. Certain as he was of the man's identity, and of what he had done, Thorne knew that there was no way on God's earth that he could prove it.

Five minutes, perhaps ten, passed as Thorne weighed it up.

He stared into the thought, into the white-hot heart of it, until at last he began to make a few decisions. Each would be dependent on the decisions of others, but as Thorne stood and gathered his things together, he felt as energised as he had in a long while. He might yet fail to cross it, but now at least he had a bloody good idea where the finishing line was.

He came out of the office and descended quickly towards the lower-ground floor. If Spike was still there, the two of them could chat while they played pool. They would have plenty to talk about.

Thorne had decided that if he was going to get off the streets, he needed to come clean . . . in every possible sense. He was going to tell Spike everything.

THIRTY-SIX

He heard the man coming long before he saw him.

The footsteps sounded hesitant; he could recognise the tread of someone unfamiliar within the network of the tunnels from a mile away. He'd heard such echoes many times before: the click-clack of heels slowing, then speeding up again as confidence comes and goes; the scrape of a leather sole against the concrete as the wearer turns to get their bearings, or decides in which direction to proceed. Or whether to proceed at all . . .

When he finally saw the man rounding the corner, Spike stood. He leaned back against the wall and waited; tried to look unconcerned as the distance between the two of them shortened, as the man moved towards him through puddles of water and deeper pools of shadow.

'Am I in the right place?' the man said. Still twenty feet or more away.

The fear would have killed any strength in his voice anyway, but with the sound moving effortlessly, as it did through the air underground, Spike had no need to speak much above a whisper. 'Depends,' he said, 'on if you've got shitloads of cash in one of those pockets . . .'

When the man stopped, it was three or four arms' lengths away from Spike. He looked around quickly. Took in his immediate surroundings. 'This is nice,' he said.

Spike said nothing.

The man nodded towards the large cardboard box behind, and to Spike's right, against the wall. 'That where you sleep?'

'It's a lot better than some places,' Spike said.

The corners of the man's mouth turned up, but it could hardly have been called a smile. 'Tell me how you got the tape.' It seemed that the small talk was at an end.

'I told you when I called . . .'

'You told me fuck all,' the man said. 'You talked a lot of crap and I've had a few days to think about it since then.'

'What's the matter? Don't you want it? That's fine with me, like. Only you seemed keen enough on the phone . . .'

'Tell me.'

It was never really silent down in the subways. There was always the muffled roar of the traffic overhead, the buzz of the striplights, the eerie beat of dripping water. These were the only sounds for several seconds.

Spike rubbed his hands across his face. Through his hair. 'What d'you want me to say?' His voice was hoarse; cracked with nerves and desire. 'You want me to tell you I'm a fucked-up junkie? Do anything to score? Desperate enough for money to shit on a mate?'

'Now you're starting to persuade me,' the man said.

'Thorne told me he was a copper, like. That he'd been working undercover because of these murders. He told me about the case, about why everyone had been killed.'

The man didn't blink.

'He talked about everything,' Spike said. 'What happened all them years ago in the fucking desert. He told me who you were and he told me about the tape.'

'Why?'

Spike shrugged. 'Fuck knows. Because it was his last night, I suppose, and the stupid bastard thought it didn't matter. He said that the bloke who did the actual killing had legged it and there wasn't anything else anyone could do . . .'

The man thrust his hands into the pocket of a long leather coat and pressed his arms close to his body. It was getting very cold in the early hours. 'So, you just sat there, took all that in, and saw an easy way to make a few quid?'

'More than a few, mate . . .'

'Don't try to be clever.' It was a simple directive. Spoken quietly, and with the cold confidence that comes from being used to having such instructions followed.

'Look . . . I was fucked off with him,' Spike said. 'For bullshitting me all that time. For making me and my girlfriend and all the rest of us look like idiots. It was a good way to get my own back.'

The man looked unconvinced. 'It was a good way to make some money.'

'Yeah, all right. Course it was. Obviously, after what he told me, I knew that the tape was valuable. That you'd probably pay a fair bit to get it back. When he said he had the tape *on* him, I started to think about it, you know? I was thinking about a shedload of smack and that. And a flat for me and my girlfriend.' Spike grinned, bounced a fist against his leg, as he thought about those things again. 'She wants us to get a place together, you know?'

'You just took it?'

'When he was asleep, I grabbed his stuff and fucked off. I know he's looking for me, but I'm pretty good at keeping out of people's way, you know?'

'He said this was the only copy?'

Spike widened his eyes. 'Thorne's fucking mental. I told you. I reckon being on the street has made him go funny, made him see things a bit twisted, like. He more or less nicked it, from what he was saying. Got some other copper he knew to hand it over to him on the quiet.'

'Why would he do that?'

'Don't ask me. He was ranting about showing it to somebody. About using it for something.'

The man seemed to think about this.

'Listen,' Spike said. 'I don't really want to know about any of it, all right? Like you said, I'm just doing this for the money.'

'Now, that I *do* understand,' the man said. 'It's what started all this in the first place.'

Spike lifted a sleeve and rubbed the sweat away. 'Starts everything, mate. Only some of us need it a bit more than others . . .'

The man peered at Spike with curiosity and disgust, as though the wreckage of an accident had been taken away and he was staring at a bloodstain on the road. 'My good fortune in this case,' he said.

Spike reached into the inside pocket of his jacket, pulled out a plastic carrier bag and wrapped it around whatever was inside. 'Tape's in here,' he said.

The man made no move to take it. 'You know that if you're fucking me about I'll find you,' he said. 'However good you think you are at keeping out of people's way. I'll *pay* someone to find you.'

'Thorne told me what's on here.' Spike shook the package. The tape rattled inside. 'I haven't watched it, but I know what you did. I know what happened back then, and what happened later on with cars and tablets and with army boots, so I know what you're capable of.' He looked across at the man and held his stare. 'I'm a junkie, and a liar, and a fucking thief. But I'm not stupid . . .'

The man seemed impressed by this. When his hand came out of his pocket it was holding a bulging, brown A3 envelope.

'How do we do this, then?' Spike held out the plastic bag at arm's length. It shook in his hand. He dropped the arm and took a breath; tried to sound casual. 'You want me to chuck it over or what?'

The man stepped forward suddenly, and kept coming as Spike moved backwards, away from him. When Spike was against the wall, the man gently lifted the package from his hand. Six inches taller than Spike, he looked down and pressed the envelope against the boy's chest. 'Quite a bit in here,' he said. 'Quite a lot of shit to put in your arm . . .'

The man's eyes swivelled in an instant to the cardboard box and at the same moment he took a step back. At the sudden noise; at the movement . . .

A week before, back at the Lift, when they'd been playing pool and talking about how it might work, this had been the moment that had caused Spike to laugh out loud. Back before Thorne had gone to Brigstocke or Brigstocke to Jesmond. Before Jesmond had gone higher to wherever the buck stopped. This had been what they'd called the 'rat' moment.

'He'll probably think it's a rat,' Spike had said. 'A fucking big one, like. He'll probably shit himself . . .'

The man's reaction when Thorne appeared from inside the box – sitting and then standing up in one smooth movement – was less dramatic than Spike had predicted, but Thorne could certainly see that he'd sprung a powerful surprise. 'I'm guessing those football tickets are out of the question now,' he said.

THIRTY-SEVEN

Alan Ward nudged his glasses, then reached to grab a handful of hair at the back of his head, as if that might be the only way to stop himself shaking it. He'd carried on moving backwards as the sides and lid of the box had burst outwards and upwards, and now he stared at Thorne and Spike across the eight or so feet that separated one wall of the tunnel from the other.

Thorne glanced to his left. 'All right?'

Spike nodded, without taking his eyes off Ward.

'This is . . . interesting,' Ward said, finally. He looked both ways along the length of the tunnel.

'No point in going anywhere,' Thorne said.

'Because . . .?'

'Because there are police officers at every exit. Why did you think it was so quiet down here tonight?'

'Stupid bastard,' Spike said.

The slow shake of Ward's head became a nod of acceptance, and, as Thorne watched, an excitement of sorts came into the journalist's eyes. Though he was clearly anxious – the muscles in his face and neck singing with it – there was also a calmness in his voice and in his manner, as though he were somehow relaxed by the tension.

He glared at Spike. 'That little fucker wired up, is he?'

Spike just smiled.

'Or have you got something set up in the box?'

Thorne nodded up at the roof of the tunnel, towards one of the small, metal PA speakers that was now more or less directly above Ward's head. 'The mike's in there,' he said. 'And the camera. Seemed appropriate to get it all on film as well.'

'You haven't got *anything*.'

'You know we've got plenty . . .'

Ward cocked his head as if he were weighing it up. Then he casually dropped the package he was carrying to the ground and began to stamp on it. The noise, as the tape's plastic housing first cracked and then shattered, echoed back along the tunnel from left and right.

Thorne waited for a couple of seconds. 'Well done,' he said. 'You've just stomped the shit out of a Jim Carrey movie.'

'I don't believe you . . .'

'Not that we couldn't have tied you to these latest killings without the tape anyway, but did you really think we'd only have *one copy*?'

Ward turned angrily to Spike.

'Since when do junkies tell the truth?' Spike asked.

Ward's unsettling calmness had all but vanished now. Thorne was aware only of the adrenaline, of a *readiness*, in the man opposite him. And something else at the furthest edge of the rush: Ward's barely concealed fury at the hopelessness of his situation.

There was nothing practical to be gained by it, but still there were many reasons why Thorne felt the need to push and to bait. To glory, and to let Ward *see him* glory at his impotence.

'So, lucky or unlucky, then?' Thorne said. 'The day you came across that tank crew. What d'you reckon, Alan?'

Ward seemed to find the question funny. Asked one in return: 'For me or those Iraqis?'

Thorne answered with a look.

'Lucky for me, definitely,' Ward said. 'Very lucky. And you can make your own luck up to a point, but it's what you do with it that makes the difference.'

'What were you doing there?' Thorne asked.

'I was driving around, monitoring radio transmissions, and I heard Callsign 40 radio through that they'd thrown a track.' Ward leaned back against the wall and looked hard at Thorne. This wasn't reminiscence. It was education. 'I heard REME telling them that the engineers couldn't get out there for a couple of hours, and I was near by, so I thought I'd head across and see what was happening. By the time I'd got there the men in the Iraqi tank had just driven up and surrendered. Popped their lids waving fucking white flags . . .'

'Very stupid of them.'

'See, I had my nice bit of luck right there, and ordinarily that's all it would have been. If all I'd wanted was to point my little camera and watch a few of our boys capturing a few of theirs, that would have been handy. But it was much more than that. Because I wanted *much more* than some boring bit of footage that might or might not have given me a bit of clout next time I was negotiating a pay rise.'

'So you . . . *encouraged* them.'

Ward was still, and focused, his eyes unblinking in the artificial light. When he spoke, it was clear to Thorne that what he said was deeply felt. The frigidity and scorn for life that Thorne knew to be at the core of this man were belied by the twisted passion of the words.

'Have you ever thought you were about to die?' Ward asked. 'Or even that you were about to be the one to take a life? Have you ever really experienced that sort of excitement?'

Thorne had little intention of answering, and Ward had even less of giving him the opportunity.

'I suppose, because of what you do, that you've felt it more keenly than most, and let me say straight away that I admire what you do. Really. Perhaps you *have* been in the sort of situation I describe, but can you even begin to imagine feeling those things for days, for weeks, on end? Constantly. Can you imagine it becoming something that you *live with*?' He flicked his eyes to Spike, spat the words out at him.

'That . . . *heightened* feeling in the body becomes something that's more powerful than any drug. And when you come down from it, you fall a very long way and you fall very hard.'

'What the fuck do you know about it?' Spike said.

Ward just smiled and turned his attention back to Thorne. 'Those boys were trained for it . . . And they *were* boys, emotionally at any rate. They were taught to expect it, whipped up into a state every day until, eventually, not seeing combat became far worse than seeing it. They needed the high, can you understand that? They were sent over there to do a job and then some of them didn't get a chance to do it. There were lads out there turning on each other. Shooting fucking camels. Anything to get *close* to that buzz.'

'You wanted it too, though, didn't you?'

Ward's eyes widened. 'I was . . . frustrated, yes,' he said. 'And me and that situation were just fucking perfect for each other. They thought it was about to happen, Hadingham and Eales and the others. They'd been told that the enemy was close, that there was every chance of engaging at any fucking moment. Then the machine lets them down and they can do nothing but watch their mates disappear into the distance. Feel that buzz disappear with them.'

'What did you do?'

'I hardly had to *do* anything,' Ward said. 'I was the catalyst, if you like; that's all. They just needed someone to give them a nudge in the right direction, to tell them that what they were thinking about doing, what they *wanted* to do, was absolutely understandable. That it was all right.' His voice had become quieter, more intense, and when he paused there was a rattle in his breath. He nodded towards the plastic bag at Thorne's feet, to the remains of the video inside. 'I don't know what you think you've seen on the tape, but I promise you that even the ones that weren't so keen to begin with, the ones that needed a bit of persuading, they got the biggest thrill of their lives that day. Ryan Eales, for one, spent the rest of his life trying to recapture it.'

'By killing for you?'

'For me, among others. He was a professional.'

'Usually . . .'

Ward nodded his agreement. 'Yes, you're quite right, of course. Usually.'

Thorne could sense Spike bristling next to him.

'He did rather fuck things up,' Ward said. 'When it came to getting *you* out of the picture . . .'

Now this *was* practical. This was not about poking at the corpse of the case for personal gratification. This was something Thorne very much wanted to know.

'How did you get my name?' he asked.

Ward said nothing, but in the smirk that transformed his features, Thorne suddenly saw *exactly* where the man standing opposite him had got his name. The source of the leak became obvious. Thorne filed the information away. He would deal with it when he had the chance.

Spike's reaction to Ward's knowing smile was altogether different, and more dramatic. He pushed himself away from the wall, the growled mutterings turning to something almost feral as he launched himself across the width of the tunnel.

It all happened before Thorne had the chance to do much more than cry out: '*Spike* . . .'

Spike was off-balance and throwing punches before he'd even reached his target, and by the time his hands, and Ward's, had stopped moving, the two were locked clumsily together, side on to the tunnel-wall.

And there was a knife at Spike's throat.

Now Thorne could see real desperation, real danger in Ward's eyes. His situation was hopeless, so there was little else for Ward to lose. Thorne knew that moments such as these were when lives were most easily, and most pointlessly, lost.

'You know you have to put that down,' Thorne said. His eyes never left the blade.

He watched it pressing against Spike's neck and wondered if Ward was thinking about what lay ahead; about slaughtering a boy who meant less than nothing and seizing this one last chance to feel that buzz.

'I can't see that I have to do anything.'

'Let me just get some officers in right now and they can take you out of here without any more fuss or any fucking about. Fair enough? Alan?' Thorne took a tentative half-step towards them. 'You know that's the clever thing to do, right?'

But Ward was not the next one to speak . . .

As Spike began to talk, Thorne became aware of the one element in the bizarre tableau facing him that he had not taken in. The most crucial detail. Down at his side, poised delicately in his right hand, Spike was holding a blood-filled syringe.

'*I've always got a weapon!*' Thorne had presumed Spike had been talking about a knife . . .

Spike eased the flap of the long, leather coat aside and brushed the tip of the needle against Ward's thigh. Scraped it across the material of the trousers. 'This'll go deep into your muscle every bit as quick as you can move that knife, like.' Spike's mouth was pressed close to Ward's cheek as he spoke. 'I don't give a fuck, really. It's completely up to you, mate. Do you want dirty, junkie blood running around in there? Mucking you up inside? How much of a fucking *buzz* would that be?'

With Ward's focus now down to where he could feel the needle, Thorne inched closer. 'Get rid of the knife and we can sort this out.'

'Do you want AIDS?' Spike whispered.

'For Christ's sake, take it easy,' Thorne said. 'Both of you.'

'How d'you fancy that?'

'Shut up, Spike . . .'

Without moving the knife, Ward leaned his head as far away as he was able from Spike's. 'Please. Keep still . . .'

'I think that should be exciting enough for you,' Spike said. 'And it'll certainly be something you'll live with every day. Though not for very long, like.'

'Don't . . .'

'What? Don't 'cause you'll kill me if I do? Or don't 'cause you're shitting yourself?'

'Drop the knife and let me bring officers in here,' Thorne shouted.

'Bring 'em in now. You can bring 'em in right now and he'll do fuck all.' Spike was gabbling, loud and high pitched; his eyes fixed on Ward, rattling out the words on fractured breaths. 'He'll do jack shit, I swear, whatever happens, because he's fucking terrified. Because he's a coward. He's a fucking coward who lets someone else clear up his mess, who pays somebody to kick men to death when they're asleep. He'll do nothing because he's all talk. Because he wants the high, but he hasn't got the bottle to do what it takes to get it. I've met his sort loads of times, like. They love to be around it, they fucking love the idea of it, but when it comes to shooting up, they're afraid of the needle. They're shit scared of it. Like he's afraid of *this* one. So bring the others in. He'll do nothing.' Spike leaned in to Ward, yelled up into his face. '*Bring them in!*'

Within a few moments of the echo dying, Thorne had made his decision. He knew that they'd be hanging on every word. That, were it not for the layout of the tunnels, which made it impossible to get close without being seen, they would have been all over Ward already. He knew that there'd be armed officers standing by. That nobody would need asking twice . . .

He looked up at the speaker and gave the order, not needing to raise his voice very much. 'Get down here . . .'

Immediately there were distant voices raised, then footsteps, and Thorne turned to see Holland, Stone and half a dozen other officers tearing along the tunnel towards them. They shouted as they ran. Making sure Ward knew they were there, telling him to drop the knife and lie down on the floor.

Ward did exactly as he was told, as Spike had predicted he would. He dropped the knife and threw himself to the floor the instant that Spike stepped away from him. But almost as soon as his face hit the concrete, Spike was on him again, flipping him over, kneeling across his chest and holding the tip of the needle an inch from his eye.

Thorne shouted Spike's name.

Holland bellowed a warning.

The rest of the team were no more than thirty feet away, and approaching fast . . .

It was a toss up as to whether Thorne or one of the others would get there first, but before any of them had a chance, Spike had fired a fine jet of blood into Ward's eyes, and, with the smallest movement of his wrist, directed it down, across Ward's lips and into the mouth that had opened to scream.

'That's for Terry,' he said. 'For Bob and all the rest . . .'

The second Spike had tossed the syringe and begun to move, Ward was seized and turned back on to his belly. An officer ran around and made a grab for Spike, but Thorne stepped quickly across and ushered the boy away. Led him down the tunnel and pressed him hard into the wall. 'Jesus . . . What d'you think you're doing?'

Spike said nothing. Regaining his breath, looking back down the tunnel to where Ward was being pulled to his feet. His hands cuffed behind him. Unable to wipe away the blood that was running down his face and chin.

Thorne was looking, too. He nodded towards Ward. 'What you threatened him with . . . Are you—?'

'Course I'm fucking not,' Spike said. 'We get tested every month, me *and* Caroline. But *he* doesn't know that, does he?'

Thorne watched, listened as Ward begged the officers around him for a tissue, a rag, a scrap of paper. *Anything*. 'Not unless somebody tells him,' he said.

Spike was calm again.

That grin.

'We've been scared to death for weeks. Now it's his turn to see what that's like. Let the bastard sweat for a while . . .'

THIRTY-EIGHT

If the sea down below him wasn't quite as smooth as glass, it was still blue. It sounded good, like a *hush*, and the sun was hot and Ryan Eales was happy enough. He lay and soaked it all in. Feeling, for the third or fourth day on the trot, that he was finally starting to get his breath back. It was a fortnight since he'd been forced to cut and run, which was longer than it would normally have taken him to recover and relax, but then it had been a kick-bollock-scramble.

Cut and run . . .

He'd had to think *so* fast when he'd come strolling up and seen the car outside the house, and right until the moment when he'd pictured the bayonet under the bed and had the idea, he hadn't been sure if admitting who he was and bringing him inside had been the cleverest decision of his life or the most stupid. Even when it was done, when the copper had slid back off the blade, he'd known that the other one was on his way. That he had to move double bloody quick.

It had taken him only minutes to get packed up and out of there, and he was proud of the way he'd done it: moving through the place at speed, but taking everything in; taking a mental inventory as he'd walked around the bedroom, gathering up only what was essential.

Passports and papers; a few clothes and all the cash. As long as he had money, he was always able to pick up the pieces.

It hadn't been the first thing he'd done, of course. He'd realised straight away that he needed to get the car out of sight; how important it would be in buying him a little time. He'd dug around in the copper's pocket for the keys; dropped the Volvo off in a side street and walked back to the flat. He'd still been in there getting his things together when the second copper had come knocking. He'd frozen then; crept to the front door and stood there until he'd heard the footsteps going back down the stairs.

'Be careful with that . . .'

A family with small children was arranged on the other side of the pool. He heard a ball bouncing towards him and the feet of one of the kids slapping on the tiles as he ran to retrieve it. Eales raised his head, reached for the ball and threw it back. The boy smiled at him. Said, 'Thank you,' when prompted by his mother.

'You're very welcome,' Eales said.

Definitely starting to relax . . .

He felt a tickle, and looked to see sweat rolling across the indigo letters on his shoulder. He thought, as he did often – as he did long before Ward had contacted him with the offer of a job – of the other three men whose bodies bore the same design. They could not have known, on the drunken evening they'd all stumbled into that tattoo parlour and gone under the needle, anaesthetised by strong German lager, how bound to one another they were destined to become.

They would live and die as a crew.

All those years before in the desert, there'd been a couple who hadn't wanted things to go as far as they ultimately had. But it never mattered. It was ironic really, he reckoned, and maybe even a bit sad, because the ones who didn't fire a shot that day ended up paying the same price anyway, thanks to one person being stupid and greedy.

It just proved, he thought, how some decisions were best taken for you by others . . .

Ryan Eales lay back down and tried to sleep.

A white spot – the retinal memory of the sun, high above him – darted behind his lids like a tracer bullet; like the point of light he'd seen two weeks earlier in the police officer's eyes, bright before shrinking.

He rolled his eyeballs, and watched as the pinprick danced across the black.

The lift carried him up towards the top floor of Colindale police station. The CID and the Burglary Squad were on the first floor, the Criminal Justice Unit and CPS offices on the second, but Thorne was heading for none of these.

He let the empty cardboard box he was carrying bounce off his knee; pictured Spike slapping out a rhythm against his legs or drumming his fingers on a tabletop in McDonald's . . .

Though it was far from official policy of any sort, Thorne had persuaded Brigstocke to dig up some money for Spike. There was a fund to pay informants, to cover the expenses of those who gave their time to help police operations, so it seemed reasonable to reward Spike for his efforts. He'd certainly earned it in that subway.

There had, of course, been the business with the blood, and once the scene in the tunnel had been cleared, it had required a major effort to keep Spike from being arrested. Thorne had worked hard to convince the team that Spike had been provoked, while at the same time admitting that the boy *had* exceeded the boundaries that had been laid down . . .

'I can't think where he gets *that* from,' Brigstocke had said.

It was hardly a fortune, but the money Thorne had wangled might pay for the deposit and first month's rent on a flat. He wasn't naive enough to believe that it would stop Spike feeling guilty about his sister's death, or help get Caroline's son back, and he was even less starry-eyed after a lesson from someone who knew how it worked far better than he did.

'It's a big step,' Maxwell had said. 'People can go from sleeping rough to getting their own flat and fuck it up straight away. They invite all their mates round for parties, let junkies and boozers trash the place, find themselves chucked back out on the street within a few weeks.'

Thorne could do no more than hope that Spike and One-Day Caroline got their big American fridge, and held on to it for a little while longer than that.

The lift doors opened and a man in a sharp grey suit stood aside to let Thorne and his cardboard box out.

The office was near the end of the carpeted corridor, and Thorne didn't bother to knock.

'Thorne . . .'

Though this was Steve Norman's only word on looking up from his desk, his face said an awful lot more: expletives mostly; the sort people blurted out when they were particularly worried.

Thorne walked towards the desk, tossing the empty cardboard box at Norman from several feet away.

Norman stood up, fumbling clumsily for the box as it knocked a photo-frame and pen set flying. 'What the hell d'you think you're doing?'

'That should be big enough,' Thorne said. 'And it's strictly for personal items only. I don't want to see any Metropolitan Police Press Office staplers going in there, all right?'

'I don't know what it is you want, but—'

'I want you to hurry up. You can write your resignation letter later on.'

Norman shook his head, squeezed out half a very thin smile. 'I'd heard rumours,' he said. 'People were saying you'd lost it.'

Thorne moved towards him quickly enough to make Norman take a step back and find himself against the wall.

'Alan Ward hasn't really started talking,' Thorne said. 'Not about *some* things, anyway. I reckon it's probably just because he hasn't been asked the right questions yet. What do you think?'

Norman looked like he was thinking about a lot of things, but he said nothing.

'I mean, obviously, they want to put the murder investigation to bed first.' Thorne leaned against the wall, his face a foot or so away and level with Norman's. 'That's fair enough, wouldn't you say? It's understandable if inquiries as to where Ward may have got certain bits of information from aren't exactly top of the list. There's even a chance that they might *never* come up . . .'

'Are you trying to threaten me?'

'*Trying?*'

'I wish you'd get on with it . . .'

Thorne's eyes flicked to the cardboard box and then back to Norman. 'Empty your fucking desk . . .'

Norman looked over to where a pattern of coloured rings was snaking its way across his computer screen, then down at his highly polished brogues for a few seconds. He sighed, irritated, as though the whole affair were some trifling inconvenience, then stepped forward and began throwing open drawers.

Thorne walked across to the window and took in the view across the RAF Museum to the M1 beyond. He spoke to Norman without turning round. 'If I thought you'd done it for money, you'd be the one going in a box, do you understand? But I think you were just trying to impress him.' He pointed out of the window. 'I could see that when I met the pair of you in the car park down there. You were like a kid who doesn't have many friends, making sure everybody knows you've got a new best mate. I'm guessing that after you'd leaked the story about there being an undercover copper out there, Ward came to you sniffing around for more information. Trying to find out exactly how much you knew. So you thought you'd show off a little . . .'

'I thought he was after a story,' Norman said. 'That's all. I thought he was angling for an exclusive. I couldn't have known what he really wanted, for Christ's sake . . .'

'He probably flattered you, right? Told you what a valuable source you were; said that the two of you worked well together. Made you think you were important. Gave you a hard-on, right?'

'He said he'd do nothing with it until after it had all come out . . .'

'So you gave him my *name*?'

Thorne saw the movement in the glass: a small nod.

'It was only to be used as part of a bigger story, once the investigation had been completed. Look, I fucked up, fair enough? Thorne . . .?'

Thorne turned, pointed to the files that Norman had taken from the drawers and dropped on to the desk. 'Into the box. You've got five minutes.'

Norman did as he was told.

'I suppose I should be grateful that you fucking up didn't get me killed. It was my good luck that it wasn't me who got kicked to death. Very bad luck for you though, because now I'm still here to make sure you answer for the man who *was* killed.'

'Terry Turner.'

'Knowing his name won't convince me that you give a shit . . .'

Norman started to move faster, his face for the first time betraying the fear that Thorne might actually do something physical. He used the edge of his hand to drag pens and paper-clips from the desktop into the box, then paused to look up. 'You were wrong about one thing,' he said. 'It wasn't me who went to the papers with the undercover story in the first place. I can't make those decisions; you know that. It came from higher up, from an officer on your side of things . . .'

Thorne knew Norman was telling the truth. It made sense. There would have been those who believed, once Thorne himself had been arrested and shot his mouth off, that the operation had been fatally compromised. That one more leak couldn't hurt.

'There was a lot of criticism,' Norman said. 'A hell of a lot of pressure. The body count was going up and it looked like we were getting nowhere. Someone decided it would be a good idea to let people know that the Met was actually *doing* something.'

Someone decided.

Jesmond . . .

Thorne turned back to the window, saw the mid-October afternoon turn a little brighter, and decided after a minute or two that he wanted to get out and enjoy some of it. At the door he turned and watched as Norman dropped the photo-frame and pen set into the box and sat down heavily in his chair.

'This might well be it,' Thorne said. 'I haven't really made my mind up. I might leave things as they are. Then again, I might go official with it if I wake up tomorrow in a pissy mood. We'll have to see how I feel, Steve. There's always a chance that I might decide to wait a while, a few weeks or a couple of months say, then turn up unannounced one night. Just pop by, somewhere you aren't expecting me, with a lump hammer or a cricket bat. See how you're getting on . . .'

He didn't wait around for Norman's reaction. He walked back down the corridor, thinking about what Spike had said in the tunnel.

'*Let the bastard sweat for a while . . .*'

Thorne stared at himself, blurry and distorted in the dull metal of the lift doors. The beard was gone. Not just the extra growth from his days on the streets, but the whole thing, revealing the straight, white scar that ran across his chin. His hair was shorter than it had been in a long time. He'd lost a little weight, too, he thought.

He'd had his old man's overcoat dry-cleaned, which had got rid of the smells he'd *wanted* rid of. And though he'd normally have preferred something a little shorter, and perhaps not as heavy, he thought it looked pretty good. They reckoned there was a cold snap on the way, so he guessed he might have to wear it a good deal from now on, and probably right through the winter. He'd need it most days, like as not.

It would go back in the wardrobe after that, as soon as the weather picked up. He'd hang it up, then maybe look at it again next time the temperature dropped; think about bringing it out next year. It wasn't really his style, after all. But he'd wait and see how he felt.

He'd wait and see how he felt about a lot of things . . .

The lift stopped at the first floor and an officer Thorne recognised got in. They'd worked together five, maybe seven, years before, on a case he could barely remember.

The man looked pleased to see him. Nodded as he reached for the button, then turned with a smile as the doors closed.

'Tom. You look well . . .'

ACKNOWLEDGEMENTS

I began work on this book in September 2003, eight months before the publication of certain photographs, the sacking of a Fleet Street editor and the scandal surrounding the treatment of Iraqi prisoners by US soldiers. Truth is not always stranger than fiction, but sometimes it's pretty bloody close . . .

Current research by organisations such as Crisis and the Ex-Services Action Group suggests that between one in three and one in five homeless people have spent some time in the Armed Forces. The most recent study revealed that up to 30% of those in hostels, day-centres and soup runs and 22% of homeless people surveyed in London on a single night, were ex-services. Despite the best efforts of those working on behalf of the homeless community and the increased awareness and activity of the services themselves, there is little to suggest that these figures are much different today.

There are, of course, many people without whom this book could never have been written. Without whose time, trouble, expertise and good advice it would have been *lifeless* . . .

Terry Walker, Gulf War veteran and author of *The Mother Of All Battles* – ISBN 190416610–5; Rick Brunwen of the Ex-Service Action

Group (ESAG); Sinead Hanks and Scott Ballantyne, co-authors of *Lest We Forget*, the Crisis report into ex-servicemen and homelessness. Above all, I want to thank Neil and Anna and the young people on the street who were willing to speak to me.

From the British Army I am hugely grateful to: Simon Saunders and Lt Col Peter Dick-Peter at G3 Media Operations, London; Major Alex Leslie (RTR); Major Ian Clooney (RTR); Major Tim David (Directorate of Corporate Communications) and all at the 1st Royal Tank Regiment in Warminster.

The support group: Sarah, Susannah, Alice, Paul, Wendy, Peter, Mike, Hilary.

And Claire. Above and beyond as always.